VOICE WITH
NO ECHO

Books by Suzanne Chazin

The Jimmy Vega Mystery Series
Voice with No Echo
A Place in the Wind
No Witness But the Moon
A Blossom of Bright Light
Land of Careful Shadows

The Georgia Skeehan Mystery Series
The Fourth Angel
Flashover
Fireplay

VOICE WITH NO ECHO

SUZANNE CHAZIN

KENSINGTON BOOKS
www.kensingtonbooks.com

KENSINGTON BOOKS are published by

Kensington Publishing Corp.
119 West 40th Street
New York, NY 10018

Copyright © 2020 by Suzanne Chazin

Excerpt from "I Was the Quietest One" by Julia de Burgos, from *Song of the Simple Truth: The Complete Poems of Julia de Burgos*, translated by Jack Agüeros, reprinted with permission from Northwestern University Press

All Kensington titles, imprints, and distributed lines are available at special quantity discounts for bulk purchases for sales promotion, premiums, fund-raising, educational, or institutional use. Special book excerpts or customized printings can also be created to fit specific needs. For details, write or phone the office of the Kensington Special Sales Manager: Attn. Special Sales Department. Kensington Publishing Corp, 119 West 40th Street, New York, NY 10018. Phone: 1-800-221-2647.

Library of Congress Card Catalogue Number: 2019953650

Kensington and the K logo Reg. U.S. Pat. & TM Off.

ISBN-13: 978-1-4967-1552-4
ISBN-10: 1-4967-1552-7
First Kensington Hardcover Edition: April 2020

ISBN-13: 978-1-4967-1555-5 (ebook)
ISBN-10: 1-4967-1555-1 (ebook)

10 9 8 7 6 5 4 3 2 1

Printed in the United States of America

To the Chappaqua Library, with great thanks for the many hours I've spent reading and writing under your welcoming roof.

I was the quietest one.
The voice with almost no echo.
The conscience spread in a syllable of anguish,
Scattered and tender, through all the silences.
—"I Was the Quietest One" by Julia de Burgos

Prologue

He crouched behind the chalk-white wall of the mausoleum, slick with dew, and peered across the moonlit rows of gravestones. He'd followed his cousin to the cemetery on his bicycle, tracking her with an app he'd installed on her phone. She was here because of the letter. He was sure of it.

She was a tiny girl. Barely five feet tall. Four inches shorter than Erick even though Erick was fourteen and she was twenty-three. Her smooth dark hair caught the moonlight like a mirror where it lay flat on her scalp. Her long braid was tucked beneath a black puffy jacket that looked as if it could swallow her whole.

The man standing before her was much bigger. Not tall, but muscular and tattooed, like the *maras* Erick's father spoke about in El Salvador. Men born dead who spent their short lives waiting for nature to catch up. His scalp was shaved close on the sides and left thick on top, like the pelt of an animal. It was cold out tonight—early May in upstate New York was seldom warm. Yet he wore only a T-shirt with the sleeves cut off. All the better to see his bulked-out arms covered in ink. To feel his power. His menace.

He'd boxed her against the side of a dark-colored sedan. The sedan's interior fabric was ripped and hanging at a slant across the rear window, making it impossible to see inside. Erick wondered whether the tattooed man was alone, or whether there were others with him. Maybe in the car or roaming the cemetery. It was an old and overgrown cemetery. All the names and dates on the headstones were from a century ago. Nobody set foot in the place anymore—especially at night.

The man's voice was low, but his Spanish had a guttural edge to it. He was demanding something from her. Money, perhaps. His cousin's replies were choked and breathy. She seemed on the verge of crying. Not girl-crying, the way women did over stuff like boyfriends. No. This was deeper. A full-chest heave, like someone drowning. Like the way his mother cried a few days ago when his father got that letter from Immigration and Customs Enforcement. Since then, Erick's dreams had been filled with men in flak vests and jack boots. He woke up slicked in sweat, his blankets in a tangle, certain that ICE had already taken his father away.

"Where is it?" the man shouted at his cousin in Spanish. She didn't answer.

The man slapped her hard across her face.

Silence. Hard breathing. A rustle of wind through the trees. Then a yelp. It took Erick a moment to realize the yelp had come from his own lips.

The man shoved her aside and turned in the direction of Erick's voice. Moonlight reflected off the white of his left eye. It wandered like a searchlight. Bulging. Freakish. Erick recoiled, slipping on the deep, spongy sod and falling back against a bush.

"Run, Erick!" she shouted.

A second man—big and stiff-shouldered, wearing a dark blue windbreaker—came up from behind. He lifted Erick off the ground, thrusting a forearm across the boy's neck.

The moon went dark. Voices faded.

Erick came to with his face pressed against the wet grass

and the thrum of an engine nearby. His cousin's cries echoed in his ears. She had to be inside the sedan.

He fumbled for his cell phone to call the police as the man in the dark blue windbreaker opened the back door and jumped in. A breeze caught his windbreaker and billowed it like a sail. Erick read three white letters stitched across the back:

I—C—E

Erick couldn't call the police.

The police were already here.

Chapter 1

The building looked like a ski lodge with its sharp-angled rooflines, skylights, and red cedar siding. Only the lettering above the main doors gave its more sacred purpose away. One word, spelled out in both English and Hebrew:

SANCTUARY

The last time Jimmy Vega stepped through these doors, it was for his daughter's bat mitzvah. Joy, who couldn't speak more than a few sentences of Spanish, stood at the bimah and read Hebrew from the Torah. Words Vega, a Bronx-born Puerto Rican, didn't know and couldn't pronounce. The rabbi praised her. His ex-wife beamed. His ex-in-laws cried.

Vega hadn't been back in six years.

He was here for something much simpler on this crisp spring evening—to give his girlfriend's elderly neighbor a ride home from services. Vega found Max Zimmerman leaning on a three-pronged cane in the lobby, just outside the sanctuary hall with its cavernous four-story cupola. Zimmerman was still wearing his black felt *kippah* and deep in conversation with three middle-aged men—none of whom looked as robust as the old man. At eighty-nine, he still had broad shoulders, a full head of silver hair, and penetrating eyes behind black-framed glasses.

When one of the men stepped back, Vega noticed another figure, also in a *kippah*, at the center of the conversation: a short, burly man with brown skin creased beyond his years and large, patient eyes.

"Ah," said Zimmerman, catching sight of Vega. "Just the man I wanted to see." Zimmerman beckoned Vega over. His words, like his gestures, carried an exaggerated air to them, no doubt a holdover from having to pick up English after a childhood of speaking Yiddish and Polish.

Zimmerman introduced Vega to the other men. "Detective Vega is a county police officer. He understands the law better than any of us. Also, he's dating Adele Figueroa, the head of La Casa. So he understands the other side too."

All the men's eyes turned to Vega. Vega felt the heat rise in his cheeks. Just because he was dating the founder and executive director of the largest immigrant outreach center in the county didn't mean he necessarily agreed with everything La Casa did. He loved Adele—not necessarily her politics.

"What do you need help with?" asked Vega, anxious to move the conversation away from his personal life.

Zimmerman pointed a bony finger in the direction of the front doors. "I was just telling Rabbi Goldberg and my friends on the board here that we call our hall of worship a *mikdash*—a sanctuary. What good is having that word above our doors if we don't live the meaning?"

"Sanctuary from what?" asked Vega.

"Mr. Zimmerman made a plea tonight for us to offer sanctuary to our handyman here," said the rabbi. He was the youngest of the Jewish men in the group, with a baby face beneath his close-cropped black beard and the wide, eager eyes of a Boy Scout behind wire-rimmed glasses. Vega had a sense the synagogue had recently hired him, this was his first congregation, and he was far more comfortable with scripture than the messiness of human interaction.

"I don't understand," said Vega, turning to the desperate-looking man in the center. "Do you have an order of removal against you?"

Several voices all spoke at once. Everyone, it seemed, but the man in the middle. The rabbi patted the air. "We were given one mouth and two ears, so we could listen twice as much as we speak."

No one paid any attention to the rabbi's words. Vega wondered if that happened often.

"We're a synagogue," said a heavyset man with a bald, sweaty head covered by a *kippah*. "I'm all for trying to get Edgar legal help—"

"*Legal help?*" Zimmerman cut him off. "Did *legal help* save my family during the Holocaust?"

"This isn't the Holocaust, Max," said a tall man with a droopy mustache and silver hair that stood up on his head like he was channeling Albert Einstein. "You, of all people, should not be comparing this to the Holocaust."

"What, exactly, is the problem?" asked Vega.

"Edgar Aviles has worked for Beth Shalom for over a decade," said the rabbi. "He got temporary legal status soon after he came here from El Salvador eighteen years ago when an earthquake devastated his country. Last year, the U.S. government took it away."

"Why?" asked Vega.

"Apparently, the federal government is doing away with the program for all Salvadorans," said Goldberg. "They've done the same to other groups. Haitians. Sudanese. Nicaraguans."

Vega turned to Aviles. He was sure the rabbi and others meant well, but he wanted the man to answer for himself. Aviles couldn't get a word in edgewise with this group.

"Have you hired a lawyer?" Vega asked the man. "Maybe tried to appeal the decision?"

"Yes," said Aviles. "I thought my lawyer was still appealing."

"Edgar's five-year-old son, Noah, has leukemia," said the rabbi. "His wife, Maria, has lupus and can no longer work full-time. We thought he was a good candidate for an exception to the new rulings. Then, a few days ago, Edgar got a letter ordering him to self-deport immediately or face arrest."

"Edgar," said Zimmerman. "Can you please show Detective Vega the letter you received? You can trust him. It's all right."

Aviles slowly unfolded an envelope from the pocket of his suit jacket and handed it to Vega. Vega noticed that the handyman seemed more formally dressed than any of the others in the group. His white shirt looked freshly ironed. His dark suit looked like one he wore to every wedding, christening, and funeral. His wavy black hair was combed stiffly into place. Only his chapped hands gave him away. They were a working man's hands.

Vega opened the letter. It was addressed to *Edgar Aviles-Ceren*—using his full, formal name that would have included his mother's maiden name, Ceren. It originated in the local Broad Plains field office of Immigration and Customs Enforcement, the federal agency better known as, "ICE." An apt name. No immigrant could hear that word and not shudder.

The letter instructed Aviles to call the Broad Plains ICE office immediately with proof that he had a plane ticket to return to El Salvador. Failure to do so within three days of receipt of the letter, it explained, would be grounds for immediate removal from the country.

Vega handed the letter back to Aviles. "Did you speak to your attorney?"

"He's on vacation," said Aviles. "His secretary says my case is still pending before a judge. How can they deport me when the judge has not heard my story?"

Vega sidestepped the question. He was no lawyer, but he knew that ICE wasn't bound by law to wait for a judge's decision. The agency could and did deport people while their cases were still on appeal. If the person won— a long shot in itself—they could come back. Almost no one did. It was simply too expensive to carry on the fight from abroad.

"Have you spoken to anyone at ICE?" Vega asked Aviles.

"My niece, Lissette, talked to an ICE agent. She is hopeful he can help."

"So . . . you filed a stay through this guy?"

"A stay?" Aviles hesitated. "I don't think so. I don't think he asked for any paperwork."

"Then what is he doing exactly?"

"I don't know." Aviles flushed and stared at his feet. He looked like a man who was used to solving his own problems. He seemed embarrassed to encounter one where he couldn't. The immigration laws were so complex, even Vega, a cop and native English speaker, didn't understand most of them.

"Look," said the heavyset bald man, focusing on all the other faces in the group except the handyman's. "No one's saying we can't take up a collection for Edgar's family. Help them out with food and rent and medical bills— whatever. But there's nothing else we can do."

"Nothing is what a man does when he's dead, Sam," said Zimmerman, dismissing the fat man with a wave of his hand. "The living must always do something."

"Something that will send us all to jail?" Sam shot back. "Something that will get Beth Shalom and the board sued? Edgar's not even legal to work at the synagogue anymore. And you want to let him *live* here? We'll spend our endowment funding a cause that many of our members won't support."

He waved an arm around the lobby. Brightly colored paintings of Jerusalem hung on the walls. Chrome and glass fixtures sparkled overhead. "Our congregation has been here for fifty years. *Fifty years.* Something like this could shut us down. You want that on your conscience?"

Zimmerman turned to Vega. "This is true?"

"It's a violation of federal law to knowingly house or employ illegal immigrants," said Vega. "So yes—the temple would be breaking federal law. There could be consequences, including arrests and fines. Would ICE arrest religious leaders? Break down your doors? I don't think so. But they could if they wanted to."

Zimmerman gestured to Vega. "See? What did I tell you?" he asked no one in particular. "Jimmy knows these things. He *knows.*" Zimmerman held a hand out to Vega. "You have a business card?"

"Uh. Sure." Vega fished one out of his wallet.

"Good. Give it to Edgar. If he needs the name of a police officer to call."

"Mr. Zimmerman, I don't know that I'm going to be much help against ICE—especially if his niece is already in touch with them. They're federal and I work for the county—"

"Better to know one officer than to know none," said Zimmerman. "Give him your card."

Vega turned it over to Aviles. The man tucked it into the breast pocket of his jacket. Vega met the man's dark, soulful eyes head-on for the first time.

"Do you have other family here who can help your wife and children if you have to return to El Salvador?" Vega asked him.

"Just Lissette," said Aviles. "But she doesn't have . . ." Aviles motioned with his hands. He wasn't about to tell a police officer outright that his niece was illegal. "She is also asking for help from her employer. He is an important man. Maybe he can help."

"Who is your niece's employer?" asked Vega.

"Glen Crowley."

"*Glen Crowley?* Our district attorney?"

"He is a very powerful man in the county, yes?"

Glen Crowley is powerful all right, thought Vega. But with the kind of power Aviles would do well to stay away from. Crowley had won multiple reelections on a strict law-and-order platform. In all likelihood, he had no idea his wife had hired an undocumented housekeeper. If Crowley found out, he'd be more likely to fire Aviles's niece than to help with her uncle's immigration problems.

"I wish you and your family good luck," said Vega, shaking Aviles's hand. He did not meet the handyman's gaze. In his heart, he knew.

Edgar Aviles was as good as deported.

Chapter 2

Vega helped Max Zimmerman into the front passenger seat of Vega's black Ford pickup.

"Thank you for driving me home, Jimmy," said Zimmerman. "I don't like driving at night anymore at my age. Wil drove me over. But he has a lab to finish at school."

Wil Martinez was a young college student who lived with Zimmerman and helped take care of him. Adele had introduced them to each other. The arrangement was working out well, but the old man was still fiercely independent. He hated asking favors.

"I don't mind," said Vega. "I'm on rotation this evening anyway. There's not much I can do except monitor my phone."

"Sort of like a doctor on call," Zimmerman noted.

"Sort of," said Vega. "Except a doctor gets called to save lives. I get called when that's not an option anymore."

"Ah, yes. Good point."

They rode in comfortable silence along the crest of a hill into town. Vega saw the rickrack rooflines of houses and churches all bathed in the warm glow of an early spring evening. He powered down his window and drank in the scent of lilac bushes and fresh-cut grass.

"I would have skipped services this evening since my

friend who usually drives me couldn't make it," said Zimmerman. "But I wanted to speak for Edgar. He's a good man in a very difficult position."

"Once ICE sends a letter like that, it's pretty much over," said Vega. "The best he can hope for is that his lawyer can argue his case while he cools his heels back in El Salvador."

"You can't . . . do anything?"

"This is a federal issue, Mr. Zimmerman. Like I told you, I don't have the authority."

"How about Adele?"

"She's had a lot of sad stories come across her desk these past few years," said Vega. "There's very little she can do."

Vega stopped at a red light. From somewhere in the distance, he heard a siren split the air. Probably an ambulance heading to a traffic accident. May was a bad month for teenage drivers. Vega hoped it wasn't a serious crash.

"Listen," said Vega, turning back to the old man. "It was very nice of you to stand up for your handyman this evening. But I agree with the other board members. Giving him sanctuary is illegal. It would put the synagogue in a very tough position."

"You think these ICE police are going to come with their guns and break down Beth Shalom's doors? Bah! They wouldn't dare."

"I don't think ICE would breach the sanctity of a house of worship," Vega agreed. "Legal or not, the backlash would be too great. But even so, wouldn't it be awkward for the synagogue? Aviles is an employee, sure. But his situation has nothing to do with the Jewish community."

"It would be a temporary measure," said Zimmerman. "Until his lawyer could help him. Or at least until his little boy improves."

"How many kids does he have?"

"Three," said Zimmerman. "A fourteen-year-old boy, an eight-year-old girl, and the five-year-old who has leukemia."

Vega heard more sirens in the distance. The musician in him heard the different pitches that likely signaled different emergency vehicles. An ambulance, perhaps. But also, a police cruiser. And maybe a fire truck. They were getting nearer. Vega wasn't sure Zimmerman could even hear them. His hearing wasn't especially good.

"It's a sad situation," said Vega. "But like your board member said, nothing can be done."

"Ach," Zimmerman waved the statement away. "Sam Lerner would look at the rain and tell you the sun is impossible."

"Maybe he's being realistic."

"Realistic is, we're all going to die," said Zimmerman. "Everything between now and then is a talking horse."

"A *what?*"

"A talking horse. You don't know the story of the talking horse?" he asked.

"No."

"Then I will tell you." Zimmerman clapped his hands together. He relished telling a good story.

"A prisoner is sentenced to die. So he says to the king, 'If you give me six months, I will teach your horse to talk.'"

They were driving through the downtown now. Two police cruisers whizzed past, their light bars dancing across the fish-scale siding of Victorians and the hanging baskets of flowers dangling from wrought-iron lampposts.

"Such hubbub," said Zimmerman, his face going from light to shadow in the passing strobe lights of police cars. "Is there some great excitement I'm missing?"

"Must be free-cone night at Ben & Jerry's," Vega joked. He wanted to keep things light with the old man. But inside, he already felt a surge of adrenaline in his veins. He repositioned his cell phone on the console between them. No messages had come in. It was probably a car crash or house fire. Nothing that required county assistance. He gestured for Zimmerman to continue his story.

"Oh yes, of course. The talking horse. So the king, intrigued, agrees to postpone the prisoner's death sentence for six months so he can teach the horse to talk."

"Which means," said Vega, "in six months, when the horse can't talk, the prisoner will die anyway."

"Maybe . . . Maybe not," said Zimmerman. "In six months, the horse could die. In six months, the king could die. Or . . . who knows?" Zimmerman spread his palms and shrugged. "Maybe the horse will talk. Why not? Plenty of jackasses do."

Vega laughed.

"The point is," said Zimmerman, "as long as Edgar stays in this country, he has a chance. To fight his deportation. To provide moral and financial support for his family while Noah goes through chemo. To be a role model to his fourteen-year-old, Erick."

"You know the family pretty well, it seems," said Vega.

"Erick helps his father on weekends at the synagogue. And I've seen Edgar's wife, Maria, with Noah and Flor. Noah has no hair right now. It's so sad."

Vega suddenly felt the weight of the handyman's crushing burden. A sick wife. A little boy with cancer. And now this—separated from his family forever. It was a lot.

"That's what the talking horse is, Jimmy," said Zimmerman. "It's hope. It's all any of us ever has."

Vega's phone vibrated beside him, A text message. Vega nosed his truck to the curb.

"I'm sorry, Mr. Zimmerman, I need to check this. It will only take a minute and then I'll get you home."

"Go ahead. I'll wait," said Zimmerman. "At my age, the only emergency I have is finding a bathroom—and I went at Beth Shalom. Nice restrooms, by the way. Very clean, thanks to Edgar. You should check them out some-time."

Vega grabbed his phone and checked the screen. One new text. From county dispatch:

10-56 reported in Lake Holly. Locals request county assis-tance. Respond via phone. Sensitive info.

10-56—a potential suicide. That's what all the sirens must have been about.

"If you'll excuse me," Vega told Zimmerman, "I've got to make a quick phone call. I won't be a minute."

"Something bad just happened, yes?" asked Zimmer-man. "It's all over your face."

"Just police business," Vega assured him. "Nothing to worry about."

Vega stepped out of the pickup and dialed the county police. Lasky, the night desk sergeant, picked up.

"I just got a text," said Vega. "About a possible suicide in Lake Holly."

"Twelve Greenbriar Lane," said Lasky. "White female. Age thirty-four. A neighbor walking her dog saw water gushing out of a basement window and called the fire de-partment. When they shut off the water main and pumped out the basement, they found the victim."

"Gunshot? Drug overdose?" asked Vega.

"She hung herself from a pipe."

"She hung herself and the water main just happened to break at the same time?"

"Initial report says it was a washing machine hose that either tore or got disconnected," said Lasky. "Lake Holly thinks it looks a little squirrelly too. That's why they're asking for county assistance."

"I understand there's some sensitive info," said Vega.

"Yeah. The victim's name is Talia Crowley."

"*Crowley?* As in the district attorney's new wife?"

"You know another Talia Crowley?"

Vega thought about the handyman's niece. "Anyone else home?"

"The DA's in Albany at a conference," said Lasky. "He's been up there since Thursday evening. The state police are escorting him back now."

"I understand they have a housekeeper," said Vega. "A young Salvadoran woman. Was she in the house?"

"Not that I heard," said Lasky. "Hey, it's Friday night. Chumps like you and me gotta work. But even the help gets off."

Chapter 3

Greenbriar Lane was blocked off by the time Vega arrived. Red and blue lights pulsed against the sprawling contemporary houses. Neighbors gathered behind police sawhorses, their voices drowned out by the rumble of pumps and generators.

Lake Holly may have labeled Talia Crowley a 10-56—a potential suicide. But that was never how Vega approached a death investigation. To him, every death was a homicide until proven otherwise, and he treated it with all the care and precision of one.

It was much easier to discard evidence you didn't need than to scrounge around later for something you did.

Vega ran through what little he knew about Talia Danvers Crowley as he pulled up to the checkpoint. She'd been a paralegal in the district attorney's office, a pretty, perky blonde Vega recalled once staying late to look up a case file for him.

At some point, she and the DA struck up an affair. Vega was betting it wasn't Crowley's first. He had a reputation for playing as hard as he worked. Still, up until Talia, he'd managed to hang on to his marriage of thirty years with his first wife, a prominent socialite from an old-line Southern family. When Talia got pregnant, everything changed.

Crowley divorced his first wife, married his paralegal, and set up house here in Lake Holly.

It was supposed to be a whole new life. Then Talia miscarried. And now she too was gone.

Vega opened the window of his pickup and flashed his badge at the Lake Holly patrol officer manning the checkpoint. Ryan Bale was his name. Shaved white head. Tree-trunk neck. Shoulders like he bench-pressed three hundred on an off day.

"You working this?" asked Bale as he handed Vega the sign-in log. "I thought you got shuffled off to pistol permits or something."

Vega felt the sting of Bale's words. It had been five months since Vega had accidentally shot and killed an unarmed civilian. He'd been cleared of all charges. And yet the shame of it stuck to him like a piece of toilet paper on his shoe, following him wherever he went. In whispers in the locker room. In new encounters with other cops. On restless nights when he couldn't sleep.

Vega said nothing as he scribbled his badge number and name on the sign-in log and handed it back to Bale. He wasn't looking to get into a pissing match. But Bale wouldn't let it go. He made a show of walking around Vega's truck and copying down not only the license plate number but the registration as well.

"I'm sort of in a hurry here," said Vega.

"It's a suicide. She'll wait." Bale smiled like a shark sensing blood. "You always were a little jumpy on the trigger."

Vega thrust out a hand. "Gimme the log."

"Huh?"

"The log. You know what you're holding, right?"

Bale handed it to Vega. Vega drew a big fat circle around the sign-in name above his: *Veronica Chang.* The assistant medical examiner. He drew another big fat circle around the time Bale had scribbled in beside it. *10 a.m.* He shoved the log back at Bale.

"Two things while I'm working here, *Officer.*" Vega leaned on the word. "One, nothing's a suicide until I say it is. And two, P.M. is night. A.M. is day. It's a simple concept. Learn it."

Vega left Bale at the checkpoint and followed the flashing lights to the end of the cul-de-sac. He parked back from the fire truck and police cruisers and snaked his way between the county crime scene van and a white sedan. An official vehicle. It had a thick blue slash angled across the rear doors and a federal eagle logo on its side. The writing across the door read: IMMIGRATION AND CUSTOMS ENFORCEMENT.

ICE was here. Had they found Edgar's niece?

The Crowley house was all peaked roofs and walls of glass. Cables snaked across the lawn. Generators spewed gasoline fumes into the night air. The flood in the basement had probably shorted out the electrical panel, forcing the cops inside to rely on portable halogen lamps to see their way around.

Vega watched firefighters packing up in front of the house, the water pushing out of hose lines, fanning across the driveway before collecting in a storm drain at the curb.

The flood bothered him on some level he couldn't articulate. He'd worked a steady stream of suicides since he'd gotten off desk duty after the shooting. Old men with debts. Jilted lovers. Teenagers who came up with permanent solutions for their very temporary problems. They took their lives in cars, bathtubs, and garages. Over bridges and in front of trains. He couldn't recall one that had flooded their house. A murderer might do it—and then commit suicide. But here, he didn't buy it.

Vega put a check in his mental notebook: *strike one.*

"Took you long enough," growled a familiar voice.

Vega saw Lake Holly detective Louis Greco barreling

toward him, encased head-to-toe in white Tyvek coveralls, booties, and blue latex surgical gloves. A clear shower cap covered his bald head. He looked like a circus tent with a couple of poles removed.

"I interrupt some hot sex between you and Adele?" Greco grunted. "I figured after a year, you two would be down to quickies."

"I figured after a year, you wouldn't care. Besides, I wasn't with Adele," said Vega. "I was driving her elderly neighbor home from synagogue. He doesn't see so well at night anymore."

"Yeah? Well, when my cataracts kick in, remind me to call you." Greco handed Vega a set of coveralls, booties, cap, and gloves. "Here. It's a mess down there."

Vega slipped into the gear and slung his badge on a chain around his neck. In all that rubber and vinyl, he felt like a walking condom. "What do you have so far?"

"Not a lot," said Greco. "Dispatch got the nine-one-one call from a neighbor out walking her dog around eight p.m. The neighbor said water was pushing out the Crowley's basement windows. Fire department showed up. Took 'em about an hour and a half to shut off the water main and pump out the basement. It wasn't until they'd almost finished, that the first-due officers—Bale and Fitzgerald—discovered the body swinging from a pipe."

"Any evidence of foul play?" asked Vega.

"No gunshot or stab wounds," said Greco.

"Find a suicide note?"

Greco snorted. "Down there? If she'd left one, it's been sucked up and disintegrated by the sump pumps by now. Same with pills. We found a broken wine bottle. No cork. She may have been drinking it. Then again, it could have been in the basement for some other reason."

"So, no note." They'd need a search warrant to go through Talia's computer files. There could be a copy of a note in there—or other evidence that she was suicidal.

Google searches of how to commit suicide. Good-bye letters to friends and family. There was a lot they didn't know. Still, the absence of a ready note bothered him. Vega put another check in his mental notebook: *strike two* on the suicide theory.

Vega noticed on the front mailbox there was a plaque from an alarm company. "The house has a monitoring system, right?"

"Electronic sensors. A keyless entry. The works," said Greco. "None of it was turned on."

"Any burglary activity in the area?"

"A few break-ins," said Greco. "Teenagers looking for pills and cash—that sort of thing. The jewelry-store heist in town is still open and unsolved. But that's a different sort of job."

"Any suspects on that?"

"One," said Greco. "A gangbanger by the name of Ortega. We lifted his prints off a glass case after the heist. But he's been a ghost since we put out a BOLO on him."

Vega stared at the house. The cold white light from the halogen lamps spilled from the windows, sucking the color from the weeping cherry tree on the front lawn. Cops' flashlights bobbed and weaved between the bushes like fireflies. The static from their walkie-talkies trailed behind—the only sound Vega could hear over the din of generators.

"What's Crowley's ETA?"

"He's on his way from Albany now," said Greco. "He should be here in less than an hour."

"When did he last speak to his wife?"

"He says she was here when he left about six yesterday. He texted her last night when he got to Albany and again this morning, but she never texted back."

"Did he say whether she had any issues with alcohol or drugs? Was she seeing a shrink?"

Greco gave Vega a sour look. "Those aren't the kinds of questions you ask the DA over the phone."

"I know," said Vega. "I'm just laying the groundwork—"

"For what? We don't know that we have anything here. This is the top lawman in the county," Greco pointed out. "We need to reconstruct the family situation tactfully. I'm already getting pressure from my chief to make this quick and painless."

"Then why'd you call me in?"

"Because suicides don't normally include missing housekeepers," said Greco. "Crowley said their housekeeper should have been here today from eight thirty to five. Nobody's seen her. She's not answering her cell. We'd like to question her." Greco jerked a thumb at the white sedan parked at the curb. "That's why I called in ICE. We believe the housekeeper's illegal."

"Probably," said Vega. "At least, that's the impression I got from her uncle."

"You know the family?"

Vega shook his head. "I don't even know the woman's full name. I just happened to meet her uncle this evening when I gave Adele's neighbor a ride home from the synagogue. The uncle's their handyman. He got a letter from ICE a few days ago, telling him he's going to be deported."

Vega felt the grind of gears as Greco sorted through that complication. "What's his name?"

"Edgar Aviles."

"Same last name as Lissette," said Greco. "Do you know where he lives?"

"In town somewheres," said Vega. "The temple would know. The whole family lives together."

"I'll get Sanchez on it," said Greco. "Maybe send him over first. ICE'll just spook 'em."

"Where is this ICE agent?" asked Vega. "Is he in the basement?"

"It's a she," said Greco. "She's got one of those long Spanish names with a million parts." Greco pointed to a figure leaning against the side of one of the police cruisers, scribbling something in a notebook.

"There she is."

She had her back turned to Vega and Greco so all Vega could see was her navy-blue windbreaker with the letters *I-C-E* printed boldly across her back. She was on the tall side, with short, kinky hair, dark at the roots and dusted blond at the tips.

Greco walked Vega over. The woman looked up from her notes, then reared back, blinking as if strafed by a beam of spotlight. Vega felt the same off-kilter sensation. Like this whole scene was taking place in his dreams.

Her full lips parted in a smile that had more to do with nerves than delight. Vega knew this because he saw her crooked eyetooth. It only revealed itself when the smile wasn't genuine. Same with him.

He never realized it was a family trait.

"Michelle." Vega's mouth felt like someone had stuffed it with cotton.

"Wow. Jimmy." She held out a hand. But instead of directing it at Vega's palm, she touched his arm and gave it a squeeze. "Of all places to run into each other."

Greco's face scrunched in confusion. "You two met before?"

"You could say that," said the woman. "Jimmy Vega is my half brother."

Chapter 4

*H*alf. *Brother.* Neither of those words sounded right to Vega. He had to think back to the last time he saw Michelle Carmelita Vega-Lopez. It was at his mother's funeral in the Bronx over two years ago. Vega hadn't invited her. He hadn't invited anyone from his father's side of the family. Not his father or Michelle or her younger sister Denise or the little one—Natasha—the child of yet another of Orlando Vega's many dalliances.

Michelle, the sibling closest in age to Vega, was the only one who showed up. Alone. Without her two kids. Without her husband—the Lopez guy. She hugged Vega afterward in the receiving line and mouthed the usual platitudes. What else could she say? They were strangers. He accepted that. What he couldn't accept was her referring to him now as her "half brother." In front of Greco. *Coño!*

"You're kidding, right?" Greco looked at Vega. Vega looked at the cops traipsing in and out of the house. He wanted to be them. He wanted to be anybody but who he was at the moment, the son of a man who gave his DNA far more freely than he gave his fidelity. Or, for that matter, his financial support.

"You work for ICE?" Vega asked Michelle. His tone sounded accusing—better fit for an interrogation room than a family reunion. "I thought you worked for the New York City Department of Corrections."

"I left," said Michelle. "Five years ago. After my divorce. ICE offered better opportunities."

Five years. Vega was embarrassed to admit that he knew more personal history about his barber and the teenager who walked his dog than he did Michelle. He felt like all the spotlights on the lawn were pointed straight at him. He needed escape.

"Excuse me," said Vega. "I need to look at the body."

Vega didn't exhale until he was inside the house. It was a beautiful house—or at least it had been until the first-due cops and firefighters trudged through, leaving a black, soggy trail of footprints. The living room had a two-story timber-frame ceiling with a fieldstone fireplace running up the height of one wall. The furniture was comfy, large and expensive-looking. Lots of linens and leathers in neutral shades. The kitchen was all white marble. On the counter was a folded *New York Times,* still in its blue delivery bag. Vega peeked inside. It was this morning's edition.

He felt a presence hovering at his elbow. He turned and saw Michelle standing there. She'd slipped white coveralls over her clothing and tucked her curls into a shower cap.

"*Ay, bendito,* Jimmy," she hissed. "Why did you have to run off and embarrass me like that in front of Detective Greco?"

"*I* embarrassed *you?*" asked Vega. "Who discussed our family relationship back there? Why not draw a Venn diagram while you're at it: all the women Orlando Vega has *chingar*-ed in his life. Literally and figuratively."

"Was I supposed to pretend not to know you?"

"You *don't* know me," said Vega. "And for the record, I don't even get why you're here. Lake Holly doesn't need the feds to find an undocumented witness."

"If she *is* just a witness," said Michelle.

Vega thought about explaining the presence of the morning's newspaper and how ludicrous it seemed for Lissette to have fetched it if she'd murdered Talia the night before. But even he knew it was too early to start speculating. Instead, he scrutinized her from across the counter.

"How many deaths have you cleared? Not counting, of course, the ones ICE caused."

She ignored the cheap shot and answered. "Twenty-seven. Nine homicides. Eighteen suicides or other causes."

Vega couldn't hide his surprise. He'd been a detective on the homicide task force for a couple of years now, not counting his time on desk duty. He had eleven cleared homicides under his belt and twice that many deaths from other causes. She had nearly the same level of expertise.

"That's impossible," said Vega. "ICE doesn't—"

"I was in charge of all death investigations for the New York City Department of Corrections before I left," said Michelle. "And unlike the civilian police, I was able to clear every one. *Every . . . single . . . one.*" She let that sink in for a moment. "So let's stop playing king-of-the-sandlot and get down to business. *Bueno?*"

They made their way down the basement steps. An odor of wet wood and diesel fuel permeated their nostrils, along with the stench of decaying flesh. Three shadows moved across the high-water mark on the buckling Sheetrock wall. Vega saw that they belonged to Veronica Chang and the two crime-scene techs, Jenn Fitzpatrick and her partner, Derek Watson. Vega gave the group a collective nod and introduced them to "Agent Lopez." Then they took in the body, still hanging from the sewer pipe.

Talia Danvers Crowley wasn't a pretty sight. She was bluish gray and stiff from rigor mortis. Her dark purple tongue protruded from her mouth—a common occurrence in hangings. Only the hardware-store rope around her neck retained its original yellow-crayon color. It felt like it was mocking them all.

Vega turned to Veronica Chang. She was a small Asian woman with pin-straight, jet-black hair and an ageless face. Vega had worked with her for years and still had no idea how old she was.

"How long do you think she's been like this?" Vega asked her.

"With immersion deaths, it's difficult to say," said Chang. "The cold temperature and movement of the water could have slowed the decomp down. On the other hand, there would have been some stagnation once the water reached the windows and flowed out. At that point, the process could have sped up."

"Ballpark figure?"

"It's reasonable to assume she's been dead at least twelve hours—if not longer."

Vega tried to judge time of day or state of mind by her soaked clothing. He couldn't. She was dressed in black yoga pants that ended mid-calf, a clingy, gray long-sleeved shirt, and black lace-up sneakers. It was almost a uniform among the upper-middle-class women Vega saw in and around Lake Holly. He couldn't say for sure if she was finishing a morning workout, just back from having lunch with friends, or lounging around watching a late-night show on TV.

She was short and slight. Five two. A hundred and ten pounds. There were blisters from rope slippage around her neck, as well as some bruising. But not enough to suggest she'd been put up there against her will or endured any change of heart. Her nails were bitten short, but absent of obvious debris that would have signaled a fight or offered a killer's DNA.

Of course, the water could have washed it all away.

"Any suspicious markings to suggest she didn't put herself in that noose?" Vega asked Chang.

"Not on first inspection," said Chang. "The only bruising appears consistent with the noose."

Vega walked the perimeter of the soggy basement. The remains of waterlogged cardboard boxes littered the floor, along with wet, grease-stained clothes, buckets and laundry baskets, trails of loose nails and rusted screws. He noted the broken wine bottle. No cork. Vega wondered if she'd been drinking it before she died. He knew Jenn Fitzpatrick and Derek Watson would bag the bottle for prints and evidence. He didn't need to tell them how to do their jobs. His job was to look for the less obvious things. The pieces of the puzzle that *didn't* fit.

Vega walked over to the washing machine.

"Everything already photographed?" Vega asked the two crime-scene techs. He knew better than to mess with the scene otherwise.

"Affirmative," Jenn Fitzpatrick answered.

Vega picked up the loose end of the hose in his gloved hands. The original installer had used a compression clamp to fasten it to the drain. There was no way to pry it off. Instead, someone had sliced the hose in half with a clean horizontal cut. Probably from a utility knife.

He didn't see the knife—a fact he pointed out to Fitzpatrick and Watson. "You bag it already?"

"Negative," said Watson. "We've come across other things. Scissors. Wire snips—"

"Lying around?"

"In a toolbox. Maybe she cut the hose and then put the tool away."

Which would make her the most OCD suicide Vega had ever seen, or . . .

. . . The tool that cut the hose was missing.

Vega circled the basement slowly, beginning at the body. He walked past the stairs to a mirrored wall where a water-logged treadmill and exercise bike sat near a rack of free weights. The weights were chrome-plated with black rubber hexagonal ends. Every weight—from three pounds to twenty-five—was there. Two of each. All of them with their poundage displayed, faceup.

All except for one twenty-five-pound weight. It was lying with the weight display a quarter turn from the face-up position. Vega couldn't say why that one weight bothered him. But it did.

So did something else.

"Where's the chair or stepstool she stood on to get a rope over that pipe?"

Watson found a wooden footstool on the other side of the stairs. He brought it over and set it beneath Talia's dangling legs.

"There," he said proudly. "She climbed on that and kicked it away after."

Vega picked up the stool and handed it to Watson. "What would you say this weighs? Fifteen pounds?"

"About," Watson said, nodding.

"How did a fifteen-pound footstool travel all the way to the other side of the stairs?"

"You ever seen that footage of tsunamis?" asked Watson. "Water can move mountains. It can certainly move a fifteen-pound footstool."

"Look at the free weights," Vega countered. "Some of them are only three pounds. They didn't move at all."

"How about this?" asked Michelle. She walked over to a plastic bucket, lying on its side. She turned it upside down near the body. It was the right height.

"Problem solved," she said.

"Stand on it," he told her.

"Okaay," she said slowly, as if humoring a crazy man. She put one foot on top. The bucket began to shake before she got close to adding a second foot.

"The problem is *not* solved," said Vega. "Not even near to being solved." He knew it, even if they didn't.

Strike three.

Chapter 5

Erick Aviles raced home and locked his bike behind the porch. He bounded up the row-frame's stairs, two at a time, and into his family's tiny second-floor apartment. His father sat at the kitchen table, still in his white dress shirt—the one he wore to funerals. His mother stood at the stove, heating up a plate of rice and beans.

"Papi!" the boy cried. "Two men kidnapped Lissette!"

Edgar Aviles pressed his meaty hands on the kitchen table and rose. "Where, *mijo?* Where did you see this?"

"In the old cemetery," Erick huffed out. "One of them choked me. When I opened my eyes, they were driving away."

Erick's father eased the teenager into one of the kitchen chairs. His mother brought him a glass of water. He downed it in one gulp.

"Take a deep breath," his father urged. He removed a handkerchief from his pocket and wiped the sweat from the boy's forehead. "When did this happen? Just now?"

"Maybe half an hour ago. I tried to chase them on my bicycle. But I wasn't fast enough."

His father tucked his handkerchief away and pulled out his cell phone. "We must call the police."

"Papi—one of the men who took her was an ICE agent."

His father's hand tightened on the phone. The only sound in the kitchen was the ticking of the big wall clock with an image of Jesus's hands clasped in prayer on the dial.

"ICE?" his father whispered. "Are you sure?"

"He was wearing a jacket with a big white *I*, *C*, and *E* stitched across the back."

Erick's parents traded glances. No one spoke for a long moment.

"We still have to call the police," said his father.

"You want to call the police? Against ICE?" asked his mother. "How will that help her? It will only hurt you."

His father sank down in a chair next to Erick. "*Mijo*," he asked. "Were *both* men wearing ICE jackets?"

"Only one," the boy replied. "The one who choked me. The other had tattoos all over his arms. He looked like a *mara*."

Mara. The word sent a new and different kind of terror across his parents' faces. *Mara. Mara Salvatrucha.* MS-13. Gangsters.

"What did they want?" his mother asked.

"I don't know," said Erick. "I couldn't hear. I think they were looking for money. The *mara* slapped Lissette. That's when I called out." Tears came to the teenager's eyes. He was embarrassed he couldn't stop. "It's all my fault for calling out!"

"No, *mijo*." His father said softly. Something in his dark eyes retreated. Erick had seen that look before, when Noah had to have something painful done to him in the hospital. His father couldn't bear to see someone he loved suffer. "The fault is mine. All mine." He pulled out his cell phone. "We have to call the police. This isn't right."

Erick's mother clasped a hand over his phone. "If you call the police, then what? These people could still hurt Lissette. And the police will just turn you over."

"We don't have a choice."

"We do," she insisted. "Maras want money. That's what they always want. We give it to them, the police never have to get involved."

His father pressed a knuckle to his lips—a habit he had when he was nervous. "I don't know—"

"*Mi vida,* please." Tears streamed down the butterfly-shaped rash across her cheeks. Tonight, her lupus looked particularly angry. "You are the glue that holds our family together. I need you. The children need you."

"Okay." A deep sigh expelled from his chest, like a beach ball deflating. "We wait."

The phone didn't ring right away. It took an hour. By the time it did, they were all nervous wrecks, huddled on the couch listening to every noise from the apartments above and below them. Televisions. Babies' cries. Slamming doors. Cars tearing up the street. Commuter trains rattling the windows in back.

The call lasted less than a minute. Erick heard only his father's panicked voice, not the voice on the other end.

"I want to speak to Lissette," his father demanded. "I will pay you whatever I can. Just please, don't hurt her."

The caller didn't put Lissette on the line. He didn't ask for money either. He wanted something else.

A phone.

"Lissette's phone?" Erick asked his father afterward.

"No. Someone else's." His father bounced a look from Erick to his mother. "Did she ever mention a special phone to either of you?"

Both of them shook their heads. "Why can't he ask Lissette?" his mother demanded.

"Maybe she won't tell him."

"Then maybe we shouldn't either," she said.

His father sank onto the couch. He looked defeated. His broad shoulders sagged. His knuckle pressed hard against his lips.

"He said they're watching our house. Watching to see if we go to the police." His father shot a glance at the two bedrooms where Noah and Flor were sleeping. "He said if we don't find the phone and turn it over, they'll hurt Lissette. Then they'll come after us. All of us—even Flor and Noah." His father's voice cracked. "Maria—he knew their *names.*"

Until that moment, Erick thought the worst that could befall his family had already happened.

He had no idea how much worse things could get.

Chapter 6

Detective Louis Greco found Vega in Glen and Talia Crowley's master bathroom, pawing through their medicine cabinet with a flashlight. The house still had no power.

"The DA's here," said Greco. "Just arrived from Albany."

"Great." Vega straightened. "Let's go talk to him."

"Not so fast." Greco blocked the doorway. "I don't like this business between you and your sister."

"She's not my sister."

"Okay, half—"

"We're distantly related."

"You share the same father."

"Trust me, that's a distant relation." Everything on his dad's side stopped being related the day Orlando Vega seduced a hateful neighbor's nineteen-year-old kid sister, got her pregnant with Michelle, and walked out on Vega and his mother forever.

Greco patted the air. "Take the temperature down, Vega. Agent Lopez is here to do a job, same as you. If I'd wanted *Family Feud*, I'd have watched it on TV. Now, I'm going to ask you a question and you're going to answer: Can you put whatever crap that's between you aside and work this case? Or am I gonna have to get someone else in here?"

"I'll behave . . . if she shuts her yap about us being related." That was as close to a promise as Vega was going to give. He closed the medicine cabinet and maneuvered past Greco into the master bedroom. It was like navigating around a steamroller.

"What are you looking for?" Greco asked.

"Psych meds. For depression or anxiety," said Vega. "So far, all I've found is a half-empty bottle of expired Valium and two vials of Viagra—all in Crowley's name."

Greco grinned. "Crowley's like, sixty. Talia was thirty-four. Maybe he's got more to be anxious about."

"He got her pregnant," Vega pointed out. "I don't see any birth control. Maybe they were trying again."

"I get the feeling the pregnancy was less, 'oh joy,' than 'oh shit,' " said Greco. "You've worked with the guy—"

"Mostly with his assistant DAs."

"Yeah. But you know him," said Greco. "Talia was one of his paralegals. I think he thought it would be another quick affair. And then . . . it wasn't."

Vega straightened. "You saying you think he was looking for a permanent way out?"

"Me?" Greco touched his chest. "Uh-uh. I'm already getting pressure from my chief to move this thing to closure. I'm just saying Crowley has a reputation for a roving eye. If it's something bigger, we'll have to do our jobs. But if it isn't, I'd like to finish up my career without turning this into some skeevy romp through his sex life."

"Gotcha." Vega shone his flashlight across the soft gray walls of the master bedroom. There was a king-size bed with a tufted white headboard, two side tables, and two sitting chairs. Vega didn't see a chest of drawers.

"Where do they keep their clothes?"

"You never been in a high-end house before?"

"Not someone's bedroom—no."

Greco walked over to one of the walls with raised white trim. There was a door handle Vega didn't see. Greco opened it. On the other side was an enormous walk-in closet.

"This one's hers," said Greco. "His is on the other side."

"Thanks."

Vega propped the door open as wide as he could and shined his flashlight on the clothes. He saw rows of black and gray leggings and shirts in various shades of cream, white, and eggshell.

"Don't women dress in color anymore?" asked Vega. "My ex-wife and daughter are the same. Twenty shades of prison commando."

Vega walked over to a chest of drawers, pulled out the top one, and raked his flashlight across a perfect honeycomb of women's bikini underwear, all neatly folded like a spread in one of those home organizing books. He began poking around. In a whole year of dating Adele, he'd never once gone through her underwear drawer.

It was the intimacy of a death investigation that got to Vega every time. He would never know another human being as profoundly as he knew every one of his homicide and suicide victims. From the scars on their flesh to the last meals in their guts. He knew the names on their speed dials. The family members in their wallets. The balances in their bank accounts. He had a front-row seat to their failed romances and fractured ambitions. He felt the weight of the unspoken pact he always made with them.

Tell me who you were and how you died—and I will get you justice.

Sometimes justice was just finding out why a person chose to take their life. Giving them one last chance to speak of their pain and longing. To be understood. In a homicide of course, it meant finding the killer. Nothing haunted Vega more than when he failed to solve a homicide.

"You want more light?" Greco called to him. He tried to maneuver the tripod closer. To do it, he needed to close the closet door. It was just a moment. But it made Vega's heart race. Made his breathing kick up a notch and his body break out in a sweat.

Greco noticed the change when he reopened the door.

"Whoa. You okay?"

"I'm fine."

"You get claustrophobia or something? My cousin has that. He passed out once at Yankee Stadi—"

"I'm fine." It wasn't claustrophobia or any other phobia. He just liked to sleep with his bedroom door open. He preferred the back rows of theaters, closest to the exit. He took the stairs instead of elevators. Checked locks on doors before he used them to make sure he could never—ever—get locked in, trapped and helpless—the way he did in his dreams.

Nothing phobic about that. Lots of people feel the same way.

Vega propped the door open wide again, took a deep breath, and moved on to the next dresser drawer. Socks. Black pairs and gray. Two with cows on them. Talia loved cows, especially the black-and-white Holstein variety. She had a whole collection of Holstein figurines on her vanity. She had salt-and-pepper cow shakers in her kitchen.

Vega had spent under an hour wandering Talia Crowley's house, but he already knew so much about her. She had a sister and two nieces she was close to. Vega saw photographs of them all over the house, always with a couple of dogs. She was an accomplished artist. Vega counted at least five framed watercolors on the walls with her signature. Still lifes of milk cans and flowers. A portrait of a girl looking through a barn window. Two paint-ings of mothers and babies. She seemed to want to become a mother very badly. Vega found a copy of *What to Expect When You're Expecting* tucked on a shelf among her jew-elry, beside a bagful of infant clothes. The miscarriage must have devastated her. She was thirty-four, married to a man of sixty. There might not be many more chances.

"Look, Vega." Greco stood in the doorway of the closet, rocking on the balls of his feet. "We've already been through the house. There's no sign of a break-in and nothing to sug-gest the place was tossed."

"That's right," said Vega. "There *is* nothing. That's what worries me." He squatted down and opened the next drawer. Sweaters. He reached his hand along the sides. "I've been doing a lot of suicide investigations lately, Grec. That's all Captain Waring seems to *let* me do. And in every one, people give off warnings. They increase their meds. Or stop taking them completely. They don't plan big events. I found two tickets to *Hamilton* on Broadway in a kitchen drawer. *Orchestra.* For the end of June."

"That's seven weeks from now," said Greco. "Seven weeks is a long time to a depressed person."

At the back of the drawer, Vega's gloved fingers brushed against something that felt like a wallet. He pulled it out. It was black with an alligator texture imprinted on the vinyl. Dollar-store quality. Vega unzipped the change purse. He found a folded ten-dollar bill and a few loose coins inside.

He lifted a small interior flap and unearthed a photo of two Hispanic girls in dark blue skirts and white short-sleeve shirts. The girls looked to be somewhere between eight and ten. They both had soft brown eyes and dimpled cheeks. Sis-ters, thought Vega. He could see a similarity in their faces. They were standing beneath a corrugated metal roof on a concrete patio. Banana trees dotted the hillsides in the background. Vega guessed the picture had been snapped in Central America. He turned it over. On the other side, in small neat print, someone had written *Deisy and Nelly, Escuela Santa Rosa.* There was no date on the shot, taken at Saint Rosa's School, but it appeared to be a few years old.

Vega showed it to Greco. "You think Talia was supporting some kids through one of those 'Save the Children' organizations?"

"Dunno," said Greco. "Could be relatives of the housekeeper's. No way to tell. We should bag it for testing and show a copy to Crowley while he's outside. Maybe he recognizes them."

They found Glen Crowley standing next to Greco's boss, Chief Battaglia. On first glance, the two men looked like they were both just working a crime scene. They were equally straight-backed and silver-haired with dark, predatory eyes and smiles that worked on cue when the cameras were rolling.

On closer inspection, however, Vega could see how Talia's death was weighing on the district attorney. He'd always had the sinewy build and intensity of a college basketball coach. But for the first time, he looked gaunt and shrunken. His bony shoulders protruded from his shirt like the spokes of a broken umbrella. His skin sagged at his neck. When he shook Vega's hand, his eyes seemed to take a moment to recognize who he was.

"Our condolences on your loss, sir," said Vega.

"Thank you," Crowley mumbled.

Battaglia bounced a look from Vega to Greco. "I think our DA has had enough for one evening. Questions can wait until tomorrow."

"Absolutely, Chief," said Greco. "Just one quick question that might help us track down Mr. Crowley's housekeeper. She's still missing, and I'm sure Mr. Crowley would want to help us find her."

"I'm happy to help you," said Crowley. "Lissette was very close to Talia. Her aunt, Maria, was my former wife's housekeeper for many years until she got ill."

"Maria—as in, Edgar Aviles's wife?" asked Vega.

Crowley hesitated. He probably had no idea who Maria's husband was. "Yes, I believe so. Charlene, my ex, could tell you more."

That was a complication Vega hadn't expected. He'd have thought Charlene Beech Crowley wouldn't want any connection to her ex-husband and his former-mistress-now-wife. But apparently, that didn't extend to sharing the help.

Rich people were different, he supposed.

Greco gave Vega a look to move things along. The chief was growing impatient. Vega whipped out his cell phone. The wallet and photo had been tagged and bagged as evidence. But Vega had the pictures here.

"We found a wallet in your wife's sweater drawer with a photograph inside," Vega explained. He pulled up the shots on his screen and handed the phone to Crowley. "Do you recognize the girls? The shot seems to indicate their names are Deisy and Nelly."

Crowley stared at the three screenshots—one of the wallet and its contents, and one each of the back and front of the photo. He kept his eyes on the shots without meeting Vega's gaze.

"This was in Talia's drawer?" asked Crowley. "Was there anything else in the wallet?"

"Just what you see," said Vega. "The photo, a ten-dollar bill, and some change."

"I see." Crowley handed the phone back to Vega. "I don't recognize the girls."

"Do you think they might be relatives of Lissette's?" Vega pressed.

"I don't know."

"But you recognize the wallet, right? It belonged to your wife."

"If it was in her drawer, it must have," said Crowley. Vega heard the irritation in his voice. The chief did too.

"You got your answer, Vega," Battaglia growled. "The rest can wait."

Chapter 7

The knocking at their front door had the insistence of a police officer. Edgar Aviles cracked open the chain to see a man in a polo shirt and khakis with a broad, brown face and a gun on his hip. He held out his gold shield. It read: DETECTIVE, LAKE HOLLY POLICE.

Aviles's stomach clenched. He prayed to God this detective wasn't here to deliver bad news about Lissette.

"I'm very sorry to bother your family at this hour, señor," the cop offered in American-accented Spanish. He was fluent, but it wasn't his language of choice.

"I can speak English," Aviles told him impatiently.

"Great," said the cop, switching to English. "My name is Omar Sanchez. I'm a detective with the Lake Holly Police. I have no interest in anyone's immigration status. I'm just trying to locate your niece, Lissette. Do you know where I can find her?"

Maria came up behind her husband and put a tight grip on his arm. Aviles got the message: *Say nothing.*

"I don't know where she is," Aviles told the detective.

"Do you mind if I come in? Ask you a few questions?"

"It's not a good time," said Aviles. If the people who had Lissette were watching his house, they'd know a police officer was here. They'd think Aviles called him in to make a report. Lissette's life—his family's lives—depended on what he did next. The sooner he got rid of this man, the better.

"But your niece, señor—out this late? Aren't you worried about her?"

Aviles tightened his grip on the edge of the door. "Why do you want to talk to her?"

"It's about her employer," said the detective. "Talia Crowley? We have a situation at her house this evening that we think your niece might be able to give us information on."

Situation. Information. The detective was hiding the real reason he wanted to speak to her. Aviles wondered if something was missing from her employer's house and they were blaming Lissette. In that case, telling the police what Erick had witnessed this evening would only make them more suspicious.

"I will let her know you are looking for her." Aviles started to close the door.

"Sir—wait." The detective stretched out a hand. He looked around, like he was waiting for someone else to tell him what to do. "Mrs. Crowley is dead."

"*Dead?*" The word came out barely above a whisper. "What happened?"

"It's under investigation."

The officer's tone was gruffer now. Aviles noticed the detective had switched from "señor" to "sir." His mind raced. In the same evening his niece had been kidnapped, her employer was dead. If it was an accident, the detective would have told him. Which meant it wasn't. The señora had been murdered. Or at least, the police suspected as much—and suspected Lissette was somehow involved. He had to disengage.

"I'm sorry," Aviles told the detective. "Tonight is not a good night to talk. I will tell Lissette to come see you."

Before the detective could object, Aviles closed the door and locked it. The detective knocked and pleaded for a few minutes, then finally gave up and slipped his card under the door. Aviles heard his footsteps echo down the stairs.

"God help Lissette," Maria whispered.

Aviles leaned his head on the door. *God help us all.*

They pulled the foldout couch into a bed so Erick could go to sleep. Then Maria and Aviles retreated to their bedroom where Noah lay curled in a cot in the corner, his bald head reflecting a nightlight by the floor, his pajama top pulled down, revealing the surgical port in his chest where doctors administered the medicine. The skin beneath the boy's eyes had a purplish tinge. No amount of sleep ever seemed to be enough. For him or his mother. Aviles wished he were the one suffering—not them.

Maria changed into a nightgown. Aviles stripped down to his undershirt and boxer shorts. He cradled his wife until she fell asleep.

He couldn't sleep. His worries hummed through his brain like a swarm of bees. He cursed himself for not asking Lissette more about this ICE agent she'd been dealing with. He'd suspected all along that the agent was corrupt. Why else would he reach out? But he'd kept telling himself that if it bought him his freedom, it would be worth it. And now, his niece was kidnapped—maybe dead—and it was all his fault.

The clock was edging up on five a.m. Saturday morning when Aviles pushed himself up from the bed. He found a pair of work pants folded atop a chair and stepped into them.

Maria awoke, propping herself on one elbow. "Where are you going?"

"To try to find Lissette."

"Please don't leave." Maria pushed herself up from the bed and placed a palm on his chest, almost like she didn't expect to feel him beneath it. Or maybe she just wanted to feel him that way one more time. She'd been the only woman in his life since she was nineteen and he was twenty-one. Not once in all those years had they slept apart from each other. Aviles felt a great rage and shame that a piece of paper might soon separate him from his family forever.

A set of headlamps strafed the closed blinds across their bedroom window, growing bigger and brighter as a car slowly coasted down the street in their direction. Aviles heard the spit of gravel from the tires and the purr of the engine.

And then it stopped.

Aviles walked back into the living room, skirting Erick asleep on the couch. He lifted a corner of the drape and peered at the street. A dark-colored compact sedan sat double-parked beneath a streetlight in front of his house. Two men ejected themselves from the front seats. One black. One white. Both had short-cropped hair and a bulk to their torsos that suggested they were wearing armor beneath their jackets. Both wore pistol holsters and military-looking boots.

The living room window was open beneath the drapes. Aviles leaned forward to listen. He couldn't hear what the men were saying, but he noticed their words had a breathy excitement to them. The black man had his hand angled like he was directing traffic.

Directing it right at Aviles's house.

The white man turned his back and Aviles saw three white letters across his jacket.

I-C-E.

Aviles felt an acid burn in his chest. His fingers and toes tingled with pins and needles. It was cold in the apartment, yet every pore bathed him in a sheen of sweat.

Maria came up behind him, saw the men, and let out a whimper. She knew—they were here for him.

"You have to leave now!" she cried.

"I can't leave you and the children like this."

"They will take you away forever if you don't. Please, *mi vida*. Please. For our sakes, you must run away."

Their conversation woke Erick. He sat up on the fold-out couch, dazed and confused. Maria told him what was happening, then she turned back to her husband. "Now is your only chance. Now!"

Aviles shoved his feet into his work boots and tried to formulate a plan. He couldn't go down the stairs. His only hope was to escape through the bedroom window, shimmy across the roof, and slide down to the back porch. He ran into the bedroom in such a blind panic that he didn't even kiss his wife and children good-bye.

The roof was steeper than Aviles had expected. A slick of pollen clung to the shingles. His boots slid as he shimmied across it. The grit on the tiles scraped his hands. The porch downspout was so dented, he didn't dare trust himself to grab it. He was thankful it was still dark outside. Had it been light, the agents surely would have spotted him.

He followed the porch roof around the corner to the back of the house. A curtain of weeds surrounded a cracked concrete patio. Several bicycles lay chained against the railing. Two grills collected a film of water that reflected the deep ocean blue of the sky. It was growing paler over the eastern hills. He wouldn't have the cover of night much longer.

He grabbed one of the column supports and slid down. He was thirty-five—not a teenager. His muscles protested. His body felt the pull of gravity. He tried to land quietly and cleanly on the back porch. But the boards were old and springy. He felt the thud of his weight right through his heels.

"Around back!" a gruff male voice shouted in English.

Aviles sprinted across the patio and hoisted himself on top of the Dumpster. On the other side of the chain-link fence ran the Metro-North train tracks. It was a minefield of deadly currents and speeding locomotives.

"ICE! *Policía!*" yelled the voice as it rounded the building. *"Levanta las manos!" Put your hands up!*

And then Aviles heard it—on the other side of the chain-link fence. The rumble of a southbound train. The first train of the morning.

"Put your goddamn hands up!" the agent shouted, this time in English. "I'm not going to tell you again."

He was white with thin, almost nonexistent lips, close-shaved brown hair, and hungry eyes so pale they looked like they were clouded with cataracts.

The train whistle pealed as it rounded the bend. Aviles heard the squeal of the tires. He was out of time. Out of options.

"Get down. Now!" yelled the agent again, pointing his gun at him.

Aviles looked to his left. He felt the blast of hot air push against his skin. He saw the headlight beams cutting through the last vestiges of darkness. The train was close enough now that he could see the engineer through the compartment window.

He looked back over his shoulder to see another agent rounding the corner of the house. The second agent's gait was slower, less urgent—like he was running because he thought he should rather than because he wanted to. He was black and older. With spreading jowls and a certain resignation in his eyes.

Two against one. If Aviles delayed his decision any longer, the men would be on top of him, cuffing him. And then it would be all over.

Aviles held his breath and jumped from the top of the Dumpster, over the fence and onto the tracks. One word looped through his brain, over and over.

Run.

It was all he'd been doing since that day, eighteen years ago in Olocuilta, El Salvador, when he found his cousin facedown in a pool of blood by the side of their fruit cart.

He knew the masked gangsters would come for him next. He couldn't afford the protection money they were demanding. So he ran—from El Salvador to Guatemala and then over the Mexican border. In Chiapas, a gang stole his shoes and he walked barefoot on bleeding soles. In Veracruz, cops beat him in the freight yards and broke his ribs. At the border, he nearly drowned crossing the Rio Grande into Texas.

His entire thirty-five years came down to this moment. A few inches one way or the other would determine his fate. Aviles took a breath and pitched forward into the path of the train's headlights. He would make it. Or he wouldn't.

One. Two. Three.

He felt nothing but the beating of his heart and the whoosh of breath in his lungs. An air horn sliced the darkness, so loud Aviles could feel it through the soles of his boots. Then it was over.

He fell to his knees in the gravel on the opposite side of the tracks and watched the train barrel past on a current of air. His legs had turned to jelly. His bowels felt weak. Bile and puke gathered at the back of his throat. He tried to shake off the sensation.

He had no phone. No money. Nothing but the clothes on his back. He looked across to the chain-link fence that sealed off his yard. The two ICE agents were pacing there like tigers in a cage.

"Go ahead and run, asshole," the agent with the cataract eyes shouted as he pulled on the fence. It puckered beneath his grip. "You're not going anywhere."

He didn't want to. That was the point.

Chapter 8

Vega rose soon after daybreak on Saturday morning. A mist still hovered over the lake, shrouding the sky. He opened his cabin's sliding glass door to the deck and let Diablo out. The only sound that greeted him was the haunting call of a loon, unseen beneath the cottony mist.

A county south of here, in Lake Holly, the maples were iridescent green with seed pods, and the magnolias and dogwoods were in full gaudy bloom. But here where Vega lived—an hour north—the air still carried the damp breath of winter. The only shoots of green came from the patches of skunk cabbage near the water.

Diablo trotted over to the back deck where Vega was drinking his coffee. The brown-and-tan mutt pushed off the bottom step with a little leap, then danced around in a circle as if chasing his tail. Vega knew what Diablo wanted. On Saturday mornings, they always took a long jog around the lake.

"It'll have to be a quick run today, pal," said Vega. "Sally will be by later. She'll take you for a long walk. And Joy will be here tonight, while I'm at the gig."

Vega hated abandoning Diablo to the pet sitter and his daughter. But Talia Crowley's autopsy was scheduled for first thing this morning and, as of last night, Greco hadn't assigned anyone in the investigation to oversee it. Not that

that was always necessary. Unless the decedent's body contained evidence, such as a bullet fragment, a report often sufficed.

But not here. Not with such a high-profile investigation. Talia's death was full of nuances that might get lost between the bloodless pages of an autopsy report. Somebody needed to be there. It might as well be him.

Vega took Diablo on a short run, showered, and then drove nearly an hour south to the medical examiner's office, a one-story building housed on the campus of the county teaching hospital. At 8:28 a.m., a deep green BMW pulled into the parking lot. An older Indian woman got out of her car.

Vega knew Dr. Anjali Gupta would be the first to arrive.

The chief medical examiner gave Vega a quizzical look over the tops of her red-framed glasses. Sunlight caught the gray streaks of a ponytail pulled back loosely at the base of her neck.

"Detective Vega?" She put a hand up to shield her eyes from the glare of the morning sun. She was dressed in a shimmery orange and pink blouse which, coupled with those bright red glasses, made her look like an extra in a Bollywood movie.

"If you're here for Mrs. Crowley, I won't be starting for another hour at least. I'm afraid you're a little early." *Mrs. Crowley.* Vega smiled. The doctor always treated the dead like patients. That's what made her so good at her job.

"I was hoping I could pick your brain beforehand," said Vega. "I have some questions going in."

"Oh?" She gave him a look that lasted a heartbeat too long. Anjali Gupta had been the chief medical examiner since Vega was in uniform. They'd known each other a long time—through many ups and downs. Her bout with breast cancer. His incident with the shooting. They had enough of a rapport that Vega knew he could ask things of her that he might not of her assistants like Veronica Chang.

She seemed to know this too. Which probably accounted for her probing expression.

"Come inside," she offered. "We can talk until my assistants arrive."

She walked Vega up the concrete steps and used her ID to buzz them through the doors. The waiting area looked like a hotel lobby with its pale peach walls, skylights, and profusion of palms and ferns. Real ones. Not dust-covered plastic. Vega learned the hard way one day when he pulled a leaf and got reprimanded by the security guard.

They signed in at the front desk. One door off the lobby led to the morgue, labs, and autopsy rooms. The other, to the administrative offices. Gupta took the administrative door, which continued the Holiday Inn vibe. There were bland floral prints on the walls and a sitting area with beige couches and low-pile carpet. The carpets smelled new. They must have gotten them in the new budget. Vega couldn't recall the last time the county police got an aesthetic upgrade. Unless you counted getting rid of the refrigerator Detective Nowicki spilled sauerkraut in three years ago.

Gupta walked Vega into the kitchen area and put on the coffee.

"You don't have to do that," Vega insisted.

"I would anyway. It's no problem." Gupta kept her back to him as she scooped the grounds into the machine. Her voice carried the singsong cadences of an Indian youth and British boarding-school education. His Bronx vowels sounded tortured by comparison.

"I haven't seen Mrs. Crowley's body yet, you understand," said Gupta. "I've read the thumbnail report and viewed the photos, but that's it. So I don't know what I can tell you."

"You know there was a flood in her basement, right?" asked Vega. "The police found her after the fire department pumped out the water."

"Yes," said Gupta. "I saw that in the report."

"So my first question is, how much forensic evidence is going to be lost because of the flood?"

"Some," said Gupta. "But if someone hung her against her will and she fought back, there should still be evidence under her fingernails—even with the flood."

"And if there isn't?"

Gupta regarded him over the rims of her bright red frames. "You sound as if you have concerns about this case."

"Lake Holly is under pressure to close this quickly and quietly," said Vega. "I don't want to feel like I rolled over on this."

"I see." She pulled two mugs down from a shelf and poured the coffee. Then she handed him a cup. "I can assure you, I will do a thorough job. As always."

"I know that." Vega wondered if he'd offended her by coming here like this. "It's not you I'm worried about. It's all the loose ends. Her housekeeper is missing. Last night, Detective Sanchez went to interview the family. They wouldn't speak to him."

Gupta thought about that for a moment. "What's the housekeeper's name?"

"Lissette Aviles."

"She's . . . Mexican?"

"Salvadoran."

"Undocumented?"

"Most likely."

Gupta stared into her coffee. "I don't have to tell you how hard it is these days to get immigrants to speak to the police. Most likely, her whole family's afraid of getting deported."

"Her uncle's in removal proceedings."

"There you go."

"You're probably right," Vega admitted. "But I feel like I'm missing something. When I went through Talia's drawers, I found this cheap wallet that didn't look like something she'd own. It was hidden at the back of her sweater drawer. Inside, there was a photograph of two little Hispanic girls. Crowley has no idea who the girls are. And Lissette's family isn't talking so we don't know if they're related to Lissette or not."

"When you say, 'Lissette's family,' do you mean a husband? Parents?" asked Gupta.

"She's twenty-three and unmarried," said Vega. "She lives here with her uncle and his family. The uncle, Edgar Aviles, is the handyman at Beth Shalom."

Gupta put her mug to her lips and paused. Her eyes got the same razor sharpness they had when she was examining a bullet fragment in a corpse. "The uncle's name is Edgar Aviles?"

"Technically, Edgar Aviles-Ceren," said Vega. "But I think he uses the Americanized version of his name here."

"Ceren . . . That's not a common Spanish surname, is it?"

"I don't think so," said Vega. "Why?"

"Come to my office," said Gupta. "I want to check something in the database."

The walls of Gupta's office—like her glasses—were a vivid shade of red. Not a color Vega would have expected for a medical examiner. But then again, nothing about Dr. Gupta was ordinary. Her shelves were filled with kitschy Third World souvenirs sandwiched in between family photographs, medical textbooks, and awards. Worry dolls from Central America. Carved wooden animals and death masks from Africa. Incense burners from India and Tibet. Over her desk was a framed quote by Voltaire: *To the living we owe respect, but to the dead we owe only truth.*

She turned on her computer and spoke over her shoulder as she scrolled through the screens.

"A couple of weeks ago, the Warburton Police found a body in the brush near the old muffler plant. No head or hands. Male. Medium-brown complexion. Approximately five-foot-eight, a hundred and seventy pounds. Heavily tattooed."

"The John Doe gangbanger," Vega remembered. "I saw the report at our weekly briefings. He had an MS-13 tattoo, as I recall."

"You are correct," said Gupta. "We sent out the DNA and got a match yesterday to a convicted burglar and gang member. But that's not what made me think of him here. It's the scrap of paper we found in his jeans when his body was first recovered. There was a list of names on it. One of them, I recall, was 'Ceren.'"

"You remember a name on a piece of paper from a dead man you autopsied weeks ago?" Vega couldn't hide his surprise. "Man, you'd be hell on wheels at a blackjack table."

Gupta swallowed a smile. Vega was flirting with her. He could tell she liked it. She went back to scanning the screen.

"Ah. Here it is."

She opened the document and turned the screen to face Vega. On it was a photograph of a torn piece of lined notebook paper smeared in grease stains and dried blood. In the center, someone had scribbled five names in black ink:

> *Cesar Zuma-Léon*
> *Jesús Monroy-Peña*
> *Deisy Ramos-Sandoval*
> *Wilmer Diaz-Garcia*
> *Edgar Ceren-Aviles*

Vega stared at the last name on the list: *Edgar Ceren-Aviles*. Was he Lissette's uncle? If so, the last names were in the wrong order. "Ceren" was Edgar Aviles's mother's last name—not his father's.

But a bigger question lingered: What was a temple handyman's name doing in the pocket of a dead gangbanger anyway?

"Do you mind texting me a photocopy of this list?" asked Vega. "I'd like to run down whether there are any connections between these names and our case."

"Certainly."

Vega gave her his cell number. Gupta copied the document and texted it over. Her landline phone rang on her desk. She took the call while Vega studied the screen. The dead gangbanger had been ID'd through a DNA match to his arrest records as twenty-two-year-old Elmer Ortega.

Ortega. Greco had mentioned a BOLO they'd put out on a gangbanger named "Ortega" after that jewelry store heist. Vega was betting this was the same guy.

Gupta finished her call and hung up. She peered at Vega over the tops of her glasses like a school principal. "That was Detective Greco."

"Did you tell him I'm here?"

"Yes. He said you weren't authorized to be."

Vega shrugged. "Somebody from the investigation needs to be overseeing the autopsy."

"Somebody is," said Gupta. "Greco called to say she's on her way."

"*She?* You don't mean Michelle Lopez?"

"That's the name, yes."

Chapter 9

Jimmy Vega caught up to Michelle in the parking lot of the medical examiner's office. She was dressed federal: dark blue blazer, white blouse, low-heeled pumps, and minimal jewelry. Only those dyed-blond curls gave her a little bit of Bronx edge.

"Exactly what do you think you're doing here?" she demanded when she saw him.

"My job," he shot back. "I had no idea Greco had assigned anyone to the cut."

"Well, he did. This morning," she said. "I'll take it from here."

She turned and headed for the front doors.

"You know what you're looking for?" asked Vega. "I don't want to see anything lost on a learning curve."

"A *learning curve?*" She spun on her heel and faced him. "Are you always such a prick with women? Or am I getting the deluxe family special here?"

Vega held up his hands. "This has nothing to do with you being a wo—"

"For your information," she cut him off. "I spent five-plus years at the Department of Corrections observing the autopsies of every inmate who died in city custody. I can tell a postmortem bruise from an antemortem. I know what a bone saw looks like. And I know that you can get a knockoff at Home Depot that will do the same job for a tenth the price. So don't give me your boys-club bullshit, Jimmy."

She turned away and headed to the front doors.

"Michelle . . ." Vega ran ahead of her and blocked her path, searching for a way to derail what his mouth had already set in motion. "I'm not the misogynist you think I am. I swear," he said. "It's just . . . seeing you like this . . . it's disorienting. This case is so much more than a suicide, if it's a suicide at all. I don't want to see anything get overlooked."

"Neither do I." She thrust her chin toward the building. "Did you find out anything I should know about before I go in?"

"A lot," said Vega. "But I have no idea if it has anything to do with Talia Crowley, or if it's just a sub-drama concerning her housekeeper. Has she turned up yet?"

Michelle shook her head. "Greco's got an alert out on her but nothing's come in. And now, it's about to become a twofer."

"What do you mean?"

Michelle glanced over at her white ICE sedan with the blue angled slash down the side. "Maybe we should discuss this in my car. I've got five minutes before I need to be inside."

Vega followed Michelle over to her car. She beeped open the doors and began speaking as soon as Vega folded himself into the front passenger seat.

"Two of my colleagues at ICE executed a removal order on Edgar Aviles at five this morning."

"He's in custody?"

"Not quite," said Michelle. "He bolted. Witnesses say he boarded a southbound Metro-North train. He could be in New York City by now. Or points beyond."

Vega let out a string of Spanish curses. He forgot that Michelle knew every one.

"Look, Jimmy," she stopped him. "This decision was made by our enforcement division. I'm in investigations. All we share in common is an administrative assistant."

"One division doesn't speak to the other? Share intel?"

"On a Saturday morning at five a.m.? No. This order probably came down several days ago—before Talia died and Lissette went missing. And besides, having Aviles in custody might have worked to our advantage. If he knows something, we'd have had leverage."

"Except—you got nothing," said Vega. "Because Dumb and Dumber couldn't catch a cold in flu season."

Michelle gave Vega a sour look. "Were you always anti-ICE? Or is this *her* influence?"

"*Her?*"

"Your girlfriend. Adele Figueroa. The head of La Casa."

"How do you know—?"

"Ryan Bale told me. He said your values were"—she put her fingers in quotes—" 'compromised.' "

"Which means that asshole also knows—"

"Relax, Jimmy. He has no idea we're related."

Vega didn't want Michelle dissecting his personal life. He had enough "personal life" with her already. He pulled up Dr. Gupta's email with that list of names from the dead gangster. He showed it to Michelle while he explained where the list came from.

"Okaay." She handed Vega back his phone. "But what's that got to do with Talia Crowley's death? Or Lissette's disappearance?"

"I don't know," Vega admitted. "And now, I never will." He slapped the dashboard in disgust. "Of all the people ICE could arrest, they had to arrest a janitor whose been in this country almost twenty years? The guy's got no criminal record. He's got a five-year-old with cancer and a sick wife. That doesn't bother you a teeny, tiny little bit?"

She glared at Vega.

"You care so much for people you don't even know,"

she shot back. "How about caring for the ones you do? You haven't asked a single personal question since we ran into each other."

"Anyone sick? Dying?"

She tossed off a laugh. "That's your idea of a personal question? No. No one's sick or dying. Denise is still teaching. I don't hear much from Natasha—I'm not even sure what she's up to. But that's to be expected, given our different mothers. My older son's turning into quite a ball player. Just like you used to be."

"What's his position?"

"Shortstop."

"Same as I used to play." Vega searched for something else to ask, but he couldn't even remember the boy's name.

"Pop's going strong," Michelle offered. "He still plays bass with his merengue band when his arthritis isn't acting up. I know he'd love to hear from you."

Vega drummed his fingers on the thighs of his khakis and said nothing.

"You can't spare an afternoon to visit your father?"

"He may be your father," said Vega. "He isn't mine."

"You have another?"

"I never had *one*."

Michelle reached into her handbag and pulled out her wallet. A shiny pink thing. Vega wondered if she caught crap for it from the other agents. She flipped it open. From a small flap on the inside, she unearthed a dog-eared photograph and held it out to him.

"Here. A reminder. For old time's sake."

It was a picture of Vega and two other boys playing stickball in the rubble of a Bronx lot. It was a color photo, but the picture was so faded and the background so stark, it might as well have been black-and-white. Two abandoned five-story tenements loomed in the background, their vacant windows dark and hollow like missing teeth. Old tires and broken refrigerators sat by a wall covered in gang graffiti, loopy bubble writing made by teenagers who were probably long dead now if they'd stayed in the life. The Bronx was a totally different place these days. Vibrant and reasonably prosperous.

It wasn't back then.

"I don't remember this picture," said Vega.

"I came across it one day in one of Pop's drawers. I didn't have any other pictures of you."

Vega had to be about six in the photograph. He was the smallest of the three boys. He was wearing jeans that were two sizes too big for him. They were rolled up at the ankles, pulled in with rope in the belt loops. Even in the photograph's muted colorings, Vega could see he looked filthy and scabbed. His jeans were smeared with dirt. His oversized undershirt couldn't possibly be called "white." His bangs hung down, nearly to the lids of his eyes.

The two older boys didn't look much better. They were closer to nine or ten. Both were rangy, almost malnourished. Their clothes were dirty, their hair uncombed. Vega had only one word for all of them: feral. They looked like nobody was raising them. Nobody at all.

Vega flipped the photograph over. Somebody had written all three boys' first and last names on the back: *Jimmy Vega, Johnny Ray Osorio, Angel Dominguez.*

"Were Johnny Ray and Angel friends?" asked Michelle.

"I couldn't tell you which was which," said Vega. "I don't have any memory of them."

"I asked Pop. He said he didn't know. I thought maybe it was when you got sent away."

"Sent . . . ?" Vega felt like the ground beneath him had shifted. The day was heating up. It was warm in the car. Yet he shuddered like he'd just walked into a room with too much air-conditioning.

"I was never sent away," Vega insisted. "Sent away for what?"

"I don't know," said Michelle. "That's what my mom always said."

"Well, she's wrong." Vega went to hand the picture back to her.

"Keep it," she told him. "It belongs to you more than it does to me."

The photograph made him sad. Worse, it made him uneasy. He was anxious to get away.

"They'll be starting the cut soon," he said. "You'd better go inside."

Chapter 10

Vega sat in his truck after Michelle went inside, staring at the dog-eared photograph of him in that vacant Bronx lot with two other boys.

You got sent away.

Michelle's words pressed against his insides like a half-remembered TV jingle from thirty years ago. From time to time as an adult, he'd catch a vague and fleeting sensation of great loss mixed with great rage. He never knew how to describe it except to say that it felt like he was standing at the bottom of a dark well while people walked above, oblivious.

Odd things triggered it. The buttery sweet smell of Coppertone suntan lotion. Old reruns of *Sesame Street*. That Kool & the Gang song, "Celebration," that always seemed happy and yet made him feel sad.

He carried tics and phobias whose origins mystified him. He grew panicky in enclosed spaces. He was almost pathologically on time for things, fearful of showing up late and being left behind. He felt a special affinity for lost children, as if somewhere, somehow, a part of him was lost.

And then there were the rages Vega recalled in early childhood. Dark, foul torrents of anger that came on in first grade. He spent much of that year in Sister Margarita's office. For throwing a stapler at his teacher. For getting into fistfights on the playground. For overturning a table full of juice cups. Once, he took a black magic marker and drew over every part of his body—even his face—as if he were trying to obliterate himself. His kindergarten teacher at St. Raymond's in the Bronx had described him as a "sunny, friendly child," who "played well with others."

His first-grade teacher said he needed a special school.

For his seventh birthday, his mother bought him an old guitar from a pawnshop on East Tremont Avenue. Music turned out to be his salvation. He practiced for hours until the pads of his fingers were as tough as shoe leather. The notes filled the hollow spaces inside of him. Gradually, the rages stopped. They were gone entirely by the winter of second grade. His mother and grandmother never spoke of them again. He'd outrun his demons.

Or at least he thought he had. Until Michelle handed him that picture.

Vega's cell phone rang in his pocket. He tucked the photograph inside his wallet and checked the screen. *Greco.* He picked up.

"What's this I hear about you showing up at the ME's office?" Greco growled into the receiver.

"I thought no one was assigned to the cut," said Vega. "Be glad I was here. I picked up some intel for you on the jewelry-store heist. Elmer Ortega, your chief suspect, is the headless and handless John Doe Warburton found down by the muffler factory a few weeks ago. The DNA just came in."

"So, you're working the burglary too? What is this? Buy-one-get-one-free week with the county police?"

"I thought you'd want to know," said Vega. "Plus, it may figure into the Crowley case."

"How so?"

"Ortega was carrying a list in his pocket when he died with five names on it. One of them was Edgar Ceren-Aviles. Switch those last names and you've got Lissette's uncle."

"And this helps us . . . how?"

"I don't know," Vega admitted. "But it's surprising, don't you think? Aviles is a handyman, not a gangbanger."

"Right now, he's a fugitive," said Greco. "Michelle told you, right? ICE tried to nab Aviles this morning. He jackrabbited."

"Maybe he's with Lissette."

"Yeah, well, let's hope so," said Greco. "In the meantime, I need you to take a ride over to the new CIC."

Vega sucked back his disappointment. He'd much rather be out talking to suspects than sifting through data at the County Intelligence Center, a fledgling unit that gathered electronic surveillance material for law enforcement. Everything from bridge-toll receipts to footage from license-plate readers.

"Something specific you're looking for?" asked Vega.

Silence. Greco seemed to be debating what to say over the phone. "Let's just say, it doesn't take three hours to drive from Lake Holly to Albany."

"Is that what Crowley is claiming?"

"Me and Sanchez just came from speaking to him," said Greco. "He says his driver, Victor Franco, picked him up at six on Thursday evening. They got to the hotel where the conference was being held at nine."

"No stops?"

"He says they caught dinner at a place called Mario's up in Taylorsville. I have a copy of the receipt. Long dinner."

Greco let that hang in the air for a second. Vega was wondering if Greco was having second thoughts about wrapping up the case quickly.

"We're having a meeting at the station house at noon," he said. "I'm texting you the license plate of the Lincoln Navigator that Victor Franco drove Crowley up to Albany in. Get the license-plate reader records and E-ZPass receipts for the vehicle. We'll talk then." Greco hung up.

Vega stared at his phone. The three-hour trip from Lake Holly to Albany got Vega curious too. He'd take a drive down to Warburton, to the former factory that now housed the CIC, and pull the records. And while he was there, he'd stop in to the Warburton Police and see his friend and drummer, Richie Solero, who just happened to work on their Gang Intelligence Squad.

Elmer Ortega's list was curious too.

It was another half hour south from the medical examiner's office to Warburton, the most industrial part of the county. The terrain grew more congested with each mile, going from bungalows to garden apartments to strip shopping malls, and finally, to a steady skyline of red-brick and sandstone mid-rises along hilly boulevards. Beyond, Vega could see the wide, gray choppy waters of the Hudson River and the wall of chiseled granite cliffs on the other side.

Solero had already punched out from his overnight shift, but he'd agreed to wait around for Vega—especially after Vega dangled the information that the John Doe at the ME's office had been ID'd through DNA as Elmer Ortega.

"Park in the precinct lot—even if you have to double-park," Solero warned Vega. "The locals see your police sticker, you're gonna have two broken headlights and a windshield covered in spray paint before you leave."

Vega couldn't find a space so he double-parked like his friend had suggested and left his keys with the desk sergeant. He waited in a stripped-down front lobby that had no place to sit—by design, Vega suspected.

A door opened a few minutes later, and Solero's head popped out.

"Only time I think I've seen you without a guitar strapped to your shoulder." Solero held out a knuckle. Vega rapped it.

"Only time I've seen you in uniform. Well, half in uniform." Solero worked undercover, but for some reason he had on his dark blue police uniform shirt over jeans.

"I had to take a new personnel photo this morning," Solero explained. "I didn't want to slip into all my gear so I just brought the shirt." Solero ripped the two halves apart. Vega pointed to the buttons.

"We county cops actually have to learn how to button our shirts, not Velcro them like preschoolers."

"Yeah?" Solero shrugged off the shirt, revealing two massive biceps and a neck that jutted from his black T-shirt beneath like a fire hydrant. "When you need your backup gun on your Kevlar vest quickly, tell me how those buttons are working for you."

"Good point," said Vega. "You come up with that idea?"

"A couple of cops at the gym gave me the idea," said Solero. "It comes in handy when I'm going from working here to working out with clients."

Solero, like a lot of bodybuilding cops Vega knew, worked a side job as a personal trainer. The money came in handy since it was expensive to train and compete on the bodybuilding circuit. Vega never understood the appeal. He liked staying in shape too. He had a weight bench right off the dining area and worked out regularly. But he never cared for the Popeye look.

Solero walked Vega through the locked entry door.

"You get the text from Danny about tonight's gig?" Solero was referring to Danny Molina, the band's keyboardist.

"No," said Vega. "What's up?"

"The groom wants us to play the 'Macarena.'"

Vega groaned. Every drunken wedding and bachelor party the band played requested it. There was a nine-out-of-ten chance that the groom would want to come onstage and sing and dance too. Maybe bring the whole wedding party up.

"Please tell me he's not a guitarist." Vega didn't want some drunk messing with his guitars. "Half these gigs— they'd do better just hiring a DJ, you know?"

"Be happy they don't."

Solero walked Vega along a faded army-green hallway past file rooms, a small kitchen, and a detectives' bullpen. WANTED posters and maps of the city lined the walls, along with personnel reminders against sexual harassment and police brutality. It was the same in every station house these days. Cops watched the citizens. The brass watched the cops. Nobody trusted anybody anymore.

"Have you talked to Chuck McCormick recently?" Vega asked Solero. McCormick was one of Solero's personal training clients. He lived up near Vega in a big house with his own recording studio. He'd given the band a special price to come in and lay down the tracks for an eight-song CD.

Vega hadn't cut a CD since before he became a cop. Back then, he harbored visions of becoming a full-time guitarist and going on the road with his band, Straight Money. Then Joy came along and he had to abandon his dreams. He was too old for the road now. His current band, *Armado*— Spanish for "armed"—was all cops with jobs and families and pension considerations that kept them from getting too serious. But he still loved the music. He and Molina had written a bunch of songs and it was exciting to put together a CD after all this time.

"I saw Chuck last Tuesday," said Solero. "He's still working on engineering the mix."

"It's been a month," Vega grumbled.

"He'll get around to it in the next week or two," said Solero. "Don't worry."

Solero opened the door to a room with a bunch of desks

pushed together. The walls were lined with more mug shots—mostly of black and Hispanic men. None of them looked to be more than about thirty.

Gang members never lived much beyond that.

"Welcome to Warburton's Gang Intelligence Squad." Solero grinned. "Though it's debatable whether 'gang' and 'intelligence' belong in the same sentence."

Solero walked over to the squad refrigerator in the corner, next to a coffee machine. He opened the refrigerator and pulled out two Cokes. He threw one to Vega. "Heads up."

Vega caught it cleanly. "Thanks."

Solero pulled out two armless chairs on rollers and gestured to Vega to take one. He spun his own backward and straddled it, resting his chin on one hand while he sipped his Coke. His bristle-short black hair sat high and tight on his scalp like a crown. He was Cuban on his father's side, but his features favored his Italian-American mother. Most people were surprised there was any Hispanic in him at all.

"The crew's not here on Saturday mornings," Solero explained. "The knife-and-gun club is more of a Friday- and Saturday-night operation. So how'd you hear about Cheetos?"

"Who?"

"Elmer Ortega," said Solero. "His gang moniker is 'Cheetos.' Word on the street was, he got the name because he tended to leave his prints on things—"

"Like the jewelry store in Lake Holly," said Vega. "They had a BOLO out on Ortega before he disappeared. You'd better check in with them."

"Will do," said Solero. "Is that your connection to the case?"

"No." Vega told Solero about catching the rotation for a 10-56—only to find out it was the DA's young bride.

"I heard," said Solero. "You're on that?"

"Just assisting Lake Holly," said Vega. "They're under pressure to close it down cleanly and quickly. If it's a suicide, fine. But her housekeeper's missing and this morning, when I was at the ME's office, Gupta told me that when Elmer Ortega's body was found, he had a list of names in his pocket. One of those names may be the housekeeper's uncle."

"Which name?"

"Edgar Ceren-Aviles," said Vega. "The housekeeper's name is Lissette Aviles. Her uncle is Edgar Aviles-Ceren. It might not be the same guy. On the other hand, Ceren's not a common name."

Solero played with the tab on his soda can while he thought about that. The tab made a tinny sound that seemed to drown out the ringing telephones and cops' voices in the halls.

"Maybe the uncle's a gangbanger."

"He was a handyman at a synagogue in Lake Holly," said Vega. "I say, 'was,' because this morning, ICE tried to arrest him on a removal order and he split. I'm trying to figure out where he went and if his niece—our witness—is with him. Were you ever able to track down any of the names on that gangster's list?"

"No hits from our gang database or criminal records," said Solero. "Mostly, we were concentrating on putting a name to the body. Now that we have one, we may be able to do something with the names."

"Got any theories?" asked Vega.

"Cheetos was a small-time drug dealer and thief—"

"I thought he was MS-13?"

"He was," said Solero. "But up here, every small-time Latin-American hood identifies himself as that. These guys aren't the Mafia, you know. They're opportunistic, impulsive thugs. So long as they pay their overlords, they can freelance all they want. My guess is that Cheetos was shaking down illegals in the neighborhood and those names correspond to people too scared to come forward."

"If that's the case," said Vega, "why Aviles? He lives in Lake Holly—not Warburton. Same with his niece."

Solero shrugged. "You said yourself, it may not be him."

"Can you do a little legwork on this for me?" asked Vega. "I know your primary focus is on getting the gangbangers who killed and dismembered Cheetos. But can you ask around on that list of names? Maybe the Avileses have connections to Warburton we don't know about. The family's not talking."

"Gotcha. Thanks for the intel. I'll check it out." Solero rose and tossed his can in the trash. Vega did the same.

"Come on," said Solero. "I'll walk you out."

Solero's black Jeep Grand Cherokee was easy to spot in the lot. It had two stickers on the rear bumper: WARNING: I BRAKE FOR DRUM SOLOS and another, with a picture of a drum kit and the words THE TEMPO IS WHATEVER I SAY IT IS.

Vega pointed to the "tempo" sticker. "Least you're honest," he teased.

"Least I'm in tune." Solero grinned and punched Vega playfully on the shoulder. Vega was sure he'd see a bruise there later. "Danny said to try and act excited when we do the 'Macarena' tonight."

Vega groaned again. "Give me Luis Fonsi's 'Despacito' any day. Or even Ricky Martin—"

"Maybe after a few drinks, they'll forget to ask for it," said Solero.

"You kidding? That's always when they ask for it."

Chapter 11

The County Intelligence Center was just a few blocks from Richie Solero's police precinct, in a rundown part of Warburton. The outside still looked like a warehouse. No signage. No windows. Cement block walls. A flat roof with fan-coil vents and razor wire. Only the elaborate security gate and surveillance cameras spoke of something more.

Vega showed his badge and ID to a cop in the security booth who scanned them into his computer and directed Vega to the parking lot. Another officer checked his ID again in the lobby, beneath the county police emblem and a sign that read: LUX ET VERITAS. *Light and Truth.*

There was more than a little irony to the CIC's motto.

"Sergeant Burke will be out in a few minutes," said the officer at the front desk.

"Thanks."

Vega suspected Sergeant Burke was either a grizzled veteran waiting to retire or a newly promoted officer dying to escape. Although the CIC was technically part of the county police, it operated independently. Recruits were often taken straight out of the academy or via some circuitous route like internal affairs. Ninety percent of the yearly budget came from civil forfeiture—confiscated cars, cash, and electronics. The so-called spoils of victory. It always left Vega a little squeamish.

Sergeant Burke was not a grizzled veteran. He was a she. A very pregnant she. With a cascade of long beaded braids— a style Vega really liked on African-American women. Leticia Burke's badge was looped around her neck. It rode the belly of her maternity blouse as she shook Vega's hand.

"Detective Vega—I don't think we've ever met."

"I don't think so." Vega wasn't sure if he should congratulate Sergeant Burke on her obvious pregnancy or pretend it didn't exist. His mouth had gotten him into so much hot water with Michelle earlier, he decided to say nothing.

"We only got the intel request from Detective Greco this morning," Burke explained. "I can give you a broad idea of what we have. But if you want a more targeted approach, we'd need another twenty-four to forty-eight hours."

"Can you take me through what you've got so far?" asked Vega. "We have a meeting at noon and I'd like to go in with something."

"Sure."

Vega followed the sergeant down a fluorescent-lit hallway with doors on either side, all locked and nameless. The CIC had only been in existence for about two years, but it already seemed to contain a massive amount of information. Every day, all over the county and beyond, small cameras known as license-plate readers or LPRs, took pictures of plates on public roads and stored that information in police computers, making it possible to track the movements of suspects and law-abiding civilians alike. Cashless tolls at bridges added another layer of surveillance. Cellular phone trackers known as Stingrays operated like cell towers and collected still more information on people's whereabouts.

In addition to these devices, the CIC had access to

dozens and dozens of databases, from both law enforcement and civilian sources. Everything from drone footage at rallies to credit scores to real-time video feeds from public cameras. And that didn't include public access databases like real estate, Google Maps, and social media, that added another layer of knowledge.

"Big Brother," Adele had groaned, when Vega told her about what the CIC could track these days.

"Maybe," said Vega. "But if you've got a snatched kid or a would-be school shooter, you want this data on your side."

At the end of the hall, Burke held up her badge to unlock another set of doors. They opened onto a large windowless room with rows of desks across the center and banks of television monitors along one wall. About a dozen men and women sat hunched behind the desks, their eyes glazed by the glow of the screens while the monitors shifted from one video feed to another in timed intervals. The whole room was physically static but visually frenzied—like an airport control tower.

On a wall opposite the monitors sat three glass-enclosed offices and a small conference room. Burke gestured to the conference room. "I've got us set up in there."

"Can I . . . carry anything in for you?" asked Vega.

Burke smiled, showing a perfect space between her two front teeth. "One of my analysts already did. Thank you."

The stack of papers on the conference room table looked like it weighed twenty pounds.

"All this stuff is for the Crowley case?" asked Vega.

"It's an inverse ratio," said Burke. "When a department knows exactly what it wants, the information is precise and targeted. When it goes on a fishing expedition, this is the result."

Vega took a seat and pulled out his notepad. "What, exactly, did Detective Greco ask you for?" Vega didn't want to start mentioning his doubts about the district attorney's alibi if Greco hadn't.

"The detective gave us three license plates and asked us to run them through our LPR database for all travel since last Monday."

Vega saw the three plate numbers on the top request sheet.

"May I?" Vega asked, pointing to the page.

"Help yourself."

The sheet indicated that one of the tracked plates was registered to a black Mercedes leased by Glen Crowley. Another was registered to a white Lexus, leased by Talia. The third was a Lincoln Navigator owned by the county—likely the one Victor Franco drove on Thursday night to Albany. Sergeant Burke had to know what Greco was trying to pin down here—even if Vega didn't expressly come out and say it.

"Did anything leap out at you?" Vega asked Burke.

"Leap?" Burke smiled. "Raw data like this doesn't *leap,* Detective. It limps. I simply don't know enough from this information to tell you if their movements were normal. I can tell you that the three vehicles didn't travel outside the state and—except for the Navigator's Thursday-night excursion to Albany—all of the travel was local. That's about it."

"Fair enough." Vega liked Burke. He decided to go out on a limb. "Here's my concern. Our district attorney and his driver claim they left Lake Holly at six p.m. Thursday night and didn't get to Albany until nine. They explain the delay by saying they stopped at a pizzeria up in Taylorsville called Mario's. I don't buy the long delay."

"You think they left later? Made more than one stopover?"

"I don't know," Vega admitted. "I just think they're covering up something. What? I can't say—except that one lie often leads to others."

Burke let the allegations settle over them for a moment. She thumbed the pages of the report until she found the one that mapped out the Navigator's journey from Lake Holly to Albany on Thursday evening.

"License-plate readers aren't GPS trackers," Burke explained. "We don't have a minute-by-minute recounting of where the vehicle traveled. But given the points we've been able to track, it backs up their statements. The Navigator left Lake Holly around six, arrived in Albany around nine, and made one detour off the New York State Thruway, passing by an LPR in the westbound lane of Route 113 at seven thirty and one on the eastbound lane, at eight thirty-five."

Vega tapped his pen on his notepad. "Can I ask you a question? Hypothetically?"

"Sure."

"Why would the district attorney go five miles off the highway to visit a crummy little pizzeria? I Googled Mario's. They're not on any Zagat-rated list. They're a take-out joint with ninety-nine-cent slice specials on Tuesdays."

Burke shrugged. "Maybe it wasn't about the pizza. Maybe they just needed a place with good Wi-Fi. Reception can be lousy on parts of the Thruway."

"True . . ."

"Maybe we can work this another way," Burke suggested. "Do you have a copy of the purchase receipt from Mario's? That would give us an exact time they were in the place."

"I don't, but I can get it from Greco." Vega pulled out his phone and texted a message to Greco. Then he thumbed the stack of printouts while he waited for a reply. He felt like a big chunk of what he really wanted to know was missing here.

"I hate to ask you to do more work," Vega began. "But . . ." He smiled his most flirtatious smile.

"What?"

"If I gave you a cell phone number, do you think you could track it?"

Her face paled. "You want the CIC to track our district attorney's cell phone?"

Vega waved his hands in front of his face. "No. Of course not. Nothing like that." Relief flooded her eyes. She was clearly counting on a long career at the CIC.

"Talia Crowley's housekeeper, Lissette Aviles, has been missing since Talia's death. Lissette's family isn't cooperating. The number I want you to track belongs to the housekeeper. I only need the period from Thursday night until now."

"You *do* realize I have no way of telling you who she called," said Burke. "Not without a court order. All I can tell you is whether her phone was on and what cell tower it pinged off of."

"I understand," said Vega. "I'll take what I can get."

Vega gave Burke Lissette's phone number. Burke left the room to ask an analyst to run the data. When she returned—with a laptop under her arm—Vega showed her Greco's reply, along with a copy of the receipt from Mario's showing the purchase of two slices of pizza and two Snapples at seven forty-five. From her wrinkled nose, Vega gathered Burke didn't buy the long lead time between Mario's and Albany either.

She flicked back her braids and opened the laptop. "Maybe Mario's wasn't his destination."

She pulled up Google Maps and typed, *Mario's, Taylorsville, NY.* She clicked on *street view.* Up came a photograph of a one-story strip mall with four stores of plate-glass windows beneath cheap signage. From left to right, Vega counted an insurance agency, a car parts store, Mario's, and a place that sold tropical fish.

"Nothing of interest there," said Burke. She hit the little arrow compass on the picture and spun the viewfinder 180 degrees, as if they were standing in the parking lot facing the other side of the two-lane county roadway. Across the street, Vega saw a gas station with a mini-mart attached. The gas was off-brand. Everything about the area looked tired and dated and slightly seedy. The concrete ramp to the gas station was cracked. The parking lot of Mario's had potholes and weeds growing around the edges.

"Guess I was wrong," said Burke. "I thought perhaps they hadn't stopped there for the food." She went to hit *escape*.

"No. Wait," said Vega. He spun the arrow back to Mario's parking lot and hit the street arrow to take him just east of the pizzeria. He saw nothing but a dilapidated trailer park. He turned the arrow around and walked it just west of the pizzeria. He came to a cement block building with weeds in front and windows covered in shades. A big neon sign on top advertised the business as RELAX SPA.

Vega zoomed in on the picture. "What day spa do you know that advertises with a neon sign?"

"They ain't licensed in shiatsu," Burke said, grinning. "That's for sure."

There was a knock on the glass. A young white guy in a polo shirt and khakis waved a piece of paper at Burke. Vega wasn't sure if he was a civilian or a cop. The CIC had civilian employees too.

Burke got up from her chair and retrieved the piece of paper. She frowned as she settled herself back in her chair.

"Lissette Aviles's phone number hasn't registered an incoming or outgoing call in the tristate area since ten p.m. last night," said Burke.

"What does that mean, exactly?" asked Vega. "That her phone's been turned off?"

"Could be," said Burke. "It could also mean she's not in the tristate area anymore. Or that she's in an area where cell phone reception is spotty. Or simply, that she ran out of juice."

"Where was her last known location?"

Burke pointed her finger at a series of codes on the page. "These numbers correspond to a cell tower up near the Lake Holly Reservoir," she explained. "That region is notoriously bad for cell reception."

Vega knew the area well. His daughter lived out that way with his ex-wife and her second husband. The houses were on acre-plus lots of land, surrounded by woods. The roads were narrow, twisting two lanes with no sidewalks or public transit. Aside from the old Magnolia Inn restaurant, there were no businesses in the vicinity. You had to crest the hill and drive through the horse farms and estates in Wickford or Clairmont before you hit anything resembling a town.

Vega scribbled *Magnolia Inn* into his notes. Maybe Lissette had a friend who worked at the inn. There were plenty of Latino busboys and waiters who might know the twenty-three-year-old and want to help her hide.

The question was—from what?

Chapter 12

The phone calls started as soon as Adele Figueroa dropped off her ten-year-old daughter at soccer practice on Saturday morning. They came from clients. From volunteers. From the weekend staff at La Casa. They were all about one thing:

"There's been another ICE raid," they told her in whispers and choked sobs.

"Where?" Adele asked them. "When?"

Last week, it had been a busboy from Guatemala. Two weeks before that, it had been a high school student from Ecuador. Now, it was the synagogue's Salvadoran handyman. The names and nationalities changed but little else.

She sat in her car in the elementary school parking lot and watched Sophia and twelve other little girls dribble and pass their soccer balls while Adele probed her callers for details. Every ICE raid felt personal. Adele had spent her entire childhood living in fear that her own parents would be deported, that a morning's kiss or bedtime tuck-in could be their last.

Her father died of a heart attack on American soil when Adele was sixteen. Her mother succumbed to cancer six years later. They never ventured farther than New York City after they left Ecuador. Yet to their dying day, they lived in fear of that early-morning knock on the door. And here Adele was, all these years later—a Harvard Law School graduate, head of La Casa, on the advisory board of an immigration think tank in Washington, DC—and she still felt as powerless as she had all those years ago.

"His wife says he ran," Adele's assistant, Ramona, explained. Ramona was first-generation American, the daughter of undocumented parents just like Adele so raids cut deeply into her psyche as well.

"Does the wife know where he's hiding?"

"If she does, she's not saying."

"What happened to our agreement with the police about courtesy calls?" asked Adele. "I thought we settled that six months ago."

Lake Holly's "courtesy calls" to La Casa began after an immigrant mother and child were seriously injured jumping out of a window during an ICE raid that they weren't even the target of. As a result, the local police began the practice of informing La Casa that a raid was in progress or had just taken place. That didn't help the target—who was already in ICE custody by the time La Casa got word. But it ensured the general safety of the community.

"Did the police call any of the board members?" asked Adele.

"No. No one," said Ramona. "Maybe they figured you wouldn't want to be woken up about it at five a.m. on a Saturday morning."

"I sincerely doubt the Lake Holly PD cares a whit about my sleep preferences."

"Wait, it gets worse," said Ramona. "When we opened La Casa at eight this morning, Officer Bale was here."

"What for?"

"He wanted to know if we were hiding the man. He demanded I let him search the center. He threatened to close us down if I refused."

"You didn't let him in, did you?" asked Adele. As both a criminal defense attorney and the director of an immigrant center, she would never submit to such a search without a warrant.

"I told him Edgar Aviles wasn't a client, he wasn't inside, and the police would have to get a warrant if he couldn't take my word for it."

"Good girl." Ramona was only twenty-four, but she reminded Adele of herself at that age.

"He left when I refused him entry," said Ramona. "But I'm worried that one of these days, the local police will just roll over and let ICE storm the whole place."

"Not as long as there is breath in my lungs." Adele checked her watch. She'd planned to do some grocery shopping while Sophia was at soccer practice. But there was no way she could let the police's behavior on this slide.

"I'm going over to the station now," she told Ramona. "This whole situation is completely unacceptable. Call me if you hear anything about Aviles."

"I will."

Adele expected the Lake Holly police station to be quiet on a warm spring Saturday, but she noticed more cars than usual in the lot. She wondered if it had to do with the case Vega had been called in on last night. He'd told her only that it was a potential suicide and he'd have to work today. He was often closemouthed at the beginning of an investigation. She supposed she'd learn more this evening when she helped him and the band set up for their gig.

She parked in visitor parking and walked through the front doors of the station house. Sergeant Foley was at a desk behind a glass booth. He was a wiry man who wore a grimace like he suffered a permanent case of hemorrhoids. He saw her, then pretended not to by busying himself writing something in a logbook. When he bent over, Adele could see his sunburned scalp between shafts of short-cropped gray hair. Lake Holly's police chief, John

Battaglia, might choke down a tamale every now and then with the Hispanic community, but the rank and file clearly considered Adele and La Casa a thorn in their side.

Adele didn't wait for Foley to pretend to notice her. She walked up to his booth and began speaking.

"Sergeant," she began. "Were you in charge of the shift last night?"

"Why?"

"Can you please answer my question."

Foley sighed. "We changed shifts at eight this morning, Ms. Figueroa." Foley drew her name out slowly, as if even having to pronounce it added a layer of paperwork to his day. "Esposito was working graveyard."

"Is Officer Bale still here?"

"He clocked out at eight too." *Which means if Bale was at La Casa first thing this morning, he was doing a little freelancing,* thought Adele. He had to have gone there right after he went off-duty.

"I'd like to find out why no one at La Casa was notified about the ICE raid in town early this morning," said Adele. "And why Officer Bale felt the need to accuse my staff of harboring the man ICE was attempting to arrest."

"I'll leave Esposito a note," said Foley.

Adele had an idea what would happen to the note. "I'd like to speak to someone about it now."

"Everybody's busy."

Adele leaned forward and caught Foley's eye. "May is Hispanic Pride Month in town, Sergeant, Cinco de Mayo and all that. I know how much your chief loves a photo for the papers of him surrounded by Lake Holly's happy Hispanics. Would you rather I wait until one of those events to bend his ear?"

Foley muttered under his breath. Adele caught the words "ball washer"—the rank and file's nickname for Chief Battaglia. Vega told her cops called him "Chief B." for short. Only Battaglia thought it was just an abbreviation of his

name and not a description of how slavishly he courted
the press.

Foley gestured to the bench in the lobby. "Wait there.
I'll see if I can get somebody to talk to you."

Five minutes ticked by. Then ten.

Two people entered the station with platters of food.
One was a well-dressed older woman with silver-blond
hair and a blue linen blazer. She was carrying a basket of
corn bread and muffins that smelled like they had just
come out of the oven. Next to her was a heavyset young
man who walked stiffly and made no eye contact. Her son,
Adele suspected. He was carrying a bowl of fresh fruit.
Adele thought the woman looked vaguely familiar.

Foley's face brightened when he saw the food. He
walked around and opened the locked door.

"Thank you so much, ma'am," Foley gushed. "You didn't
have to do this."

"Nonsense," said the woman in a honey-glazed Southern
drawl. "Y'all are working so hard to help Glen get closure
during this trying time. It's the least Adam and I can do."

Glen . . . Glen Crowley? Our district attorney? This had
to be his former wife. And his son. Adele recalled he had a
disabled son, though she couldn't remember either the son
or ex-wife's names. She waited until they'd left to ask
Foley about the situation.

"Is the district attorney all right?"

"Yep." Foley's eyes got that flat cop look to them. Adele
had seen it before in Vega when he didn't want to answer
a question.

"Then what was all that about?"

Foley seemed to be debating whether to answer when
the lobby door swung open and Detective Greco breezed
in. He was deep in conversation with a female cop Adele
had never seen before. She was a dark-skinned Hispanic,
pretty and on the tall side, with curly hair frosted at the
tips. Adele noticed a gold badge clipped to her hip near

her gun holster. Not Lake Holly. Not the county police either.

ICE.

She had to be involved in Aviles's arrest. Which meant Greco was too. Adele excused herself from Foley and walked over.

"Pardon the interruption," Adele told Greco. "But I need to speak to both of you. This won't take long." Her voice was forceful. Her manner, direct. Adele was shy and reserved when it came to her own life. Hesitant to voice her needs or feelings. But not when it came to advocating on behalf of others. For that, she'd walk through fire.

Or ICE, as the case may be.

"I'm busy here," Greco muttered. "Whatever you got can wait."

"I have *been* waiting, Detective," Adele shot back. "And I am *through* waiting. ICE conducted a raid at five this morning here in Lake Holly and the only notification I got about it was when one of your officers showed up at La Casa to accuse my staff of harboring the man."

"Well—were you?" asked the female agent.

Adele gave the woman a withering look. "No, we were not. I don't know what ICE office you come from, Agent, but around here, we obey the law—and expect the law to treat everyone in turn with courtesy and respect. That includes informing interested parties of police activity in the town and not bullying my staff into granting an illegal search."

Greco's jaw went slack. The anger that had been percolating in him just seconds before was now replaced by a look of confusion. He alternated an index finger between Adele and the other woman. "You two . . . you don't know each other?"

Adele and the woman looked at each other and shrugged.

"You *really* don't know each other?" Greco asked again.

A slight grin creased the corners of his lips as if he were trying hard to hold it in. He stretched a hand the size of a
baseball mitt in the agent's direction. "This is ICE Super-
vising Agent Michelle Lopez."

Michelle Lopez didn't extend a hand to Adele. Adele
didn't expect one. She'd met Wayne Bowman, the local
field office director of ICE, a few times. They'd exchanged
pleasantries when they had to. It never got chummier than
that. She didn't know his underlings.

Greco turned to Michelle Lopez. "This is Adele Figueroa,
founder and executive director of La Casa."

Agent Lopez's eyes widened. She stepped back. Adele's
name and title didn't usually have any effect on ICE
agents.

Greco laughed, a low rumble like a generator kicking
in. "Better get this catfight out of the way before Vega
shows up."

"What are you talking about?" Adele felt like she'd
missed a punch line somewhere. This whole conversation
had derailed her. She'd come in to find out why Lake
Holly didn't tell her about the raid—and now she was
caught in some sort of private joke between Greco and this
ICE agent.

"My maiden name is 'Vega,' " said the woman. " 'Vega,'
as in—"

"She's Jimmy's half sister," Greco blurted, unable to
contain his glee any longer. "And Michelle? As you've already guessed, this is your brother's girlfriend."

The two women stared at each other. The only sound
was Foley in the background, oblivious as he fielded calls
on the station house phone and munched on a muffin.

"We've got a briefing in ten," Greco said to Michelle.
"I'll leave you both to it. Just . . ." He bit back a grin. "No
guns or knives." He sniffed the air. "What's that delicious
smell?"

* * *

Michelle Lopez was taller than Adele. With kinky hair that was nothing like Vega's soft waves. Yet Adele couldn't deny a certain family resemblance. She had a ropy, kinetic quality to her limbs and an easy physical grace, even with that gun on her hip, that reminded Adele of Vega. Her lips were a little thicker, her eyes, less hooded. Her gaze, more direct. Not so moody-looking, but that last one probably had less to do with Vega's DNA than his innate disposition.

"Does . . . Jimmy know?" Adele asked finally.

"That I work for ICE? That I'm in town?"

"Both," said Adele.

"He does as of last night," said Michelle. "I'm working the Crowley case. I'm surprised he didn't tell you."

He didn't even tell me there WAS a Crowley case, Adele wanted to say. She still had no idea who'd committed suicide. She had to assume, by process of elimination, that it was wife number two. Talia. But she couldn't say for sure.

She could understand Vega not divulging police business. But not telling her he'd run into his sister? Adele had spoken to him last night—albeit briefly—before he turned in. It wasn't like she didn't know he had three estranged half sisters. That whole side of his family lived ghostlike on the periphery of their lives. Why keep the encounter a secret?

Especially since Adele was no secret to Michelle.

"You knew," said Adele. "About Jimmy and me."

"I knew, because one of the cops on duty last night told me," said Michelle. "Jimmy never said a word."

"Speaking of what the cops told you," said Adele, trying to regain her bearings, "I'm assuming ICE informed Lake Holly of their presence in town this morning. Why wasn't La Casa informed?"

Michelle shrugged. "I'm in investigations, not enforcement and removal. I have no idea. Perhaps Donovan and

Tyler didn't know the protocol in town. Perhaps the sergeant on duty couldn't figure out who to call it in to. Or maybe"—she met Adele's gaze head-on—"he thought at five a.m., you might not want to know about some illegal we're picking up."

Illegal. The word burned in Adele's gut. That's what people like Michelle called her parents.

"First of all," said Adele, "Edgar Aviles had temporary protected status before the government yanked it away. So he wasn't in this country illegally. And second, no person is illegal."

"Temporary means, 'not forever,'" said Michelle. "If his status was revoked, then he was here illegally. Which makes him an illegal. What part of what I'm saying don't you understand?"

"Maybe if you saw these people up close," said Adele, "worked with them like I do, listened to their hopes and dreams for themselves and their children, you wouldn't be so callous and dismissive."

"And maybe if you'd spent ten years in corrections like I did, watching criminal aliens get released only to break the law and come right back again," said Michelle, "you would."

Michelle folded her arms across her chest and walked her gaze down Adele. "How long have you and Jimmy been dating?"

"About a year," Adele said stiffly.

"Is it serious?"

Adele didn't answer. The question felt invasive. Everything about this woman felt invasive.

"It's not a trick question," said Michelle. "I'm genuinely curious."

"We enjoy each other's company."

Michelle uncrossed her arms. Her face softened. For a minute Adele saw the woman, not the cop.

"Jimmy's a hard guy to get to know. A good guy. But . . ."

he's had a hard life. If it's working out between the two of you, I'm glad."

"Thanks," said Adele. "Is there anything you can do for Edgar Aviles?"

"The illegal you came here about?"

Adele stayed silent. This was not the time for semantics.

"Like I said, I'm not in removals. And even if I was, the guy split," said Michelle. "He's a fugitive now. I couldn't do anything even if I wanted to." She glanced over Adele's shoulder at the parking lot.

"You want to ask anything else, you should probably talk to Jimmy. He's headed this way."

Adele spun around and saw Vega walking toward the building. He had a distinctive walk—loose-limbed and rangy with a cocky confidence in his stride. Before Adele ever saw him dance, she felt the rhythm within him, the way it telegraphed something sexy and slightly dangerous that drew her in every time.

Michelle reached over and gave Adele's arm a squeeze.

"Take care of him, all right?"

The gesture was so unexpected, Adele didn't process it until Michelle had walked over to Foley, who buzzed her through the security door.

Adele exited the building just as Vega reached the front steps.

"*Nena?*" The "babe" slid affectionately from his mouth. He froze in his tracks, one tactical boot on the bottom concrete step. "Everything okay?"

"There was a raid in town this morning," she said. "ICE tried to arrest the handyman from Beth Shalom, but he fled across the Metro-North tracks."

"I heard," said Vega.

"The police are supposed to notify me. They didn't," said Adele. "I just spoke to Greco about it."

"Good."

"I spoke to the female ICE agent as well—the one you're working with."

Adele watched her words work their way across the muscles of Vega's face. She knew. He knew she knew.

Vega rocked his boot on the bottom step without meeting her gaze. "She told you, huh? About our family connection?"

"The question is—why didn't you?"

A siren cut the air. It seemed to be headed their way. Vega swept a gaze around the parking lot. Adele supposed that sirens were Pavlovian to a cop. Once they heard one, everything else stopped.

"I was going to tell you on the way to the gig tonight. I swear," said Vega. "I just have a lot on my mind."

Adele heard another siren, this one accompanied by a fire truck's air horn. Two uniforms hustled out the front doors of the station house and over to a patrol car. Vega turned to them.

"What's going on?"

"DB on the Metro-North tracks," said one of the officers, referring to the dead body. "Looks like the dude got killed trying to cross."

Adele felt something tighten in her gut.

"You have a description of the victim?" asked Vega.

"Hispanic. Thirtysomething. Broadly built. That's all we know."

Chapter 13

Vega left Adele with a promise to update her later. He hustled into the police station just as Greco, Sanchez, and Michelle were walking out.

"I just heard about the DB," Vega huffed out. "Is it Aviles?"

"Dunno," said Greco. "We're headed there now. Grab a ride with Lopez."

Vega followed Michelle wordlessly to her government-issued sedan. She unlocked the doors and they hopped inside. She turned on the dashboard flashers and made a three-point turn out of the lot. Vega waited for her to bring up Adele and was glad when she didn't.

"I've got a call in to the two agents in charge of apprehending Aviles," said Michelle. "Donovan and Tyler. Last I heard, Aviles was headed to New York City. Maybe this isn't him."

"If it is," said Vega, "ICE blew it. Aviles was our best link to Lissette. Lissette might be the only one who can help us figure out what happened to Talia."

Michelle nosed through a light just as it turned red. Vega held his breath. Even with their dashboard lights flashing, he didn't want to chance getting hit by some distracted civilian.

"I know what happened to Talia," said Michelle. "I was at the autopsy this morning, remember?"

"What did you find out?"

"Cause of death was strangulation. The mechanism was the garden rope you saw, consistent with the ligature marks on her neck. No DNA present from any other parties."

"The killer could have been wearing gloves," Vega pointed out. "What about the time?"

"Around nine p.m. Thursday," said Michelle.

"Someone could have visited. Or broken in."

"They could have," Michelle admitted. "But here's the kicker: Gupta ran the tox screen. Talia had a blood concentration of .8 milligrams of diazepam and .12 of alcohol at the time of her death."

"Valium and booze," Vega muttered. It was a potent combination. But if anything, it argued against Talia hanging herself.

"She's doped up on sedatives, how the hell did she have the coordination to tie a slipknot and cinch that rope over the basement pipe?" asked Vega. "Not to mention having the balance to stand on a chair or stool and then kick it away."

"Someone wants to kill themselves," said Michelle, "they'll find a way."

Vega watched the town speed by like a movie on fast-forward. The turrets and bay windows of gingerbread Victorians. The wrought-iron street lamps with flower baskets dangling from their hooks.

"So what's Gupta's conclusion?" he asked. "That the manner of death was suicide?"

"Gupta left it as undetermined," said Michelle. "Pending the outcome of our investigation. She said the flood diluted the quality of the evidence."

"Yeah. No kidding." Vega told Michelle what he'd found at the CIC. "Crowley made a pit stop at a parlor, all right. Only, I'm betting it was the massage kind—not the pizza."

"That's conjecture."

"Sure, it's conjecture," said Vega. "Every piece of evidence starts as conjecture. We gotta build it from there. Same for Lissette. Her last cell phone transmission was Friday night at ten p.m. in the vicinity of the Magnolia Inn."

"Where's that?"

"It's this big old eighteenth-century farmhouse restaurant up by the Lake Holly Reservoir," said Vega. "Most of the help is immigrant Hispanic. That should be our starting point in finding her."

Michelle was quiet for a moment as they pulled into the Lake Holly train station parking lot. She stared past the century-old timber-frame building with its green clay tile roof to a spot about two hundred feet beyond the platform where all the emergency vehicles had gathered.

"Greco's not going to let you investigate the DA's sex life," she said slowly.

"What if it's the key to the case?"

"God," she whispered. "I hope not."

Vega and Michelle got out of the car and followed Greco and Sanchez over a low wall. They signed in on a log sheet and slipped into bright orange vests before moving onto the tracks. The Metro-North cops had already erected a privacy barrier around the body. They'd stopped all trains in both directions and turned off the juice to the third rail.

It was a quick, clean kill, as train accidents go. The victim was lying in a fetal position on the gravel by the edge of the outside rail. All his limbs appeared intact. He must have been knocked aside by the momentum of the train. The impact left deep bruising on his back and shoulder and tore his shirt. Vega noticed gravel deeply embedded in one arm. But at least it wasn't the usual bloody mess. The man's family could have an open coffin, for once.

From this vantage point, he looked like Edgar Aviles. Medium brown skin. Broad shoulders. Dark hair.

Everyone introduced themselves with quick nods and grunts.

"What's the engineer telling you?" Greco asked one of the Metro-North investigators, a man with buzz-cut blond hair and a waxed handlebar mustache like something out of the 1890s.

"He said the guy casually walked in front of the train," said the investigator. "He wasn't running. He wasn't pushed."

Greco nodded. Most train deaths in the county were suicides. It was rare for someone to accidentally wind up on the tracks. And, even if they did, the trains never ran more than every ten or fifteen minutes—plenty of time to escape if it was an accident.

Vega crossed to the other side of the rail and squatted down to get a better look at the victim's face. He straightened.

"It's not Aviles."

Greco picked his way over the rail bed and came up behind Vega. "You sure?"

"Sure, I'm sure," said Vega. "I met him last night. This isn't him."

"Vega's right," said Omar Sanchez, stepping up beside Vega's elbow. "I know this man. He's a painter in town. He was the foreman for that paint crew"—Sanchez looked at Greco—"remember? The ones I interviewed after the jewelry-store heist? They painted the store about two weeks before the heist."

"I thought you cleared them," said Greco.

"I did," said Sanchez. "But I decided to take another crack at them when Elmer Ortega went MIA. I kept trying to reach the foreman. He never answered my calls."

"We didn't find a wallet or ID on the body," said the investigator with the handlebar mustache. "But we found this."

He held out an evidence bag to them that contained a typewritten letter and envelope. Vega recognized ICE's blue eagle logo on the upper right of the stationery. The letter was a boilerplate denial for a stay of removal with an order to leave the United States immediately or face arrest and deportation. It was addressed to a Cesar Zuma-Léon with an address in Lake Holly.

"That's the guy," said Sanchez. "Cesar Zuma."

Zuma. Vega pulled out his phone and called up a picture on his screen. He handed it to Sanchez.

"This is a list of names the Warburton Police found in Elmer Ortega's pocket when his body turned up. Cesar Zuma's on the list. And maybe Edgar Aviles's as well."

Sanchez and Greco read the names:

> *Cesar Zuma-Léon*
> *Jesús Monroy-Peña*
> *Deisy Ramos-Sandoval*
> *Wilmer Diaz-Garcia*
> *Edgar Ceren-Aviles*

"Well," Greco grunted. "Least we know who Ortega's inside man was on the jewelry-store heist. This will help clear the case." Greco handed the phone back to Vega. "Text me a copy of that list. I'll run it past the Warburton Police."

"That's it?" asked Vega as he forwarded the list.

"What do you want us to do?" asked Greco. "Invite them all to Zuma's funeral?"

"These names are connected to a dead MS-13 gang member," said Vega. "One of them is now dead himself and directly linked to a crime in town. Another could be the uncle of Talia Crowley's missing housekeeper—"

"Which, outside of the jewelry store heist, helps us,

how?" Greco interrupted. "That is, assuming the name on the list even corresponds to Edgar Aviles. The last names are reversed."

"I know that," said Vega. "But shouldn't we track down those other names? Figure out if there's a connection?"

"If I was the Warburton Police? Investigating Ortega's murder? Sure," said Greco. "But I've got enough on my plate without taking on freelance. Zuma's death is between Metro-North and Lake Holly. Your priority right now should be finding Lissette Aviles and closing Talia Crowley. Nothing else."

Vega and Michelle left Greco and Sanchez at the scene to confer with Mr. Handlebars. On the way back to the car, Michelle confronted Vega.

"What's this about meeting Aviles?" she asked. "You *know* him?"

"No, I don't *know* him," said Vega. "I just happened to meet him last night when I was picking someone up at the synagogue where he works. I'm sure your enforcers already know his place of employment."

"Don't call them 'enforcers,'" said Michelle. "It makes them sound like mafiosos."

Vega didn't reply. He thought in some respects, it was an apt comparison.

"Why didn't you mention this earlier?" she demanded.

"I told Greco," said Vega. "I didn't think it mattered. You said Aviles ran to New York City. Besides, wouldn't ICE have checked out where he works already?"

"I don't know what they've checked or haven't checked," said Michelle. She picked up her phone and began punching in a number. "What's the name of the synagogue?"

Vega felt an acid knot tightening in the pit of his stomach. He wouldn't even have known where Aviles worked if not for Max Zimmerman. His friend. Adele's neighbor. Vega's cheeks grew hot as he recalled what Zimmerman had said to Aviles last night:

You can trust Detective Vega.

"Jimmy—the law is the law. You need to tell me."

Vega closed his eyes. He heard nothing but the rumble of fire trucks as they left the station parking lot. His breath stilled in his chest. He was Max Zimmerman's friend, sure. But he was also a police officer. He swore an oath. He took a deep breath and forced himself to say the words. Each one felt like a lead weight on his tongue.

"Edgar Aviles is the handyman at Beth Shalom."

Chapter 14

Edgar Aviles crouched in a corner of the toolshed, behind the lawn mower and leaf blower, shivering. The adrenaline from his run had worn off, his white undershirt was soaked. The damp early morning chill made him shiver. He felt like he was back in Olocuilta, standing over the bloody corpse of his teenage cousin. His best friend. The food cart they'd pooled their money to buy was supposed to be their ticket out of poverty. Instead, it spelled their ruin. When they couldn't make their protection payoffs, the local gang killed his cousin. Sliced him fifteen times with a machete.

Aviles left Olocuilta that same day and never looked back.

He wiped an arm across his sweat-slicked forehead and tried to think about what to do next. He felt a deep well of shame hiding in the shed of his employer. On a normal Saturday morning, he'd be unlocking the front doors of the synagogue and running a mop along the raised stage so it sparkled for Saturday worship. He'd be dusting the front of the great carved cupboard—the ark—where the religious scrolls were kept, and polishing the bimah, or lectern, where they were read.

His favorite job was shining the glass panes of the lamp—

the eternal light—that glowed brightly above the ark. Aviles liked the way the lamp was always lit, even when the sanctuary was empty. Rabbi Goldberg said it was to remind people that God was always present, even when people couldn't feel Him.

Aviles prayed that that was true. He sorely needed God's presence now.

Most Saturdays, there was a bar or bat mitzvah. The pews would fill with the relatives of the young boy or girl celebrating this Jewish rite of passage. Rabbi Goldberg would read Hebrew from the Torah. Cantor Bloom would sing. The songs were mostly bittersweet—nothing like the bright, rousing tunes Aviles knew from the assembly he went to with Maria and the children. And yet both worship halls filled him with wonder and reverence. A sense that no matter how dark things got in the world, there was still hope and goodness. He just had to find it.

He stayed in the shed for a long time, listening to the birds in the trees and the distant whoosh of cars along the main road. And then, he heard it, the sound of a car slowly pulling into the temple parking lot. Just one car. He knew whose car it would be. The second car to arrive on Saturday mornings—after Aviles's.

Rabbi Mark Goldberg.

Aviles watched from a crack between the shed frame and the door as the rabbi got out of his Dodge minivan. Rabbi Goldberg was a lean man with a close-cropped beard and wire-rimmed glasses. He was thirty-five—the same age as Aviles—yet he felt both older and younger.

The rabbi's hands were soft, almost girlish, with long, double-jointed fingers that seemed to move of their own accord, like beach grass. He was shy with audiences and sometimes mumbled when he read from the Torah. He had no stomach for containing some of the older and more difficult members of his congregation. They tended to walk all over him—unlike Rabbi Weiss, now retired, who had a voice like God and knew how to control them.

Yet Aviles had also seen how tender Rabbi Goldberg was when he spoke to Mrs. Teitelbaum, now addled by dementia. Or when he helped the Klugers, who'd lost a son to drugs. He seemed sincerely drawn to his faith, not out of a desire to speak or lead but from a deep-seated belief that he himself was being led. He didn't talk so much as listen.

If Aviles ever needed someone to listen to him, it was now.

He took a deep breath and slid open the aluminum door of the shed. It echoed like an empty oil drum. Rabbi Goldberg's head swiveled at the sound. His face registered a moment of relief seeing Aviles, then puzzlement at the fact that his custodian's white undershirt and uniform pants were covered in grass stains and dirt.

"Edgar? Where's your car?"

Aviles noticed that Rabbi Goldberg wasn't traveling alone this morning. His wife, Señora Eve, was in the front passenger seat. Their two little girls, ages three and five, were strapped in car seats in back. The girls blinked at Aviles. The señora got out of the minivan. She put her hands on the hips of her long, flowing dress, her narrow shoulders backlit by the sun. Her wavy brown hair rippled across her shoulders like water, amplifying every movement.

"*Mark*," she chided her husband in her lilting French accent. "Can't you see that something's wrong?" She set her eyes on Aviles. Dark, kind eyes that searched for an answer that might not be found in his words. "Is Noah all right?"

Her oldest, Sarah, was the same age as Noah. Of course she'd think of the boy first.

"He's fine. Thank you, missus." Aviles shoved his hands in his pockets and stared down at the blacktop. A blacktop he'd helped repave two years ago. He was too ashamed to face their scrutiny. "It's me," he choked out. "This morning, two men—two agents—came to my door—"

"ICE?" The señora was a beat ahead of her husband, as always. "Are you saying ICE tried to arrest you?"

"Yes, missus. I ran. I didn't know what else to do."

"You ran *here?*" the rabbi's voice cracked on the last word.

"Of course he ran here, Mark," said the *señora*. "Why shouldn't he run here? He's been part of Beth Shalom longer than you've been its rabbi. We need to get him inside—"

"Do you think that's wise?" the rabbi asked his wife. Then he turned to Aviles. "I'm sorry, Edgar. You are a good man. And a loyal employee. I want to help. If it were up to me alone . . . But last night, you heard what the board said—"

"*A broch* on what the board said!" his wife interrupted in disgust. "The board is five men and a hundred and five opinions. Look at him, Mark. He's cold. He's frightened. Whatever is or isn't going to happen, he's our employee. Our friend. He deserves to go inside, warm up, and eat. Feeding someone a bagel isn't a federal crime."

Her words had the desired effect. Rabbi Goldberg turned to Aviles. His tone was almost apologetic. "My wife is right. Let's get you inside and figure out what to do next."

Aviles followed the Goldberg family into the synagogue. It was a beautiful building, paneled in blond wood with walls of windows and plenty of skylights that made even the grayest day feel sunny. Plush red carpets covered the lobby floors and bright oil paintings of Jerusalem covered its walls. A chandelier sparkled outside the door to the sanctuary. A large bronze plaque listed dozens of names of families who'd made large contributions to the synagogue. Some of the families were two and three generations.

"I'm going to need to make some calls about this," said the rabbi. He excused himself to his paneled office.

"Come," said the señora, taking the girls by their hands and beckoning Aviles to follow. "Let's go downstairs to the preschool. The girls can play and we can eat and talk."

On the building's lower level, bright yellow walls welcomed them to the preschool, along with pictures of children's artwork beneath letters of the Hebrew alphabet. There were two big playrooms, complete with pint-size bathrooms and a full-size kitchen—one of two in the building. The building was built on a small hill, so even though the preschool was down a flight of stairs, it was on the ground floor in back. Large windows and sliding glass doors overlooked a playground.

The señora flicked on the lights in one of the big playrooms, revealing two long tables with little chairs stacked upside down on the tables—just where Aviles had left them yesterday afternoon when he'd finished cleaning.

Sarah and Carly ran over to a shelf with red, blue, and yellow bins and pulled the red one out. It was full of half-naked Barbie dolls with tangled hair and glittering gowns. The two girls settled into play while Señora Eve walked into the kitchen and put on some coffee. She took two bagels from the freezer and stuck them in the toaster.

"I think there's a clothing donation bin down here somewhere," she said, her French accent soft and buttery—so much more pleasing to Edgar's ear than the sharp consonants of English. "We can probably find you a warm shirt."

She began opening cabinets until she found the one she wanted. "Ah. Here it is." She rummaged through one of the bags and pulled out a dark-green flannel with the name *Ralph Lauren* inside. She held it up. "I think this will fit you."

"You don't have to do all of this," he told her.

"Nonsense," she said, pressing the shirt into his hands. "You need to eat. You need clean clothes. You might be here a while."

"Maybe in a day or two, ICE will give up."

She tucked a thick strand of wavy hair behind one ear and studied him for a long moment. "You don't really believe that, do you?"

Aviles slipped into the shirt. It was a lovely soft cotton. The sleeves were too long, but they were easy to roll up. "Thank you," he said. "I won't stay here beyond today."

"Where will you go?"

Aviles kept his eyes on his hands as he buttoned the shirt. He had no idea. He felt a rising panic in his chest and tried to swallow it back.

"You have to stay here," she told him softly. "You can't leave your family. They need you."

The señora's two little girls chatted away behind him. Aviles felt a sharp pain slice his heart thinking about leaving his own children behind. Especially now. After that call. Those threats. And Lissette missing. But he couldn't tell the señora any of that. She wouldn't understand. It would only frighten her. So he said nothing. And neither did she.

There was no answer.

She poured coffee and spread cream cheese on two toasted bagels. She did not eat the second bagel but split it in half and set it on one of the children's tables for the girls, along with some juice.

"You're not eating?" Aviles asked her.

"I had breakfast earlier," she said. "But you? You need to keep up your strength." She gestured to the stairs. The rabbi's voice floated above them. He was still on the phone. It did not sound like things were going well. When he was reading scripture, his voice was musical and pleasing. When he was dealing with people—especially difficult people—it tended to get thin and hesitant. His wife seemed to hear it too.

"I swear," she said, gesturing to the stairs. "If those men had been around when Moses was leading our people out of Egypt, the Red Sea would have parted and un-parted again before they made a decision."

Aviles smiled. She seemed delighted she could get him to smile.

"Please. Eat." She gestured a hand to his plate.

Aviles wasn't sure he could. His teeth felt like they had forgotten how to chew. His stomach didn't seem to recognize the taste of food. But he didn't want to be rude. Eve Goldberg had always been so kind to him. She passed along clothing from her sister's children to Noah and Flor. She got Maria an appointment with a good lupus doctor through her uncle, who headed a hospital in Broad Plains. She wrangled a scholarship that allowed Erick to attend sleepaway camp for two whole weeks last summer. But this problem here? This went well beyond kindness and they both knew it.

"I have an idea," she said, pulling out her phone.

"Who are you calling?"

"Max Zimmerman," she said. "If Mark is going to have Sam Lerner and David Stern and Ben Levine and Leo Hirsch over here this morning, he should have Max as well."

"Missus, please," said Aviles. "The señor is an old man. I don't want to upset him."

"Nonsense," she said. "You need someone to speak for you. And I can't do it alone."

A thump on the window made both of them jump. A man in a beard and *kippah* held a clipboard in his hand.

"It's the caterer for the kiddush," she said.

Aviles had worked so long for the temple, he knew many Hebrew words and traditions. The kiddush was the prayer meal after Saturday morning services. Since the temple was celebrating a bar mitzvah today, the boy's family would be paying for the kiddush and it would likely be substantial: lox and bagels and trays of hot appetizers.

"I need to handle this," said the señora. "Why don't you go about your chores for the morning—pretend it's a normal day—and Mark or I will fetch you before services to talk some more?"

"Yes. Thank you," said Aviles. "Only . . . can I ask a favor? Can you call my wife and tell her I'm okay? I ran without my phone."

"I can do that," she said. "But if I do, she'll know where you are. And then perhaps ICE will too."

"She won't say anything," Aviles assured her. "I don't want her to worry."

"In that case"—the señora held out her phone to him—"why don't you take a few minutes to speak to her in private? I can wait."

Aviles felt both better and worse after speaking to Maria and the children. Better, because he was able to reassure them he was okay. Worse, because Lissette still hadn't come home. Not that he could call the police. Not with a gang watching his family. How could he protect them from inside the temple? Or worse, locked away in some detention center?

He tried to lose himself in the rhythms of work after that. Scrubbing the bathrooms. Polishing the chrome banister of the staircase that led to the sanctuary. Vacuuming the rugs. He heard Cantor Bloom singing snippets of prayers that made him feel both sad and full of wonder at the same time. Like a movie where you know the hero will die, but you watch and root for him anyway.

Aviles was mopping the floor of the side entranceway when the señora came up to him.

"Mark and the board are all in the conference room," she told him. "They want you to go talk to them."

Aviles leaned on his mop. His knees felt weak. He had a heavy Spanish accent and a fifth-grade education. What could he say to these powerful, educated men that would convince them to risk their temple—their reputations—on him?

He took a deep breath and tried to steady his nerves. "Have they decided?"

"I don't think they can agree on the weather," she said. "So no—they haven't. Which is why you need to help them decide."

Aviles stared at his hands. "My English is not so good. I don't know what to say."

"Your English is fine," she assured him. "Tell them about Noah. About Maria's condition. About why you need to stay here for your family. They will understand family."

Aviles washed his hands and face and finger-combed his hair. He smoothed out the creases in his borrowed Ralph Lauren green plaid shirt. His tongue felt like sandpaper as she led him to the conference room. The door was closed. Aviles could hear a murmur of voices on the other side. All of a sudden, the door flung open. Sam Lerner barreled out of the room, throwing his hefty arms over his bald head and turning back at the now open door.

"We'll all go to jail, at this rate. This is *mishegoss!* Crazy! I cannot support it."

Rabbi Goldberg ran after him, his wire-rimmed glasses bouncing off the bridge of his nose. Aviles felt embarrassed standing there. Like he was witnessing a family quarrel. Worse, he was the cause.

"Sam!" the rabbi shouted. "We're talking about a few nights! Just until we can sort something out. Ben might be able to tap a colleague who can draft some kind of legal appeal. We owe that much to Edgar. To his family."

Sam Lerner spun around. He didn't seem to notice Aviles standing there. Or maybe he did. Maybe that was the point.

"He told us his lawyer already filed an appeal," said Lerner. "It didn't help. Why would ours? It's enough for us to take care of our *own* people. In our *own* house."

David Stern and Leo Hirsch nodded in agreement.

"We can't take on unsolvable problems like this," Lerner continued. "It's like"—he waved his arms, wound up with the effort—"like trying to empty the ocean with a tin can. Let his own people help him, if they're so inclined. This is not our war."

There was a moment of hushed silence. All Aviles could hear was Sam Lerner's heavy breathing. Then came the sound of a cane slowly thumping down the hallway. A voice rose up from the direction of the sanctuary—thin and sharp, like a snapped branch in winter.

"He who can protest and does not, is an accomplice in the act."

The men all turned their heads in the direction of the speaker. No one needed to guess who it was. Aviles recognized the Eastern European accent, the slight tremor in the vocal cords. Max Zimmerman shuffled toward them.

"Max," said Rabbi Goldberg. "What are you—?"

"Eve called me, so I drove right over," said Zimmerman. He and the señora exchanged a knowing glance. "What? I'm supposed to sit around watching reruns of *Judge Judy* while a man's life is at stake?"

"We can figure this out without your input," Lerner

told him. "Or your quoting of the Talmud. Jewish law doesn't apply here, Max. This isn't about our people."

"Not about our people." Zimmerman mumbled and shook his head. He raised a bony finger. "As the great Talmudic scholar Hillel once asked, 'If I am only for myself, what am I?'"

"Sam's right," said Leo Hirsch. He was a thin man with pendulous ears and a salt-and-pepper beard that only made his lean face look longer. "We can't use Jewish teachings to solve a problem rooted in U.S. immigration law. If Ben can file a different sort of appeal, let him file it. If our congregation can raise money for legal and medical expenses, let them raise it. But these charitable deeds should be the extent of our involvement."

Everyone began to talk at once after that. The rabbi. The señora. The fat man, Sam Lerner. Leo Hirsch, the man with the pendulous ears. Ben Levine, the attorney. Aviles couldn't understand their words. They just blended together in one giant soup of English.

And then they heard it. Beyond the hallway. Banging. Someone was banging on the entrance doors to the synagogue. The doors weren't locked. Why wouldn't the person just open them?

Rabbi Goldberg checked his watch and frowned. "The Cohens are here for the bar mitzvah? Already?"

"Maybe it's the caterer," Leo Hirsch suggested.

"He's already in the building," said the señora. "I saw him and his workers setting up in the kitchen."

Rabbi Goldberg poked his head around the corner and stared down the short set of stairs to the wood-paneled doors inlaid with glass. A flash of red light from the other side of the glass lit up the rabbi's pale, bearded face and reflected across the lenses of his wire-framed glasses. The rabbi's placid, expectant smile vanished. He took a step backward. The pounding came again.

The rabbi turned his face to the board members, all hushed and expectant as children. He skipped over Aviles's searching eyes and looked at his wife. Aviles saw something cross the rabbi's soft features. Deep love. But also, deep need. God wasn't the only one the rabbi turned to in times of stress. Rabbi Goldberg took a deep breath.

"I'm afraid we'll need more than holy books for this."

Chapter 15

The meeting in the conference room of the Lake Holly police station frustrated Vega. He felt like the case was getting away from him. Aviles was holed up—at Beth Shalom or somewhere else. Lissette was still missing. A house painter and a gangster—both of whom may or may not be connected to the case—were dead. And none of that got Vega any closer to figuring out what happened to Talia Crowley.

"I feel like the ME's office is playing tag with us," said Greco. "Everything Dr. Gupta found suggests Talia committed suicide, plain and simple." Greco ticked the evidence off on his thick fingers. "The alcohol and Valium in her blood. The lack of evidence of a struggle. The absence of foreign DNA beneath her fingernails. Yet Gupta's not calling it. She's shifting this hot potato to us."

"She's not shifting," Vega argued. "The science doesn't support a hard and fast determination. This case is far from conclusive."

"No evidence of a struggle seems pretty conclusive," said Sanchez.

"She was doped up on booze and Valium," Vega argued. "Maybe too doped to fight. And that's not all," he continued. "What about the housekeeper, Lissette? If it's a simple suicide, where is she? How come her cell phone's last activation was at ten p.m. last night in a part of town she doesn't live in and can't easily access?"

"She's probably got a boyfriend who works at the Magnolia Inn," said Greco. "For all we know, she's shacked up somewhere with him right now. It may have no bearing on the case."

"What about Crowley's motives?" Vega countered. "That massage parlor Sergeant Burke and I uncovered up in Taylorsville? I checked with the county sheriff's office. They've had a number of prostitution complaints about the place."

Silence. Sanchez doodled on his notebook. Michelle played with her bracelet. Greco sighed heavily, the patient teacher who'd run out of patience.

"Look, Vega, if we get even a shred of evidence that Crowley's possible—underlined, *possible*—extracurricular activities have any bearing on Talia's death, I'll be the first to let you run with it. Until then, this conversation is off the table. I want to finish this case, not have it finish me."

Vega sat in the conference room listening as everyone took turns filling the others in on their part of the investigation. The air-conditioning unit rattled full-blast in the window behind Vega, circulating chilled air that felt clammy and humid. Vega jotted down notes and then stared at the two pictures of Talia tacked to the investigation board.

One was a candid shot, taken on a lounge chair without makeup. The other was at some political event with her husband. Vega preferred the candid shot, the way Talia looked straight at the camera. She was a naturally pretty woman with dark blond shoulder-length hair, large charcoal blue eyes, full lips, and a symmetrical face. But she lacked that preening self-awareness that so many pretty women have.

She'd been a paralegal in Crowley's office. Then his mistress. Then his pregnant wife. She and Crowley had been married only four months when Talia miscarried. Vega couldn't escape the question: Was Crowley relieved to move on? He was sixty—a hard-charging prosecutor with a socialite ex-wife and grown children, including a disabled son. Was he really looking to start over? With a paralegal from the wrong side of the tracks?

According to Sanchez, Talia Danvers Crowley was the daughter of a truck driver from western Pennsylvania. She worked two jobs to put herself through college and train as a paralegal. She'd had a brief first marriage—no children—in her early twenties. Friends said she was excited to become a mother—and devastated by the loss.

"Devastated enough to take her life?" asked Vega.

"That's what we need to find out," said Greco. "She's got a sister named Lori Danvers who owns a pet-grooming business in Broad Plains. I want you and Lopez to take a ride over there, see what you can find out. I understand they were close."

"We're on it," said Michelle, rising from her chair. Vega stayed seated.

"How 'bout Lissette?" he asked. "Shouldn't we be focusing on her as well?"

"Me and Sanchez will be interviewing a friend of Talia's who lives up near the Magnolia Inn. We'll swing by the place, show Lissette's picture around. If she's got a boyfriend there, he'll turn up."

"We don't know that she was actually *at* the inn," Vega pointed out. "Only that the cell tower in that region was her last point of contact."

"I'm telling you, Vega—she'll show up. I wouldn't be surprised if the Avileses know where she is and they're not saying."

When the meeting broke up, Vega signed out an unmarked brown Ford Taurus. He twirled the car keys around his finger, bunching them in his fist like brass knuckles as he walked into the station house parking lot with Michelle trailing one step behind.

Twirl—grab—jingle. Twirl—grab—jingle.

He was going to spend a whole goddamned day with the woman who'd helped him betray Max Zimmerman's confidence. And more importantly, Adele's.

"You want to drive to Broad Plains?" Vega asked her. "Or can I?"

"You can drive," said Michelle. "I need to check my texts and see if Tyler and Donovan had any luck arresting Aviles."

"Luck." Vega snorted. "Right."

Michelle grabbed Vega's elbow and pulled him between two empty cruisers.

"Listen up, Jimmy—I'm only going to say this once. I'm doing my job. And you're doing yours. So cut the bullshit."

Vega straightened and stared at her, unsure of what to say.

"It's not like anyone's going to know," she said.

"Know?"

"That you tipped off ICE. That's what you're worried about, isn't it? You're afraid Adele will find out."

"You think I'm that much of a coward?" Vega felt like he'd been slapped. "You don't know me at all, Michelle. Stop pretending you do."

Vega stormed ahead. He was inside the vehicle by the time Michelle folded herself into the shotgun seat. The Taurus smelled of disinfectant and cigarettes despite the department's no-smoking rule. Vega stuck the key in the ignition, punched in a code on the dashboard computer console, and nosed the car out of the lot.

They headed south to Broad Plains, a soulless collection of high-rises, strip malls, and highways that was also the county seat. The trip to the pet grooming store, Paws and Claws, should have taken twenty minutes, but their GPS showed an accident on the highway so Vega had to take the back roads, which added another fifteen minutes to the journey.

They didn't speak. They were like passengers on an airplane who shared nothing but a destination. Michelle pulled out her cell phone and began scrolling through her text messages.

"Yes," she muttered, under her breath.

Vega's heart sank. "Tyler and Donovan arrested Aviles?"

"Huh?" She looked up. "No. No word from them yet. I just won a year's supply of dog chow."

"You have a dog?"

"My landlord doesn't allow dogs, much to my sons' disappointment."

"Then why—?"

"It's my hobby," Michelle explained. "I enter contests. It costs nothing and you can't believe how much stuff I've won over the years. Tickets to shows. Cruises. Meals. Electronics."

Up ahead, a road crew was repairing potholes. Traffic narrowed to one lane. A woman in a bright orange vest stopped them for oncoming traffic.

"Ever win a car?" Vega asked over the idling engine. That's what he needed. Something to replace his aging pickup.

"No. But last week, I won a case of hot sauce."

Vega laughed. "What are you going to do with a case of hot sauce?"

"Same as I'll do with the dog chow—trade it for other things. Free haircuts. Manicures. Car tune-ups—"

"So, you do it for the economic benefits."

"Not really." Michelle considered the question. "I do it because when I win something, I feel lucky and special. Sometimes, it lasts for just an hour. But it's a boost to get me through the day. Know what I'm sayin'?"

Michelle turned her gaze from Vega and stared out the side window at a landscape of acid-green trees that seemed to go on forever, broken only here and there by the rooflines of houses and church steeples. "When I was a girl, I used to enter my mother's name in vacation contests. I wanted to get out of the Bronx so bad."

Vega remembered the feeling, especially in summer when the streets would sizzle and the tar would turn sticky beneath his sneakers. The tenements were like ovens. People slept on their fire escapes and hung out on their stoops well into the night. Sometimes, his mother would take him on a long subway ride out to Rockaway Beach in Queens. The sand burned his feet and the waves were strong. Mostly, he ran beneath a spray of water from the fire hydrants that dotted the sidewalks. When his mother first moved them to Lake Holly with its crystal waters and green lawns, he felt like he was on vacation every day.

You got sent away.

"That's where you got the idea from," Vega mumbled.

"What idea?"

"That I got sent away. I didn't get *sent*. We moved," said Vega. "From the Bronx to Lake Holly."

"That wasn't it," said Michelle. "I was, like, eight when you moved up to Lake Holly. I remember that. You got sent away when I was really small." She was silent a moment. Thinking. "You want," she said, "I can just ask Pop."

"No," Vega growled. "I don't want anything from that man. And besides, what would he know about me anyway?"

"Oh, come off it, Jimmy. You act like Pop walked out and never saw you again. Until your mom moved up to Lake Holly, we saw you all the time."

"He didn't support me—"

"He barely supported *me*," she replied. "Am I angry about it? Hell, yeah. The neighborhood gave men a pass. It still does. And it's wrong. But Mom's made peace with the past, and I'm trying to as well. I force myself to focus on the happy stuff."

She snapped her fingers. "Hey—remember Corn Dog? That old wino who used to curse at me and Denise and throw things at us for playing jump rope on the corner?"

"You were scared of him," Vega recalled.

"Damn straight, I was. Remember how you mixed up a packet of Kool-Aid and water, sprinkled it on him, then convinced him that that old lady at the botanica had poisoned him?"

Vega flushed at the memory of that cantankerous old drunk trying to scrape the "devil's spell" off his jacket.

"I was a mean bastard."

"You were a good brother," said Michelle. "Or whatever you want to call yourself. You must've been about ten at the time. I must've been about seven and Denise, five. We laughed so hard, remember? He slept in the park after that. Never bothered us again."

Vega smiled. "I can't believe you remember that."

"I can't believe you forgot."

Chapter 16

Paws and Claws was in a strip mall on the approach into downtown Broad Plains. There was a colorful sign out front with whiskers and pawprints all over it and a display window full of the accoutrements of the well-heeled pet: fancy leashes, ergonomic feeding bowls, dog toys that cost more than a new video game.

Vega once made the mistake of buying a really nice dog toy for Diablo. A green rubber artichoke that the vet said would keep him from chewing up Vega's hundred-dollar running shoes. Diablo buried the twenty-dollar artichoke the first day he got it—and promptly returned to chewing Vega's sneakers. Now, Vega just left out an old pair and accepted the consequences.

Vega told Michelle the rubber artichoke story as he pulled into the parking lot. She laughed.

"You're so lucky to have a landlord who lets you keep a dog."

"I don't have a landlord," said Vega. "I own a little cabin on a lake up in Sullivan Falls."

"Wow. That's like being on vacation every day," said Michelle. "All my boys ever get to see is my apartment, my mother's apartment, and *Tía* Gloria's place."

Gloria. Vega stiffened at the name. He hadn't thought

about Michelle's aunt in years. Michelle must have caught the change in his demeanor.

"Come on, Jimmy. You can't still be sore at Gloria. She had nothing to do with my mother and your father getting together. She was as broken up about it as your mother."

"I don't know about that either way," said Vega. "What I do know is that her stupid cat nearly blinded me in one eye when I was in kindergarten. Then she accused my mom of poisoning him."

"Did she?"

"How the hell do I know?" said Vega. "I was five."

Michelle lifted her chin to the sign for Paws and Claws. "Good thing we're visiting dogs."

A chorus of barks greeted Vega and Michelle as soon as they entered Paws and Claws. It came from the glass-enclosed playroom on the other side of the store. A white girl barely out of her teens with a nose ring and tattoos came out of the room.

"Hey there," said Vega. "Is Lori Danvers in? I believe she's expecting us."

The girl's eyes turned glassy.

"I can't believe what's happened," she said. "I just saw Talia last week in the store. She seemed fine."

"She didn't have a dog, did she?" Vega hadn't noted any evidence of an animal in the house. No leash or feeding dishes or dog hair.

"I don't think so," said the girl. "She just came to visit Lori."

A second door in the back opened and a woman in her late thirties stepped out. Vega recognized her from the photographs in Talia's house. Her hair was dyed very blond—much blonder than Talia's. She'd obviously been dying it for many years because the shafts were stiff like doll hair and the ends were shredded and frizzy. But there was no mistaking a family resemblance. She had Talia's same big charcoal blue eyes that looked straight at him without guile or pretense, just like the picture of Talia he'd seen at the station house.

She brushed a hand down a black apron covered in dog hair.

"I just finished trimming a yellow Lab. They shed everywhere. You're not allergic, are you?"

Vega and Michelle shook their heads. "No, ma'am," Vega answered.

"Good." Lori extended a hand to Michelle first and then Vega. Vega had told Michelle in the car that whoever Lori Danvers shook hands with first should take the lead. So the ball was in Michelle's court. For now, anyway.

"Thank you for seeing us," Michelle said. "Our condolences on your loss."

"Thank you. This is all sort of a shock right now." The skin beneath Lori Danvers's eyes twitched, but she fought back the urge to cry and turned to the girl with the nose ring. "Harrison's in the playroom if Mrs. Lawrence returns while I'm in back."

"I'll take care of him." The girl looked adoringly at the playroom window where a big yellow Labrador retriever stood up on his hind paws, licking the plate glass until it was a blur of slime. "Who was a good boy for his haircut?" she cooed. "Yes, you are, Harrison! Yes, you are!"

Lori led Vega and Michelle past the dogs into a small break room. Even back here, Vega could smell the dogs and hear their barking. Lori gestured for Michelle and Vega to take a seat at a round plastic table in the center of the room. She brushed off the crumbs of what looked like a morning muffin and offered Vega and Michelle something to drink. They both declined.

Vega expected they'd have to work up to the death. Family members often spent a good deal of time sharing random details about their loved ones—things that mattered only to them. Last meals together. Favorite vacations. Childhood memories.

But not this time.

Lori walked over to a corkboard above the coffeemaker and pulled down a postcard with a photograph of a golden retriever eating a pizza on the front. She handed it to Michelle, who flipped it over. On the back, in girlish print, were the words: *Saw this card and thought of Roscoe. See you for dinner Saturday! Love, Talia.* Vega noticed the postmark on the card was from this past Tuesday—only forty-eight hours before she died.

"You see this card?" asked Lori, fixing both Vega and Michelle in her gaze. "I got this yesterday in the mail. Tal and I were supposed to meet for dinner this evening. Does that sound like a woman who would hang herself? Somebody did this to her. I'm sure of it."

"That's why we're here," Michelle assured her. "To look at all the possibilities."

Vega gestured to the postcard. "If you don't mind, ma'am, I'm going to need to take this into evidence."

Lori's face crumpled. "Oh please, Detective. It's my last correspondence from her. There's nothing of importance on it. Roscoe's my dog."

"I understand," said Vega. "I can assure you, you'll get it back. But we need it to do a thorough investigation. Look, why don't I snap a photo of it now and send it to your phone? That way, you'll have my cell phone contact and the postcard together."

That seemed to mollify her. She gave Vega her cell number. Then she found him a clean zippered sandwich bag. He took a photo of the front and back of the postcard and texted it to her. He tucked the postcard inside the bag and slipped it into their evidence folder.

Lori stared at the photos Vega had just texted to her and wiped a hand across her eyes. "I have all these photos of her on my phone. It's like she's still here."

"The dinner date you scheduled for this evening," asked Michelle. "Was it a regular thing?"

"We got together when we could," said Lori. "I tried to be here for her a lot after the miscarriage. I guess you'd call it more a 'stillbirth.' She was seven months along when it happened."

"How was she handling it?" asked Michelle.

"She was depressed. Who wouldn't be? She talked to a shrink a couple of times."

"Did the doctor prescribe any medications?"

"I don't know." She seemed to register the line of questioning. "You didn't find drugs in her system, did you?"

Michelle shot a questioning look at Vega. Cops like to hold back as much information as they can, but it's always a juggling act. Sometimes, giving information is the best way to get it. Vega gave a slight nod of the head and Michelle continued.

"The medical examiner found alcohol and Valium in her system," she told Lori. "The alcohol was probably only a couple of glasses of wine or the equivalent. But the Valium was more on the order of four days' worth of tablets. Mixed with wine, that's a potent sedative."

Lori stiffened. "My sister did not have a drug or alcohol problem, if that's what you're suggesting."

"Not suggesting," said Michelle. "Only asking." Clearly, they'd touched a nerve. "Was her husband supportive when she miscarried?"

"Huh." Lori rolled her eyes. "More like, relieved."

Michelle and Vega exchanged glances. Lori's tone was much colder when she spoke about Crowley.

"He didn't want to become a father again?" Michelle pressed.

"I think he intended Talia to be a fling," said Lori. "But when she got pregnant . . . she was thirty-four. How many more chances do you get at thirty-four?"

"Did her husband try to talk her out of having the baby?"

Vega noted that Michelle repeatedly referred to Crowley as "her husband." Not "Glen." It was a nice touch. It kept everything centered on Talia. Michelle was an able interviewer—far better than Vega would have expected.

Lori sat back in her chair and took a moment to ponder the question.

"Glen didn't pressure her to end the pregnancy. Nothing like that. But I know he wasn't overjoyed either. He has two grown children from his first marriage. His daughter's a prosecutor in New York City. But his son's . . . I guess you'd say he's autistic."

"Did they argue about her continuing the pregnancy?" asked Michelle.

"They might have at some point. I know he had a temper."

"By temper, do you mean, he shouted? Hit? Vandalized her things?"

Lori picked at some dog hair on her apron. She responded without looking at either of them.

"I never saw any marks or bruises."

Vega thought that was a funny way to answer the question. Almost like she was convincing herself. Vega thought the question was too central to the investigation not to lean a little harder on Lori for an answer.

"Ms. Danvers," said Vega. "Did your sister ever indicate that her husband might be physically abusing her?"

Silence. Vega heard a customer in the front of the store collecting one of the dogs, maybe Harrison, the Labrador retriever. He could hear the jingling of dog tags and the bark of other dogs echoing down the hall. Lori shot a glance over her shoulder as if she hoped her assistant might come in to fetch her. When she looked back, Vega saw something haunted in her eyes.

"Look," Lori began. "When I said I thought my sister

didn't commit suicide, I wasn't saying I thought Glen did anything to her. I mean—my sister's life changed in so many ways after she married Glen. There are probably all sorts of things I don't know."

"We're not accusing anyone," Vega tried to reassure her. "But if there's something you recall—some interaction that you think would be helpful for us to know—we'd like to hear about it."

"She wanted to hire a private investigator."

The words ripped like an electric current through Vega's veins. He could see that Michelle felt it too.

"Did she tell you why?" asked Michelle.

"No," said Lori. "We were . . . I guess you'd say we were closer before she and Glen got married. After, Talia was just . . . in a different world. Socially and economically."

"She told you she wanted to hire a private investigator but she didn't tell you why?" asked Michelle.

"I think it had to do with Glen. But no, she didn't say."

Vega found that hard to believe.

"Listen," said Lori. "The only reason I know she wanted to hire a private investigator is because my ex-boyfriend's one and Talia asked for his number."

"What's his name?" asked Vega.

"Billy Kelso. He's a former cop out of the forty-eighth precinct in the Bronx, but he lives here in Broad Plains. I don't even know if Tal called him in the end."

"Can you give me his contact information?"

Lori scrolled through the contact tab on her cell phone until she found it. She texted it to Vega.

"Did your sister think her husband was cheating on her?" Vega asked.

"That's what I figured." Lori smiled sadly. "It'd be karma, right? My sister stole another woman's husband. And someone else steals hers."

"Do you know if Talia ever cheated?" asked Michelle.

Lori looked surprised at the directness of the question. "No," she said. "She was 'the other woman' and all before they were married. But no. Talia wasn't like that. She was in this for real, even if maybe Glen wasn't. I mean, Talia wasn't the first woman Glen Crowley cheated with."

"Talia told you that?"

"I think she just knew. Or maybe she knew because Charlene, Glen's first wife, told her."

"*Charlene* talked to Talia?" This surprised Michelle.

"Often. That's like, freaky, right?" Lori looked at Vega and Michelle for confirmation. "I'm sure, behind closed doors, Charlene was embarrassed and angry at what happened. I know I would be. But publicly, she was all honey and smiles. You've met her, right?"

"Only in passing," said Vega. "At law enforcement events."

"I met Charlene this morning," said Michelle. "At the Lake Holly police station. She was bringing the cops fresh-baked muffins to thank them for their help with the case."

"That's Charlene." Lori tossed off a laugh. "Martha Stewart on steroids. But she's a good mother to Adam."

"Adam's the DA's son?" asked Vega.

"Yeah," said Lori. "He works as a stockroom clerk at a shoe store in Lake Holly. My sister had him over for dinner regularly. I think Charlene appreciated that." Lori shrugged. "Like I said, Talia and Charlene brokered some sort of truce. They even shared housekeepers. Well, sort of. Tal's housekeeper, Lissette, was the niece of Charlene's housekeeper, Maria."

"Speaking of Lissette . . ." Vega opened his phone and showed Lori a copy of the photograph of the two Hispanic girls he'd found in Talia's drawer. "Do you recognize them? Maybe they're related to Lissette?"

"I don't recognize them," said Lori. "But like I said, Talia didn't tell me everything."

Chapter 17

Rabbi Goldberg walked down the short flight of carpeted stairs to the front doors of the synagogue. Red flashing lights lit up the wall in front of Aviles, bouncing off the glasses on the faces of most of the board members.

Nobody said a word. The only sounds Aviles could hear were Sam Lerner's steady wheezes and the ding of a text coming from Leo Hirsch's phone—which was turned up all the way. So much for his pendulous ears. He was obviously hard of hearing.

The rabbi's voice was tight, devoid of its normal authority. He was speaking to a man—no, two men—at the front doors. The men's words didn't travel up the stairs where Aviles could hear them. But their tone did. There was something muscular about it. An insistence that lacked negotiation or compromise.

These men wanted something—and they had every intention of getting it.

"Well, I'm not standing here like a scared rabbit," said the señora, her French accent, as always, making the words seem inviting even when they weren't.

"Me neither," said Max Zimmerman, his Eastern European accent less melodic, but no less firm. The señora held out an arm to Zimmerman and together, they walked down the stairs, leaving Sam Lerner and the three other board members—Leo Hirsch, David Stern, and Ben Levine—standing there, hiding in the hallway. With Aviles. The only one who had reason to hide. The four board members all became self-conscious at once and followed.

Edgar Aviles hung back, listening to their voices. He could hear now that they were also joined by the cantor, Rachel Bloom. Everyone started talking at once. The flurry of voices blocked out the two visitors' conversation.

Aviles retreated down the hall to the conference room. He peered out a corner of the window onto the parking lot. At the curb, he saw a dark blue sedan—the same one, he was pretty sure, he saw in front of his house this morning. The sedan had no lettering on the side, just a portable lightbar pulsing insistently against the windshield glass, bouncing off the cedar siding of the temple. Still, he knew in every fiber of his being who they were.

ICE.

Had the rabbi called them? Had one of the board members? Aviles supposed it didn't matter. They were here now. The synagogue would turn him over. He couldn't get away.

His limbs felt shaky. The back of his neck turned slimy with sweat. He wasn't afraid for himself. He didn't care if they sent him back to El Salvador. His life was worthless without his family anyway.

But he cared for their sakes—for the danger he'd be leaving them in. His stomach began a slow twist as he thought about that phone call last night. Those threats. Lissette was gone, maybe even dead by now—he didn't know. What he did know was that men like that were capable of anything. He'd seen their *anything* in El Salvador. When he closed his eyes, the memory of his dead cousin came flooding back to him. The way his blood pooled and glistened like spilled engine oil all over the street and into the gutters. There was so much blood running down the street that day, it was a wonder it all came from one skinny little teenager.

No police department in the world could protect his family from men who could do that. Not in El Salvador.

Not here either.

He heard footsteps walking up the stairs and tried to compose himself. To feel nothing. That's how he did it when he walked his way from El Salvador to the United States. He willed himself to feel no hunger or thirst. No pain or fear. *Be a stone,* he used to tell himself. *A stone feels nothing.*

A stone does not have a wife with lupus and a son with cancer, thought Aviles.

The footsteps came closer. Aviles expected the heavy, insistent tread of cops. But the steps were light, almost hesitant.

"Edgar?"

It was the señora. Aviles willed his feet to walk to the conference room door and poke his head out. Their eyes met from a distance of maybe ten feet. She stopped and studied him, tucking a strand of wavy, flowing hair behind one ear.

"I assume you know who's downstairs," she said softly. "I want you to know, the temple didn't call those men. Not my husband. And not the board either. I have to assume they came because they know you work here."

"Yes. I understand." His voice sounded weak and blocked. He cleared his throat to make it stronger. "It's no one's fault."

The voices had gone quiet downstairs—all except for one. Max Zimmerman's. Aviles could hear the accent. He had no idea what Zimmerman was saying, but the old man sounded angry. And not just at the cops. It sounded like he was speaking Yiddish—or maybe Hebrew—Aviles wasn't sure. Which meant his anger wasn't just at the ICE police. It was directed at the board members in his own congregation.

"The two agents promised if you leave with them now, they won't give you any trouble," said the señora. "We'll make sure the congregation knows. We'll collect money for your appeal. For Noah's and Maria's medical bills."

"Thank you."

She looked at him with tears in her eyes. "Edgar—if I could do something, you know I would. But there's nothing—"

"I understand."

"I'm just the rabbi's wife. I have no say in any of this. And even Mark—he's an employee of Beth Shalom. Their spiritual leader, yes. But still an employee. Like you."

Aviles took a deep breath and willed himself to walk with her. The terra-cotta tiles he'd so often mopped felt like pebbles beneath his work boots, like he was crossing a raging river that was about to suck him under. He shot a glance at the sanctuary to his right. The heavy double doors were open. The eternal light above the ark glowed serenely over the empty worship hall with its cavernous ceiling. God was supposed to be present here. But maybe God only listened to Jews in a synagogue and to Christians in a church. Maybe it was like having a ticket to the wrong movie.

Or maybe God didn't listen at all, no matter which movie you bought your ticket for.

Aviles put a hand on the chrome banister he always polished and stepped onto the red carpet he'd just vacuumed this morning. All conversation stopped on the landing below. In the doorway, he saw the same two ICE agents who'd chased him this morning. The white man with no lips and pale, cataract-looking eyes, and the black man with loose jowls and a bored expression. Aviles froze.

The black man with the loose jowls called up the stairs. "You come down now, you hear? Game's over, man." His voice was friendly and casual, but there was no mistaking the way he fingered the handcuffs on his belt that he was growing inpatient.

The rabbi looked up the stairs at Aviles with pleading eyes. He spread his palms.

"We didn't call Immigration, Edgar. I swear." His voice was thin and his face looked especially young in the flashing strobe from the police lights. "Mr. Zimmerman called La Casa before he came over here this morning. They're trying to reach Adele Figueroa to see if there's anything she can do."

Aviles didn't know Adele Figueroa except by reputation, but he doubted she could help him if his own lawyer couldn't. And yet he thought he saw something cross the two agents' faces at the mention of her name. Like they'd eaten something they weren't sure of, and they couldn't tell if they were getting heartburn or food poisoning.

Were they *afraid* of her? Of La Casa? They were the law. They didn't have to be afraid of anybody.

Or did they?

The black agent straightened, his voice trying to relocate its casual tone without success. "Makes no nevermind who you called," he said. "This illegal alien is under arrest." The agent lasered his eyes on Aviles. "Come on down here. We're through playing around."

Aviles trudged down the stairs. He passed by Zimmerman, who gripped his elbow with his bony fingers. "Don't step outside," Zimmerman muttered in Spanish. "Wait for Adele. She'll come. You'll see."

Aviles wasn't sure what surprised him more—the old man speaking Yiddish-accented Spanish or the firm, strong grip a man pushing ninety could have on Aviles's elbow.

"Whatever the hell you're saying, you keep out of this, *Rabbi*," the white agent barked.

"I am not the rabbi," said Zimmerman. He pointed to Rabbi Goldberg. "He is."

"Doesn't matter, old man," said the agent. "You all look like rabbis to me."

There was a moment of stunned silence. The men's postures turned rigid. Something electric seemed to travel through the group. Zimmerman's grip on Aviles's elbow became even firmer. Like they were glued together. Sam Lerner—the man who couldn't wait to turn Aviles over—stepped in front of both of them.

"Just who the hell do you think you're speaking to here, Agent"—Lerner squinted at the badge strung around the white agent's neck—"Donovan."

"Stand out of the way," Donovan barked. "And get your people here to do the same."

Donovan attempted to step around Sam Lerner's girth and over the threshold, but the rabbi and Ben Levine blocked his path.

"Please, Agent Donovan," said Rabbi Goldberg, patting the air. "I ask that you not enter the synagogue. This is a house of worship. A *mikdash*—a sanctuary."

A vein in Donovan's neck bulged. His face turned red. He glanced at his partner, who held up his hands and backed off. This wasn't a fight the black agent was willing to pursue—not here and now at least. But Donovan was. He narrowed his gaze and fanned a look across the crowd. The contempt in his pale eyes a minute ago had just been for Aviles. Now, it was for all of them.

"You are in violation of Title Eight, subsection one-three-two-four," Donovan hissed at the rabbi. "Which makes it a federal crime to attempt to shield, harbor, or conceal from detection any illegal alien in *any* building or form of transportation. That law applies to you"—Donovan pointed a finger at the rabbi—"just the same as it applies to anyone else. Your *people,*" he leaned on the word, "are not above the law, even if they think they are."

Aviles could feel the tension rising in the group. Donovan wasn't just speaking to him anymore. He was speaking to them. American citizens. American citizens with a painful history of their own.

Ten years ago, when Aviles started work at Congregation Beth Shalom, he knew nothing about Judaism or anti-Semitism. He had a fifth-grade education from a third-world country. He'd never even heard of the Holocaust until Rabbi Weiss, now retired, took him aside one day and gave him a Spanish-language copy of the *Diary of Anne Frank*. Aviles brought it home, too embarrassed to admit that it would be a struggle to read it. But his wife, Maria, did. She filled his head with the stories and images of that poor little girl and her family in hiding—not just from the Nazis but from Dutch neighbors who sympathized with the Nazis.

Until Aviles heard those stories, he assumed that only his own people could be so cruel and ruthless. After that, he began to develop a special feeling of kinship toward his employers and their families. He got angry if someone he knew tossed off an anti-Semitic remark. He learned some of the traditions and stories of these people who'd always treated him with kindness. And sure, there were a handful in the congregation who acted like he was invisible. Or their personal servant. But so many others passed along clothes and toys and books for his children. After Noah was diagnosed, they raised an astonishing $18,000 to help with his medical care. Many still came up to him to ask about Noah's progress.

Donovan was probably so used to treating the people he arrested with contempt, he gave no thought about extending that to others. But it had been a grave mistake here. If

Aviles's ten years at Beth Shalom had taught him anything, it had taught him the special and fragile history of the Jewish people. For all their wealth, education, and citizenship, they were only a few generations removed from the fear of men in uniforms like Donovan. The ICE agent's words had brought it all back.

Everyone started shouting at once after that. About lawsuits and defamation and words Aviles didn't know in English or Spanish. Aviles said nothing. The noise of their voices drowned out the sound of a car pulling behind the agents' sedan. A pale green Toyota with a few dents on the doors. A Latina got out. She was short and pretty and dressed in casual jeans and a bright blue cotton sweater. Her black silky bob of hair caught the sun. She cupped a hand across her eyes to shield them from the glare.

"Hello?" she called from the steps. She had to say it twice before anyone heard her. The black agent turned. The muscles in his face tightened. His bored gaze snapped to attention.

"Ma'am," he growled. "Do *not* interfere. This is a police matter."

"Then don't 'ma'am' me," she replied. "You know damn well who I am. And you know damn well that I could call every major TV station in the area and have them here in five minutes filming federal agents trying to forcibly remove the father of a grievously sick child from a house of worship. A *synagogue*. After the media has its way with you, the Anti-Defamation League and the ACLU will keep you tied up in court so long, you'll be collecting your pension from a witness stand."

"That's Adele Figueroa, head of La Casa," Zimmerman whispered to Aviles. Aviles nodded. He'd figured as much.

"The synagogue is in violation of federal law," Agent Donovan shot back. "They need to turn this illegal alien over."

"Do you have a signed judicial warrant for Mr. Aviles's arrest?" asked Adele.

The two agents exchanged glances. Donovan's lips thinned into pencil lines.

"What are you, his lawyer now?" Donovan jerked a thumb in Aviles's direction. "Dude's probably got a dozen of them in there already."

"Keep going, Agent"—she squinted at his badge around his neck—"Donovan . . . and"—she turned to the black man—"Tyler . . . You are both doing a great job of making the Anti-Defamation League's case for them. Now, I ask you again—do you have a signed judicial warrant for Mr. Aviles's arrest?"

"Aw, for crying out loud . . ." Tyler turned to Donovan. "Show her the damn paper."

Donovan whipped out a folded piece of paper and flung it at Adele Figueroa. She slowly unfolded it and read the document. Then she folded it up again.

"Did you break down this man's door when you attempted to arrest him this morning, Agent Tyler?"

"Huh? No! We didn't break down any—"

"Did you force your way into his building?"

"He ran." Donovan sneered at her. "Like a scared rabbit. You've got nothing on us."

"That's right." She smiled and handed Donovan back the paper. "Just as you know, you've got nothing on Edgar Aviles."

A murmur went up through the figures in the doorway. Adele turned to the rabbi.

"Agents Donovan and Tyler just showed me something called an administrative warrant," she explained. "It's basically a piece of paper issued by ICE that gives its agents the authority to arrest someone in a public place. Repeat—*a public place*. It does not allow them to break down anyone's doors and haul them away." She turned to the agents and smiled sweetly. "If I'm not mistaken, gentlemen, those restrictions against arrest also include schools, hospitals, and houses of worship—Jewish or otherwise."

"What does that mean?" asked Rabbi Goldberg. "Does that mean he's free?"

The smile on Adele's face faltered. Donovan answered.

"Your boy's not free. Not by a long shot," he sneered. "He steps one foot outside that door, he's ours."

The rabbi looked at Adele. "Is that true?"

"For the moment," she said.

"Damn right, for the moment," said Donovan. "Aviles is getting deported. Today. Tomorrow. Makes no difference to us—it's just paperwork. We'll get a signed judicial warrant. And then we'll be back. Nothing you say"—he pointed to Adele—"or you say"—he pointed to the rabbi—"will make any difference. In the meantime, you want your precious illegal alien? You got him. Twenty-four hours a day, seven days a week. Enjoy, *Rabbi*. Your congregation's gonna *love* you after this."

The two agents got into their car and drove out of the lot. The group unclenched. Rabbi Goldberg shook Adele's hand and Max Zimmerman patted her on the shoulder and beamed.

"What did I tell you?" he asked no one in particular. "She has chutzpah. And integrity and honor, besides. I knew she could do this."

Adele Figueroa stood in deep conversation with the rabbi and his wife for a few minutes. Aviles had a feeling the picture wasn't quite as rosy as Mr. Zimmerman seemed to think. He waited until they'd all said their piece. Then Aviles approached her.

"Thank you, señora," he said. "I cannot begin to tell you how grateful I am. Can I go home now and see my family?"

She shook her head. "I don't think that's a good idea."

"But you just told the agents that they can't break down my door and arrest me."

"With an administrative warrant, they can't, no," she explained. "But two things are going to happen now. The first is, if you go home, they'll harass and threaten anyone and everyone who goes in or out of your building until you surrender. They'll tell your friends and neighbors that if you don't surrender and ICE gets a judicial warrant, they'll arrest everyone in that building who doesn't have papers."

"Can they do that?" asked Aviles.

"Yes, unfortunately," she replied. "Once they have the legal authority to enter your premises, they can arrest and deport anyone and everyone who can't prove legal status—whether they have a removal order against them or not. So going home can hurt a lot of people and cause a lot of bad feelings."

Adele flicked her eyes across the room. Not at the rabbi. At his wife. "That's why you need to stay here for a while. The synagogue has plenty of space. You already work here and can keep on earning some money to help your family."

"But I can't live here forever."

"That brings us to the second thing," said Adele. "You need to file a request for an administrative stay of removal. A stay is basically a request that ICE stop proceedings to deport you."

"But my lawyer already filed," said Aviles.

"He filed a judicial appeal," she explained. "He asked a federal court to overturn ICE's order of removal against you and maybe grant you some long-term protected status. Appeals like that can take a year or more. In the meantime, ICE can still deport you. That's been the law since 1996."

Aviles felt like his head was spinning. Immigration law was hard for people with a lot of education. It was especially hard for a man like him with very little. He'd always been so self-reliant his whole life. It pained him that he was so powerless in this.

"This stay," said Aviles. "How do I file it?"

"You file it at the local ICE office—in this case, the one in Broad Plains," Adele explained. "ICE will consider a stay if you can prove immediate humanitarian concerns. In this case, your son's cancer. Your wife's medical issues. I can help you file but you need to gather all the paperwork and we need to act quickly."

"Thank you, señora," said Aviles. "I would appreciate that. If we do this, will ICE grant this . . . *stay* . . . as you call it?"

"It's hard to predict," said Adele. "In your situation, they might. As I understand it, you have no criminal record. You have steady employment. You were previously protected under temporary status. And your wife and children are all American citizens."

"Yes. That's correct." Aviles felt hopeful. But he could see that the señora didn't look quite as hopeful as he did.

"The thing is," she continued, "a stay is just that—an extension. Usually six months to a year. The government could still deport you after that. And you have to check in with them periodically. But at least it would allow you to keep fighting your legal appeal in the meantime."

"I want to file a stay," said Aviles.

"Good." She smiled but there was something forced around the edges. "Speed is everything now," she explained. "If those two agents can get a federal judge to sign the order for your removal before we can gather the paperwork and make an administrative appeal, ICE can arrest you anywhere—including in this synagogue."

"Would they do that?"

He saw something flicker in her eyes. And he realized, of course, that he was not the first person to ask Adele

Figueroa for help, nor was he likely the last. As head of La Casa, she'd probably witnessed miraculous family reunions and excruciating separations. The memory of each seemed to linger in her eyes. No one could say which Edgar Aviles would turn out to be.

She grabbed his hand. Her palms were sweaty. "If you are a praying man, now would be a good time."

Chapter 18

Lori Danvers's ex-boyfriend, Billy Kelso, wasn't work-ing on this beautiful Saturday afternoon. He was play-ing softball with a team of cops from all over the area called the Blue Avengers. They were leading five to two against a group of firefighters called the Red Devils. Firefighters could hit—but nobody could run like a cop.

Getting shot at made every officer fast on his feet.

The baseball field was in a park just north of Warbur-ton that had once been a factory. The land had the sani-tized look of an EPA cleanup site. All the trees were the same stunted height and the earth so pancake flat and free of stones, it had to have been backfilled.

"You still play?" Michelle asked Vega when they pulled into the parking lot. "I remember you were good."

"Pickup games here and there," Vega replied. "I'm more about my music now. Got a wedding gig tonight with my band, Armado."

"You call yourselves the Spanish word for 'armed'?"

"We're all cops."

"I see," said Michelle. "Truth in advertising, I sup-pose."

They both slipped on sunglasses and walked to a set of metal bleachers on the other side of the dugout. The benches were pitted and dusted with pollen. Vega took a seat and texted his daughter to make sure Joy was still pet-sitting Diablo tonight. Michelle kept her gaze on the game.

"I texted my mom and asked her about that photograph I gave you."

"And?" Vega looked at her.

"She told me to mind my own business and not ask Pop. She said it might upset him."

"What kind of response is that?"

"Not one I expected."

"Did she . . ." Vega had to force himself to say the words. "Did she say anything about me getting sent away?"

"I didn't even get that far. She practically hung up on me." Michelle lifted her sunglasses and massaged her eyes. "I'm sorry I gave you that picture, Jimmy. I didn't think it would be a big deal."

Vega was happy he was wearing sunglasses himself. It gave him something to hide behind. He searched the field. The cops were at bat. Kelso had told Vega he'd be wearing the number 23 on his jersey. Vega spotted him now. He was a big white guy with wavy brown hair going gray on the sides and muscle just starting to turn to flab. He was on deck, swinging two bats above his head—totally unnecessary. It was never strength that made the play. It was timing. Connect too early, the ball limps in as a grounder. Connect too late, it's a fly pop. Baseball, more than any of the other major sports, was physics in motion. It had a rhythm all its own. Maybe that's why the musician in Vega liked it so much.

It was the top of the fifth inning. The Avengers had no outs. Vega and Michelle would just have to wait until Kelso struck out, was tagged out, or brought in a run.

Michelle's phone dinged with a text. She looked at the screen.

"You were right," she mumbled. "Aviles was at the synagogue."

Vega felt the air leave his lungs. "So, he's in custody?"

"Negative." Michelle scrolled through the message. "It seems your girlfriend intervened. Told Tyler and Donovan they needed to get a judicial warrant." Michelle narrowed her gaze at Vega. "You didn't . . . tip her off or anything, did you?"

"I haven't spoken to her since I saw her at the station."

"Well, somebody did."

"It wasn't me," said Vega. "And not for nothing, if ICE wanted to arrest Aviles, they should have gotten an order signed by a judge, same as I'd have to."

"ICE is allowed to arrest on an administrative warrant," she reminded him.

"On the street," said Vega. "But Aviles wasn't *on the street*. You talk about the law—where's the law in that?"

"Aviles is an illegal alien," said Michelle. "Not an American citizen or legal permanent resident."

"He's a janitor with no criminal record and a sick kid."

"That doesn't change the fact that his status has been revoked," she countered. "What do you want us to do? Open the borders to everyone?"

"No."

"So? Somebody's going to be kept out. Or sent back. That's why we have laws. So we can control who gets in and who doesn't."

Kelso swung at the first pitch and missed. The umpire called a strike.

"All I'm saying," Vega grunted, "is that the laws don't work. Average folks are getting hurt while the mutts walk free."

"It's our duty as Americans to keep unwanted intruders out of our country."

"Those unwanted intruders pick our vegetables, mow our lawns, bus our dishes, and care for our children," said Vega.

"Then let them get in line for a visa like everyone else."

Vega watched the ump call a second strike on Kelso. He turned to Michelle and raised his mirrored sunglasses so she could see his eyes.

"All right," he said. "Hypothetical situation. Say there was a boat full of immigrants heading to your shores. A thousand men, women, and children. Good people who wanted to apply for valid visas. But there was a wait list that stretched for years and the quotas were so small, there was no way they'd be admitted anytime soon. If they returned home, there was a good chance they'd be subjected to violence. Maybe even killed. Would you let them in? Or turn them away?"

"Hypothetically?" Michelle seesawed her head. "I'd tell them what I just told you—wait your turn for a visa."

"A visa that might never come?"

"Yes," she replied. "A visa that might never come." Even Michelle knew that the odds of getting into the United States legally from many countries was next to impossible. Short of great wealth, marriage abroad to an American, or a Nobel Prize, it wasn't going to happen.

"That's just what the United States did," said Vega. "In 1939 when a passenger ship full of European Jews sailed from Germany to Cuba. Cuba wouldn't take the refugees so they pleaded with the United States. We turned them away. More than a quarter of those men, women, and children died in concentration camps."

Max Zimmerman, a Holocaust survivor himself, had told Vega that story one night over dinner at Adele's. Vega sat transfixed as Max described what it must have been like to sail so close to Miami that the people on board the ship could see the lights of the harbor. Vega couldn't imagine their anguish as they sailed away, many to their doom.

"I guess, in retrospect . . ." Michelle's voice trailed off.

"It would have been good if the United States had eased restrictions a little. But okay." She slapped her thighs. "Let's go the other way. Let's say we took in every single person in Europe back then who was facing potential death. Jews. Gypsies. Gays. Communists. People in war zones. People facing starvation or bombings or other war atrocities. You overload a lifeboat? Everybody drowns. There is no good solution."

Vega turned back to the game. He had no answers. He much preferred the sweet simplicity of sports where everyone played by the same rules and there was always a ref to remind you what they were. He watched Kelso reject a third pitch that went low and make contact with the fourth—a high pop—that the third baseman caught.

They waited for Kelso to notice them on the bleachers. He walked over.

"Mr. Kelso?" Vega rose and extended a hand. "Detective Jimmy Vega, county police. This is my partner, Agent Lopez."

Kelso wiped his sweaty palm on his uniform pants and shook their hands.

"Call me Billy. Billy's fine."

He was tall and broad-shouldered with blue eyes and a dimpled grin. The kind of man who probably turned all the girls' heads in high school. His features had widened and coarsened since then. The blue eyes had grown suspicious—as they always did in cops. The wavy hair, stubborn and bristly. The dimples looked like puckers in flesh just beginning to sag.

"What's a county detective teaming up with ICE for?" Kelso asked them cheerfully.

Kelso's grip slid away when Vega told him.

"You're kidding," said the ex-cop. "I just spoke to Talia the other week."

"Well, that answers one of our questions," said Vega. "Maybe we should take a little walk. Can the team spare you for a moment?"

"Sure."

There was a track on the other side of the rec field. A soccer game was going on in the center. Moms with strollers were walking the perimeter. Vega, Michelle, and Kelso stood on the side and watched them.

"So how did it happen?" asked Kelso. "Gunshot? Drugs? Must be bad for you to walk me over here to talk."

"We'd like to keep this conversation between you and us at the moment," said Vega. "She was found hanging in her basement."

"Holy . . ." He let out a whistle. "Lori must be a basket case. They were close."

"We interviewed her sister this morning," said Vega. "She said she used to date you."

"A while back, yeah." Kelso didn't elaborate. The breakup must have been mutual—or at least, mutual enough that there were no bad feelings.

"Lori said you used to work for the NYPD and you're a private investigator now."

"That's right," said Kelso. "I left about four years ago. Took a bullet in a robbery and said, 'I'm outta here.' "

"Sorry to hear that," Michelle offered.

"It was a graze," said Kelso. "No permanent damage. I was burned out by that point and glad to leave."

"You like PI work?" she asked.

Kelso shrugged. "I don't get shot at, which is good. Most of my cases are cheating spouses and divorcing couples who want to find their partner's hidden assets."

"Did Talia fall into either of those categories?" Vega slid the question in smoothly. Talia was dead, but Kelso could still invoke client confidentiality in absence of a court order. Vega and Michelle were hoping to avoid that.

"Look, guys." Kelso ran a hand through his bristly hair. He seemed nervous all of a sudden. "Talia spoke to me. But I didn't do any work for her. As a matter of fact, I brushed her off."

"Why?" asked Vega. "What did she want you to do?"

Kelso hesitated. "I don't want to be your source on this. I don't want the blowback."

"You don't have to be our source," said Vega. "Just tell us what she said. If it was something really out of the ordinary—"

"That's just it," said Kelso. "It wasn't. It was the sort of bread-and-butter work I do every day. I just didn't want to do it for the DA's wife. I gotta operate in this county, you know?"

Vega and Michelle traded looks. They both saw where this was headed.

"Are you saying Talia wanted to hire you to catch her husband cheating?" asked Vega. "He had another mistress?"

Kelso tossed off a nervous laugh. "He ain't into mistresses these days. Least not after getting his former one knocked up."

"Hookers," Michelle muttered under her breath.

Vega thought about that massage parlor up in Taylorsville. He'd sensed all along he was on the right track.

"That's not even the worst of it," said Kelso. "Talia thought at least one of them was underage. A human trafficking victim."

"Holy . . ." Vega felt like he'd grabbed a live wire. Everything inside of him thrummed with nervous energy. They'd just gone from marital problems to misdemeanors to felony charges with federal implications. "Did she provide you with any evidence?"

"I didn't *want* any evidence," said Kelso. "I told her to

call the police. This wasn't a PI case. A PI case brings down a marriage. She was talking about bringing down the man. The last thing I wanted was to go up against the DA."

Vega wondered if that was the last thing Talia Crowley wanted too.

Chapter 19

Fourteen-year-old Erick Aviles was biking home Saturday evening, balancing a bag of milk, vegetables, and tortillas from Claudia's bodega on the handlebars of his bike. He was happy to have someplace to go and something to do. Anything to avoid being inside his apartment with his weepy mother, his little brother and sister, and the endless parade of neighbors and friends who tried to console them and offer advice.

Edgar's employers will help him . . .
La Casa has lawyers on staff . . .
Noah's doctors can write a letter . . .

Erick felt like he was drowning in good intentions. No one could help them. Not really. His father's immigration troubles were the only part they knew about. The rest, his family was covering with a lie. Each time the question of Lissette came up, his mother would look away and say she had "gone to visit friends."

Over and over, Erick replayed the events at the cemetery, like a level in a video game he couldn't get past. Everything that happened was his fault. If he hadn't cried out, maybe those men wouldn't have taken his cousin. Maybe Lissette could have just given them whatever they wanted and they'd have let her go.

At the top of the hill, Erick drank in the scent of damp

earth and green shoots. It reminded him of a time, not so long ago, when spring meant grabbing his soccer ball and running out to play with friends. He wanted to feel like that again. Like the boy he'd once been.

He pushed off the pavement and let his feet dangle away from the pedals as he coasted down the hill, feeling the exhilaration of unbridled speed as the bike gained momentum. The road had just been paved so the asphalt was as smooth as icing. The crews hadn't even painted yellow stripes down the middle yet. The wind hit his face, raking his hair in every direction. He turned his eyes upward and watched the streetlights play peekaboo between the lush canopy of trees.

He was so focused on the trees that he didn't notice the big black SUV until it pulled up alongside his bicycle—so close that Erick saw his own reflection in the dark tinted glass.

The back door swung open. Rap music poured out. A burly Latino in a well-worn leather jacket eyed Erick. He had skin like a jicama—all pitted and uneven.

"*Métete,*" the man commanded in Spanish. *Get in.*

Erick backed away from the door.

Jicama-man cursed. "Nobody's gonna hurt you, okay?" He spoke in English this time, with a Spanish accent. "I'm here about your cousin. I'm here to tell you she's fine. Get in and I'll show you." He smiled, showing two gold teeth.

"No."

"Look, *cipote,*" the man said in a weary voice, using the Salvadoran slang for "child." "If I wanted to hurt you, I could do it anywhere. Anytime. You think I'm gonna pick a busy street? With you on your bike? Leave the bike. Bring your groceries and get in the car. We talk and then I'll drop you back here."

Erick looked up and down the street. The dry cleaners behind him was already closed at this hour on a Saturday.

So was the nail salon and the barbershop. Cars drove by, but the big black SUV shielded them from seeing Erick. He could run—but like the man with the pitted jicama skin and gold teeth said, he could find him anywhere.

And besides, Erick owed it to Lissette to help her. It was his fault this *mara* had her in the first place.

He set the bike down on the sidewalk, grabbed his groceries, and climbed inside the vehicle. The interior smelled of weed and body odor. The driver pulled away sharply from the curb. Erick could only see the back of the driver's head and his tattooed neck, but he recognized the pelt of hair that rested on top. The driver looked at Erick from the rearview mirror and Erick saw his crazy eye track outward as it had done that night in the graveyard. He immediately regretted getting into the vehicle. His voice broke when he tried to speak.

"Where are we going?"

"Like I told you. Around the block." Jicama-man pushed Erick down and grabbed both of the boy's arms. He shoved a grease-stained hand into the front and back pockets of Erick's jeans and the pouch of his hoodie.

"Hey!" the boy cried. "Stop!"

The man tightened his grip as he pulled Erick's cell phone from the pouch of his hoodie.

"That's my phone," Erick cried.

The man examined the phone, then pocketed it. "You'll get it back," he said. "Where's the other phone?"

"I don't have any other—"

"Is it in your apartment?"

"Lissette has a phone. She had it with her—"

"Not hers, *baboso*. The one from her employer."

"I don't know about any other phone."

"Well, you better know," said the man. "You better find it." He flung Erick against the inside of the car door. "Your cousin's life depends on it. Your whole *family's* lives depend on it. I don't get that phone, it's not just Lissette you gotta worry about anymore. It's your brother. Your mother. Your sister. Even your father. We can get to him too. Make no mistake."

Erick started to shake. The SUV turned the corner and cruised down a block of bungalows with basketball hoops over their garages and American flags over their front doors. Erick smelled someone cooking hamburgers on a grill. Everything looked so tranquil. So safe.

Erick felt a million miles away—like he was in another country. In a way, he supposed, he was.

Jicama-man grabbed Erick's hoodie tight around his neck. "Listen up," he growled. "That phone is your life. You find it and turn it over, you live. You don't, you die. And don't get any ideas about turning it over to the police. We'll know if you do. You'll be dead before the first cop car shows up."

The SUV turned the corner and turned again. They were coming up to the spot on the pavement where Erick's bike lay on its side, untouched, like a dead body. The SUV pulled to the curb. The man with pitted skin released his grip on Erick's hoodie and flung open the back door. Traffic pushed past them, headlights reflecting in the rearview mirror, then bouncing back on the man's scarred face. His eyes looked like two black river stones, slick and cold. He threw Erick's bag of groceries on the curb.

"We'll be watching, *cipote*," he grunted, shoving the boy's cheap cell phone back into his hoodie pocket. "You. Your family. You want them to live long, happy lives? Find that phone. We'll be in touch." The SUV turned the corner and sped off.

Erick stood frozen on the curb next to his bike and bag of now-bruised vegetables and leaking milk. All that stood between him and his family's safety was a phone. A phone that wasn't in their apartment. He knew. He'd looked. He had no idea where it could be. Only Lissette knew. And either she wasn't telling—

Or she couldn't anymore.

Erick felt something warm trickle down one leg of his jeans. The warmth quickly turned cold and clammy. And he knew as he stood there, shivering in shame, that his fear wasn't just for what the men had done to him.

It was for what they could still do. To all of them.

Chapter 20

Vega and Michelle sat in the Taurus in stunned silence after they left Billy Kelso.

"We have no proof that anything that private investigator just told us is true," Michelle insisted. "It's not like Kelso did surveillance on Crowley and caught him having sex with human trafficking victims."

"I know," said Vega. "But if it's true and Talia was planning to go to the police, it provides a strong motive for Crowley to kill her."

"Crowley was in Albany when his wife died," Michelle reminded him. "If he hired someone else to kill her, where's the evidence of forced entry? Of Talia resisting? Why is the housekeeper missing?"

Vega had no answers, especially regarding Lissette. He turned over the Taurus's engine and nosed out of the ballfield parking lot.

"You update Greco," Vega told Michelle. "He thinks I'm a broken record with my suspicions about Crowley."

Michelle dialed Greco's cell and filled him in while Vega drove north, tapping the steering wheel and brooding about the case. He kept coming back to Lissette. She was at the heart of everything.

"Ask Grec whether he and Sanchez had any luck at the Magnolia Inn."

Michelle relayed Vega's question, then fielded his reply. "He says he and Sanchez showed Lissette's picture around. Nobody there knew her. He did, however, find a taxi driver who dropped Lissette off at the Crowleys' house on Friday morning."

Vega was pleased by the confirmation that Lissette was likely the one who brought in that *New York Times.* Yet the question still remained: Why didn't Lissette call the police as soon as she discovered Talia's body? Or, if she was afraid to call the police, why didn't she at least call Glen Crowley?

Because she knows something about Talia's death, thought Vega. *Something she isn't supposed to know.*

Vega thought about Elmer Ortega's list with those five names. Two, at least, had been facing deportation—Cesar Zuma and Edgar Aviles. Now Zuma was dead and Aviles was on the run. *What about those other names on that list,* Vega wondered? He couldn't shake the sense that that list was the key to finding Lissette. And Lissette was the key to finding out what happened to Talia.

Vega made a right and headed east, away from the direction of Lake Holly.

"You missed your turnoff," said Michelle.

"No, I didn't," said Vega. "I want to make a stopover in Broad Plains and run those names from Elmer Ortega's list through the ICE database."

"What? *Now?* Do you know how big a job that is?" asked Michelle. "We don't have birth dates or addresses. We don't even know if we have their names in the right order."

"All I'm asking is for you to input the names into the database."

"It's almost three," Michelle argued. "We've got statements to write up from Lori Danvers and Billy Kelso. You've got a gig tonight. I've got two hungry kids at home—"

"You'll still see your kids and I'll make my gig. Come

on," Vega urged her. "It's a Saturday. The place will be empty. How hard can it be to type five names into a computer?"

The Broad Plains headquarters of Immigration and Customs Enforcement was housed in a ten-story brown-brick office building that looked like it had been fashioned out of a shipping carton. It was cut-rate and government-issue all the way, from its faded flags in the lobby to its dim lighting in the hallways. Vega and Michelle parked in an underground lot, signed in with a security guard, and took the elevator to the fifth floor.

The waiting area had a big blue ICE logo on the wall and not one but six American flags in various sizes and configurations. Rows of plastic chairs lined the waiting area where desperate immigrants waited on weekdays to plead their cases. Everything was quiet on a Saturday afternoon.

Michelle swiped her pass and led Vega through a locked door and into a space full of fabric-partitioned cubicles. The desks were nicer than the ones Vega saw in all the police stations he'd been in, including his own. They had a shiny blond veneer of wood and the partitions were a soft cream color—not the usual beige or gray. It gave the whole operation a touch of class that seemed out of keeping with ICE's street image.

Michelle walked Vega past an open desk with a big dish of candy and a banner full of flowers and bunnies that read, HAPPY SPRING, across it. Vega swiped a miniature Snickers bar from the candy dish.

"Is that okay?" he asked. "I'm not breaking some federal law that's gonna get me deported?"

"Really Jimmy." Michelle pulled a face. "We're not like that. Especially Karen, our administrative assistant. She's like a den mother around here. She's the one who puts up our holiday decorations and bakes cupcakes for people's birthdays."

"We don't have den mothers at the county police," said Vega. "When we have a birthday, someone on the squad sticks a flashlight in a roll of toilet paper and props it next to a doughnut."

Michelle laughed. "We should loan you Karen."

The walls of Michelle's cubicle were covered in pictures of her sons. She caught Vega looking at them as she turned on her computer.

"I think Artie Junior, my older one, looks like you," she said. "Both of you have Pop's eyes."

Vega saw it too. The pucker of flesh beneath the lower lids when the boy smiled. That unruly arch of black eyebrows.

"Is he the shortstop?"

"Yeah."

Vega wished he could think of something more to ask, but words failed him when it came to family. He whipped out his phone and pulled up Ortega's list. He showed the names to Michelle. She took a deep breath.

"Okay. Let's get started."

Vega thought he heard some disappointment in her exhale. She wanted things from Vega that he didn't know how to give.

She turned to her computer and typed in *Cesar Zuma-Léon.*

"Here he is," said Michelle. "Age thirty-two. Birthplace: Honduras. Occupation: housepainter. No criminal record. One driving citation."

Vega bent over the screen and looked at the mug shot next to the information. It matched the man Vega had seen lying on the tracks. "That's him, all right."

Michelle squinted at the screen. "It says here, he was cited five years ago for driving without a license."

"Was that when he came to the attention of ICE?"

"Looks like it," said Michelle. "He applied for asylum. It was denied two years ago. He missed his court date on the appeal."

Or more likely, ran out of money and figured it was a lost cause, thought Vega. "When did he go into priority removal?"

Michelle clicked onto another screen. "Huh," she murmured.

"What?"

"He didn't. There's no indication he was ever shifted into priority removal. That's not to say ICE wouldn't have picked him up in a raid and deported him. But we weren't gunning for him."

"I saw the letter in his shirt pocket," said Vega. "It said he had to deport immediately."

"I know," said Michelle. "But there's no record of anything like that here."

Vega read the next name on the list to her: Jesús Monroy-Peña. Again, she was able to call it up on her computer. Monroy was a thirty-eight-year-old Guatemalan who worked as the foreman on a horse farm in Wickford. He'd come to ICE's attention after his employers asked him to apply for legal status. His application was denied. But again, there was no record that ICE had put him into priority removal.

Vega leaned over Michelle's computer to get a better look at Monroy's mug shot. He noticed the name of the farm in Wickford where Monroy worked: Springdale.

"That farm rings a bell," said Vega. "I think they had a break-in there a few months ago. The county was called in to help. The owner kept a lot of guns, as I recall."

"Did they catch the suspect?" asked Michelle.

"I don't think so, but I'd have to check. It wasn't my case." Vega took out a pen and made a note to call Wickford to see if they'd ever spoken to Monroy.

Michelle moved on to the next name, the only female on

the list: Deisy Ramos-Sandoval. Age: sixteen. Birthplace: El Salvador. No criminal record. No infractions of any kind.

"It says here, Deisy crossed the border three years ago as an unaccompanied minor," said Michelle. "A judge issued her temporary asylum while her application for permanent asylum makes its way through the courts."

Vega leaned in closer and looked at the mug shot on the screen. It showed a young teenage girl with soft brown eyes and dimpled cheeks. Vega reared back.

"It's her."

"Who?"

"Deisy. Deisy and Nelly." Vega fumbled for his phone, scrolling until he found a copy of the photograph he'd seen in Talia's drawer. The one of the two little girls on that lush green hillside in Central America. He showed it to Michelle.

"It's the same girl, all right."

"It's more than the same girl," said Vega excitedly. "It's the direct connection we've been looking for. Deisy Ramos. Her picture was sitting in a wallet in the back of Talia Crowley's dresser drawer. Her name is on Elmer Ortega's list."

"Yes, but why?" asked Michelle. "Was Talia involved in helping this girl? Was the girl connected to Lissette?"

Vega read the file over Michelle's shoulder. It said that Deisy lived in Port Carroll with her mother, stepfather, and two half brothers. There was no mention of a "Nelly." Maybe Nelly was a cousin still residing in El Salvador.

"I don't understand what a sixteen-year-old asylum-seeker would be doing on that list," said Michelle. "Cesar Zuma was illegal. So is Edgar Aviles since his TPS was rescinded. But Deisy—she has temporary asylum. She doesn't need some gangbanger to help her avoid deportation. If anything, he'd hurt her chances."

"Maybe someone convinced her otherwise." Vega thought about the removal letter from ICE that the Metro-North police found in Cesar Zuma's pocket. He mentioned it to Michelle.

"Do you think it was real?" he asked.

"It had to be."

"I don't remember who signed it," said Vega. "You've got no record of it in your files."

"Greco must have a copy he can text to me," said Michelle. "If someone from our office signed it, I'd recognize the name."

They split up after that. Michelle texted Greco to ask about that letter and finish inputting the names into the computer. Vega called his contacts in Wickford about the Springdale Farm break-in.

"You can use Karen's desk," Michelle offered. "Just don't eat all her candy."

Sitting at Michelle's administrative assistant's desk felt like visiting someone's grandma. There were potted plants and tiny crocheted stuffed animals scattered about the desktop. There were dozens of snapshots and Bible quotes pinned to a partition. Karen Hurst appeared to have a very big and very loving family. Vega tried to move as few things as possible as he attempted to track down the threads to a case that seemed to be multiplying by the minute.

He started by calling Mark Hammond, a detective friend at the Wickford Police. Hammond was playing golf, this being a sunny spring Saturday. But he was happy to fill Vega in on the details of the robbery from the thirteenth hole.

"It was quite a haul," said Hammond. "The thieves got away with two shotguns, one pistol, and about thirty thousand dollars in cash and jewelry."

"Any indication it was an inside job?" asked Vega.

"Every," said Hammond. "The thieves had the alarm code."

Vega asked Hammond if they'd interviewed Monroy.

"The foreman? Sure," said Hammond. "He's worked for the Eldridges for eight years. Takes care of all their horses. He has the alarm codes for everything so we looked at him closely."

"And?" Vega heard the thwack of balls and the stutter of sprinklers in the background. Hammond's mind was on the game. It was an effort to get him to connect to the messiness of crime while he was surrounded by so much manicured greenery.

"We couldn't find anything that tied him to the heist," said Hammond. "He had a solid alibi the night of the break-in. He was helping his brother at a catering gig. A hundred people saw him there. Plus, afterward, he didn't start flashing around a lot of cash or new purchases—which is usually the case in these things."

"No drug use?"

"None."

"Talk to him again," said Vega. "Tell him his name is on a list we recovered from the pocket of a dead gang-banger by the name of Elmer 'Cheetos' Ortega, the chief suspect in the jewelry-store heist in Lake Holly a few weeks ago. See what he says."

"Will do," said Hammond. "Thanks for the tip."

Vega hung up and wandered back to Michelle's cubicle. He found her staring at her computer screen with a frozen look of disbelief on her face. In front of her was the ICE file of the fourth name from the list: Wilmer Diaz-Garcia. Age: Forty-two. Birthplace: Ecuador.

"Well?" asked Vega. "Don't tell me he's a suspect in a crime as well?"

"No," said Michelle. "But his wife, Nelda, was."

"What?" Vega pulled up a chair and sank into it.

"Nelda Diaz was questioned by police in the break-in of her employer, a CEO who lives in Quaker Hills."

"Why is that showing up in Wilmer Diaz's file?"

"Because Nelda confessed," said Michelle. "She told the

Quaker Hills police that an ICE agent contacted her and showed her an order of removal for her husband, Wilmer. She said the agent promised her if she gave up the alarm code of her employer's residence, her husband could get his deportation order reversed."

"Did she have the agent's name?"

"She said he didn't give it."

"How convenient," said Vega. "You think it's a cover story? Or someone really scammed her?"

"It must be a scam," said Michelle. "I can't even find an order of removal for Wilmer Diaz before this happened."

"What do you mean, *before?*"

"A day after Nelda confessed, both Diazes were rounded up in a raid and subsequently deported back to Ecuador."

"*Ay, puñeta!* Do you think that's just coincidence?"

"I don't know," said Michelle. "It seems like every person on that list believed they were imminently in danger of being deported—even when the files suggest they weren't. Someone was playing them. A con man or . . ."

Or an agent inside ICE.

Vega sat back in his chair and thought through the implications. It felt like he and Michelle were looking at a modern-day version of the Greek Trojan horse. A seemingly innocuous gift with treachery at its core. What better way to gain inside information about alarm codes, valuables, and the comings and goings of wealthy homeowners and upscale businesses than through low-level immigrant workers such as maids, gardeners, and housepainters? What better way to ensure those workers cooperated but to threaten them with deportation if they didn't?

"What about Aviles?" asked Vega. "Did you run his name?"

"I ran the surnames as they appear on the list and in reverse order," said Michelle. "The only one in New York that turned up was Edgar Aviles-Ceren."

"I'm assuming his priority removal is legit," said Vega.

"He's on the list. But he was only moved there about a week ago."

"Who moved him?"

"I don't know. There are no initials next to his change in status."

"Is that common?"

"It happens," she admitted. "Names move so quickly through the system, people make mistakes. Agents forget to enter their initials. Names are misspelled. Records are entered into the wrong file."

Michelle's phone dinged with a text. She opened the screen. "It's Greco," she said. "He sent a copy of Cesar Zuma's removal letter."

Michelle pulled up the letter. A puzzled look crossed her features.

"What's wrong?"

"Daniel Wilson signed the letter a month ago."

"He works here, doesn't he?"

"Worked—past tense," said Michelle. "Dan Wilson retired from ICE five months before this letter ever went out."

Chapter 21

"Daniel Wilson ordered Cesar Zuma's deportation five months *after* he retired?" Vega was incredulous.

"There must be some mistake," said Michelle. "Maybe the letter got waylaid and someone else signed his name to it."

"Or maybe he's found a novel way to supplement his retirement income."

"Not Dan Wilson," Michelle insisted. "He's a true believer. Me and a lot of the other agents joined ICE for the benefits, pay, and job security. We believe in our jobs and all. But it's not a mission. Dan considers it his patriotic duty. I can't see him blackmailing illegals into committing crimes. This has to be a mix-up or something. Zuma simply caught a five-month break."

"What if it's not just Zuma?" asked Vega. "What if all these people got removal letters signed by Dan Wilson—including Edgar Aviles."

"Impossible." Michelle typed Edgar Aviles's name into the system and pulled up his removal letter. "You see?" Michelle pointed to the signature. "Marcus Tyler signed it last Monday. He and Lyle Donovan are the agents trying to apprehend Aviles now."

"Does that mean Tyler's the one who put Aviles into removal proceedings?"

"Not . . . usually," she admitted. "Tyler and Donovan

are enforcement agents. They act on directives generated from the database. Those directives tend to happen higher up the food chain."

"So we're back to not knowing who threw Zuma and Aviles into priority removal."

"My boss will know," Michelle assured him. "We can trace it. We just need time."

"Time Aviles doesn't have."

Vega and Michelle typed up their statements from Billy Kelso and Lori Danvers. They included a brief summary of their findings from the ICE database, highlighting Deisy Ramos's name and her connection to the wallet picture in Talia's drawer. They sent one copy of their summary to Greco, one to Vega's boss, Captain Waring, and one to Michelle's boss, Wayne Bowman.

Vega dropped Michelle off at her car in the Lake Holly lot, then signed in the Taurus and texted Adele that he was on his way to her house. They had an hour to shower, change, eat, and pack his gear for his gig tonight. Vega was glad to be playing this evening. He needed the distraction—not only from the case, but from the unease that gnawed at him ever since Michelle showed him that childhood photo of himself and told him he got sent away.

He hadn't told Adele about that photo. One of many things he hadn't told her lately. He felt the weight of every one.

Adele stood on her porch in stockinged feet as Vega nosed his pickup into her driveway.

"You've heard, right?" she asked as he got out of his truck. "That Edgar Aviles is seeking sanctuary at Beth Shalom?"

"I heard."

Vega walked up the porch steps and took Adele in his arms. Her blouse was untucked. Her black reading glasses rested low across the bridge of her nose. It felt good to feel the press of her flesh between his hands. "Heard you got ICE to back down too."

"Hardly. All I've done, I fear, is bought him the weekend."

Vega stepped inside. He smelled chicken and rice simmering on the stove. Reflexively, he looked up the stairs for Sophia, then remembered she was at her father's for the rest of the weekend.

"Jimmy, I know we said we'd spend Sunday together. But I'm going to be snowed under tomorrow. I've got to help Edgar get the paperwork together to file a two-forty-six—a request to ICE for an administrative stay on humanitarian grounds."

"Do you think they'll grant it?"

"I don't know," she admitted. "It's a race against the clock at this point. The two agents who showed up at Beth Shalom only had an administrative warrant. They'll probably go before a judge on Monday and get a real one. I have to get Edgar in front of someone at the ICE field office with all his paperwork in order before then or things could get ugly. I mean, ICE isn't going to want to bust down the doors of a synagogue. But they could."

Vega walked into Adele's kitchen and washed his hands and face. Adele put a hand on his back. "Why don't you take a shower and change, *mi vida*? I'll put the salad and chicken together."

"Are you sure? I can help."

"You've still got to load your gear into the truck. We don't have a lot of time. And besides, what's a roadie for?" Adele loved helping the band set up for gigs. Vega even bought her a shirt that said *#1 roadie.*

Not that Armado had any others.

Vega showered quickly and changed into a plain black T-shirt and black jeans—the same outfit he wore for every gig. Adele was quiet over dinner, playing with her food more than eating it.

"You okay?" Vega asked her.

"Yeah," she said. "Just worried about Edgar and his family. His niece is still missing."

"I know," said Vega. "We're working on it. But the family won't talk to the police. I have to think they know where she is."

"They're probably too scared to say. I mean, look at all they've been through." Adele put down her fork. "What I can't figure out, is how ICE knew Edgar would be at Beth Shalom. I mean, sure, he works there. But they seemed so—certain, somehow—that they'd find him there. It was like someone tipped them off. My money's on one of the board members. According to Max, some of them were against this whole arrangement from the start."

Vega felt like a white-hot spotlight was pointed directly at him. He closed his eyes. He had to tell her. He wasn't a coward, despite what Michelle believed.

"*Nena.*" He reached across the table and took her hand. "I'm the one who tipped ICE off."

"You . . . ?" She yanked her hand away. ". . . Why?"

"It's my duty as a police officer."

"Your . . . *duty?*"

"I didn't know he was there. Not for sure. But I can't hold back information just because I don't like the outcome. Aviles ran from law enforcement. His family refuses to cooperate with the police about his niece's disappearance. It's my duty—"

"Screw your duty." Adele pushed her plate away. "What about something higher than duty? What about conscience? His little boy has cancer. The child's got to go to the hospital next week and his father may be halfway to El Salvador by then—never to return. Where's your *duty* in all of that?"

"I'm sorry," said Vega. "Believe me, I am. I wish ICE had never tried to collar Aviles. But they did and we're stuck with the results. I wanted to be totally honest with you."

She gave him a sour look. "This is her doing, isn't it? Your sister."

"This is *me, nena. My* values. The same values I've had since you first met me. And second, she's not my sister."

"Okay, half."

"I barely know the woman!" Vega threw up his hands. "I barely know myself anymore."

"What's that supposed to mean?"

"Forget it." He pushed himself up from the table and took his plate to the sink. "I'll understand if you don't want to help me at the gig tonight. I get that you have your code of ethics. But I have mine."

He was aware of Adele's eyes on him. When he turned to her, she was leaning in the doorway of the kitchen, arms folded across her chest, staring at him.

"This isn't about ICE trying to arrest Edgar Aviles," said Adele. "Or Talia Crowley. This is something else. What's going on?"

"Nothing." He moved between the dining room and kitchen, carrying in plates and running them under hot soapy water. He needed somewhere to focus his attention.

"You want to be totally honest with me, Jimmy? Then *be* totally honest and tell me what's on your mind. I'm coming with you tonight, one way or the other. So you might as well stop playing the wounded loner here."

"It's got nothing to do with you."

"I'm not going until you tell me what's on your mind."

"It's nothing. Stupid stuff."

"All the more reason to share it."

Vega turned from the sink and dried his hands on a dish towel. He fished his wallet out of his back pocket and opened the billfold. He pulled out the dog-eared photo Michelle had given him and handed it to Adele.

"Michelle gave me an old picture of myself this morning." He held it out to her as a peace offering, hoping to bridge the enormous distance right now between them.

She examined the glossy pre-digital-era snapshot, bouncing her head between Vega and the smallest boy in the picture. "I can definitely tell it's you," she said. "Where was it taken?"

"I have no idea." Just showing Adele the photograph of him all dirty and unkempt in those oversized jeans made Vega feel naked and ashamed. He was a cop. He was used to exerting control over situations. Yet here, he felt as vulnerable as a child.

Adele turned the picture over and read the other two names. "Angel Dominguez . . . Johnny Ray Osorio . . . do you remember them?"

"No," said Vega. "Not the faces or the names."

"You look like you're about five or six." She handed back the photo. "It's . . . a little on the depressing side."

"Michelle says she thinks it was taken when I got"— Vega put his hands in quotes—"sent away."

"Sent away where? For what?"

"I don't know. Foster care? Behaving badly? I know I had these terrible rages in first grade," Vega recalled. "I hit people. Threw things. Maybe I got sent away on account of that."

"Nonsense." Adele dismissed the claim. "I don't believe it. How would Michelle know anyway? She's three years younger. She's just messing with your head. Don't let her."

Vega stared at the photo again, as if it had the power to suck him back to that time.

"She's not wrong." He looked up from the picture to Adele. "You know that feeling you get when you first wake up and sort of remember your dream? But the more you try, the more it slips away?"

"I've had that. Sure."

"That's what this feels like," said Vega. "Not just the picture. That whole period in my life. Every now and then, I get these odd, freeze-frame images. Of a cop with squeaky black patent leather shoes. Or this big green wooden door with the handle removed and fingerprints all down the sides. Sometimes it's not an image at all. It's a smell. Wet towels. Coppertone suntan lotion."

"Was that when your father walked out?"

"No," said Vega. "He left when I was two. This happened a few years later. When I was about six. I have a vague memory of the time period because our neighbor's cat scratched my eye badly a few months before. I remember wearing an eye patch and then getting it removed. I'd finally gone back to playing ball. The neighbor, by the way, was Michelle's aunt. That's where her mother was living when my father seduced her."

"*Ay, caray!* Sounds like the plot of a telenovela," said Adele.

"No kidding." Vega shoved the photo back in his wallet. A part of him wanted to throw it out but couldn't bring himself to.

"I'm sure Michelle could clear up the mystery by asking her mother," said Adele. "Or your father."

"When Michelle asked her mother about the photo today, her mother practically hung up on her. She told Michelle not to mention it to our father because it would upset him too much."

"How about tracking down those other boys in the picture?" asked Adele. "You're a cop. I'll bet you could find them if you wanted to."

"Don't know that I want to." Vega checked his watch. "It's getting late. I'd better load up the truck." He was anxious to be on the road and have nothing in his head but his music.

Adele slipped her hand around Vega's waist and gave it a squeeze, her tender feelings for him overcoming her frustrations earlier.

"Michelle's wrong," she assured him. "I never knew your mother or grandmother. But from everything you've told me, they sound like loving people. You were the center of their world. Whatever Michelle says, I refuse to believe they sent you away."

"Yeah. You're probably right." Vega kissed the top of Adele's head and didn't say what he was thinking: *Then I was taken.*

That was worse.

It meant that his mother or grandmother had done something really bad to him. It had to be really bad because in Vega's neighborhood, getting nailed by your mom or *abuela* with a *chancla*—a rubber sandal—was practically a rite of passage. Vega recalled both women taking swipes at him from time to time. But there was no real violence attached to their anger. These weren't beatings. They were wake-up calls. Frowned on in today's society, perhaps. But necessary for a single mother raising a boy in the Bronx back then. The streets were full of temptations. It didn't hurt to know that your mother's and grandmother's wrath awaited at home.

But what if it was something more, Vega wondered? *What if it was something truly evil?* Just because Vega couldn't remember the circumstances, didn't erase the doubts. They grew like a cancer inside his brain. To kill them, he had to face them. Head-on. Without flinching.

At what cost to my family's memory? he asked himself. *At what cost to my own?*

Chapter 22

Vega's band was playing a wedding reception at the Grand Marquis, a catering hall in Broad Plains. It was off a stretch of four-lane, around the corner from Lori Danvers's Paws and Claws. The outside was poured concrete and painted in flamingo pink. Two gold lampposts fronted the oval driveway. The inside had all the charm of a cut-rate hotel. Low ceilings. Carpets that felt like Astroturf. No windows—probably because there was nothing worth looking at. Only the wall of mirrors and chandeliers overhead gave any indication this was a party space.

"It's not very romantic," Adele whispered when they were unloading Vega's amps and guitars.

"The bride and groom were in a hurry," Vega explained. "He's getting shipped out with the First Infantry next month. And she's, shall we say, a teeny, tiny bit pregnant."

"How teeny tiny?"

"Let's just say, if they'd left it any longer, Katie and Mike Grande would be spending their honeymoon in the delivery room."

"Ah." Adele grinned. "Well then, you'd better do the 'Macarena' early."

"I hate that song."

Three of the band members and the sound engineer were already inside, setting up. Danny Molina, Armado's keyboardist and founder, was doing mic checks with Tony Furci, their sound engineer. Brandon Cruz, their bassist, and Chris Feliz, their sax player, were setting up amps and running through their riffs.

"Where's Richie?" Vega asked Molina.

"On his way, I hope. What can I say?" Molina paused a beat. "Timing has never been his strong suit."

Vega snorted. Every band piles grief on their drummer—most of it deserved.

Adele walked off to help Brandon Cruz and Chris Feliz unfurl amp cables and microphone wires. Vega pulled out his pedal board and began attaching the pedals to create different sound effects. He owned a total of sixteen pedals but never brought more than eight to a gig. Tonight, he'd brought his favorites—the wah-wah and the reverb and the overdrive, which created a clean, warm tone.

Molina grabbed a roll of black duct tape and began taping down Vega's sound cables and amps. "Where the hell would we be without the invention of duct tape?"

"Unemployed," said Vega. They could deal with a broken string or missed cue, but if somebody accidentally kicked out a power cord, their whole set was sunk.

Molina eyed the back doors, searching for Solero.

"Richie will be here," Vega assured him. "I saw him this morning at his precinct. He knows we have a gig."

"You helping Warburton with a case?"

"No. Lake Holly," said Vega. "But Warburton may figure into it. And Port Carroll too, come to think of it."

"Yeah?" Molina was born and bred in Port Carroll and now walked a beat there. "What's the case?"

Vega pulled out his phone and scrolled to the picture of the two Hispanic girls taken from Talia's drawer. He showed it to Molina.

"You ever seen either of these girls around Port Carroll? The one on the right is Deisy Ramos-Sandoval. The picture's old. She's sixteen now."

Molina pinched his meaty fingers together to magnify the girls' faces on the screen. He was a talented keyboardist, but you wouldn't know it from his thick fingers. He had the hands of a butcher.

"That's Deisy all right," said Molina. "Her mom's a waitress at the Port Carroll Diner." He handed Vega back his phone. "Do you know where she is?"

"I was going to ask you that," said Vega. "Doesn't she live in Port Carroll?"

"She ran away from her mother's apartment a couple of weeks ago." Molina's eyes screwed tight in their sockets. He paled. "Please tell me you haven't found a body."

"No. Nothing like that," said Vega. "The girl's a missing link in a case of mine and I'd just like to speak to her. Her name appears on a list found in the pocket of an MS-13 gang member who was murdered in Warburton about a month ago."

"What's the mutt's name?"

"Elmer 'Cheetos' Ortega."

"Cheetos." Molina nodded. "I've heard of him. He used to work with the Ramirez brothers. Carlos and Ramon. Small-time hoods. Mostly into burglary, car theft, and prostitution. They owned a chop shop in Port Carroll until we closed it down a few years ago."

"What happened to them?"

"Beats the hell out of me." Molina called over to Cruz to toss him another roll of duct tape. "The brothers went dark. They could've moved operations to Long Island or up to Buffalo. I'd like to think they hightailed it back to El Salvador. But if Ortega's been murdered, you have to wonder."

Molina fiddled with the positioning of a speaker. Vega thought it was in a good place already, but he knew that Molina, as the band's manager, got the grief if the speakers blasted the audience. It was always a struggle to keep the music loud enough to be lively and soft enough so people could talk over it.

"Do you know if Deisy was the sort of girl to get mixed up with a guy like Cheetos?" asked Vega.

"She had a rough adjustment when she came here three years ago as an unaccompanied minor," said Molina. "All these kids do. The crossings are brutal. So many of the girls are sexually assaulted. By the time they reunite with their families, they're a ball of anxiety, depression, and rage."

"So you're saying, she fell apart."

"For a while," said Molina. "Hilda, her mom, came to me and I got the girl into therapy. It seemed to be doing the trick. She was going to classes. Getting good grades. She even made the high school's varsity volleyball team. And then, a couple of weeks before she ran away, her mother said she got real quiet and secretive. She missed curfew a couple of nights. Then she lost her phone—"

"She lost her *phone?*" Vega knew that most young girls would sooner lose a limb than their phones.

"She wouldn't tell her mother where she was when she lost it," said Molina. "They had a big fight and the next morning, Deisy was gone. No note. Nothing. Hilda came to me and I put out a BOLO. You're the first sighting I've had."

"I'm not a sighting," said Vega. "All I've got is that old picture and Deisy's name on a dead *mara's* list." Vega thought about the photograph. "Do you know who the other girl was in the snapshot? It said 'Nelly' on the back."

"Nelly?" Molina got a panicked look on his round, normally cheerful face. "Let me see the picture again."

Vega pulled it up on his screen. Molina cursed under his breath.

"This is bad," he said. "Something terrible has happened to Deisy."

"How do you know?"

"Because Nelly was Deisy's younger sister," said Molina. "Deisy would never have parted with this picture you're showing me. Not voluntarily."

"Why?"

"Nelly Ramos drowned three years ago when the girls were crossing the Rio Grande into Texas," said Molina. "That's part of the reason Deisy was such a mess when she arrived. She watched her kid sister get swept away."

They set up their equipment with a sort of grim determination after that. Like they were laying a supply line for an invasion. Molina walked Vega through the story of Deisy Ramos while they worked. His voice carried a weariness to it. They'd both heard versions of the same sad history dozens of times. Kids left behind in Central America who risked everything to be reunited with parents they hadn't seen in so long they were strangers. Parents who'd built new lives with new spouses and children and didn't always welcome their resentful, foreign offspring. What started out as a fairy-tale reunion seldom had a fairy-tale ending.

They were interrupted by a pounding on the back doors.

"I'll bet that's our fearless drummer," quipped Molina. "The knocking just speeded up."

They opened the doors to see Richie Solero pushing a cart piled high with equipment. He looked like he was moving the entire contents of his apartment. Vega never got over how much time and effort it took to make a few hours of music.

"Hey, Jimmy," Molina shouted across the cart. "What do you call a drummer who's late to his own gig?"

"A deadbeat," said Vega, right on cue. "Hey Danny—how do you know the drum solo's coming up?"

"Half the audience runs to the can."

Molina held out a knuckle and Vega rapped it. They

were corny jokes that Solero had heard a thousand times before, but they usually elicited a grin from him. Or, at the very least, a middle finger. This evening, Solero didn't even seem to hear them. His eyes, which always carried a vague sleepiness to them in the best of times, looked especially lost this evening. His face was flushed and sweaty.

"Hey, Richie—you okay?" Molina asked.

"Yeah. Sorry. Me and Kim were sort of going at it again."

Kim was Solero's ex-wife and the mother of his two children. Money—or the lack of it—seemed to be a constant source of conflict between them. So much so, it had spilled over into Solero's budding romance with Jenn Fitzpatrick, the crime scene tech, and ended their affair a few months ago as well.

"Come on," Vega said to him. "We'll help you set up."

Molina and Vega each grabbed a drum box while Solero began setting up his stand. From the kitchen, Vega heard a crash of dishes followed by a string of Spanish curses. The catering staff was having their own problems at the moment.

Molina pulled the kick pedal out of a soft zippered case and handed it to Solero to screw into place.

"Jimmy was just telling me about that dead *mara* who turned up in Warburton. Cheetos Ortega. And about that list of names you found in his pocket when he died."

"What about it?" asked Solero.

"One of the names on that list is a runaway from Port Carroll," said Molina. "A sixteen-year-old Salvadoran girl named Deisy Ramos. I know the mom. She's a waitress at the Port Carroll Diner and she's desperate to find her. If you know anything . . . ?"

"Sorry, Danny," said Solero. "I don't know anything more than you do." He shot Vega a questioning look. "If anything, I know a whole lot less."

The facility's wedding planner—a pasty-faced man in a dark, well-worn suit, gestured to Molina that he needed to speak to him. Molina excused himself to talk to the man. Solero waited until Molina and the others were out of earshot to speak.

"You get reassigned to Warburton or something, Jimmy?"

"Huh? What do you mean?"

Solero pulled a keychain from his pocket and removed a T-shaped key. His drum-tuning key.

"When I saw you this morning, you'd only just confirmed that the body at the ME's office was Ortega's."

"That's all I knew then," said Vega. "This afternoon, I got access to ICE's database, so I ran the names. Turns out Deisy Ramos's name is not only on that list. Her picture's in a wallet I found in the back of the DA's wife's sweater drawer. I don't know what the connection between the two cases is. But I feel like there is one."

Solero inserted his drum key into one of his tom's tension rods and slowly tightened it, moving diagonally from one side of the drumhead to the other.

"So how come this is the first time I'm hearing about it? I walk in, and you're telling Danny before you even tell me?"

"I'm telling you now," said Vega. "I just happened to see Danny first. Deisy Ramos is from Port Carroll. His beat."

Solero grabbed a drumstick and banged the head of his snare while he tuned it to pitch. He didn't meet Vega's gaze.

"Look," said Vega. "It's not just Deisy I found out about. Every name on that list is an immigrant with uncertain legal status. Several appear to have been the targets of some sort of scam."

"What kind of scam?"

"I'm not sure," said Vega. "But it looks like somebody's going around blackmailing immigrants either by pretending to be ICE or by trading off some real connection to the agency. A mutt like Ortega wouldn't have the know-how. But he may have been working for someone who does.

That might be a good investigative angle for Warburton to pursue."

Solero snapped his drum key back on his keychain and straightened. He met Vega's gaze head-on. His normally sleepy eyes had a spark of something unfamiliar in them. Anger. Vega had seen that anger in Solero for his ex-wife. But never for a band member.

"Listen, Jimmy. You and me—we're friends and all. So I'm gonna say this in the nicest way possible."

"Okaay."

"Don't go into another man's house and reprogram his TV remote."

"Huh?"

"Cheetos' murder is Warburton's case. That list, those names—they're all part of our case—"

"You're gonna play turf battles with me? When we've got dead bodies on our hands? I'm not trying to steal your case. I'm trying to get answers—"

"Which Warburton will do," said Solero. "I'm happy to pass on intel to you and Danny. I'm happy to see if we can find this runaway kid. But you are way overstepping your bounds here, partner."

"And you're getting into a pissing match while the building burns down."

Molina heard their raised voices. He ran over. "Guys! Guys!" He tamped down the air. "Cool it. We got a gig to play." The rest of the band and Adele hung back, gawking at the commotion. They never normally argued.

"Take a look at that list," Vega sputtered, ignoring Molina. "Cesar Zuma threw himself in front of a Metro-North train this morning. Deisy Ramos ran away. Edgar Aviles is holed up in a synagogue, awaiting deportation. Things are happening fast. You want Warburton to get the credit? I'll give you all the credit you want. But we can't afford to let the situation get away from us."

A swirl of voices rose up from the other side of the dining room's double doors. The bride and groom and guests were beginning to arrive.

"Guys!" Molina hissed, holding up a meaty hand so both Solero and Vega could see. He wiggled his fingers. They looked like dancing sausages. "What do we always say?"

Solero sighed. "Armado is five fingers all joined at the hand. If the fingers don't work, the hand doesn't either."

"We're a family." Vega extended a knuckle. Solero rapped it. Then Molina. Then Brandon Cruz and Chris Feliz. Then Tony Furci and Adele. The music was what mattered. It was all that mattered.

"Now"—Molina clapped his hands together—"let's rock and roll."

Chapter 23

The thing about performing, Vega realized years ago, was that it was impossible to play and keep anything else in his head. Music wiped the slate clean. When Vega stepped onstage and heard those first notes, he felt transported. He lost himself in the rhythm that swayed his body and quieted his mind. In the emotions he brought to words he could utter precisely because they weren't his.

The stage and acoustics at the Grand Marquis stank. And yet, for some reason Vega played like he was on fire. Every note was clean and pure. Every word reverberated in his chest until his entire body felt like a tuning fork. Even that stupid "Macarena" song. He knew why blues musicians were so damn good. Music channeled pain. And pain made music better.

By the time Vega stepped off the stage, he'd forgotten he and Solero had even had words that evening. He felt calm and spent. Eager to pack up, go home, and make love to Adele. The music had flushed out everything else in him.

It had been that way for him since he was seven years old when his mother came home with his first guitar. She'd bought it secondhand from a pawnshop on East Tremont Avenue in the Bronx. Vega had no idea what made her buy it. He just knew that as soon as he wrapped his right arm over that sound box and strummed those nylon strings, all the rage he'd been feeling went quiet and still.

Where had that anger come from? For years, Vega had no idea. And now, he thought he did:

You were sent away. Your mother and grandmother did something terrible to you that got you sent away.

Being onstage tonight had drowned out that voice in his head. But after, lying in Adele's bed, listening to her soft breathing, it came back.

He didn't want to wake Adele. She had all that work to do with Aviles tomorrow. He didn't want to drive home either. Joy was at his place. She wasn't expecting her father until the morning. His sudden presence would alert Diablo and wake her up. So he got out of bed, slipped into a clean T-shirt and sweatpants, and padded softly down to Adele's kitchen to make coffee.

He pulled out that picture of himself from his billfold while he waited for the coffee to brew and placed it in front of him on the table, across from Adele's laptop, closed and plugged in to charge.

He recognized nothing in the photograph. Not the empty, garbage-strewn lot with its old refrigerators and car parts strewn about. Not the abandoned five-story tenements behind him, their vacant windows as dark and hollow as an addict's eyes. He couldn't even tell which boy was Angel Dominguez and which was Johnny Ray Osorio. He knew only that both were Hispanic—Puerto Rican like him. Or maybe, Dominican. One was stocky, with a spare tire of flab that threatened to balloon over the waistband of his jeans. The other was tall and lean, with kinky hair, hawkish eyes, and big ears that stuck out on the sides of his head. Neither boy was more than ten.

The coffeemaker clicked off and Vega poured a cup, then dumped in two sugars. He thought about what Adele had said to him earlier, about how easy it would be for a cop like Vega to track down the two people in the photograph. That was true—if Vega were tracking them down as part of an investigation. But on a personal matter? Those databases were audited regularly. He didn't want to chance getting charges. Not now. Not when he was finally back to full duty.

There was no harm in him doing a civilian search, however. Vega opened Adele's laptop and typed in her password. Then he pulled up her Google search engine and typed *Angel Dominguez*. Dozens came up—both males and females. He found poets and artists. A Realtor in Texas. A chiropractor in California. A football player for Michigan State. None of them felt or looked like either boy in the picture.

He tried the same with *Johnny Ray Osorio*. He found plenty of John Osorios and Jonathan Osorios. But only one entry contained the name Johnny Ray.

An obit. From a weekly newspaper in the Bronx, dated two years ago.

Vega's heart sank as he read the few brief lines that said that Johnny Ray Osorio, age forty-five, an employee in the maintenance department of Montefiore Hospital in the Bronx, had died after a long illness. Vega scoured the few lines of text for survivors. No wife or siblings or parents were mentioned, only a daughter, Cecilia.

Vega typed *Cecilia Osorio* into the search engine. He had no idea how old she was or whether Osorio was even still her last name. He found a student in Belize and a journalist in Venezuela—neither of which, he suspected, was the right Cecilia.

He scrolled down page after page of mentions that weren't quite right. And then he found something that caught his eye. A letter to the editor in a trade publication called the *Journal of Emergency Nursing*. The letter writer was commenting on a study of prophylactic treatment for rape victims. Next to her name, Cecilia Osorio, were the initials BSN, RN, CEN. None of that meant anything to Vega, though he suspected the RN was Registered Nurse. But it was what was below it that caught his eye:

Emergency Department, Lake Holly Hospital, Lake Holly, NY

Cecilia Osorio worked right around the corner.

Vega closed the screen. He could stop right now. Maybe that was the sensible course. The boy in the picture with Vega was likely dead. This woman, at best, was only his daughter. What could she possibly tell him? Certainly nothing about his own past or why he was sent away.

He pulled out his cell phone. He could call the hospital. At least find out if Cecilia Osorio still worked there. There was no commitment in that.

He bypassed the main switchboard and called Sharon Lamont, an admitting nurse he knew who worked the night shift. No big deal. He was a cop. He called the hospital all the time on cases.

He was glad when Sharon answered.

"Hey there. It's Jimmy Vega—"

"Detective Vega," she said warmly. "How can I help you?" She assumed he was working on a case. It made the whole interchange easier.

"Do you know if an emergency room nurse by the name of Cecilia Osorio still works at the hospital?"

"I'm not sure if she's on duty tonight. Let me check." Sharon put him on hold and then returned to the line. "She's in the ER right now. Would you like me to transfer you?"

"No!" This was all happening too fast. He wasn't ready.

"So you're going to stop by instead?" asked Sharon.

"Uh . . . yeah. I'll stop by." Vega couldn't believe how incompetent and nervous he sounded. Like a teenager asking out his first date.

"I'll let her know you're coming," said Sharon. "Can I tell her what it's about?"

"That's okay," said Vega. "I'll do that myself."

Vega left Adele a note, telling her he couldn't sleep and went home. He was going to wish her luck with Aviles tomorrow but decided that was a sore spot between them he'd do better to stay away from for the moment.

In the hospital's parking lot, he tried to steady his nerves and remind himself again that Cecilia probably couldn't tell him anything about the picture. All she could do was fill in the blanks about her father and maybe offer up a little of their family history.

He found Sharon when he walked into the admitting area and made small talk while she tried to track down Cecilia and find out when she had a break to talk.

"She asked if you have a court order," said Sharon.

"A court order? Why?"

"I don't know. She just seemed to think you'd need it."

As soon as Cecilia appeared, Vega knew he'd found Johnny Ray's daughter. She was in her late twenties and dressed in blue nurse's scrubs and sneakers. Her black kinky hair was pulled back tightly into a ponytail that exposed her oversized ears—obviously a family trait. She greeted Vega with a wary handshake and a look of uncertainty in her hawkish eyes.

"Detective? Sharon said you wanted to talk to me."

Vega felt the heat rise in his cheeks. Cecilia Osorio seemed to be expecting some big police interview. Vega didn't know how to break it to her that this was personal.

"Can I buy you a cup of coffee in the cafeteria?" Vega asked. "I promise not to take up too much of your time."

"Sure."

The cafeteria was empty at three thirty in the morning. Even the night-shift doctors and nurses didn't seem excited about hanging around in it. Maybe it was the bright fluorescent lights that made the room feel harsh and unwelcoming. Or the lingering smell of tomato soup that felt too overpowering at this hour.

Vega bought Cecilia a cup of herbal tea and another coffee for himself. She began speaking as soon as they sat down.

"You're investigating Talia Crowley's death, right?"

"Uh, yeah." Vega had no idea how she knew that.

"Do you have a court order?"

"A court . . . No. Why?"

Cecilia folded her hands in front of her. "I knew it was only a matter of time before someone from the investigation showed up. I'd like to help. Believe me, I would. For the wife's sake. But HIPAA regulations—"

"Wait." Vega was tired. It was taking his brain extra time to process things. "You think I'm here on the Crowley investigation?"

"Aren't you?"

"Should I be?"

She smiled. She looked so much younger when she smiled. She brought her tea to her lips and cradled it like she was protecting a small, delicate bird. Vega had a sense she'd be good with patients.

"I think we're playing a game of 'Who's on First?' " said Cecilia. "Why don't you tell me why you're here and then maybe I can help you."

"Okaay," said Vega, drawing out the word in a long, extended breath. "Here goes." He felt like he was diving into very cold water. "I'm looking for the daughter of a man I had contact with in the Bronx when we were kids. His name was Johnny Ray Osorio. I found what I think is his obit and it mentioned a daughter. Then I found you."

She put her tea down without sipping it and stared at Vega a long moment. She had a strong jaw and a direct gaze. There was something about her that made Vega think she played sports in college. The articulated shoulders. The physical confidence, even when she was blindsided.

"How did you know my father?"

"That's what I'm trying to figure out," said Vega. "This is my only clue." He fumbled in his wallet and handed her the picture. She held it gently by a corner, as if sensing its value.

"That's my dad all right." She bounced a look between Vega and the shot. "You're the smallest kid in the photo, I take it."

"Yeah. But that's all I know."

She turned the photo over and read the third name. "Angel Dominguez. Do you know him?"

"No. I haven't been able to track him down."

She handed the photo back to Vega. "Why is it important?"

Vega had fooled himself into thinking before he came here that there would be a way to find out all about Johnny Ray Osorio's life without revealing his own. But he saw now, in Cecilia's questioning gaze, that that would be impossible. To open her up he would first need to open himself.

"I may have been in foster care for a short while when I was very young. I can't remember. My mother and grandmother never spoke about it. I was hoping that by finding the other boys in that shot, I'd know."

"You don't have any family who can tell you?"

"No." Vega had come to ask the questions. He felt frustrated that he was the one doing all the answering.

"If you don't remember, isn't that sort of a blessing?" she asked. "My dad spent most of his childhood in foster care and the rest of his life trying to forget."

Her words made Vega feel jumpy and expectant. If nothing else, she'd just confirmed what Michelle had told him: *You were sent away.* He hoped that that realization could put the matter to rest. But he realized with a pang of clarity that the really big question was one even Johnny Ray Osorio and Angel Dominguez couldn't have answered: *Why?*

Vega tried to deflect the conversation away from himself. "Were you and your dad close?" he asked.

"I didn't grow up with him," she admitted. "He and my mom split when I was a baby. They were both so young. My father had a lot of demons, but he was trying to make things work between us when he died."

"Cancer?" asked Vega.

Cecilia nodded. "Esophageal. He'd been a heavy drinker and smoker his whole life. He'd had drug problems too, though he was long over them when the cancer came along."

"I'm sorry."

She took a sip of tea. "I wish I could tell you something to help you in your search," she said. "But my dad never spoke about his childhood. His mother was a junkie. He never knew his dad. I think he was like, three or four when social services took him away."

"Do you know why they took him?" asked Vega.

"He was beaten by one of his mom's boyfriends after he wet the bed. She just kind of watched, I guess. Or at least, that's what I gathered. My dad was very angry at her for abandoning him like that. He never forgave her." Cecilia shrugged. "I don't know how bad it was compared to other homes in the 'hood. But I guess it had to be pretty bad for child services to take him away. I mean, this was the Bronx in the early eighties, not *Mr. Rogers' Neighborhood.*"

Vega felt the sting in her words. Like she was describing his own worst fear. *It had to be pretty bad . . .*

"In any case," said Cecilia, "after that, my father cycled through a series of foster homes, never staying in any one of them very long. I'm betting that if he were alive and you showed him that picture, he might not be sure himself which home he was in at the time."

"Sure. I understand." Vega stared at his coffee. He needed someplace neutral to rest his eyes. He didn't want her to see the pain in them.

"So . . . this was why you came tonight?"

Her words set Vega on solid footing again. He was a cop. He was investigating a death. When they first sat down, it was clear Cecilia Osorio had information pertaining to the case. He leaned in.

"About that . . . other matter," said Vega.

"I can't talk about that."

"But you thought that's why I was here," Vega pointed out. "You thought I wanted to talk to you about Talia Crowley. Why?"

"Sharon said a county homicide detective wanted to talk to me," said Cecilia. "The only death investigation in Lake Holly I'm aware of at the moment is Talia Crowley's."

"But why would you think I would contact you?"

Cecilia shook her head. "I'm sorry, Detective. I have to follow HIPAA rules."

"All right. Fair enough," said Vega. "But you can deduce. So can I. You're an ER nurse. You know something about Talia Crowley's medical status. I have to assume she came into the hospital's ER at some point and you treated her. I have to assume it was recently, or you probably wouldn't have put it together with my visit. So it's not about her pregnancy. That ended several months ago."

"I can't tell you anything," she said. "Not without a court order."

"But to get a court order, I need to know what I'm looking for."

Cecilia tossed a glance over her shoulder. Two hospital orderlies walked into the cafeteria. They were talking baseball with the cashier. Nobody was paying any attention to Vega and Cecilia.

"She was in the emergency room maybe two weeks ago," Cecilia said softly.

"For what?"

She stirred her tea. Vega went on a hunch.

"Was she beaten? Was Crowley abusing her?"

Cecilia shook her head. "Not . . . in the way you're thinking."

"What? He raped her?"

She took a deep breath. "She was suffering pelvic pains."

"From the miscarriage?"

"That was long over."

"Then what?" asked Vega. "Appendicitis? A punch to the gut?" He leaned forward. "Help me here, Ms. Osorio—"

"Cecilia—"

"Cecilia," said Vega. "Nobody's gonna know. I promise." Vega made a cross on his chest. "Hey, I just bared my soul to you. I think you can trust me."

"She was suffering from pelvic inflammatory disease."

Vega gave Cecilia a blank look. He had no idea what that was.

"It's an infection in the female reproductive organs," she explained. "Usually from an untreated sexually transmitted disease."

Vega took a moment to process what Cecilia was telling him. "Talia had an STD? From long ago? Or from recently?"

"It couldn't have been from long ago because every newly pregnant woman gets tested for STDs during her first OBG visit, usually when she's two or three months pregnant. So she didn't have one six months ago."

"In other words," said Vega, "she didn't have one before she married Glen Crowley."

Cecilia said nothing. Her silence was confirmation enough.

"I guess that leaves only two options," said Vega. "Either Talia got an STD from an extramarital lover or Crowley did. Which means at least one of them was cheating."

"Judging from her reaction at the time," said Cecilia, "I don't think she was cheating."

"So we're down to one assumption."

Chapter 24

Vega awoke in his lakeside cabin at ten thirty the next morning to the smell of bacon—a surprise in itself, since Joy was a vegetarian.

He pulled on a pair of sweats and stumbled down the wood plank stairs onto the first floor of the cabin. Joy was in the kitchen area, frying something on the stove. She looked well rested. Vega was glad. He'd waited until a respectable six a.m. this morning to sneak into the house, giving Diablo a treat to keep him from waking her. He fell into such a deep sleep after that that when he awoke, he forgot his daughter was here.

"Hey, *chispita*," Vega called out, using her childhood nickname, "little spark," in Spanish. "That smells delicious."

Joy turned to him, her lower lip sagging in disappointment. "I was going to serve you breakfast in bed."

"I'd rather eat down here with you." Vega came up behind her and gave her a hug. He looked in the pan. Strips of something thick and gray swam in a sheen of olive oil. "I thought you were frying bacon."

"It's tempeh," said Joy.

"What the hell's tempeh?"

"Compressed and fermented soybeans."

"Looks like fingers from a corpse," said Vega.

"Daad! It's healthy for you. Bacon's full of carcino-gens."

Vega didn't want to criticize his daughter's attempts at feeding him. Joy had been going through a rough patch these past few months after an attempted sexual assault back in January. She'd regressed a little since the incident—as Wendy, her child psychologist mother, said she would. She'd taken to collecting stuffed animals again and watching TV shows from her childhood. She was also spending less time with college friends and more time with her parents.

Vega loved seeing Joy. They did all the things they used to do when she was younger—going for jogs around the lake, playing board games, cuddling on the couch and watching the Yankees. But he hoped he wasn't helping her hide from the world.

"Hey," he said, putting his hands on her shoulders. "If you made this teepee, I'm sure I'll love it."

"*Tempeh,* Dad. It's called tempeh."

Vega gobbled down the fried eggs and potatoes Joy made him but fed the tempeh to Diablo when she wasn't looking. He drew the line at herbal tea and made coffee instead.

"So, what are your plans today?" he asked her.

She shrugged. "Study for finals. Binge-watch TV."

Vega put down his coffee mug. "Isn't there something on campus you'd like to do? A concert? A lecture? Dinner with friends?"

"Maybe. I'll see."

Joy lived with her mother and Wendy's second husband in Lake Holly. Valley Community was only twenty minutes from their house. When Joy started there last September, the plan had been for her to go for two years and then transfer to a better college. Now, Vega couldn't imagine her feeling secure enough to move away.

"*Chispita.*" Vega leaned forward and searched her big dark eyes. "It's been almost four months now since the . . . incident." He didn't know what to call it. He felt embarrassed even talking about it and he knew she did too. "You're barely nineteen. You should be out seeing friends, maybe dating—"

"You want me to *date?* Every boy I ever brought home wasn't good enough."

Vega studied the black sheen of his coffee. That was true. But that was before . . .

"I want you to go back to having a life," he explained. "I love spending time with you and I know Mom does too. But we don't want you to be afraid of the world."

Joy pushed her eggs around the plate. "I'm not . . . afraid," she said slowly. "I just . . ." Her voice trailed off.

"Just what?" Vega held his breath. Joy rarely opened herself like this. He didn't want to blow it.

"I'm having a hard time putting it behind me." She pushed her plate away. "I wish I could just wash it out of my brain and forget. But I can't."

"I know." Vega patted her hand. "Life should come with an erase button. But it doesn't. Sometimes, the only way past something is straight through it."

He hadn't planned on telling her about that photo in his wallet or Michelle or his meeting with Cecilia Osorio, but all of a sudden, he found himself doing just that. He thought she might be annoyed that he was mixing her turmoil with his own. But it seemed to help her. She leaned over and hugged him.

"Oh, Daddy," she murmured into his neck. She never called him that anymore. "You must be so torn up about this."

Vega felt his pulse quicken at her words. He *was* torn up. And just like Joy, he couldn't seem to move on from it.

"Why don't you visit your father and ask him?" Joy suggested.

"I can't," said Vega. "There's too much baggage there."

"But you need to know what happened," said Joy. "If not through your father, then through Michelle. It's like you just told me—the only way past this is through it."

Vega hated when she used his words against him.

"You want me to be strong, Dad. Maybe we can be strong together."

They cleaned up the dishes and took Diablo for a jog around the lake. A light rain had fallen earlier and the clouds still hovered low and dark like steel wool. It felt good to be with Joy. Vega had never felt closer to her. *This is what matters,* he told himself. *The here and now. Not the past.* But he knew that his daughter was counting on him to be a role model. If she was going to get past her trauma, then he'd have to do the same.

After she left, Vega called Adele. She was on her way out the door, first to meet with Aviles's wife, Maria, at their apartment, and then to go to the synagogue to meet with Aviles. Vega wished her luck, then told her about tracking down Cecilia Osorio at the hospital last night and how Joy had encouraged him to call Michelle and get the facts.

"I agree with Joy," said Adele. "You don't want these questions forever weighing on you."

"I may just be exchanging one hell for another," said Vega.

"I refuse to believe anything bad about your mother or grandmother," said Adele. "If you got sent away, it was because of a mistake. I'm sure your father could set the record straight."

"He can't and he won't," said Vega. "Think about it. If

my mother or grandmother abused or neglected me, the first place the courts would have sent me was my father's. But they didn't. Even though Michelle and Denise were living with him, *I* went into foster care. Which means my father and Michelle's mother bailed on me too."

"Oh, *mi vida*," Adele said gently. She had no other words and neither did Vega. They both knew the logic of what he was saying. When they hung up, Vega sent Michelle a text:

Found Johnny Ray Osorio's daughter last night. He's dead but the daughter confirmed I was probably in foster care. Ask your mom for details. I deserve that.

Michelle didn't respond. Vega wondered if a busy single mother even checked her messages on a Sunday. He moved on to work. He needed to get ahold of Greco. Cecilia Osorio's conversation had done more than fill in the blanks in Vega's life last night. It had filled in some blanks he didn't even know he had in Talia Crowley's. Or Glen's, for that matter. Vega thought about what that PI, Billy Kelso, had said about Talia being convinced her husband was seeing prostitutes. Getting an STD was pretty damning evidence she was right.

Louis Greco's cell phone went to voice mail so Vega dialed his home. His wife, Joanna, picked up.

"He's fishing up on the Brighton Aqueduct," she told him.

"In this weather?" Vega looked out the sliding glass doors at the steady rain now beating down on the back deck.

"He'll fish in just about anything. He says the trout are easier to catch when it's raining."

"He's not answering his phone."

"He probably didn't hear it." She was too diplomatic to tell Vega what he already suspected—Greco had screened his call.

"If you speak to him, tell him I'm heading over there now. He can pick up his phone or we can shout across the lake. But one way or the other, we're talking."

* * *

The Brighton Aqueduct was a collection of adjoining bodies of water north and west of Lake Holly. It was a hilly area with steep granite cliffs where loons and cormorants fished the waters, and deer and coyote—even an occasional red-tail fox or black bear—roamed the densely wooded trails. The land surrounding the aqueduct was wild and would likely stay that way, thanks to the fact that the area supplied New York City with drinking water. Only aluminum rowboats were allowed in its lakes, which were liberally stocked with walleye and trout. Vega suspected Greco came out here as much to get away from visiting grandchildren and pesky colleagues as he did to actually fish. He didn't even like the taste of seafood.

The rain had tapered off by the time Vega pulled his truck onto the muddy gravel turnoff. Greco's Buick LeSabre was the only vehicle there. Vega had dressed in dark-colored khakis, a collared golf shirt, hiking boots, and a weatherproof windbreaker, but he felt the damp chill right through everything. Early May was like that in New York. Yesterday, he could have broken out the air-conditioning. Today, he'd turned on his heater on the ride over.

Water dripped from the curtain of pines as Vega negotiated the soft ground down to the edge of the lake. The sky was so low and dense, it felt like the trees could pierce the clouds. The water was choppy and gray, pricked here and there by a few drops of rain, as if Mother Nature were wringing it out of a dish towel. One rowboat bobbed on the water. A solitary figure hunched beneath a dark green rain poncho that seemed to spread in every direction, like candlewax. He was seated facing the shore. He could definitely see Vega.

Whether he wanted to see him was another matter.

Vega pulled out his phone and dialed Greco's cell.

"Do I look like I want to talk to you?" Greco growled into the phone.

"Talia Crowley may have caught an STD from her husband," said Vega. "Who may have been visiting prostitutes. *Underaged* prostitutes. Those are the highlights. Come in, and I'll tell you about the missing teenage girl in that photo from Talia's drawer."

For a moment, Vega thought Greco had hung up on him. He heard nothing on the other end. Not even breathing.

"How do you know all this?"

The rain seemed to pick up again. Vega cupped a hand and looked at the sky. "I'm not about to stand out here and take an outdoor shower, Grec. You want the details, row in. You're not catching Moby Dick out there."

Greco cursed and hung up. Five minutes later, Vega helped him pull his boat ashore and chain it up. He had three good-size trout in his bucket.

"I coulda had two more, if not for you," he grumbled.

"You don't even like fish."

"I like fishing!"

"You like escaping," said Vega.

"That too."

Greco dumped out his bait and threw his rods and the bucket of fish on a thick plastic sheet in his car. Greco was obsessed with keeping his car clean. Even his driver's seat had plastic on it so he wouldn't get it wet or fishy on the drive home.

"Better do this in my car," said Greco. "I'm geared up for the mess."

"Fair enough." Vega slipped into the passenger seat. The inside smelled of pine air freshener mixed with the scent of damp clothes and fish. The rain came down hard as soon as he closed the door. Vega pointed to the windshield. "You owe me. I saved you from that."

"Out of the frying pan and into the fire," said Greco. "What's this crap about Crowley giving his wife the clap?"

"I don't know *what* he gave her exactly," said Vega.

"Gonorrhea. Chlamydia. Warts. We'll need a court order for that. But a lot of things are stacking up to suggest that Glen Crowley may have had plenty of good reasons to hire someone to silence his new bride."

Vega suspected—correctly—that Greco hadn't read the report he and Michelle left him yesterday. So he took the Lake Holly detective through Billy Kelso's claims, then followed it up with his conversation with Cecilia Osorio and her off-the-record comments about Talia's ER visit.

"So last night, you just decided, 'what the hell?' and went to visit the ER?" asked Greco.

"No," said Vega. "I was there on another matter."

"*What* other matter?"

"It's personal, okay? Family crap."

Greco held up his hands. "Say no more. I'm dealing with enough of your family crap already."

Vega told Greco about him and Michelle running those immigrant names through the ICE database and how three of the five people on the list seemed to match up to crimes. "Except Aviles and the girl, Deisy Ramos," said Vega. "I don't know what the scam was on them but I'm sure there was one."

"And how, exactly, does any of that matter to our case?'" asked Greco. "All these damn hyphenated names. Jesus! The whole Hispanic community's like a bad Russian novel."

"Forget the names for a minute, Grec. Just concentrate on the connections. Aviles is the uncle of the Crowleys' missing housekeeper. Deisy's the girl in that picture in the back of Talia's sweater drawer. Coincidence? I think not."

That intrigued Greco. And scared him at the same time. He reached across Vega, opened the glove compartment, and pulled out a bag of red licorice Twizzlers—his addiction. He thought and chewed.

"We're under pressure to close this case down," said Greco.

"At the cost of compromising our ethics?"

"No," said Greco. "If I saw something that suggested Talia was killed, I'd put the brakes on everything. But all you're bringing me is gossip, Vega. Gossip that Sanchez and I didn't hear from any of Talia's friends or her husband. Not even from Charlene, his ex-wife. If anybody's gonna give you dirt, it's an ex-wife."

"If Crowley likes to whore around," said Vega, "I very much doubt he or the very proper Miss Charlene Beech would ever tell you about it."

"True. But I'm not going on insinuations here," said Greco. "The hard facts of the case are that even a very, very strong person would have had one hell of a time stringing Talia up on that pipe against her will."

"She was doped up on alcohol and Valium—"

"Which would have made her dead weight to lift," Greco pointed out. "There's no sign of a break-in. No defensive wounds to her hands—"

"Who cuts the hose to their washer and floods their basement right before they kill themselves?"

"An angry, depressed woman who miscarried her child and believes her new husband is cheating on her," said Greco. "Everything you've brought me just bolsters the suicide claim. Now, as far as the immigrants getting scammed, I think that's a separate case. One that the Warburton Police should look at while they go after Ortega's killer."

"You sound like my friend with the Warburton Police—"

"Well . . . he's right."

The car windows began fogging up. Greco tapped the steering wheel, deep in thought. "Dr. Gupta is leaving the manner of death as undetermined. I'm going to gather up the reports and present the police conclusion as a suicide on Monday—"

"Tomorrow?"

"Tomorrow," said Greco. "To enable the ME's office to release the body for funeral arrangements."

"What would change your mind?"

Greco regarded Vega beneath his bushy brows. "Hard proof. Find me something that proves Talia wasn't alone in that house the night she died. A witness. A piece of evidence. That's what I need to put the brakes on this."

Chapter 25

A witness. A piece of evidence.
Vega had less than twenty-four hours to find one or both of those or Lake Holly was going to close down the investigation and label Talia's death a suicide. Vega sat in his truck, feeling the weight of Greco's decision and the promise he always made to victims:

Tell me who you were and how you died—and I will get you justice.

So far, he'd failed Talia Crowley. He knew only one way to rectify that. *Go back to the beginning. Start over.*

Vega left the aqueduct and drove to Greenbriar Lane, hoping that seeing the house again might help him recall something he hadn't Friday night. The house was still surrounded by yellow crime-scene tape, now sagging from the rain and the endless crisscrossing of cops. A piece of tape had come undone across the driveway, the loose end now swimming in a murky puddle.

Vega got out of his truck and knotted the tape in place again.

"He's not here," a voice called across the driveway to him.

Vega turned to see an older white woman by the curb. She was carrying an umbrella and walking a miniature hairball of a dog. The dog was wearing a little raincoat that looked nicer than Vega's.

"He's staying with his ex in Wickford," she added. "In their carriage house. Funny arrangement, if you ask me." The woman wrinkled her nose. She had sharp eyes that seemed to take everything in and pass judgment on most of it.

Vega stepped over the tape and extended a hand. "Detective James Vega. Do you live on the block?"

"Edith Walker. I'm the one who called nine-one-one. I live next door."

She pointed a bony finger at a contemporary house about a hundred feet away. "I was walking Walter and saw the water gushing out their basement window. At first, I thought they were watering their lawn. But who waters their lawn at eight at night?"

"Did you know them well?" asked Vega.

"Who knows their neighbors anymore? People are so busy these days. All this social media." She offered a disapproving look. "They only moved in a few months ago. He was never here. I guess that's to be expected for a district attorney. And she was always dashing off—probably to some exercise class or whatever. I saw their maid more than I saw them."

"Lissette?" asked Vega. "Did you talk to her at all?"

"I saw her. I didn't say I spoke to her."

"What was she doing when you saw her?"

"Oh, just . . . you know . . . sweeping the driveway. She came out when FreshDirect delivered their groceries. And of course, I saw taxis and cars pick her up and drop her off."

"How about on Friday?" asked Vega. "Did you see her come or leave?"

"No."

"How about Thursday night?"

"I didn't see anyone there at all," said Walker. "That house was dark all night. Not a single light on. I already told the police all of this," she said, a note of irritation in her voice.

Vega's cell phone rang in his pocket. Walker nodded to the sound. "That's the problem these days. Everyone's too distracted."

"You're right," said Vega. He wasn't in the mood for a lecture. And besides, the caller was Michelle. He was anxious to speak to her. "Well, thanks for clarifying everything, ma'am," said Vega. They parted. Vega walked back to his truck as he picked up the call.

"Michelle?"

"So listen . . ." She began. "Can you drive down to the Bronx today?"

"Drive . . . all the way down there?" He hopped in his truck and shut the door. He didn't want to be having this conversation out in the open. "If you were able to find out something, I'd rather just hear it over the phone."

"It's not that simple," she explained. "My mother and Pop won't tell me anything. My mother yelled at me to quit asking."

"This is my *life* we're talking about. They're denying me information that is rightfully mine."

"I agree," said Michelle. "So I found another solution." She cupped a hand over the phone. Vega could hear her sons' voices in the background and Michelle yelling at them to "hush up!" Then she un-cupped the phone.

"I have this friend," she began. "Yvonne Peters. Well, she's not really a friend. She's the grandmother of my son Alex's best friend. But she works in records at ACS."

"What's ACS?"

"The Administration for Children's Services. What used to be called the Bureau of Child Welfare. If you were in foster care, Jimmy, your records would probably be with ACS. And you're a cop. You wouldn't have to jump through a million hoops to see the file."

"But it's a Sunday."

"Exactly," said Michelle. "Even a cop has to fill out a

lot of forms and leave a paper trail. ACS is closed today and Yvonne can just walk you in there. All you have to do is drive down."

Vega's breath clouded the windows of his truck. He ran the sleeve of his jacket across them. He felt paralyzed by the choice before him. He liked his life. It had taken so much time to build it. To find a woman he could truly be himself with. To make peace with his daughter. His ex. His past. He felt like Lot's Biblical wife. If he looked back at who he'd once been, he might turn into a pillar of salt. Become bitter and unmoored. Fall back into the bottom of that dark well he'd crawled out of so many years ago.

Then again, he'd made a promise to his daughter. If he wanted her to make peace with her past, he had to do the same.

"Come," Michelle pleaded. "We'll make it fun. I'll drop my kids with my mom and we can grab a bite at Mama Linda's after."

"You want to go to a *cuchifritos* joint?" Mama Linda's had been around since Vega was a boy. The deep-fried pork snacks could still conjure the aroma of his mother and grandmother's kitchen.

"You need to get back to your roots more often," she chided him. "When the roots go, the leaves begin to die."

"Only at Mama Linda's could someone mention food and death in the same breath."

"*Ay, bendito!* You are sooo suburban," she teased. "I have my doubts whether you can even parallel park anymore. So do we have a date? I can text you the address of ACS and when you get there, you can text me and I'll bring Yvonne Peters."

Vega took a deep breath. "Okay. You're on."

"Trust me, *mano*, going to ACS won't be half as bad for your digestion as Mama Linda's."

Mano. Bro. Not quite a brother but close enough. The

word kindled something inside of him. His whole life, he'd considered himself an only child. He'd gone through everything alone. His grandmother's death. His move to Lake Holly. His divorce. His mother's murder.

Maybe—finally—this was one thing he didn't have to go through as an army of one.

Chapter 26

The rain had stopped entirely by the time Vega reached the Bronx. The air became humid with the promise of warmer weather. In the park, children climbed the monkey bars beneath the broad green leaves of sycamore trees and old men wiped down the benches and chessboards. Along the streets, neighbors gathered on their stoops. Everything felt warmer down here. The temperature. The pavements. The people. Spanish chatter rose on street corners. Car horns and boom boxes played a melody in counterpoint.

Vega didn't trust his out-of-city police parking decal to shield him from a ticket. He drove past the address for ACS on Leland Avenue and navigated the streets until he found a parking spot. Then he doubled back on foot, past dollar stores and bodegas and liquor marts that felt as timeless to him as the five-story tenements with their zigzag fire escapes and Puerto Rican and Dominican flags in the windows.

He texted Michelle that he was close by. She texted back that she and Yvonne were running twenty minutes late. **Ok,** he replied. They were on neighborhood time. He could wait. He put his phone away and turned the corner.

The street was familiar. He saw that now as he stood on the curb between two parked cars and gazed across at a five-story brown brick tenement with a pale crown-shaped design above each window and an even bigger one above the door. He allowed his eyes to wander up to the third floor, to the windows on the right.

They had childproof security gates across them now. They didn't when Vega lived there.

He should have recognized the building—if not from memory, then certainly from photographs. He lived there until he was in first grade. Until his mom and grandmother moved to the other side of East Tremont. He shoved his hands in his pockets and rocked on his heels, feeling a wash of conflicting emotions. Warm memories of his mother and grandmother frying *alcapurrias*—meat fritters—in the kitchen. The scratchy salsa that played from their eight-track tapes—the same ones Vega's grandmother taught him to dance to. Hot days when his legs stuck to the plastic slipcovers on the couch. Cold nights when he cuddled with his mother under the crucifix that hung over her bed.

Not every memory was happy, however. He remembered the hissing tomcat. Its sharp claws and ready pounce. The patch he had to wear over his left eye for weeks until his cornea healed. The arguments between his mother and Michelle's aunt afterward. Did his mother really poison Gloria Rodriguez's cat? Vega couldn't say. It was all so long ago.

He crossed the street and leaned a foot on the bottom step of the front stoop, feeling a wave of nostalgia for the place. He remembered thinking as a boy how high the stoop was and feeling so brave when he jumped off the top. He remembered the girls with their double-Dutch jump ropes. The boys with their basketballs forever thumping by their sides. The salsa and rap that blared from passing car windows, dissipating in the stench of fried food and exhaust.

An old, heavyset woman with wiry gray hair maneuvered around Vega and slowly began lugging a small shopping cart up the stoop. She wore lace-up sneakers and a flowery housedress that hung loosely over her big-bosomed frame.

"Here," said Vega. "Let me help you with that."

The old woman eyed Vega like he was a mugger.

"I used to live here," Vega explained, hoping to ease her fears. "When I was a boy."

He picked up her cart and carried it up the steps to the front vestibule doors. The outer door opened to mailboxes. The second door was locked. A pale, urine-colored light washed across the stairs. So many of the old tenements had burned down or been knocked down, but this one stood, sturdy as ever. The banister was covered in layers of dark brown paint. The steps were worn smooth from decades of feet. The beige walls had scuff marks running along the plaster.

The woman stared at Vega. *"Conoces a alguien aquí?"* she asked. *Do you know someone here?*

Did he? Vega poked his head into the outer vestibule and scanned the brass mailboxes and buzzers on the wall. He searched the names, then saw it. The mailbox to an apartment on the third floor. *G. Rodriguez.*

Michelle's aunt still lived in the building.

The woman in the flowery housedress held Vega's gaze a beat too long. "You can come inside if you like," she said in Spanish.

"No. That's okay."

"Please. I would like that." Something swam in her eyes. *Sorrow?*

Vega took in the woman's wiry gray hair. The spread of her features that time and gravity had softened. His mouth went dry. His heart felt like it was beating outside of his chest.

He knew.

She knew he knew.

"I'm sorry," Vega answered in English. "My mistake. I have the wrong building."

He turned on his heel and retreated down the steps. There were ghosts inside that place.

Ghosts he couldn't even name.

The Administration for Children's Services building was a gray four-story square with tinted windows. It looked like a layer cake that had been moldering in the back of someone's refrigerator for a year. The lobby was staffed by a bored security guard playing games on his phone. Vega thought he'd have to wait around, but Michelle was already there with Yvonne Peters in tow. She was an older African-American woman with kind eyes that were magnified by thick glasses.

"Thank you for coming," Vega told her.

"We'll find the paperwork, Detective. Don't you worry." She spoke like he was a lost child instead of a cop. Vega supposed that directly or indirectly, she'd had a lot of experience with very lost children.

Yvonne showed the security guard ID and they all signed in. Then they took a lumbering elevator to the fourth floor. There was a reception area and behind it, a door to the file room. Yvonne unlocked it.

"Will you get in any trouble for taking us back here?" Vega asked her.

"If you were a civilian? Maybe," said Yvonne. "But you're a cop—"

"I'm not carrying official paperwork or a court order," said Vega.

"And you think Officer Candy Crush downstairs is going to notice?" She laughed. "You can't remove anything from the files. But you can certainly look."

Vega felt like he was stepping into a research library.

There were rows upon rows of black metal shelves filled with Pendaflex folders separated out by decades.

"So many abused and neglected children," said Vega.

"And these are the ones we know about," said Yvonne. "There are so many more we don't. Still, you gotta thank the Lord that some of 'em survive and turn out okay." She gave Vega an approving once-over. He wanted to insist that he was never an abused or neglected child. But he couldn't say that anymore. Not with any certainty.

She walked over to a computer by the door and switched it on. "I need your full name as it appears on your birth certificate, your Social Security number, and your date of birth," said Yvonne.

"James Orlando Vega-Rosario." Vega spelled it for her. "We dropped my mom's maiden name, 'Rosario,' later, to make me sound more American. But I think it would be this way in the computer." He gave Yvonne his date of birth and Social Security number.

Yvonne typed it in.

"So, I'll be in the computer if I was in foster care?" asked Vega.

"No, honey," she explained, forgetting once again, it seemed, that he wasn't one of her charges. "Your name will show up here if you ever came to the attention of ACS. Or rather, the Child Welfare Administration as it was known back then. It doesn't necessarily mean you were placed in foster care. Social workers could have decided to close out the case with no action. That's the most common route."

"But all of that will be in the computer, right?"

"Files from the 1980s are kept on paper," she explained. "But your name, birth date, and case number would be registered here. That will give us a starting point to see if you're in the system."

Yvonne made humming sounds as she clicked between

screens. "Here we go," she said cheerfully. "J-16. Case CWA 6282."

He was here. He felt the shame and anguish in those numbers.

Yvonne fished a pad out of a desk drawer and copied down the case number. Then she walked Vega and Michelle down a long, tiled hallway past rows and rows of files, all representing other long-ago children. The ones in this section would be Vega's age now. Had they grown into responsible adults? Had they married? Did they have families of their own? Vega felt sad that a certain percentage—the ones far less lucky than he'd been—had not. He wondered how many files in one row begot files in another. He shuddered at the thought.

"Here we are." Yvonne pulled out a thick folder.

"That much?" Vega felt queasy.

"This is nothing," said Yvonne. "I got kids whose folders take up half a shelf."

She carried it over to a table in the back and opened it. "I'd love to tell you that you could look at it uninterrupted, but I have to stay. I'm responsible for making sure everything goes back in the file."

"I understand," said Vega. He gave Michelle points for hanging back.

The first few pages were basic information Vega already knew. His name. His mother's and father's names. His birth date. His mother's address and phone number. The name of his grandmother who also lived in the home. The name of the medical clinic his mother took him to. His record of vaccinations. The forms filled him with dread, not because of what they said, but because they confirmed that this was really and truly him.

He turned several pages of basic information until he came to a familiar form. Familiar to him, at least. He used a version of the form all the time. It was a police incident report. This one was NYPD, but the county police forms were so similar, Vega knew just which box to scan to find out what incident was being reported. And there it was, on the upper left, in the black-pen chicken scratch of an NYPD officer's handwriting: *Suspicion of child abuse.*

Vega knew this was coming. He knew it the moment his name showed up in the system. But it was different somehow reading those words. It was different seeing the date and doing the math. Realizing he was barely six years old, just finished with kindergarten, when it happened. Vega searched the box with the officer's name and badge number. Dennis Walsh. He was long retired now, if he was even still alive.

Vega tried to pretend he was viewing the report as a cop, not a former victim. He tried to take a dispassionate look at the information. According to Officer Walsh's notes, someone had called the child welfare hotline to anonymously report that Vega was being physically abused. When Walsh responded to Vega's mother's apartment, the officer noted "visible swelling" on Vega's left cheek and "bruising and discoloration" on his side.

Mother insists child's injuries came from playing baseball, the officer wrote. *Child questioned whether mother ever hits him. Child said yes.*

Ay, puñeta! Did he really say that? It was true, of course. Everybody's mother and grandmother in the neighborhood gave them a swat now and then. But Vega never recalled either of them hitting him in the face or leaving bruises on his body.

"My mother . . ." Vega felt the words bunch up in his chest. "She never . . ."

"Damn straight, she never," said Michelle. She looked over Vega's shoulder at the report. "Your mother was telling the truth. I'm sure of it. That's not child abuse. That's a sports injury. You played a lot of ball—with boys older than you. Those games were rough. Kids got bruised by balls and bats, bloodied over disputed scores. And if that wasn't enough, the trash in those lots could finish you off."

"But . . . somebody called this in," said Vega. "Somebody thought I was getting beat up. And the cop—he certainly did."

"He could have been a rookie," Yvonne mused. "We had a case not long ago. A young cop arrested a mother because a teacher reported bruise marks on the child. Turns out, the child had leukemia. It wasn't diagnosed until after the mother's arrest."

"I didn't have cancer," said Vega.

"Still, the officer could have overreacted," said Yvonne. "Back then, there wasn't as much training as there is now. Cops and case workers don't just look for injuries anymore. They look for patterns. Is there food in the house? Is the child clean and well fed? Do other children in the house have similar poorly explained injuries? It looks here like none of that took place."

"But who would make such a charge?" asked Vega. "They must have thought I was in danger."

"They probably did," said Yvonne. "But there's no way to find them and ask them. We keep hotline calls anonymous for a reason. You call in a report on a violent parent, that parent could come after you next."

Vega flipped through the pages. It was like reading someone else's story. He remembered none of what followed. His mother's arrest and subsequent posting of bail. A family court judge's decision to place Vega in foster care.

Why foster care? Where was his grandmother? For that matter, where was his father?

The pages provided the answers in bloodless detail. His grandmother was visiting her sons—his mother's brothers—in Puerto Rico. She couldn't get back in time. Nor did she understand the legal issues involved. She didn't speak English. And his father?

There was no mention. No mention at all.

"Why didn't they call Orlando?" Vega asked Michelle. He didn't say "my father." This was one more reason why he never would.

"I wish I could tell you," said Michelle. "But my mother and Pop won't talk about it."

"Of course they won't talk about it," said Vega. "Because they refused to take me in."

Carmen Rodriguez would have been about twenty-two at the time, an unwed mother with a three-year-old and a baby, being asked to take on a third child—the son of her lover's angry, jilted wife. With zero support from her lover. As always.

Vega had asked and answered his own question.

Vega thumbed ahead, anxious to be through with this hateful exercise. It raised more questions than it answered. Another piece of paper showed that he'd been placed with a foster family on Melrose Avenue. Joel and Miriam Bonilla. The dates of Vega's time in their home corresponded to the summer of his year between kindergarten and first grade. Eight weeks.

Eight weeks. That was a lifetime to a six-year-old.

"Do you remember them?" asked Yvonne.

"No," said Vega. "Nothing. Not the place or what they looked like. Nothing."

Vega searched for other information about the foster couple. There was nothing in the file. Only a thin piece of paper showing the charges dropped against his mother and that she'd retained a lawyer and had to sue the family courts to get Vega back. The court delays and paperwork took eight weeks. That explained the time period. There was one follow-up report from a social worker after that. Then the case was closed.

Vega shut the folder and turned to Yvonne. "Can you tell me anything about Joel and Miriam Bonilla? The file doesn't contain much information."

"Let me see what I can find in the computer."

She refiled Vega's paperwork, then typed in Joel and Miriam Bonilla's names and address into the main computer.

"Huh." Yvonne frowned at the screen.

"What?" asked Vega.

"Their files have been removed from the system. There is a lock on the data."

"What does that mean?"

"Usually, it means there has been some kind of legal action. Let me try another way." She switched screens and typed their names and address again.

"This is a list of homes certified as acceptable for foster placements. I'm trying to see if I can find anything here."

She let out a long breath of air. Vega read something defeated in the exhale. "It says here that the Bonillas had their foster care certifications revoked about two years after you were placed in their care."

"*Revoked?* Do you know why?"

"Usually, it's because social workers found something that rendered them unacceptable as foster parents. It could be anything from falsifying records, to a change in the adults living in the house, to neglect, to . . ." She hesitated.

"To what?"

"Abuse. Physical or sexual."

"Is there a way to find out more?"

"Not unless criminal charges were filed," said Yvonne. "But I'll tell you now, that rarely happens."

"Why is that?" asked Vega.

"Because DAs are reluctant to prosecute foster parents for anything less than very serious crimes. First, because it's difficult compiling evidence. The kids move around so much, their memories are flawed. And second, the city doesn't want to scare potential fosters away."

"So you're saying that even if Joel and Miriam Bonilla abused the children in their care, they were never held accountable?" Vega felt tight with rage. Here he was, ripped from his mother over a baseball game, while these monsters got off scot-free.

"It's not that simple, Detective," said Yvonne. "The Bonillas may not have been directly responsible for whatever happened. Sometimes, it's an incident between two children in a foster parent's care. Sometimes, it's a relative who moves into the home. I can't tell you. All I can say is that when foster parent names are removed, it's usually an in-house decision and the paperwork on it is sealed."

"So I'll never know what happened to me," said Vega.

"According to these records, you were in foster care for eight weeks," said Yvonne. "The Bonillas weren't removed from the system for another two years. My guess is, given the time frame, nothing terrible happened while you were there."

"Nothing terrible happened?" Vega felt a slow burn of fury building inside him. "Some person I will never know called in false information on my mom that got me sent to people deemed unsuitable to care for children two years after caring for me. You think that's *nothing terrible?*"

"Jimmy," Michelle cautioned. He was overstepping his bounds and he knew it. But he was angry at what ACS or CSA or whatever the hell they called themselves did to him. To his mother and grandmother.

"I'm sorry," Vega told Yvonne. "I don't mean to take it out on you. It's not your fault. But I feel violated. I feel like my family was violated."

He rose from his chair. "Thank you for your time, Ms. Peters. Sorry to have troubled you."

He walked to the file room door, opened it, and kept

walking. He bypassed the elevators for the fire stairs. He wanted out of this building. The walls felt like they were closing in. A vague image of a locked green door with no knob and dirty fingerprints came to him again. The same image he'd known all his life. It mixed with the memory of wet mildewed towels and the rich buttery scent of Coppertone.

It wasn't a dream or a random phobia. He knew that now. It belonged to that dark time in foster care.

A place he never should have been but for an anonymous caller and an inexperienced cop.

Chapter 27

The rain had stopped by the time Adele pulled her pale green Toyota Prius into the parking lot of Beth Shalom. She parked near Rabbi Goldberg's white minivan and got out. It took both arms to heft the accordion folder full of paperwork from her front passenger seat. It was crammed with copies of the Aviles family's tax forms and medical records and doctors' reports that Adele hoped would form the bulk of her appeal on Edgar Aviles's behalf. She'd spent the whole morning with his wife, Maria, compiling them.

She walked up the front steps of the synagogue and rang the bell with her elbow. She leaned her face close to the glass. Rabbi Goldberg looked relieved as he opened the door.

"Thank you for coming," he said as she stepped inside. He held out his arms. "Here. Let me help you."

Adele gratefully surrendered the heavy folder.

"Edgar's downstairs in the preschool, repainting one of the bookcases," said the rabbi. "I told him he doesn't have to do that. But I think work helps keep his mind off things."

"How is he doing?" she asked.

Rabbi Goldberg seesawed his head. "He's trying to stay hopeful. We all are. His family came last night to see him.

I don't know if that made him feel better—or worse."
Rabbi Goldberg gestured to a hallway off the sanctuary.
"Would you like to work in the conference room?"

"That would be great."

"Good. We'll drop off all this stuff and then I'll take
you to Edgar."

Edgar Aviles was hunched over a small bookcase, painting the wood a vivid shade of turquoise, the color of the
Caribbean Sea. He put the paintbrush down, wiped his
hands on a rag, and forced the muscles of his face to look
pleased at seeing Adele.

"Thank you for all you are doing, señora," he said.

"Don't thank me until I'm successful," said Adele. She'd
meant the words to be light and playful, but they came out
dark instead.

"Ms. Figueroa has all your materials in the conference
room," said Rabbi Goldberg. He turned to Adele. "Can I
get you anything before I leave?"

"No, thank you," said Adele. "We'll be fine."

"Then I guess I'll go home." The rabbi made a show of
checking his watch. "Eve left you dinner in the refrigerator, Edgar."

"Thank you," Aviles said shyly.

"I'll call you later," Adele promised the rabbi. "And let
you know where we stand."

"Yes. Good. Well—see you tomorrow."

Aviles put his paintbrush into the sink to soak, then
washed his hands and walked Adele back up the stairs and
into the conference room. Bookcases along the walls held
thick texts in English and Hebrew. A large colorful oil
painting hung between them. It depicted a tree full of different kinds of fruit with Hebrew writing winding up the
trunk.

"That's a beautiful painting," said Adele.

"I believe the quote says something about devotion to

faith," said Aviles. "At least, that's what Rabbi Weiss once told me. He's retired now."

"You've worked here a long time," said Adele.

"Over ten years, yes." Aviles sighed. "They are good people. I feel terrible that I am putting them in this situation."

Adele took a seat at the conference table and gestured for Aviles to join her. "Then the sooner we can get this situation settled, the better for everyone. Would you be more comfortable if we did this in Spanish?"

"That would be easier. Thank you." Aviles pulled out a chair and sat catercorner to her. His eyes were bloodshot. Shadows pooled beneath the rims. He leaned on his elbows on the table and pushed his knuckles into his lips, biting down on the tender skin—a nervous habit, she supposed.

She opened the folder to the top sheet. It was the printout of ICE form 246. Across the top it read, *Application for a Stay of Deportation or Removal*. Adele translated the words into Spanish for Aviles though she suspected she didn't need to.

"Your wife and I went through the form this morning to gather the paperwork for your application," she explained, patting the folder. "I have your Salvadoran passport and a copy of your birth certificate here, as well as copies of medical records relating to Noah's condition and your wife's."

"That's good, yes?"

"We're going to have to hope it's good enough," said Adele. "Ideally, I'd like to see letters from Noah's oncologist and his pediatrician, attesting to how important it is that you remain here during his care. I'd want a similar letter from Maria's doctor, explaining why her condition makes caring for Noah impossible without your help. Maria put in calls this morning to the doctors' answering services to try to get those letters, but I fear they won't come in time."

"We need to present everything tomorrow morning, I guess," said Aviles.

"Nine a.m.," said Adele. "As soon as the ICE office opens in Broad Plains. I want to get in there before those two agents you saw yesterday get their removal order signed by a judge."

Adele looked up from her paperwork and met Aviles's bloodshot eyes head-on. "I'm not going to lie to you. It's a risk. If ICE approves, you will be issued something called an Order of Supervision, which will probably involve showing up at that office every three months or so. At any of those meetings, ICE could decide to rescind the order and immediately deport you. They don't even have to show cause."

"This is the bad news?" asked Aviles.

"No," said Adele. "This is the good. A temporary reprieve."

"Then what's the bad?"

"We show up tomorrow," said Adele. "They reject our application and handcuff you immediately. In which case, I've coaxed you out of sanctuary and basically handed you over for deportation."

Aviles frowned at his callused hands. Adele noticed two small smudges of turquoise paint on them.

"I am very grateful for all you are doing for me, señora," he began. "Please forgive me these questions. I am not an educated man."

"You can ask me anything," she assured him.

"Okay." He took a deep breath. "Can you file this paperwork without me?"

"No. They will likely reject the claim if you do not file in person," Adele explained. "I've seen them reject a claim if a person sends in the wrong fee. Or fails to include an apartment number in their address. Or forgets to sign their application. We don't want to give them *any* reason to reject you. So yes, you would have to accompany me. And yes, that might mean that you would be walking right into their hands. Doing Tyler's and Donovan's jobs for them. But I don't see a choice," she said. "If you stay here, they'll come back. And I wouldn't count on the synagogue to give you indefinite sanctuary. Some, like Max Zimmerman, would do it in a heartbeat. But others would not."

Aviles pushed his knuckles to his lips again and bit down as he stared at the table. "This is all my fault."

"The powers that be in Washington took away your temporary protected status," said Adele. "This is not your fault."

"Not the removal," said Aviles. "Lissette."

Her name came out a whisper. It hung in the air.

"Your niece?" asked Adele. "How is her disappearance your fault?"

An ambulance sped by in the distance. The sirens made Aviles jump. Sweat beaded on his forehead. This wasn't ICE he was afraid of. This was something else. Something he didn't seem to want to tell her.

"Señor," Adele said, leaning forward. "While I may not officially be your attorney here, I am functioning like an attorney. Anything you say to me will not go to the police."

"I understand," said Aviles. "But some things, I cannot say. Even to you. At least, not until I know I can protect my family."

"You mean if you're deported?" Adele exhaled. "Your wife and children are American citizens. ICE can't do anything to them."

Aviles regarded her from beneath his bushy eyebrows. "But there are people who can."

"*Maras?*" Adele dropped her pen and stared at him. "Are you being threatened by gangsters?"

Adele saw the truth in his trembling lips.

Chapter 28

Michelle caught up to Vega a half block from the ACS building. He had his hands in his pockets and his shoulders hunched like he was fighting a stiff wind.

"Jimmy! Slow down!" She came up behind him and slipped her arm beneath his elbow. "*Ay, bendito,* you really know how to make an exit."

"I'm sorry," he mumbled. "It's not that I don't appreciate what you did—"

"I'm furious."

"I didn't mean to walk out like that—"

"Not at you, *mano.* At Pop. At my mother." She stopped in her tracks, forcing him to do the same. She spun him around to face her. "They should've taken you in and cared for you after that cop arrested your mother. It was a misunderstanding. Anyone who knew how rough ball games in our neighborhood were would have understood that. My parents should have stepped up."

Vega could see she was genuinely upset. It touched him. He felt something well up in his heart for her. He wasn't expecting that. He put his hands on her shoulders.

"Your mother was very young, Michelle. I didn't realize that then. As a little boy. But now? With a nineteen-year-old daughter myself? I get it. She had two babies. Three, if you count our father. She didn't need another—especially the child of her lover's angry ex.'"

"Yeah, but Pop—"

Vega's father was harder to forgive. He was pushing thirty at the time. But even there, he knew.

"Our father is like water," said Vega. "He follows the path of least resistance. And I'm quite sure your mother put up a lot of resistance. Probably, they had no idea it would take eight weeks for my mother to get me back. Probably, they thought it would be a few days."

Michelle gave him a shocked expression. "Are you saying you forgive them?"

Vega shook his head. "Not forgive, perhaps. Just . . . understand."

People walked past them with shopping carts and strollers. Car horns sounded. Teenagers huddled on the corner by the bodega, smoking. Michelle barely registered any of it. She was a city girl. This was her home. It wasn't Vega's anymore. He tried to remind himself just how long ago all this was.

"I don't think I'll ever know who called in that child abuse accusation on my mother," said Vega. "Or what the Bonillas did to me. But at least I know that my mother and grandmother didn't abuse me. For that, I thank you, *Nita*." Short for *hermanita*—little sister. Vega had no idea if he'd ever called her that before, but it suddenly felt right.

Michelle smiled, relieved. "Are you still up for Mama Linda's?"

He wasn't. Not really. But he felt he owed her something for all she'd done for him today.

"Okay," he said, tapping her shoulders. "Let's do this."

"We're not going on a raid," Michelle giggled.

"No, but we'll need a can of it before we're through," said Vega. "And a case of Tums."

* * *

Vega couldn't recall the last time he'd been to Mama Linda's. The place hadn't changed in forty years. Roll-down metal gates sat like eyebrows above two plate-glass windows smeared with grease. Blinking neon signs advertised lottery tickets and *cuchifritos* in the same oversized lettering.

Inside, the air was heavy with the scent of deep-fried pork, garlic, onions, and chilis. There was a line at the counter. There was never *not* a line at Mama Linda's. Women with rollers in their hair. Men in do-rags. A cluster of regulars by the lottery machine. On the tile wall behind the counter, a Board of Health designation hung in a grease-spattered frame. Impossible to read. Probably just as well. Vega suspected it was about as spotless as the criminal records of some of Mama Linda's customers.

There were no menus. Everything was on the order board—none of it explained. If you had to ask what it was, you probably wouldn't want to eat it anyway. Michelle ordered *chicharrón de pollo sin hueso*—boneless fried chicken chunks—with a side order of *maduros*—fried sweet plantains. Vega went with the comfort foods of his youth: the *mofongo*—Puerto Rican-style pork stuffing—with red bean gravy, two *alcapurrias,* and a piece of slow-roasted pork shoulder known as *pernil.* They both ordered Medalla Lights, a Puerto Rican brand of pale lager.

"My treat," said Vega, waving her money away.

"Thanks," said Michelle.

They took their trays to a small Formica-topped table that sat elbow to elbow in a row of three tables. Privacy was not Mama Linda's strong suit. Nor was tranquility. At a booth in back, people played scratch-off lottery games—almost as much of a draw as the food—while heavily syncopated reggaeton music blasted over a tinny loudspeaker.

"I'm not going to eat for a week after this," said Vega as he dug into the food. "I can't believe I ate like this all the time as a kid. Only, it was my grandmother's food—not Mama Linda's."

"Your grandmother was a fantastic cook," said Michelle.

Vega gave her a puzzled look. "How would you know?"

"When my mom was in high school, after her mother died, she lived with Gloria across the hall from your family," Michelle explained. "Sometimes, your grandmother would feed her. This was, of course, before . . . everything."

Vega put down his knife and fork. "You're kidding. I guess that's how my dad got to know your mom."

Michelle stared at the grease forming little islands across her heavy white china plate. A fire truck passed by outside, its red flashing lights bouncing off the windows, sucking all the color from the room.

"Pretty crappy family history, huh?" asked Michelle. "I don't blame you for hating all of them."

Vega ran his finger along a bottle of hot sauce on the table. "I don't know what I feel," he admitted. "Mostly, I feel for my mother. For what they did to her. I guess if I hate at all, it's on her behalf."

"Your mom was long past it," said Michelle. "You know that, right? She was on good terms with Pop before she died."

"She was?" That was news to Vega. An image of his mother flashed through his head. The way the light caught the lenses of her glasses, magnifying those big dark eyes that took in everything. That slight inhale of breath she used to give before she spoke, as if her words could never entirely express what was inside her. She was a private woman—private, even to him. There was a lot his mother never told him after she moved back to the Bronx. She had to die for him to know she'd had a secret lover all those years.

"Pop wanted to come to your mother's funeral," said Michelle. "But he figured it might upset you. That's why I

came alone. Hell, my whole family would've come otherwise. Even my mom."

"Your *mom?*" asked Vega, surprised. "I wasn't even allowed to say her name growing up."

"That's ancient history, Jimmy. They were over it at the
end. They both understood that Pop couldn't stay faithful
to *any* woman. That's not right, I know. But they stopped
taking it personally."

The heat inside Mama Linda's was stifling. Or maybe it
was just the heavy food and heavier conversation. Vega
pushed his plate to one side. He was anxious to get his mind
off all this ancient drama and back on the case. "There's
some stuff I found out last night about Talia Crowley," said
Vega. "You want to walk and talk?"

"Too many eyes and ears?" she asked.

"No," said Vega. "I can't hear myself think."

She grinned. "You're getting old, *mano.*"

Outside, a train rumbled by on an elevated track.
Michelle waited to speak until after it had passed.

"Can we walk over to Rosedale?" she asked. "My boys
are staying with my mother this afternoon."

"Your mom lives in the projects?"

"The rent's reasonable," said Michelle. "My boys prefer
it to our building because of the basketball courts and
playground. And besides, there are a lot of good people
there."

"Yeah, but it's the bad ones that make life hell for everybody else." Michelle was right. He was getting old and
suburban.

On the walk over, Vega filled Michelle in on Talia Crowley's pelvic inflammatory disease and undiagnosed STD.

"You know," said Michelle, "pelvic inflammatory disease can cause infertility."

"She was pregnant when they got married."

"Sure. When they got married," she said. "But Talia was thirty-four. She lost the baby. PID might have been a factor."

"You think?"

"It's possible," said Michelle. "If Crowley gave it to her, he might have cost her any chance at *ever* having a baby. That could make a woman pretty angry. Maybe angry enough to want to ruin the man who did it."

Ahead of them loomed four ten-story tan-brick buildings. The Rosedale Projects. A chain-link fence surrounded a playground and four half-court basketball courts in the center. Vega heard the thump of balls bouncing on concrete and the soft swish of chain mail as they cleared the nets. As a boy, Vega and his friends used to refer to a half-court game as "shooting some chink," based on the sound of the balls in the nets. It wasn't until Vega saw an Asian man blanch at the phrase that he understood how he and his friends must have come across.

"What you're telling me," said Michelle, "is that Talia might have threatened to expose the DA—which is reason enough for him to kill her."

"Except he's got an ironclad alibi," Vega reminded her.

"Then he got someone else to do it."

They found an empty bench near the playground and sat down. Rap music blared from the windows of a passing car, the bass notes loud enough that Vega could feel them through the soles of his boots.

"I told Greco everything you're saying to me," said Vega. "He said my findings could just as easily prove why she committed suicide."

"So that's it?" asked Michelle. "He's just going to shut us down? With all our unanswered questions?"

"Unless we can find some hard evidence that Talia wasn't alone the night she died," said Vega. "So far, I'm coming up empty-handed."

Michelle went to speak, but her attention was drawn to

something over Vega's shoulder. He turned and followed
Michelle's gaze to a Hispanic couple walking out of one of
the buildings. The man was dressed in basketball shorts
and a sleeveless top, his prison-chiseled biceps covered in
tattoos. He had his arm around a girl in a shiny pale pink
jacket and skimpy hot pink shorts, propping her up like
she was drunk or high or both. He was half walking, half
dragging her to the street corner.

"You know those two?" asked Vega.

"I don't live here," said Michelle. "But no, I don't recognize them. She looks doped up."

Vega agreed. The young girl's head flopped back. Her
ponytail had hair sticking out of it. The man with the tattoos looked nervously down the block, like he was expecting a ride that was already late.

Vega rose from the bench. He couldn't, in good conscience, allow an obviously intoxicated young woman to
be dragged into a car.

"You're not going to intervene, are you?" asked Michelle.
"This is the Bronx, Jimmy. People have to be visibly hemor-
rhaging before I call nine-one-one."

"I just want to see what's going on."

"Then I'm coming with you."

Vega kept his hand on his hip as he approached. He didn't
have his gun. He didn't carry in New York City—the paperwork for a concealed carry was a nightmare. But the man
holding on to the girl wouldn't know that.

The girl was young. She had thighs like saplings and
very high heels. One of the straps wasn't buckled properly.
She didn't put those shoes on. Someone else did.

"You there!" Vega called. He flashed his badge. From
this distance, the man would think he was NYPD. "What's
wrong with that girl?"

The man turned his head. One dark eye looked straight
at Vega, the other wandered like a marble in a tin can. He
removed his tattooed arm from the girl's shoulder. She

dropped hard to the sidewalk, her pink jacket riding up, showing nothing but a black halter bra beneath.

He ran.

"Call nine-one-one," Vega yelled at Michelle. "Stay with her."

Vega raced ahead. He was in the wrong frame of mind for a chase. He was off-duty, unarmed, and out of jurisdiction. His heavy, greasy lunch sloshed around in his stomach like a football in a washing machine. His boots were better suited to navigating the mud around the Brighton Aqueduct this morning than the gritty pavements of the Bronx. Most of all, he wasn't wearing a Kevlar vest. If the man he was chasing had a gun and decided to use it, the game was over.

The man dashed across a busy street, barely skirting a gypsy cab, the driver giving him both the horn and the finger. Vega was betting that wasn't his girlfriend he'd dropped to the pavement back there. It was some junkie he'd sold a lethal mix of heroin to. Or maybe a prostitute he'd just paid in dime bags. Vega noted the girl's hot pink shorts. Then again, his own daughter walked around in hooker chic half the time. All the teens did these days.

Vega tried to cross the same corner as the tattooed man with the lazy eye, but he couldn't get past the traffic. Up ahead, a dark blue sedan screeched to the curb. The man jumped in and the car roared off.

Vega raced back to Rosedale. A crowd of people had formed a circle in the courtyard by the playground. Young men in basketball shorts. Kids with skateboards. Mothers with babies on their hips. Vega looked around for an ambulance. Or at least, a police car. But this was the Bronx. Patrols arrived slowly. Ambulances, sometimes not until you didn't need one anymore.

He pushed his way through the crowd to see Michelle hunched over the girl, performing CPR. "Stay back!" she huffed out between compressions. "Give her room!"

Vega knelt beside Michelle. She was sweaty and exhausted from the effort.

"I'll take over," said Vega. He shrugged off his jacket and leaned over the girl, pressing down on her slight rib cage, counting out the compressions to the Bee Gees song "Stayin' Alive," as he'd been taught. Her skin and lips were blue. But even so, Vega registered a familiarity in those dimpled cheeks. The same ones that stared back at him from that photo in Talia Crowley's sweater drawer, and again, on her asylum application at ICE.

Deisy Ramos-Sandoval.

They'd found the missing Port Carroll teenager.

They'd found her too late.

Chapter 29

"We have to call the police," Adele told Edgar Aviles, pushing herself up from the conference table. "We have to tell them that gangsters are threatening your family."

"If ICE grants me a stay of removal tomorrow, I will tell the police everything," Aviles promised. "But until then, no. I have to be able to protect my family. I can't leave them defenseless."

"The police can protect your family."

Aviles stared into his hands without answering.

"Is this about Lissette?" Adele asked him. "If there's something I can pass on to the police—something that will help them find her—"

"There is nothing." Aviles cut her off. "Please, señora. You must give me your word that you won't say anything about what I've told you until after the meeting at ICE tomorrow."

Sixteen hours. That's all he was asking for. Adele took a deep breath.

"Okay. We'll wait until after the meeting."

She gathered up her papers and shook his hand. He walked her down the stairs and as far as the front door of the synagogue.

"What time will you be back here?" he asked.

"Eight a.m.," she said. "Do you have a suit?"

"My wife brought it over earlier."

"Good. See you tomorrow then—and lock the door."

She walked down the steps, stopping for a moment to hear the click of the lock. Satisfied, she headed over to her car, unlocked the doors, and hefted the paperwork on the front passenger seat. Then she walked around to the driver's side, stuck her key in the ignition, and drove out of the lot.

A little yellow warning light lit up on the far right of her dashboard. Adele had noted it on the drive over, but she hadn't wanted to stop. The car drove normally. It had to be an electronic malfunction.

A half mile down the road, however, the right side of her car began to shudder. Adele pulled onto a quiet dead-end street and got out. Her rear right tire was flat. She bent down to examine the rubber and noticed a nail head poking out from the now-flattened tread. *Ay, caray!* She couldn't afford a flat tire right now—not with all she had to do.

She pulled out her phone to dial AAA. She suspected that on a late Sunday afternoon, it would take at least forty minutes before a tow truck got here.

She started to dial when her peripheral vision caught sight of a black-and-white Lake Holly Police cruiser pulling onto the street. The patrol officer turned on his flashers and pulled up behind Adele's car. The cruiser door swung open, sending a crackle of dispatch voices across the quiet street. A figure in uniform stepped out. He was tall, broad, and sculpted like a granite cliff. Mirrored aviators covered his eyes even though the sun was tilting into the trees. Not that she needed to see them.

She knew who he was.

He pressed a hand possessively on the taillight of her car.

"Good afternoon, Ms. Figueroa." His tone carried an authoritative edge to it. Like he'd caught her doing something she shouldn't be.

"Good afternoon, Officer Bale."

Ryan Bale walked around the edge of her car. He whistled when he saw her rear right tire. "Don't you check your tires occasionally?"

"It was fine this morning. I was going to call Triple A. Do you know of a tow service that might be closer? I'm sort of in a hurry."

"A hurry, huh?"

Bale squatted down on the opposite side of her car. She couldn't see him, but she gathered he was examining all of her tires. When he straightened, he switched on his body cam. All the cops had personal body cameras these days. Adele hoped she didn't make some offhand comment that ended up circulating around the police station.

"Your other tires look sturdy at least," said Bale. He brushed his dusty palms along the sides of his uniform pants.

"Perhaps I should just call Triple A," she said again.

Bale gestured to her rearview mirror with an Ecuadorian flag hanging over the mount. "You know that's illegal in the state of New York."

"What is?"

"Hanging anything from your rearview mirror."

"Really?" *And how about demanding to search an immigrant center without a warrant?* Adele bit her tongue. He'd surely write the ticket if she provoked him. Plus, the whole encounter would be on video.

Bale folded his arms across his Popeye chest and stood in front of her, blocking out the sun. "Look, Ms. Figueroa— I'm not going to ticket you—"

"Thank you."

"In fact, if you want, I can change your tire for you."

Adele looked up at those mirrored shades. She saw only her own face in the lenses' reflection.

"I thought the police didn't change flat tires."

"As a policy? No," said Bale. "But it's a slow evening. You're a local resident and . . ." He ran a glance down her slacks and blouse. "You don't look dressed to change a tire."

He walked over to her trunk as if the matter had just been settled. "You got a doughnut and jack in back, right?"

"I guess." Adele was embarrassed to admit she'd never checked.

"The Shell station's open for another hour," said Bale. "They could probably mount a brand-new tire for you if I put the spare on now and you get over there right away."

"Thank you," said Adele. "I'd appreciate it."

"Pop the trunk."

She pulled out her electronic key fob and beeped it open. Bale gestured to a gym bag full of Adele's workout clothes and another with Sophia's soccer cleats and ball. "May I remove these? I'm going to need to take this stuff out to get to the doughnut," he explained.

"Of course."

Adele took the bags and threw them in the rear seat of her car. She walked back to the trunk and watched Bale lift up the piece of carpeting to expose two storage compartments over the doughnut. He went to pull the first compartment out when his hand froze in midair.

"What do we have here?"

"Pardon?" Adele poked her head inside. She hoped Sophia hadn't left a candy bar to melt.

Bale pulled the storage compartment closer and nudged something with his finger. Adele wondered if the dealership had sold her a broken jack. She'd had the car four years and never needed it. *Figures.*

But Bale's face looked more concerned than it might for a broken jack. He reached into the compartment and pulled out a clear plastic gallon-size ziplocked bag. Inside the bag were bundles of palm-size square envelopes, each bundle fastened with a rubber band.

Adele's mouth went dry. Her heart raced. She knew what those bundles looked like.

They looked like heroin.

Bale began to count the bundles through the bag. *One . . . two . . . three . . . four . . .*

"Those aren't mine," Adele protested. "I've never seen them before."

Bale ignored her. *Five . . . six . . . seven . . .*

"I've never even checked to see if I had a spare or a jack."

. . . Eight . . . nine . . . ten . . . eleven . . .

"This is crazy!" Adele stammered. "Do I look like a junkie to you?"

. . . Twelve . . . thirteen . . . fourteen. Bale finished counting and looked at her. Fourteen bundles. Each bundle contained probably ten hits—half a gram. Which added up to seven grams in total.

Felony weight.

Adele worked hard to find her voice. "I swear, Officer, I don't know where that bag came from."

"Right." Bale told her not to move while he went back to his vehicle and fetched a field drug test. He dropped a small amount of powder from one of the packets into a test tube. The solution turned cloudy.

Adele threw up her hands. "This is ridiculous!"

She wanted to prove that this was all a mistake. But she didn't know how. Heroin use was rampant in the county. Where once it had been solely the province of hardcore addicts, it was now being snorted and injected by plenty of people whom no one would suspect. Business executives and lawyers and Ivy League college students home on break. Having no needle marks meant nothing. Snorting was more common than injecting anyway.

"Officer, please." Adele felt her voice rise in pitch. All her years of Harvard legal training went out the window. "This isn't mine. I don't know how it got there, but it's not mine!"

"Turn around, ma'am. Place your hands on your vehicle."

Bale didn't wait for Adele to comply. He grabbed her by the shoulder and spun her into position, kicking her legs apart until he had her under his control. She heard the jingle of handcuffs and felt the cold steel of a bracelet lock around one wrist and then the other behind her back. Her shoulders burned from the sensation. In all her years of dealing with criminal defendants and detained immigrants, she'd never once experienced what it felt like personally.

"You are under arrest for possession of heroin," Bale grunted as he ran his thick hands down her body, looking for—what? A gun? A joint? More heroin?

"I don't think I need to read *you* of all people your Miranda rights," said Bale. "But let's run through them anyway. You have the right to remain silent . . ."

Bale droned on. Adele's mind raced. The lawyer in her knew she shouldn't say anything from this point forward. But the human being in her was panicked—and angry at herself. Why in God's name had she allowed a police officer to go through the trunk of her car? Why had she consented to a search?

And then she remembered: All of Aviles's papers were in that accordion folder on the front passenger seat. His Salvadoran passport. His birth certificate. Copies of Noah's and Maria's medical records. Everything she needed to make his case tomorrow for a stay of removal.

Adele's arrest not only imperiled her freedom and future. It imperiled Edgar Aviles's as well.

Bale gathered all the evidence from Adele's trunk and walked Adele over to his patrol car. He placed a hand on the top of her head and pushed her down on the seat in back. He closed the self-locking door. She was in the equivalent of a cage now. Her heart beat wildly.

Bale got on his radio and ordered a tow truck. A police one, this time. And of course, this time, they'd come. Her car was now part of a police investigation. Worse, a *felony* police investigation. It could go into civil forfeiture. Adele might never see it again.

But it wasn't the car that worried her most at the moment. It was what was still in it.

"Officer." She tried for her most cooperative voice. "There are some papers in a folder on the front seat of my car. Legal papers that have nothing to do with my arrest. Can I please ask that you remove them from my car before it's towed?"

"No can do," Bale grunted. "The contents are part of a police investigation. For all I know, those papers contain the name of your supplier."

"Officer," Adele tried again. "A man's life—his family's lives—are at stake here. You don't have to turn those papers over to me. You can turn them over to my attorney if you'd like." Adele's best friend, Paola Rosado, was a criminal defense attorney. If she couldn't represent Adele, she'd find someone good who could. "I don't want anyone else's case held up because of my arrest."

Bale said nothing. He got out of his patrol car, walked over to Adele's vehicle, and opened the front passenger door. Adele watched through the cruiser's front windshield as Bale leaned in to examine the papers. She held her breath, waiting. Then he straightened, closed the door, and walked back to his patrol car, empty-handed. He stuck his chiseled face through the driver's-side window and lifted his mirrored aviators.

"You want those papers? You'll have to go through a judge," said Bale. "Edgar Aviles is a fugitive. I'm not going to help one criminal aid and abet another."

Chapter 30

It took nearly ten minutes for the first patrol car to show up to the Rosedale Projects—and another five before an ambulance arrived. By then, it was too late.

Sixteen-year-old Deisy Ramos was dead.

Vega and Michelle were sweat-soaked and exhausted from performing CPR. They collapsed onto a bench while two young NYPD officers—a man and a woman—took their statements with the bored expressions of cops who'd already seen too many junkies die.

Vega explained that Deisy was a witness in a death investigation they were involved in. He offered up Deisy's mother's name and the fact that she lived and worked in Port Carroll.

"I don't have the mother's address," said Vega. "But she works at the Port Carroll Diner. You should be able to get a home address from Daniel Molina. He's a Port Carroll police officer." Vega gave them Molina's cell number. "He knows the family," said Vega. "It would be great if the NYPD could authorize him to be the one to notify the mom."

"We'll run it by our superiors," said the black female cop. She was a little older than her white male partner and clearly the one in charge. She asked the questions. He wrote down the answers.

"So"—the female cop flicked a finger between them—"you two came down here to speak to her?"

"Not exactly," said Michelle. "My mother lives in Rosedale. We just happened to recognize her."

Vega gave them a description of the lazy-eyed man Deisy was with and the car he got away in. "I don't have the tag number," Vega apologized. "I couldn't see it."

The male cop stopped writing and made eye contact with Vega. "Back up a moment. You're partners, you're not on duty, and you're "—he gestured to Michelle with his pen—"visiting *her* mother?"

"I live in the neighborhood," said Michelle.

"And you?" The female cop looked at Vega. "You live here too?"

"No," said Vega. "I live upstate. In Sullivan Falls."

"I see." She and her partner exchanged smirks.

"It's not like that," Michelle stammered. "Detective Vega and I . . . we're not . . . That is, we're—"

"Honey," the woman said to Michelle. "It's no skin off my back. So long as your IDs and phone contacts check out, makes no never-mind to me what you do on your own time."

IDs. Cell phones. That's when it hit Vega.

"We didn't find any ID or a cell phone on the girl," said Vega.

"I'm guessing the dealer/boyfriend she was with took her purse," said the female cop.

"No," said Vega. "I saw him. He wasn't carrying anything. And she wasn't either. Hell, my teenage daughter won't go to the bathroom without her cell phone."

The two NYPD cops got the implication. Wherever Deisy Ramos was going with this man with the wild eye, it hadn't been voluntary.

"Crazy Eye was no boyfriend," said Vega after the cops

and ambulance had left. "He was her dealer. Or maybe her pimp."

"Looks like she got herself mixed up with some bad people," said Michelle. "Her mother's going to be devastated. I hope they let your friend in Port Carroll break the news to her."

"Me too," said Vega.

He stared at the spot where the young girl's body had been. In the suburbs, a dying woman would excite an aftermath of conversation. Here, the crowd scattered as soon as the body was loaded into the ambulance. Mothers went back to nursing babies on park benches. Young men huddled in groups, smoking and eyeing the girls. The courts refilled with the sound of thumping basketballs.

Vega didn't move, struck as he was, by the purposelessness of her death. She'd traveled two thousand miles and endured God-only-knew what sort of traumas to end up like this. Dead on a Bronx pavement. The journey to the U.S. had ended up costing both sisters their lives. And for what?

Still, Vega couldn't shake the sense that this was more than a young girl making bad decisions. He didn't buy a teenager going from varsity volleyball player one week to hooker and addict the next. A voice rose up from deep inside him. *Somebody did this to you. Used you up and threw you away.* But why?

"Would you like to meet my boys?" asked Michelle. "They're upstairs with my mother."

"Your boys?" Vega felt a panic grip his chest. He wasn't ready. He wasn't sure he'd ever be. "Maybe some other time."

She looked disappointed. Vega felt guilty.

"You're going to Port Carroll, aren't you?" she asked.

Vega shrugged. "It's on the way home." Not really. Not even close. It wasn't like he could interview Deisy's mother.

Not now—given that he and Michelle were witnesses to her daughter's death. It would be a breach of protocol. But he still felt the need to talk to Molina.

"Well." Michelle let out a slow exhale of air. "Let me know what you find out." She turned to go inside. Vega grabbed her hand.

"Thanks for everything today, Michelle. I mean it."

"Sure." She smiled, but her eyes looked sad. For her, for him—for Deisy Ramos—he couldn't say.

Vega called Adele when he got back to his truck. Her phone went to voice mail. He supposed Aviles was taking up more time than she'd intended. He called Danny Molina next and told him about Deisy Ramos. He knew the NYPD wouldn't get around to making a notification for at least several hours.

"I can't believe it," said Molina. He sounded stricken.

"It looked like a drug overdose," said Vega. "Did her mother mention any drug problems?"

"No," said Molina. "Not that that always means anything. But she really had turned a corner and was getting her life together."

"Was she the target of any gangs?" asked Vega. "She was dressed . . . well, like a prostitute. Not that all the girls don't dress provocatively these days. But I got the sense that the guy with her wasn't a boyfriend. He was a pimp or a dealer. She didn't have a purse or ID or even a cell phone on her when she collapsed. And I didn't see the mutt run off with anything."

"This mutt," said Molina. "What did he look like?"

"Hispanic," said Vega. "Late twenties, perhaps. Muscular. Full sleeves of tattoos. He had a left eye that wandered."

"A left . . . ?" Molina's voice got a breathy excitement to it. "You got time to come into the Port Carroll station today?"

"I'm in the Bronx," said Vega. "But I can swing by on my way home. You have a dirtbag in mind?"

"Yeah," said Molina. "Ramon Ramirez. His nickname is *Ojo Loco.*"

Crazy eye.

"Is he one of the Ramirez brothers you were telling me about last night?" asked Vega.

"Affirmative," said Molina. "So much for going back to El Salvador."

"These guys never do."

The sun was setting by the time Vega drove into Port Carroll. The harbor, normally stagnant, had gone golden. Even the long-shuttered bakery plant had a peachy glow like an artist's rendering. It made Vega think of the stories Adele used to tell him about growing up here, when the yeasty scent of fresh bread used to waft up from the plant and seep into everything. Clothes. Closets. Even people's hair.

Vega pulled off Main Street and made a right into the visitor parking lot of the Port Carroll police station. The station was built around the same time as Lake Holly's—right after the Great Depression—and it had the same optimistic view of government in its design. Everything was sturdy brick and built to last forever.

Vega asked for Danny Molina. Instead, a detective came out to greet him.

"Carl Rafferty," said the man. He had the extra-hardy handshake of a used-car salesman and a shelf of eyebrows large enough to park a Mack truck on top. "Danny will be here soon. He and I just came from making the notification to Hilda Ardon. He wanted to stay with her a few extra minutes, seeing as they're friends."

"The NYPD signed off on Port Carroll making the notification?" asked Vega.

"I think they were only too pleased to be relieved of the burden," said Rafferty.

The detective ushered Vega back to his desk. The walls were covered in pictures of golf greens and cartoons about golfing. Vega wondered if he knew Mark Hammond, the detective in Wickford. Golf was like its own branch of policework.

"Did Hilda say whether Deisy was abusing drugs?"

"She insisted she wasn't," said Rafferty. He raised one of his thick eyebrows. "Of course, every parent says that. And these kids who came over on their own from Central America . . ." He shook his head. "Some of them have seen and done everything long before they arrived."

That was probably true, thought Vega. Still, Deisy was a sixteen-year-old girl. Whatever her life before, she was still considered a child here.

"Did her mother mention a boyfriend?"

"She claimed Deisy didn't have one."

"How about her clothes?" Vega pressed. "Did you take a look in her closet? See if she tended toward suggestive clothing?"

"You think that stuff's just going to be hanging there?" asked Rafferty. "Next to her confirmation gown and her prom dress?"

No. Vega didn't. But even if a girl is concealing a second life, some part of it was bound to show up someplace in her room. If only Rafferty had bothered to look.

Vega was already getting the sense that this guy lived for golf. Investigations were a sideline.

"Did you mention that when she was found, she had no cell phone or ID on her?"

"Molina mentioned it," said Rafferty, stifling a yawn. "The mom said she'd lost her cell phone and wallet a couple of weeks ago. So it has nothing to do with her running away."

Vega recalled the story Molina had told him about Deisy losing her phone—and how, right after that, the girl had run away. But the mention of the wallet was new.

And then it hit him.

Vega pulled out his phone. "Is Danny still with Hilda?"

"The mother?" asked Rafferty. He'd already forgotten her name. "I think so."

Vega dialed Molina's cell. "Hey, man. It's Jimmy. Where are you?"

Molina said he'd already left Hilda Ardon's apartment and was heading to the station.

"I'm going to text you a picture when I hang up," said Vega. "I need you to go back to Hilda and show it to her. Ask her if the wallet in the picture belonged to her daughter. The wallet has a cell phone compartment. Ask her if that's where Deisy kept her phone."

Vega hung up and texted Molina the picture of the wallet. His gaze settled on the compartment that was designed to hold a cell phone. It was empty. He didn't want to think of the implications.

"You county hotshots really like to take over, don't you?" said Rafferty.

"I'm not taking over. Deisy Ramos was connected to a case I'm working on."

"Yeah? Well her death ain't your case, Vega. It ain't even ours. It belongs to the NYPD. You're here as a favor to Danny."

"I'm *here*"—Vega pressed a knuckle on the table—"to ID Ramon Ramirez. You want? I can do it with your chief."

Rafferty's brows narrowed until they were one continuous dark mark separating his forehead from the rest of his face. He turned to his computer and punched in the password like each key needed to be personally hammered down. He pulled up a mug shot and turned the screen to face Vega.

"This is Ramon Ramirez. Is this the mutt you saw Deisy with in the Bronx?"

Vega stared at the picture. There were things he hadn't been able to take in about Ramon Ramirez at a distance. The sloped forehead and low brow, like he was posing for one of those *National Geographic* renderings of prehistoric man. The dark pelt of hair resting high atop his scalp. That slight upward thrust of his chin that suggested he'd never met an adversary he was scared to take on.

But the one thing Vega couldn't forget was that eye. The way it wandered like a lighthouse searchlight.

"That's him," said Vega. "I'm sure of it. He has brothers?"

"One we know about," said Rafferty. He pulled up another mug shot on the screen and showed it to Vega. The brother was leaner and slighter with a turn of the lips that suggested he was mocking the camera. He had pitted, acne-scarred skin and eyes that looked like they registered slights easily. Vega suspected he was the brains to Ramon's brawn.

"This one is Carlos Ramirez," said Rafferty. "Also known as 'Chucky.' Like the doll from the horror movies."

Vega looked over the rap sheets on both men. Both had been arrested numerous times. For possession of stolen property, possession of narcotics, and pimping. But either the charges were thrown out or bargained down. There were no charges for the past three years.

"It's like Danny said," Vega noted. "The gang went dark. I guess they moved to the Bronx and paid the right people."

"Or they found a scam we haven't been able to catch them at." Rafferty tucked his hands behind his head and leaned back in his chair. He'd surrendered to the notion years ago, it seemed, that some criminals couldn't be beaten.

"With a record like this, how come the Ramirez brothers haven't been deported?"

"They're American-born, my friend. Raised in El Salvador with a deported mom but born right here in the good ole U.S.A. Some dirtbags, you can't return to sender."

Vega's cell phone rang in his pocket. He looked at the screen, assuming it was Molina calling about the wallet. But it wasn't Molina. It was Adele's best friend, Paola Rosado. Vega picked up on the first ring. His mind raced at all the terrible reasons Paola—instead of Adele—would be calling him.

Never could he have imagined the real one.

Chapter 31

The cops in the station house acted like schoolkids when Officer Bale brought Adele inside. All conversation stopped. They flattened themselves against the walls, mouth breathing as Bale led her down the hall for booking. She could feel their eyes watching her while they pretended not to. She had a sense the entire station had heard the report over the radio. They all knew what she'd been stopped for.

Adele tried to hold her head up with dignity and remind herself that she'd never used heroin in her life. She'd barely puffed a joint—and that wasn't until she got to Harvard. She was so boringly clean, the first time she tried pot, she choked on the fumes, got nauseous, and ended up nursing a Diet Pepsi while everyone else laughed over nothing and stuffed their faces with potato chips.

This was a sham arrest. In time, everyone would know that.

In the meantime, how would she explain this to Sophia? Her ten-year-old was bound to find out. Arrests were a matter of public record. This one was likely to spark the interest of the local press. Not to mention a barely veiled mention on the Lake Holly Moms Facebook page. Parents would gossip. Kids would overhear.

Bale walked her over to a bench in the hallway. He un-cuffed her hands from behind her back. Adele felt a burn-ing in her shoulders and pins and needles along her biceps.

"Sit," said Bale. Adele obeyed and Bale cuffed one wrist to the bench. Then he walked away.

"Wait. You're leaving me?" she asked. "I want to call my lawyer."

When people say, *I have the kind of best friend who'd spring me from jail, no questions asked,* they mean Paola Rosado. Literally. Not that Adele ever expected to take her up on it.

"This isn't the Hilton," Bale growled. "You'll get your call when I'm ready."

Lake Holly wasn't a hotspot of crime, especially on a Sun-day evening. There were two uniformed officers sitting at a counter, doing paperwork. The entire detectives' division and all the brass had gone home. The place looked dead. Adele was sure Bale was doing this just to humiliate her.

Nobody spoke to her. She was a bag of trash to them. Only Fitzgerald, the rookie, seemed mildly uncomfortable with the situation.

"You want a coffee?" he offered.

"No. Thank you," said Adele. "What I want is to call my lawyer." Adele had left her handbag in her car. Her wallet, keys, and cell phone were inside. She had noth-ing—not even a way to reach her daughter and tell her where she was. She was glad she knew Paola's cell number by heart.

It took twenty minutes for Bale to appear again. He was nursing a can of Red Bull when he returned.

"I want to call my lawyer," Adele repeated.

"You don't need a lawyer," said Bale. "You can go home right now."

Adele waited. She knew there was a catch.

"Just sign an affidavit that the heroin is yours and I'll

get you a desk appearance ticket," Bale assured her. "Get you released on your own recognizance. It's a first offense. The judge is just going to order you into treatment, anyway."

He was lying and Adele knew it. He didn't catch her with one baggie of heroin. He caught her with 140 baggies. Felony weight. Either way—one baggie or a 140—Adele wasn't confessing to anything.

"I want my lawyer," she said again.

Bale rocked on the balls of his feet. Like a lot of weight lifters, he didn't look especially agile. All those muscles might pack strength, but they made him look awkward and heavy-footed. He let out a tense breath of air like he'd just bench-pressed a buffalo.

"You want to do it the hard way? Fine. Let's get this over with."

He took out a key and unlocked the cuff that was attached to a ring on the bench. Then he attached it to her other wrist in front. He walked her down the hall to a small room with a glass window that looked out on the detectives' bullpen. He pushed her shoulders down in a chair across from him and powered up a computer. He scrolled the screen until he came to what looked like some kind of intake form. He asked Adele for her full name, address, Social Security number, and date of birth. He pecked them into the computer without looking at her. The glow of the screen lit up a look of surprise in his beady eyes as something opened on a window in the right-hand corner.

"You were arrested before?"

Adele didn't answer. It was all there. When she was at Harvard, she'd participated in a demonstration against stop-and-frisk tactics being used in Cambridge on people of color. She'd been arrested on a misdemeanor charge of unlawful assembly. The citation was almost twenty years old.

Bale ran a hand across his shaved head and smiled at her like a shark zeroing in on prey. "Sure you don't want to reconsider my offer? You go to trial, it's going to be on felony weight."

Adele didn't answer. Bale gave up and finished typing in her basic information. Then he uncuffed her hands and scanned her prints into a digital scanner. At least she wouldn't have ink-smudged hands. When Bale was finished, he stood her up in front of a height board and took front and profile photographs. Even if the case was dismissed, Adele's prints and mug shot would forever show up in the system.

"You know," said Bale, while he was setting up the shots. "You give me your dealer on this dope, I could make this whole case a lot easier on you. Hell, you probably know half a dozen dealers in Lake Holly through that immigrant center of yours. You could pick one out at random."

Was that what this was about? Adele wondered. Had she been set up because the cops thought some immigrants were dealing heroin and figured she had insider knowledge?

Bale couldn't delay the inevitable. He took Adele over to a phone on the counter, punched nine to get an outside line, then let her make her call. Adele got Paola on the first ring. Her best friend was rightly shocked and promised to be over as soon as possible.

"Can you make two phone calls for me first?" asked Adele. "Can you call Peter and tell him what's happened. Tell him not to tell Sophia. Just say I had car trouble and I need her to stay with him tonight."

"Of course."

"And can you also call Jimmy for me?"

"Will do."

Bale walked Adele down to the basement holding cells after she'd made her call. He unlocked a metal door and swung it open. A stench of sweat, mixed with the odor of mildew and urine, assaulted her. The heating ducts thrummed overhead.

There were three cells, measuring about six feet by nine, each with a concrete bunk covered over in a thin, ripped vinyl pad that Adele didn't even want to sit on, much less lie down on. Across from the bunk was a stainless-steel toilet—right there in the open for every cop on camera to watch. There were no windows—only fluorescent lights that blazed twenty-four-seven, and a TV in a corner tuned to whatever the cops wanted it tuned to. Right now, it was Fox News.

God, she hated Fox News.

Adele was relieved that at least she was the only one down here on a Sunday evening.

"When is Judge Keppel coming in for the arraignment?" asked Adele.

Bale unlocked the cell closest to the door and motioned for Adele to step inside. He slammed the bars shut with a little too much gusto. "Sometime tomorrow morning."

"Tomorrow . . . ?" Adele felt a moment of panic surge through her. "But he lives in town. He could come in right now if necessary."

"I'm not calling the judge in on a Sunday evening," said Bale. "Besides, I think he's away for the weekend."

"This is absurd," she fumed. "You could release me on my own recognizance right now and let me just show up tomorrow morning."

Bale gripped the bars as if testing their strength. His neck bulged. His jaw tightened. He was like one giant rubber band pulled too taut.

"You're a lawyer, Adele," he sneered. "Don't tell me you don't know the law. The police have twenty-four hours to bring charges—habeas corpus and all that crap. Which means you got two choices. You can park your corpus here until nine a.m. tomorrow. Or you can take our chauffeur-driven limo to the county lockup."

Not the jail, thought Adele. She wanted to stay as far away from that hellhole as possible.

"I'm staying here until my lawyer can get me out."

"Well then." Bale pushed himself off the bars. "Have a good night."

Paola showed up in under an hour—the longest hour of Adele's life. Bale was out on patrol when she arrived. Fitzgerald, the rookie, brought Adele up from the holding cells and into one of the interrogation rooms. The station didn't have a formal room for suspects and their lawyers to confer.

Paola was already seated at the flimsy Formica-topped table. Her long, glossy black hair was pulled into a tight bun. Her white blouse and navy slacks looked Supreme Court ready. She wore only lipstick this evening—she probably didn't have time to do more. But she looked cool and professional as always.

Growing up, Adele was the girl who sweated every assignment and got places through her fiery intellect and sheer force of will. Paola worked less, charmed more, and ultimately achieved the same success. She went to an Ivy League law school—University of Pennsylvania instead of Harvard. She became a criminal defense attorney at a top law firm. She was on track to make partner in about four years. Adele sometimes wondered if sweating all the small stuff had really worked out in the end.

It certainly didn't look that way now.

"Thank you for coming," said Adele.

"You think I wouldn't? I'm as outraged as you are." Paola opened up a large black leather briefcase and took out a notebook and pen.

"First things first," she said. "I spoke to Peter. He's keeping Sophia for the night. She's angry that you're 'working' again"—Paola lifted her fingers in quote marks—"but she'll survive."

"Until some PTA mom who subscribes to the local online rag reads the arrest log."

"Let's worry about that when it happens, shall we?" said Paola. "I spoke to Jimmy too. He's doing a little leg-work for me." Paola set the notebook and pen in front of her. "Now. Tell me what happened—from the beginning."

Adele gave Paola some background on Edgar Aviles and his situation at the synagogue. Then she walked her through her flat tire, Bale showing up and offering to change it and then finding the bag of heroin bundles when he went to re-trieve the spare.

"Needless to say, I've never seen those bundles before in my life," said Adele. "I don't even know if they *are* heroin. The field test could be bogus. This could be some ridicu-lous prank."

Paola's eyes darkened. She tapped her pen absentmind-edly on her notebook. "I checked with Bale on the phone before I drove in. He tested a second sample here at the station. It also came back positive for heroin and fentanyl. If this goes to trial, I'll insist all of it be tested, but for now, we have to assume we're dealing with about seven grams of the real thing."

Adele cursed under her breath. "I feel like an idiot. I mean, I had no idea there were narcotics in my car. But even so, I'm a criminal defense attorney. I should know better than to allow a police officer access to my car with-out a warrant. What the hell was I thinking?"

"You were a stranded woman with a flat tire and a client's troubles on your mind," said Paola. "You didn't expect to find yourself in this situation. Which reminds me—how exactly *did* Officer Bale come to your rescue?"

"He just happened by."

"I see," said Paola in that slow defense-attorney way. Like Adele, she always viewed the police with suspicion.

"What? You think Bale set me up?" asked Adele. "I watched him open my trunk. I think I'd have noticed if he'd been carrying a bag of heroin."

"True," said Paola. She flicked a manicured hand in front of her. "We probably shouldn't pursue that line of questioning anyway," she reasoned. "It could get ugly unless we had solid proof. And motive. I mean, I get that you and the Lake Holly Police don't have a cuddly relationship. But why on earth would one of them go out of his way to sabotage you? He'd be jeopardizing his own job—and for what?"

"I know," said Adele. "But where does that leave me? *I* didn't put that heroin there. So who did?"

"Have you or La Casa been threatened recently?"

Adele tossed off a laugh. "Try, every week. But it's usually limited to Internet trolling and anonymous letters."

"Still, people around town know your car. They know where you live and work. It's not hard for someone to take a slim jim and pop the lock then unlock your trunk."

"La Casa is under video surveillance," said Adele. "We have so many people in and out of that lot, it would be next to impossible to do all that to my car unnoticed."

"How about at home? You keep your car in the driveway usually, right?"

That was true. Adele's garage was at the back of her property, unattached to her house. Plus, it was filled with junk. It was much easier to park right next to her house. She had no alarm system—inside or out—despite Jimmy constantly badgering her to get one.

"My neighbors live very close to me," said Adele. "Mr. Zimmerman is always keeping an eye on my house."

"He's pushing ninety, Adele. He probably goes to bed after *Wheel of Fortune*."

"But still," Adele countered. "It's a big chance to take."

"Not if someone knows your schedule," Paola countered. "Maybe saw you drive away in Jimmy's truck. When's the last time you left your car unattended in your driveway for all or most of a night?"

"Last night," said Adele. "Jimmy had a wedding gig in Broad Plains. We took his truck. It had all his gear. We came back very late. But who would know that?"

"I don't know," Paola admitted. "I'm just spinning my wheels here." Her eyes lit up with another idea. "Has any mechanic worked on your car recently?"

"I've had my oil changed—stuff like that. But nothing where they'd need to pop the trunk. Besides, that's a lot of heroin. If a mechanic put it there, wouldn't he try to get it back?"

"He may have," said Paola. "And been unsuccessful."

Both women went quiet for a moment. Adele dropped her head into her hands. "I'm scared, Paola. This could affect my whole career, not to mention that I could lose custody of Sophia."

"I wouldn't go there just yet," said Paola. "You are well-known in this town. People respect you. They also know you may be a target for some. I think we can work this out."

"But even if we do," said Adele, "I've got a more immediate problem: Edgar Aviles. He's got an order of removal against him. If I don't get him down to ICE's Broad Plains office first thing tomorrow, he's as good as gone."

"Can someone else do it for you?"

"All his documents are in my car," said Adele. "The police have impounded it. Even if someone else drove him down tomorrow and argued on his behalf, they'd have none of his paperwork. It would be an automatic rejection. ICE would take him into custody right then and there."

"What if he just stays where he is in the synagogue until you can get his papers back?"

"And ask the synagogue to go against a judicial warrant?" Adele shook her head. "There are people on the board who aren't comfortable giving him temporary sanctuary—even without the warrant," Adele explained. "If

ICE comes with the power of U.S. law behind them, they'll feel obliged to turn him over."

"Okay. I get it," said Paola. "We need that paperwork and we need it right away."

"Bale's not going to let you have it," said Adele. "He hates La Casa and everything it stands for."

"And unfortunately, he's under no legal requirement to produce anything from the car since he could claim it's part of the investigation." Paola pulled out her phone. "That's why we need Judge Keppel."

"Bale said he's out of town."

"Well, fortunately, we're not dependent on Officer *Bale's* word on things." Paola punched in a number and spoke into the phone. "I'm with her now," she said. "Did you find Keppel? Well, better than nothing. I'll let you tell her."

Paola handed over her phone. "It's Jimmy."

Adele took the phone and held it to her ear. She'd been so strong all this time but hearing his voice, she wanted to dissolve into tears.

"Nena? Are you okay?"

Adele cleared her throat. "About as well as can be expected. I'm sorry to get you involved."

"I wish I could do more," he told her. "Listen, I called around to find Keppel. He's at some Boys and Girls Club fundraiser at the Wickford Country Club this evening. I'm headed there now to try to sweet-talk him into coming into the station and handling everything tonight."

"Thanks," said Adele.

"And *nena?*"

"Yeah?"

"One question. Those envelopes of heroin—did they contain any stamp on them?"

"Stamp?"

"Like a brand name. *Lucky. Zombie. Thunder.* Used to be, all the dealers liked to stamp their product to build a following. Now, they don't so much because they're afraid cops will be able to link all their product."

Adele thought about it. "No," she said finally. "I didn't see a stamp on any of them. But the little baggies were distinctive."

"How so?"

"They had a pale blue line running down one side. It was very faint."

"All right," said Vega. "Sit tight and take a deep breath. We'll get through this, I promise."

Chapter 32

Vega pulled his aging Ford pickup to the wrought-iron gates of the Wickford Country Club. A parking attendant appeared at his window.

"Sir? Are you a guest?" The attendant took in Vega's dark khakis, polo shirt, and windbreaker. Vega flashed his badge.

"I'm looking for a judge named Clarence Keppel. He's supposed to be attending the fundraiser tonight. You know who he is? You remember parking his car?"

"No."

Vega handed the valet his keys. "Never mind. I'll find him myself."

The Wickford Country Club was a sprawling turn-of-the-century mansion surrounded by a golf course, tennis courts, pools, and cabanas. Vega had been to "the Wick," as it was called, only twice. Both times were on Adele's arm, at fundraisers.

He followed a footpath past cherry blossoms in gaudy bloom. His phone rang in his pocket. *Danny Molina*. He'd been so distracted with Adele's arrest that he forgot he'd asked Molina to check out whether that wallet he'd found in Talia's drawer belonged to Deisy. Vega stopped beneath a tree and retrieved the call.

"Jesus, Jimmy—what did you get me into here?" Molina asked by way of greeting. "You told me to run that wallet by Deisy's mother. You never said you found it in Crowley's house."

"So the wallet's hers?"

"Yeah. It's hers. And that's not all," said Molina. "Deisy's best friend told me Deisy lost it, and her phone, a couple of nights before she ran away. Doing—get this—undercover work for a federal agent."

"You're shittin' me." Vega got a stern look from a couple strolling past.

"I'm not saying it's true, Jimmy. I'm telling you what her best friend told me. This girl wouldn't even speak to me after Deisy ran away. But now that Deisy's dead, she poured out this crazy-ass story Deisy swore her to secrecy over. She said some federal agent told Deisy he could get her permanent asylum if she went to this rich guy's house and recorded herself having sex with him. By the way, those 'rich guy' words are hers, not mine."

"Did she give you a name? A contact? A physical description?"

"The story's secondhand. She wasn't present for any of it," said Molina. "But I don't think she's blowing smoke. She said the man knew Deisy's whole immigration history. He showed her a letter of removal if she didn't comply."

Music wafted out of the country club. A light, jazzy cocktail riff. Men in dinner jackets smoked cigars beneath strands of white lights glittering on the porch, backslapping one another with false bravado. Vega felt a million miles away.

"Where's the removal letter?" Vega asked Molina.

"I don't know. The friend doesn't know. And neither does Hilda. I'd say it's the stuff of an overactive teenage imagination. Except you showed me Deisy's name on that dead gangbanger's list. And now I find out her wallet was inside Crowley's house."

Molina dropped his voice. "You know what this looks like, don't you, Jimmy?"

A cherry blossom fell to Vega's shoulder. He brushed it off. Neither he nor Molina wanted to utter their biggest fear: This wasn't just a "rich guy" Deisy recorded on her missing phone. It was the DA.

"Let's take this one step at a time," said Vega. "Shoot me a copy of this girl's statement and Hilda's ID of the wallet. Leave any mention of the implications out of it. Just straight fact. We're a long way from proving anything."

"I hope you're right," said Molina. "I've got young kids, Jimmy. I need this job."

Vega disconnected. His head was spinning. If Deisy's friend's fantastical tale was true, then the teenager was coerced into becoming a human trafficking victim by someone pretending to be a federal agent. Someone with access to the ICE database who wanted dirt on Crowley. But that scenario created more questions than it answered. How did Deisy's wallet end up in the back of Talia's sweater drawer? Did Lissette find it? Did she walk in on Crowley and Deisy?

Most importantly, where was the phone?

Vega tried to push those thoughts out of his head and concentrate on finding Judge Keppel and getting Adele out of jail. That was priority one at the moment. He followed the crowd of men in tuxedos and women in glittering evening attire into the clubhouse, which could only be described as robber-baron chic. Persian rugs. Chandeliers. Gilded-framed oil paintings of rolling hillsides and fox hunts. Waiters walked through the crowd with trays of hors d'oeuvres and flutes of champagne while a pianist, bassist, and drummer rolled out fine, sweet jazz.

Beyond the room, Vega could see an even bigger room decked out in white linens, gold-rimmed china, and towering vases of fresh flowers. The party was still in the cocktail hour—which was bad news for Vega. He'd be pulling

Keppel away from an excellent meal that the judge probably contributed handsomely toward.

Vega studied the sign welcoming guests to the fiftieth
annual Boys and Girls Club Gala. Adele always joked that
"gala" stood for "Give Away Lots of Assets." Not that she
herself didn't depend on the same thing for La Casa.

"You should be wearing oxfords."

The comment was delivered in such a flat, robotic voice,
Vega was certain the speaker was addressing someone else.
Then he heard the comment again and turned. A young,
heavyset man with curly dark hair stood close to Vega, staring at Vega's black duty boots, still encrusted with mud on
their rubber soles from his trek to the Brighton Aqueduct
this morning.

"Pardon?"

The young man's eyes stayed focused on Vega's shoes.
"Those are tactical boots. Only police officers wear those."

Vega realized belatedly that the young man had cogni-
tive issues.

"You're right. They're tactical boots. I'm a cop." Vega
reached into his back pocket and produced his badge. He
thought the young man might be excited but nothing registered on his face.

"You're supposed to wear oxfords to a formal event.
Not Derby shoes or loafers. Or tactical boots."

"Thanks. I'll remember that." Vega wouldn't know an
oxford from a Derby. But it occurred to him suddenly who
this young man might be. "Are you Glen Crowley's son?"

"Yes," he said woodenly. "What size shoe are you?"

"Nine-and-a-half medium," said Vega. "You work at a
shoe store in town, don't you?"

"Berber Shoes."

"I know the store," said Vega. "I used to take my daughter
there to get shoes when she was little. What's your name?"

"Adam. I'm a twelve wide. My mother says I'm a difficult fit."

Vega wondered if she was referring to more than Adam's feet. "Do you know a judge named Clarence Keppel?"

"What's his shoe size?"

"I don't know." *Ay, puñeta!* Vega didn't have time for this right now. He scanned the crowd for an old white man with thinning white hair and a neck like a turkey.

He had only about a hundred matches.

"Adam." A female voice called out. Vega turned as a woman with silver-blond hair strode toward them, a lean, striking figure in a dark blue off-the-shoulder gown. She offered Vega a questioning smile that was more polite than friendly.

"I hope my son wasn't bothering you," she drawled in a soft, Southern twang. "Are you . . . security? I didn't think we'd hired security."

We? So Charlene Beech Crowley was one of the organizers of this charity dinner. Vega wasn't surprised. Even after her divorce from Glen, Vega regularly saw her name attached to society events. The Junior League. Museum fundraisers. Scholarship grants.

"I don't know if you hired security, ma'am, but I'm not it." Vega flashed his badge and introduced himself. "I'm looking for Judge Keppel. Clarence Keppel? I understand he's here tonight?"

"I believe I saw him earlier. Is there a problem?"

"Nothing Judge Keppel can't solve." Vega smiled as he said the words. He didn't want to offer up any details, but he didn't want to be rude either. He spotted Keppel on the other side of the room, near the jazz trio.

"There he is." Vega went to step forward. Charlene thrust an arm out to her son. It was a subtle gesture, but one guaranteed to deliver the point—*I don't want a police officer wandering through our private event.*

"Adam?" she drawled in her sweetest Southern voice. "Can you please ask the judge to come over here? He's the one standing next to the woman in the red sandals. He's wearing the black wing-tipped oxfords."

"Those aren't oxfords," Adam grunted. "They're brogues."

The young man trudged across the room without another word. Charlene's pale skin flushed with color.

"You'll have to excuse my son," she said. "He's autistic. He has his own . . . interests, I guess you'd say."

"It's totally fine."

A waiter passed by with a silver tray full of white wine. He stopped in front of Vega and Charlene—an awkward moment. But like a good hostess, Charlene motioned for Vega to take a glass.

"No, thank you," said Vega.

"Ah. You're on duty."

Vega didn't answer. He didn't want to dissuade her—or Keppel—who might be more reluctant to come over if he thought the problem was personal.

Charlene took a glass for herself, sipped it, and ran his name across her lips. "Vega . . . Detective Jimmy Vega . . . I've heard that name before."

Vega suspected she knew his name the same way everyone did—from that shooting last December. He felt the heat rise in his cheeks and changed the subject.

"I'm helping the Lake Holly Police with the investigation." Vega didn't mention Talia's name. He could be discreet too.

"Of course," said Charlene. "Two detectives interviewed me this afternoon."

"Louis Greco and Omar Sanchez."

"I think that was their names," said Charlene. "Nice gentlemen. The older one has a fondness for my sweet potato pie."

"That would be Greco," Vega laughed. "You may have a regular customer."

"I promised I'd bring a pie down to the station for him

sometime," said Charlene. "Adam and I brought over some corn bread and muffins yesterday morning. Glen is so grateful for the care and consideration y'all are giving him. It's such a terrible tragedy."

Vega couldn't hide his surprise. "Pardon me, ma'am, but isn't this the woman who . . ." His voice trailed off. He didn't know how to say it in such a genteel setting.

". . . Auditioned for the part of wife number two while Glen was still married to wife number one?"

That was a classy way of putting it. Vega wished he could have been half as classy when Wendy "auditioned" Alan—and then awarded the man with twin boys for the effort.

Vega glanced at Charlene but she kept her eyes on the crowd. Her lips barely moved. Her smile never faltered. "I can't say I approved of his choice," she said. "But there was no ill will between any of us, Detective. If anything, I liked Talia. She was extremely kind to Adam."

"You're not angry? Bitter?" Vega felt like he was showing his own hand. He pulled back before he said something he'd regret.

"Of course I was upset," she said. "But there are worse things than that."

"I can't think of one."

"Humiliation. A loss of social decorum." Her jaw tightened imperceptibly. "There is nothing more pathetic than someone who allows private matters to escape into the public domain." Charlene offered Vega a slow, appraising look. "Are you asking as a police officer? Or as a man?"

"Both, I guess," Vega admitted.

"Mmm." She pressed her pale pink lips together. "I've learned to forgive and forget. It's much less taxing on the mind."

Adam did not return to Vega and Charlene. Vega noticed him standing in a corner by the piano, staring at the musicians' black lace-up sneakers. Vega was sure Adam didn't approve.

"Detective?" Keppel's small blue eyes tightened as he walked over. "Something with the case that can't wait until tomorrow? I was just about to head into dinner here."

"Sorry, Judge. Can I speak to you privately for a moment?"

Keppel turned to Charlene. "Keep my dinner warm."

"My pleasure," she replied.

Vega wondered if it would be anybody's "pleasure" when Keppel found out he would likely not be returning.

Keppel suggested they walk outside. Night was closing in. The earth had gone shadowy, cut only by the twinkle of security lights along the circular driveway and the reflected golden glow from inside the clubhouse. Above, the sky remained a bruise of colors. The soft hues of overripe fruit and spilled wine. A cool breeze fanned the manicured grass, a current of air with Canada in its address.

"I thought the Talia Crowley case was being closed down?" said Keppel. "Treated as a suicide?"

"It is," said Vega. "For now, at least. Actually, I'm here for another reason. This afternoon, Adele Figueroa was arrested."

Vega had been in front of enough judges to know how their minds worked. They were used to controlling the flow of information and forming their own opinions. If Vega spilled out everything at once—the crime, the circumstances, his belief that Adele was innocent and possibly even framed—he'd tick off the judge. Maybe even turn Keppel against Vega for coming over here like this and using his leverage. So Vega stood very still and waited for the judge to ask the questions.

"Arrested? Hmmm." Keppel stopped in his tracks. "Was there a civil disturbance in town today? A protest march?"

"No," said Vega. "She was meeting with a client about an

immigration matter." Vega decided to leave out the "sanctu-ary" stuff. Keppel might not approve. "When she left, she noticed she had a flat tire. Officer Bale happened by and of-fered to put her spare on for her. When he pulled apart her trunk to get to the spare, he found a bag full of heroin."

Vega kept his words flat and devoid of emotion. He could see he had the judge's attention.

"How much heroin are we talking about?"

"Seven grams," said Vega. He didn't need to add "felony weight." They both knew.

Keppel whistled but said nothing else. Vega knew what he wanted to add—that Adele had never used heroin in her life. But Vega could prejudice the judge and Keppel could end up recusing himself as a result. Vega didn't want that. Still, he had to keep up the momentum.

"She's in a Lake Holly holding cell now, Judge. Her lawyer's at the station house. They're talking about keep-ing her overnight until you can arraign her tomorrow morning. She has an important meeting with her client at nine a.m. at ICE that she'll miss. If there was any way you could see her tonight—"

"You mean, inconvenience *my* schedule so she doesn't have to inconvenience hers."

"No, sir. Not at all," said Vega. "This isn't about Adele. This is about her client. If she misses that meeting, then *he* misses it and it could be very damaging to his legal situa-tion."

"I see."

A door to the clubhouse opened and someone stepped outside to smoke a cigarette. Laughter and chatter poured onto the lawn and then died just as quickly as the door shut again. Keppel turned to the clubhouse, his pale, scrawny face and turkey neck bathed in the glow. He seemed to be debating his choices.

"This heroin," said Keppel. "Do you know if it had a

stamp on it? A brand name?" Vega noticed Keppel didn't ask where Adele got it from or if she got it. He was trying to keep himself neutral.

"I asked," said Vega. "She said it didn't have a stamp on it. A lot of the stuff doesn't these days. Dealers don't want to get caught if one of their buyers OD's. She did say she noticed a pale blue line down one side of the dime bags when Officer Bale pulled the bundles out of the car."

Keppel's face pivoted from the clubhouse to Vega. "A pale blue line? Nothing else?"

"That's correct. I'm out of narcotics investigation these days," Vega admitted. "The pale blue line means nothing to me."

Keppel sucked on his teeth. Vega had a sense the pale blue line did indeed mean something to him, but judicial impartiality prevented him from explaining.

"You're a county detective, correct?"

"Yes, sir."

"Call someone on your narcotics squad and mention it to them. This shouldn't be coming from me." Keppel looked back at the clubhouse and shook his head. "I'm going to miss a lovely dinner."

Chapter 33

"Okay," said Paola as she took a seat next to Adele at the defense table. "Judge Keppel's in the building and changing into his robes. McMillan's downstairs getting coffee with the court stenographer. The judge ordered them in." Arthur McMillan was the town prosecutor.

"Where's Jimmy?" Adele's cell phone was still in her handbag—which was still in her impounded car. She had to rely on Paola to communicate with him.

"He's got a call in to a detective in county narcotics."

"Why?" Adele couldn't see where anything another cop said could help her right now.

"He didn't say. But he promised he'd be up here as soon as he's through."

Paola pulled a yellow pad full of notes from her briefcase and settled herself at the table. The courtroom was on the second floor of the Lake Holly police station, up a flight of worn steps. There was a judge's bench, two tables—one for the defense and one for the prosecution—a table on the side for the court stenographer, and a bunch of flags: U.S., state, and county. The whole place resembled an elementary school auditorium but without any spectators. The few seats behind the tables were empty at this hour on a Sunday night.

This little show was just for Adele.

"Where was the judge?" asked Adele. "At home?"

"No," said Paola. "Just about to sit down to a charity dinner at the Wickford Country Club."

Adele groaned. "I cheated him out of a good meal. He's going to be hungry—and angry."

"Let's hope Jimmy got him here tactfully."

The rear door opened. Adele and Paola turned. Arthur McMillan grunted out something that vaguely sounded like "hello" and walked over to the prosecutor's table with his paper cup of coffee. In court, he normally favored three-piece suits and a liberal use of aftershave. This evening, he was wearing only dark khakis, an oxford shirt, and a hastily knotted tie.

The court clerk, an older woman Adele had seen before with baby blue glasses on a chain around her neck, took a seat at her table and texted something on her phone. She was here but she wasn't. This was just a quick way to earn a little extra overtime.

McMillan settled himself at the prosecution table and angled his body in Adele and Paola's direction. "Never thought I'd see you sitting there, Adele, if you don't mind my saying."

"We mind, Mr. McMillan," said Paola. "I invite you to reserve your statements for the judge."

Adele flushed. She felt acutely embarrassed. She knew she was innocent, but she felt like someone was holding a sign above her that read: GUILTY.

It wasn't the first time that Adele had internalized the opinions of others, right or wrong. When she was twelve, shy and bookish, two classmates that other girls considered "cool" took Adele under their wing. One day, she accompanied them to a local five-and-dime and watched in horror as the two girls stuffed candy bars and chewing gum down their blouses. When the store manager shouted at them, they ran. Not Adele. She stood there with empty pockets, frozen by the enormity of what she'd just witnessed.

The store manager clasped a hand on Adele's shoulder and prodded her to the back of the store where he made her pull down her pants to prove she hadn't stolen anything. Then he proceeded to feel inside her underwear.

"To make sure you're not hiding any candy." He didn't stop touching her until she began to cry. Then he pushed her away. "Mexican trash," he hissed. "You better not tell your parents you're a thief. Your whole family could get deported."

Adele told nobody what happened to her in the five-and-dime that day. She was easy prey—the poor daughter of undocumented immigrants. She knew it. Her parents knew it. Her Harvard Law degree was supposed to protect her against such things now. And yet here she was again, small and defenseless before powerful men who made her feel guilty for things she hadn't done.

A door opened behind the bench and Judge Keppel climbed the steps to his seat. He hooked a pair of wire-rimmed glasses over his face and banged his gavel.

"Court is now in session. We are presiding over the arraignment of Adele Eugenia Figueroa on the charge of criminal possession of a controlled substance in the fifth degree, a class D felony. Ms. Rosado, how does your client plead?"

Paola rose. "Your Honor, we would like to request that these charges be set aside. There is no evidence my client abuses drugs or had any knowledge that those drugs were in her vehicle—"

McMillan interrupted. "Your Honor, even children understand that possession is nine-tenths of the law. Ms. Figueroa is the legal owner of the Toyota Prius in which the drugs were found. She gave Officer Bale permission to open the trunk of her car. Those facts are indisputable."

"She is a pillar in this community," Paola shot back. "A mother of a ten-year-old child. The founder of La Casa. An attorney—"

"Ms. Rosado," Keppel interrupted. "Ms. Figueroa's pedigree doesn't automatically exempt her from anything here. Sadly, I've seen a lot of 'pillars' in this community succumb to heroin addiction lately."

"Your Honor, if I may," said McMillan. "Prosecution realizes that this is a first-time offense. The people are willing to reduce the charge from felony possession to misdemeanor possession with a recommendation of probation in return for a guilty plea right now and an agreement that the defendant submit to drug counseling and regular testing during the probation period."

Adele was thankful that Paola didn't even entertain the offer. "Your Honor, my client is willing to submit to a drug test right now to prove she's not using—"

"Your client has been locked up since this afternoon," McMillan countered. "Maybe she planned to go home and nod off."

"She's not a drug abuser," said Paola. "She maintains that those drugs were planted in her car without her knowledge or consent. She is a defense attorney, Your Honor. Do you really think she would have consented to Officer Bale opening her trunk if she'd known those drugs were in there?"

"She can plead to a misdemeanor and she won't automatically get disbarred," said McMillan. "I don't see what the problem is."

Keppel turned to McMillan. "Mr. McMillan—your offer to the defense is a fair one. But this is an arraignment, not a plea-bargaining session. Let's take this one step at a time. Ms. Rosado—has EMS ever been dispatched to your client's house for issues related to an overdose?"

Adele knew that Keppel was asking a question he wasn't

technically allowed to ask because it violated patient privacy. But she also understood that he was trying to establish whether Adele did indeed have a drug problem.

Paola looked at Adele. "No," said Adele. "I have never had EMS visit my house for any reason other than the time my daughter Sophia fell down the stairs about four years ago."

"Is anyone in your extended family dealing with any drug issues?" Keppel realized he was overreaching. He clarified. "I'm just trying to figure out if there is a reason for those drugs being in your car without your knowledge."

"No, Your Honor," Adele said again. "To my knowledge, no one in my family or friend circle is abusing drugs."

The rear door of the courtroom swung open. Adele turned and saw Vega striding down the center aisle with a piece of paper in his right hand.

"Your Honor," said Vega. "I have some information that I think might figure into the court's consideration of the charges against Ms. Figueroa." He spoke formally, without glancing in Adele's direction. Adele understood. To help her, he had to act as neutral as possible.

"Please enter your name, title, and reasons for being here into the record," said Keppel.

"James Vega. Detective, county police," he said. "I have nineteen years' experience as a police officer. I am currently assigned to the homicide task force but prior to this, I worked five years as an undercover officer in the narcotics division." Then, belatedly, Vega added, "I am also familiar with the defendant."

"You are dating the defendant, is that correct?" asked Keppel.

"Yes, Your Honor. I am. But I'm not here to vouch for her character, although it's unimpeachable. I'm here to make the court aware of the pedigree of the heroin found in the defendant's possession."

Vega and Keppel locked eyes for a moment. Adele got the sense the judge knew what was coming.

"You have examined the evidence?" asked Keppel.

"I have."

Adele wondered which officer cut Vega a break. Definitely not Bale.

"I sent a cell phone snapshot of one of the bundles to Lieutenant Nicholas Giordano, a top-ranking officer in our county narcotics squad," Vega explained. "Lieutenant Giordano just texted this reply. May I approach the bench and show you his response?"

"Please," said Keppel.

Vega handed his cell phone to the judge.

"Your Honor, as you can see, Lieutenant Giordano says the pale blue stripe on the side of the bundle is identical to a heroin/fentanyl mixture seized six months ago in a multi-agency raid. A raid Lieutenant Giordano and his officers were involved in."

"The dealers could have made more," said McMillan.

Vega shook his head. "Lieutenant Giordano says the ring was closed down. The players are in jail. The only way someone could get this heroin right now would be from a police evidence locker."

McMillan was on his feet. "Your Honor—there is no evidence of any kind that a police officer planted that heroin." He gestured to Vega. "Unless the detective here is telling you he's the one who did the planting."

"Of course not!" said Vega. "I'm not even assigned to narcotics anymore. What I'm saying is that this particular brand of heroin and fentanyl disappeared off the streets six months ago. Nobody's seen it since. What junkie do you know who buys fourteen bundles of heroin and then just stores it away? That stuff isn't hers."

Keppel handed Vega back his phone. "Please make a printout of the lieutenant's statement at the adjournment of this proceeding so that it can be included in the record."

"Yes, Your Honor. Thank you."

Keppel folded his hands in front of him and sat like that for a long moment. In his black robes, his beady blue eyes magnified behind wire-rimmed glasses, he looked like an enormous vulture eyeing his prey.

"Well, this certainly begs the question, how did that heroin end up in Ms. Figueroa's car?"

Silence. Adele and Paola knew better than to fall into the trap of pointing fingers. However much it looked like Adele was set up, they'd undo all the court's good will by suggesting that without proof. And yet Keppel was too good a jurist not to be troubled by the fact that the drugs may have been in police hands before they were in the trunk of Adele's car.

Keppel addressed the prosecutor.

"Mr. McMillan? Please inform the Lake Holly PD that I will be making a recommendation that the district attorney's office investigate the origin of these confiscated narcotics. Lieutenant Giordano's statements are troubling."

"Yes, Your Honor," said the prosecutor.

Keppel's eyes then zeroed in on Adele. "Ms. Figueroa, I'm inclined to think that these drugs are not yours, despite being found in your vehicle. While I'm disinclined to countermand a police officer's arrest, in this case, I'm going to make an exception—"

"Thank you, Judge—"

"Not so fast." Keppel raised a finger. "I'm releasing you on your own recognizance and setting a court date for three months from now. In the meantime, you will submit to routine drug testing. If the tests all turn out negative, I will vacate the charges in three months and order the arrest stricken from your record."

"Your Honor," said Paola. "My client will have this hanging over her head until then—"

"That is unfortunate, Ms. Rosado. But if your client is

as clean as you say she is, she has nothing to worry about. It's an inconvenience—nothing more."

"Your Honor," Adele said, jumping up. She knew she was supposed to go through Paola, but this was too important not to address herself.

"What is it, Ms. Figueroa?" Keppel asked wearily.

"The police impounded my car—"

"I will sign an order of release," said the judge. "But it's up to them whether they want to release the car now or in the morning."

"But my wallet and keys are in there," said Adele. "Along with a folder of important client documents."

"I'm sure if you explain the situation, the officers can give you back those things, even if they can't release your car until morning." Keppel banged his gavel. "Court adjourned. Hopefully, I can get back to the Wick for dessert."

Chapter 34

It took another hour for Vega to cajole the Lake Holly Police into releasing Adele's car. He pointed out that Adele hadn't been charged with a felony—and hopefully wouldn't be if she stuck to the terms Keppel had outlined and her lawyer, Paola, had agreed to.

"I have to pee in a cup for three months to prove what anybody who knows me already knows?" Adele grumbled as they left the station.

"Better peeing in a cup than peeing in a jail cell toilet," said Vega.

Adele's car wasn't at the police station. It was in an impound lot on the north end of town. Adele said her goodbyes and thank-yous to Paola. Then Vega drove her there. They had to call a number on the fence and wait for the tow truck driver to come back from his nightly rounds.

They sat in Vega's truck with the heater on. The rain today had been followed by a temperature drop.

"Maybe we should come back tomorrow," Vega suggested. "It's not like you can drive your car far anyway until you get a new tire."

"If it was just a matter of getting my car back, I wouldn't have even dragged you here," said Adele. "But all of Edgar's paperwork for his administrative stay is inside. I've got to fetch it and find someone who'll lend me their car so I can drive him down to Broad Plains tomorrow morning."

"Can't someone else handle things for once?" Vega could hear the exasperation in his voice. He was tired. He thought Adele took on too much. "What about La Casa's attorney? Frank what's-his-name?"

"Espinosa." Vega could tell it irritated her that he'd forgotten the man's last name. He never forgot a witness's. "He can't," she said. "His wife's going in for surgery. Besides, either way, I need the paperwork."

The tow truck driver showed up about twenty minutes later. Even though Adele's charges had technically been set aside, she still had to pay for the tow: $75. At least someone had put the doughnut on so she could drive home. Vega followed her back to the house and carried the big accordion folder of papers inside, hefting them onto her dining table. She began pawing through them. Vega gently kissed her neck.

"*Nena,* go to bed. You'll handle that in the morning."

She didn't seem to be listening. She tilted the folder sideways and allowed the contents to spill across the table, nearly knocking over her colorful Talavera pottery candlesticks.

"It's not here," she said in a tight voice.

"What's not here?"

"Edgar Aviles's Salvadoran passport. His birth certificate. They were in this folder when I left Beth Shalom."

"You want me to check the car? Maybe they fell out?"

"They didn't fall out."

"Are you sure?"

"Of course I'm sure!" she snapped. "Without his original birth certificate and passport, there's no way ICE will grant him a stay of removal tomorrow."

"Can you delay the application?"

"I delay the application and Edgar is as good as deported," said Adele. "He was nearly deported on Saturday. It was only because those two goons didn't have a signed judge's order that I was able to intervene. Tomorrow morning, they'll have the order. What then?" Adele slammed a fist down on the table. Vega had never seen her so angry.

"God damn that Ryan Bale! I know that bastard took those documents."

"Adele . . ." Vega patted the air, trying to calm her down. He didn't want to say what he was thinking—that she was being paranoid. Sure, the majority of cops Vega knew held strict law-and-order views. They didn't like lawbreakers of any kind—and that included illegal immigrants. But that didn't mean Ryan Bale would cross the line and tamper with evidence. That was a felony. A firing offense. And for what? Edgar Aviles was one of millions of illegals in the country. Why would Bale put his job on the line for this one?

"In all likelihood, those documents are somewhere in the impound lot," said Vega. "I'm sure we'll find them tomorrow. I can go back now if you want."

"They're not in the impound lot, Jimmy. I'm sure of it. Bale stole them. Maybe that's what this whole arrest was about."

"Oh, come on." Vega pulled a face. "I don't like the bastard either. But cops don't risk their jobs—their *pensions*—over petty crap like this."

"You think?" She turned to him. "Then explain why Bale tried to bully his way into La Casa on Saturday morning to arrest Aviles after he ran from the two ICE agents who tried to arrest him."

"He was being thorough."

"He'd just gone off-duty, Jimmy. That's more than thorough. Stop with all this 'brothers-in-blue' crap and open your eyes. Something's going on."

Vega stared at his face in the reflected glass of the dining-room windows. The streetlights outside didn't illuminate so much as taint the darkness.

"Look, Adele," Vega began. "I get what you're saying. But why would Bale risk himself like that? What's in it for him? Aviles is a janitor. And—not that you're not a great attorney and all—but I think the guy's going to be deported no matter what you do."

Adele pulled out a dining room chair and sank into it. "You're probably right." She studied her thighs. The seams of her pants looked grimy from the jail cell. There was a spot of something on her blouse. Her makeup had gone blurry around her eyes. Bale had clearly put her through the wringer with this arrest.

"The thing is," said Adele, "I had a bad feeling the moment he pulled up. Like I knew even before he offered to change my tire that something was off. And yet nothing he did was improper. I was standing there the whole time. I saw him open the trunk. I saw him discover those bundles. I even saw him switch on his body camera before he walked to the trunk."

"*Right* before?"

"That's right," said Adele. "Why?"

Vega pulled out another chair and straddled it backward, facing Adele. He braced his hands across the back and balanced his head on his knuckles, deep in thought.

"I was out of uniform before body cams came into being," said Vega. "But other cops I've seen always switch their units on as soon as they get out of their vehicles on a call. Some forget, obviously. But Bale doesn't strike me as the type to forget."

"He did switch it on," said Adele. "Just not until he walked to the trunk."

"What did he do before?"

Adele thought a moment, then rolled her eyes. "He told me the Ecuadorian flag hanging from my rearview mirror is a traffic violation in the state of New York."

"That's all?"

"No . . ." She massaged her forehead. "He walked around the car and checked all my tires."

"Was he visible the whole time?"

"Not the *whole* time," said Adele. "I remember him squatting down on the other side. For a moment I lost sight of him. I figured he was just being thorough. When he stood up, he turned on his camera."

"Huh."

"What's that 'huh'?" asked Adele. "You always say that when you're thinking of something and don't want to tell me."

She was right. Vega took a deep breath. He hated conjecturing like this about a fellow cop.

"Wherever the drugs came from," said Vega, "they were already in your car when Bale pulled up."

"I know that already," said Adele.

"Maybe, so did Bale."

"What?"

"I'm trying to think about how I'd set someone up for a bust," Vega explained. "I'd take a slim jim to their car, pop the trunk, and put the contraband in when they weren't home to catch me. Then I'd stick a nail in their tire. Not too big a nail. Something that would produce a slow leak."

"But I could have developed that flat anywhere."

"Not if I let just enough air out of your tires," said Vega. "I could time it."

"You still wouldn't know where I was," Adele pointed out.

"I would if I put a tracking device in one of your wheel wells—then removed it when I showed up."

Vega let the words hang in the air for a moment. The only sound was the hum of the refrigerator in the kitchen.

"Do you really think that's what he was doing on the other side of my car?"

Vega threw up his hands. "I don't know. This is all me

conjecturing. But this is how I would do it. Those GPS devices are magnetically mounted and small enough to fit into a man's palm, so it wouldn't be hard for him to pretend he's checking out your tires and take the GPS back."

"He knows we can't catch him either," said Adele. "He turned his body cam on after he stood up so there's no proof any of this happened."

"Not . . . quite," said Vega.

"What do you mean, 'not quite'?"

Vega pushed himself out of the chair and paced the floor. It went against every fiber in his being to accuse a fellow cop. For nineteen years, his work life had revolved around trusting his brothers and sisters in uniform. At traffic stops. On stakeouts. When he was working undercover. They held his life in their hands and he held theirs. But he loved and trusted Adele even more. And he knew something was very wrong here.

"Body cams are designed to record thirty seconds of footage before an officer physically turns them on," said Vega. "The idea being that an officer might not remember to switch on his camera in the heat of the moment."

"*Every* body cam?" asked Adele.

"Every one I've ever encountered," said Vega. "There's no audio in those thirty seconds, but there's video."

"So you're saying that whatever Bale did when he was crouched by my wheels would have been recorded?"

"If it was in those thirty seconds before he turned that sucker on, yeah."

"Can we get that footage?"

Vega shook his head. "Not without a court order. If you went to trial, then I imagine, it would probably be part of discovery for your defense."

"So, by not getting charged, Bale walks."

"Wait. Hold up," said Vega. "This is all me spinning wheels. I have no reason to believe Ryan Bale would take a risk like this. For what? So some handyman gets deported?"

"Maybe he's not just a handyman," said Adele. "Maybe he's a witness."

"What do you mean?"

"He told me this afternoon that gangsters are threatening his family," said Adele. "He wouldn't say why—not until he gets a reprieve from deportation. But he seemed genuinely scared. I think there are things he's not telling the police."

About Lissette's disappearance? That would be Vega's guess. If Crowley was entertaining underage prostitutes at the house, Lissette would have known about it. Maybe Aviles did too.

Vega swept a gaze over Aviles's case file now fanned across the table. Crowley had ample reason to want Aviles deported. Vega wouldn't put it past Bale to help grease the skids if he was on the take with the DA. But still—neither of them was ICE. If Aviles was put into priority removal, someone in ICE had to put him there.

"Did Aviles give you any indication why he was put into priority removal?" Vega asked Adele.

"None," she replied. "I know the government's doing away with temporary protected status for Salvadorans. But I have no idea why they targeted Aviles in particular. The letters explain nothing."

"Letters—plural? Aviles was only put into priority removal a week ago."

"Yes, but they've been threatening him for a while."

Vega blinked at her. "ICE doesn't threaten, Adele. They do. Or they do not."

"Well, this time, they threatened. See for yourself."

Adele rose and pawed through the paperwork. "Here's the most recent letter." She handed it to Vega.

The letterhead contained a blue embossed ICE seal at

the top with an eagle logo. It was the letter Aviles showed Vega at the synagogue Friday night, advising him to self-deport immediately or face arrest. Vega had seen the same letter in Michelle's ICE files yesterday. It was signed by Marcus Tyler, one of the two agents involved in his arrest.

"Here's the other from a month ago."

Adele handed Vega a letter with the same logo. Much of the wording was the same, with the exception of the last line demanding that Aviles deport immediately or face arrest.

It did, indeed, appear to be a threat, rather than an immediate demand.

One other thing was different too. The signature. Not Marcus Tyler's. Not Lyle Donovan's. The name was so forgettable that Vega wouldn't have recalled it if not for the fact that the same ICE agent signed the letter in Cesar Zuma's possession when he died.

Vega handed Adele back the letter. He felt hopeful for the first time all day.

"I think I just figured out a way you can help Edgar Aviles."

Chapter 35

"Daniel Wilson," said Vega, pointing to the name of the ICE agent who'd signed the letter to Edgar Aviles.

"What about him?"

"He signed this letter a month ago," said Vega. "There's just one problem. He retired *six* months ago."

"How do you know that?"

"Michelle told me," said Vega. "And that's not all. You know that immigrant who died on the Metro-North tracks yesterday? The one we thought was Aviles?"

"Yes," said Adele. "Cesar Zuma." It figured Adele would make a point of learning the man's name—even if he'd never been a client of La Casa's. She reached out to everyone in the Hispanic community.

"Cesar Zuma had a letter just like this. Signed a month ago by the same Daniel Wilson. And get this—according to ICE's files, Zuma wasn't even slated for immediate removal."

"But Edgar is," said Adele. "Tyler and Donovan—those ICE agents who came for him—mean business."

"I know they mean business," said Vega. "ICE put Aviles into priority removal. But we don't know who made the decision or why. If Michelle can track down Daniel Wilson and prove that either he didn't write that letter or he did but it was misdated or intended for someone else, you might be able to argue for an emergency stay."

"Would Michelle do that? Go to bat for the opposing team?"

Vega winced. "Come on, Adele. It's not like that. She's a good person. And a good cop. She'll do what's right."

Adele lifted an eyebrow. "She and I have different versions of what's right."

"Yeah? Well, you don't know her."

"I thought you didn't either."

That stopped him. Like a wet towel across the face.

"I guess . . ." He didn't know how to put what he was feeling into words. He felt a great comfort in Michelle's presence that he hadn't expected to feel. He hadn't even acknowledged it until this moment.

"Look," said Vega. "Let me worry about Michelle. You just concentrate on Aviles."

"I can't bring him to ICE if they're just going to slap the cuffs on him."

"Then don't," said Vega. "Go to Beth Shalom in the morning and stay with him there. I'll ask Michelle to track down Daniel Wilson and call you with an update." Vega pulled out his phone. "I'm texting you her cell now."

"What if the gestapo shows up?"

"Tell them to speak to Michelle. Tell them you're working this out. And for God's sake, Adele, *don't* call them gestapo."

"Some would beg to disagree," she muttered. "Where will you be tomorrow?"

"Trying to convince Greco not to close Talia Crowley's death investigation," said Vega. "Everything we're coming up with ties into that."

"How will you convince him?"

"I don't know."

*   *   *

He checked all her doors and windows and made sure she was secure for the night. Then he sat in his truck and texted Michelle about the situation with Aviles. He didn't mention Adele's arrest. He was pretty sure Adele wouldn't want that broadcast.

You've got to get someone at ICE to issue Aviles an emergency stay, Vega wrote Michelle. **We need Aviles as a witness. ICE needs to speak to Daniel Wilson. Call me or Adele and let us know if you got the stay.**

It was late. He didn't expect a text back tonight. But at least she'd get it in the morning. He turned on his ignition and pulled out of Adele's driveway. A left would take him north. To the highway. Home. Diablo. His comfy bed. A right would take him through town, east along the hill and up to Greenbriar Lane.

Five minutes, he told himself. He was pulling a Hail Mary at this point. He knew he needed something to convince Greco not to close down the case. He didn't have a goddamn clue what that might be.

He parked at the end of the cul-de-sac, staring past the yellow crime-scene tape across the driveway. A pale wisp of moon lit up the flowing tendrils of the weeping cherry in the front yard. Aside from that slash of light, all was dark. The house was as black as the mouth of a cave.

Vega got out of his truck and stood at the foot of the driveway, shivering in the cool breath of deep night before him. He thought of Talia's neighbor, the old woman with the bony fingers and that tiny dog in a raincoat. Ethel or Edith or something. He was so tired, even witnesses' names escaped him. But he remembered her words. He remembered her telling him about the water pushing out the basement windows of the darkened house when she dialed 911.

Not a single light was on.

Vega replayed her words in his head. Then he said them aloud. Once. Twice. A slow warmth spread through his body, melting something heavy that had settled around his heart. The weight of a promise he didn't think he could keep. But he could now. He knew it.

Greco said he needed hard proof that Talia wasn't alone in the house on the night she died. And tomorrow, he'd get it.

Chapter 36

They met up when the dew was thick on the grass. Before the school buses and garbage trucks started their morning rounds. Greco lumbered out of his white Buick LeSabre, looking tired and ill-tempered. Vega skirted the yellow crime-scene tape across the driveway and pressed a coffee into the big man's hands. The steam rose like mist, sparkling in the early morning sun. Greco's jaw set to one side.

"Is this an apology for getting me up extra early? Or for wasting my time?"

"Take me inside before you tell me it's a waste of your time."

Greco took a gulp of coffee and left the rest in his car. He retrieved a key from the seat. Both men slipped into blue latex gloves.

"You couldn't just *tell* me what you found?"

Vega shook his head. "You need to see it for yourself."

They stepped over the yellow crime-scene tape and walked up the driveway.

"What's this I heard about Adele getting arrested yesterday?" asked Greco.

Vega decided to give Greco as neutral a recounting as possible. He was a friend, sure. But like Vega, he tended to side with a brother-in-blue.

"Adele got a flat tire. Bale showed up and offered to

change it for her. When he popped her trunk, he found seven grams of heroin in the spare tire compartment."

Greco offered a long, low whistle. "Not my business," he said. "But did she give an explanation?"

"Would you? If you'd never seen something before?"

"*Officer, it's not mine,* is the oldest defense in the book," said Greco. "And it doesn't usually work."

"It doesn't need to," said Vega. "The evidence backs her up. One of my lieutenants ID'd the confiscated heroin as part of an inter-agency sting six months ago. The drugs were all taken off the street and thrown into police evidence lockers throughout the county."

"Which argues that either you're doing a little extracurricular dealing," said Greco. "Or someone with a cop connection put it there."

"I think you know the answer to that one."

"Never a dull moment with you, is it, Vega?"

Greco peeled back a piece of yellow crime-scene tape across the front door and unlocked it. The two men stepped inside.

A death investigation is all bright lights and bodies in motion when it first happens. The aftermath, however, is entirely different. Like a stage once the actors have departed. The first thing Vega noticed was the smell. A mixture of mold from the wet basement mingled with a faint whiff of decay, like Parmesan cheese that had gone rancid in the back of someone's refrigerator. Sunlight streamed through the long windows ahead of them in the living room. But all Vega could see was the dust motes in the air—detritus from all the bodies that had traipsed through Friday night, leaving a trail of dirt that crusted the carpets and floors.

Everything else was silent. Light-filled and silent.

Vega followed the grimy path past the living room, into the kitchen and over to the open door of the basement. He peered down. Even in the basement, light penetrated through the small casement windows. It wasn't bright like the living room, but it was light enough to see. Vega gestured for Greco to take a look.

"What, exactly, am I looking at?"

"Everything," said Vega. "Do you agree that you can see everything? Without switching on a light?"

"So?"

"I checked with the fire chief this morning before I drove here," said Vega. "When his guys arrived on Friday night, there were no lights on in the Crowley house. That was *before* they cut the power. The neighbor who called in the flood? Edith Walker? She told me the same thing."

Vega pointed to the light switch at the top of the basement stairs. It was in the off position.

"Dr. Gupta said Talia Crowley died at nine p.m. on Thursday night," said Vega. "You tell me how she managed to string herself up down there in the dark. Because there's no way that woman climbed these stairs and turned off this light switch afterward."

Greco frowned at the switch plate. "Maybe Lissette did it when she came here Friday morning."

Vega gestured to the light pouring in through the windows.

"Why would she reach for a light switch at all on Friday morning? I checked the weather. It was sunny. You can see for yourself, there's plenty of light in the house. If anything, we'd have been more likely to find a light on that Lissette *didn't* notice."

Greco stuffed his hands in his pockets and circled the island counter in the kitchen. He didn't like complications. On the other hand, he was too good of a cop to let them pass.

"What you're saying is—someone else turned off the lights on Thursday night after Talia was strung up—"

"That's exactly what I'm saying," said Vega. "You asked for hard evidence to prove she wasn't alone when she died. Well, here it is."

Greco cursed under his breath. "This doesn't just prove that someone was in the house," he grunted. "It proves that whoever was here more than likely killed her."

"That about sums it up."

"Jesus." Greco drummed his fingers on the marble countertop of the kitchen's center island. "You got any theories?"

Vega began laying them all out, beginning with Talia's STD that she likely caught from her husband and ending with Deisy's wallet in Talia's drawer.

"You've got a wife looking for revenge," said Vega. "You've got a fragile immigrant teenager worried about losing her asylum bid. You've got some con man with inside knowledge of ICE who manages to convince a vulnerable teenager that all she has to do to avoid getting deported is sleep with some rich dude at his house. And boom—you've got more than a messy divorce. You've got a human trafficking charge that'll take down the DA. That's more than enough motive for murder in my book."

"So where's the girl's phone that proves all of this?" asked Greco.

"I don't know," admitted Vega. "But I think Talia did. That may have been what got her killed. And maybe Lissette too. There are so many pieces to this, the only person who can tell us all of them is Glen Crowley."

"All right." Greco slapped the counter. "Let's go."

"Where?"

"You've been dying to get a crack at Crowley since this case began. Now's your chance."

Chapter 37

Adele drove her Toyota to Mike's Tires and begged a mechanic she knew to mount and balance a replacement while she waited. She texted Rabbi Goldberg from the waiting area:

Tell Edgar we're not going to ICE this morning. Ask him to sit tight. I'll explain when I get there.

Beth Shalom was busier than Adele would have expected on a Monday morning. Then she remembered why: the preschool. She could hear the happy chirp of little voices drifting up from the lower level of the building as she walked to the rabbi's office. His secretary, a grandmotherly woman with stiff dark hair and glasses perched at the end of her nose, told Adele that the rabbi was on the phone.

"Edgar's in the sanctuary, waxing the floor. Would you like me to fetch him?"

"That's okay," said Adele. "I'll find him myself."

"The rabbi said you could use the conference room if you like."

"Thanks."

Adele dropped off her accordion file of papers in the conference room, then made her way to the sanctuary. She'd never been in Beth Shalom's sanctuary before. It was a majestic space, all blond wood and high ceilings, like a concert hall. Sunlight streamed down from skylights four stories above where a catwalk encircled the windows. The only sound was the steady whoosh of Aviles's mop across the stage.

"Señora?" Aviles put down his mop and gave her a panicked look. "Rabbi Goldberg said we weren't going to ICE this morning. I didn't change into my suit."

"We aren't going. Not yet, at least."

Adele stepped into a shaft of sunlight and glanced up. Three long gold chains cradled a lamp that twinkled in a delicate filigreed container.

"What a beautiful light," she said.

"It's the eternal light," said Aviles. "It's always lit to show God's presence."

"We need Him now." Adele gestured to the rear doors of the sanctuary. "Rabbi Goldberg said we could use the conference room to talk. Is this a good time?"

"Of course."

Aviles stowed his mop and walked with Adele back to the conference room. Adele began speaking in Spanish as soon as Aviles closed the door.

"We have a problem," she began, taking a seat. "But I'm hopeful we also have a solution." She told Aviles about her arrest last night, feeling red-faced and guilty all over again. She felt worse when she had to tell him that someone had rifled through his paperwork and removed his passport and birth certificate.

"The police?" Aviles whispered. He closed his eyes, as if absorbing the blow.

"I know where I put those documents and they're not there," said Adele.

"Can we go to ICE and explain?"

"That would be futile," she told him. "They'd just arrest you right away. There is hope, however."

Adele thumbed Aviles's case file and pulled out the letter signed by Daniel Wilson. She placed it in front of Aviles.

"This letter you got a month ago? Informing you that you were in danger of being removed? Do you recognize it?"

"Yes," said Aviles.

"It was signed by an agent named Daniel Wilson," said Adele, pointing to the signature. "Mr. Wilson retired from ICE five months before he signed that letter."

Aviles gave Adele a puzzled look. "How can that be?"

"One possibility is that he signed that order before he retired, it got lost in the system, and someone changed the date and sent it out a month ago. The other"—she paused and settled her eyes on his—"is that he signed that letter when he was no longer an ICE agent—or someone not authorized signed it for him."

"But I have that other letter signed last week by a different agent," said Aviles.

"Marcus Tyler," said Adele. "One of the agents who came to arrest you. I know. But he and Donovan were probably working off an order already put into the system."

"By Daniel Wilson?"

"Maybe. Maybe someone else." It frustrated Adele how sloppy the government's record-keeping was. She'd heard so many horror stories of naturalized Americans and lawful green-card holders being arrested—even deported—because the Department of Homeland Security forgot to update their files.

"The thing is," said Adele, "because your temporary protected status has been rescinded, you are always at risk of deportation. Still, someone put you into priority removal. If you were put there by mistake or by someone not authorized to do so, we can maybe put the brakes on this."

"But you're saying that even if the government made a big mistake—they could still deport me."

"I'm afraid so," said Adele. "The good news is, I have a connection at ICE. I'm hoping she can plead special circumstances and get us an extension so we can replace your passport and birth certificate." Adele checked her phone again for the umpteenth time this morning. Michelle still hadn't called.

Aviles exhaled. He looked defeated. He pushed himself back from the conference table and rose.

"There is something I want you to see, señora. If the ICE agents come. If they take me. Someone needs to know."

Aviles walked over to the colorful painting of the tree with Hebrew words running along it. He scanned the bookshelf of texts in English and Hebrew. Then he moved two aside and pulled out a padded manila envelope. It looked frayed and dirty around the edges like it had been sitting out somewhere for a long time. It was addressed to Lissette Aviles.

"My son, Erick, found this and gave it to me when he visited yesterday," said Aviles. "My family doesn't know where Lissette is. But we know she was taken. And now, we know why. This."

Aviles opened the envelope and tipped a cell phone on the table.

"Is this Lissette's cell phone?"

"No," said Aviles. "Turn it on and see for yourself. I did."

Adele powered up the screen. She saw a selfie of a young and pretty Hispanic girl with dimpled cheeks and large, dark eyes. The girl couldn't have been more than fifteen or sixteen. Adele showed it to Aviles. "A relative?"

"I don't know who she is," said Aviles. "But Lissette must have. The gangsters who took her called me and told me to hand over a phone. We didn't know what they were talking about. Last night, Erick went back to the cemetery where he saw them grab her. He found this envelope hidden behind one of the mausoleums there. The only thing inside was the phone."

Aviles sank heavily into a chair. "This is what they want, señora. I'm sure of it. They said they will kill my family if I don't turn it over. The problem is—I don't know if this phone is keeping my family alive or putting them at risk."

"We should call the police about this—"

Aviles put a hand over hers. "No police. I don't trust the police."

"Because of my arrest yesterday?"

"Even if you weren't arrested," said Aviles. He folded his hands in his lap and tried to gather his words. "The two men Lissette met with on Friday—Erick saw them. One was a *mara*. But the other . . ." His voice trailed off.

"Was what?" asked Adele. "A police officer?"

"He was wearing an ICE agent's jacket."

Adele froze. She could hear the children downstairs singing a song in Hebrew and Rabbi Goldberg's secretary talking on the phone down the hall. It all felt so innocent, so removed from the dark grip of paranoia that had become both their lives.

"Now do you see why I cannot go to the police?" asked Aviles. "They could be involved in this. At the same time, I can't just leave this phone here if I'm taken, knowing it might be the one thing that can save my family."

"What do you want me to do?" asked Adele.

Before Aviles could answer, there was an urgent knock on the door.

"They're here," said the rabbi in a choked voice. Neither Aviles nor Adele had to ask who "they" were.

Adele's breath quickened in her lungs. Her heart beat so loud, she heard it in her ears, echoing like a chant through the sanctuary. Aviles tucked the phone back in the envelope and returned it to the bookshelf. Adele opened the conference room door. Rabbi Goldberg looked like he was delivering a death notice.

"Do they have a judicial warrant?" asked Adele.

"They claimed they did," said the rabbi. "I didn't ask to see it. But I have to assume if they're here again . . ." Rabbi

Goldberg shot a glance in the direction of the stairway that led to the preschool below. The children must have been having snack. Adele could hear the scrape of chairs and some sort of pre-food prayer in little voices.

"Adele," Rabbi Goldberg said, looking at her. "We have small children on the premises. The agents told me they're not going to break down our doors. They don't want to make a scene. They just want to do their jobs."

"What do you want to do here?" Adele asked the rabbi. This wasn't her call. She could fight for Aviles. But she couldn't ask others to do the same.

Rabbi Goldberg winced like someone had just stuck him with a needle. He hesitated. It was Aviles who spoke.

"I must go, señora." Aviles stood up on shaky legs and moved to the doorway. "I can't ask any more of the rabbi and his congregation. They have done enough."

Chapter 38

Glen Crowley was living above the carriage house at the home he used to share with his first wife, Charlene, in Wickford. And okay—he wasn't sleeping in the same bedroom with her or sharing his-and-hers sinks, but it still seemed a little weird to Vega. He'd rather take a tent in the woods than move back in with *his* ex.

Then again, nobody could do "forgive and forget" quite like Charlene Beech Crowley.

"We're going to need to get creative here," said Greco on the drive over. "Make a script, catch him in some lies, and then go back and fill in the blanks later." They were back in the unmarked brown Ford Taurus with the sticky stains on the floormats. The dispatch radio hummed with petty callouts. Locked keys in a car. A loose dog growling at pedestrians. A fender bender in front of the supermarket.

"Are you suggesting we pull a good cop, bad cop on him?" asked Vega.

"More like a Dumb and Dumber," said Greco. "You know how DAs think. We're all blue-collar morons who can't spell."

"So who's Dumb and who's Dumber?"

"Seeing as I got one foot on a banana peel and one foot in a fishing boat in Florida somewhere, I'll take the lead," said Greco. "Crowley spared your ass from a grand jury proceeding last December. You've got more to lose."

Vega powered down his window. The air smelled like hay and horse droppings. Old money smells. They were in Wickford, after all.

"We can get him," said Vega. "I know a way."

"How?"

"Let's assume for a moment that Deisy Ramos recorded her encounter with Crowley on her missing phone," said Vega. "Crowley cops to that, we've got motive."

"But we don't know where the girl's phone is," said Greco. "Or whether she recorded the encounter."

"True," said Vega, "but neither does Crowley."

The Crowley estate sat on a bluff surrounded by horse farms and pasture. It was a century-old classic white clapboard Colonial with a wide front porch, a dormered third floor, and a slate-tile roof.

"No way did Crowley divorce his wife and leave her all this," grunted Greco as he turned onto the long driveway. Flowering apple trees shaded the approach, along with oaks so big, it would take three adults to encircle their trunks.

"She comes from old Southern money, I guess," said Vega.

"Looks like a big chunk of it migrated north."

The carriage house was behind the main house. Greco thought it would be better to check in before they went sauntering back.

"Edgar Aviles's wife, Maria, used to work here as a maid," said Vega. "Before she got sick with lupus."

"Huh." Greco gazed up at the rows of leaded glass panes. "Hope she didn't do windows."

Greco parked the Taurus on the edge of the circular driveway. They got out and bounded up the steps of the front porch to ring the bell. They'd expected a maid to answer, but Charlene herself greeted them at the door.

"Detective Greco?" She flipped her silver-blond hair girlishly behind her shoulder. "To what do I owe the pleasure of your company?"

Vega had done thousands of interviews with victims, witnesses, and suspects over the years. Not one had ever described these meetings as a "pleasure."

"I still have some of my sweet potato pie left," she added. "Just for you."

Vega swore he saw Greco blush. If Vega didn't know better, he'd say the big man had a crush on Charlene Crowley.

"We're here to wrap a few things up with Mr. Crowley, ma'am," said Greco, then belatedly remembered that Vega was standing beside him. "This is my partner, Detective Vega."

"Of course." Charlene smiled but not quite as warmly as she did at Greco. "We met last night at the Wick."

"I was at the country club fetching Judge Keppel," Vega explained. He was happy when Greco made the connection fast enough to let the matter drop.

"Come in," said Charlene. "I'll let Glen know you're here."

The hallway had polished wide-plank floors, high ceilings, and brass sconces. Vega peeked into the rooms. Flowing draperies framed long, mullioned windows. Oil paintings of seascapes hung over buttery leather couches. Charlene led them to a room with built-in mahogany bookcases and large potted ferns. A framed navigational chart hung over the fireplace. French doors offered a panoramic view of the pastures and woods beyond. It looked like the sort of house with a million nooks and crannnies.

"Glen will be in shortly," said Charlene. "Can I get y'all anything? Coffee? Tea? A slice of my sweet potato pie?"

"Nothing ma'am, thank you," said Vega before Greco could speak. Greco gave Vega a dirty look when she left.

"What's wrong with being hospitable and eating her food?"

Vega looked pointedly at Greco's waistline. "Any more hospitable, and I'm gonna have to trade the Taurus for an RV."

Vega heard footsteps shuffling in the hall. He motioned for Greco to be quiet as he rose from the couch and peeked around the corner.

"Adam?"

The young man was standing right outside the doorway, his curly hair standing up like he'd yet to brush it this morning. The kid had a creepy sense of personal space.

"Sorry, I didn't realize you were here," said Vega.

"Berber Shoes is closed on Mondays," said Adam in a flat voice. "They're open on Saturdays. Mr. Berber says more people buy shoes on Saturdays than Mondays."

"Sure. That makes sense," said Vega. "Do you remember me? We met last night?"

"Size nine-and-a-half tactical boot." Adam looked at Vega's feet. "You're still wearing them."

Vega felt embarrassed, almost like he'd been called out for wearing the same underwear two days in a row. He stepped back from the door and gestured for Adam to come in. "We're just waiting to talk to your dad. This is Detective Greco." Vega looked at Greco. "This is the DA's son—"

"I know who he is," said Greco. "I buy my shoes at Berber's. Hey, Adam. How's business?"

Adam looked down like he was too busy concentrating to hear the question. "Size eleven wides. You like Hush Puppies Gilstrap loafers and hate white sneakers."

"Yeah. That's right." Greco jerked a thumb toward Adam and looked at Vega. "Pretty amazing, huh? I haven't been in Berber's in probably two months and he remembers."

That gave Vega an idea. "Hey, Adam," Vega asked. "What kind of shoes does your dad like to wear?"

"Lace-up oxfords. Cole Haan. Size ten, narrow."

"How about Talia?"

Adam looked up from the floor at Vega. He had an odd habit of either not making any eye contact or making too much, like now.

"Talia is dead."

"We know," said Vega. "We're sorry for your family's loss. Did you spend a lot of time with her and your father?"

Adam seemed not to hear Vega's question. Or maybe he just couldn't process it.

"She liked sandals and ballet flats and espadrilles."

"What are espadrilles?" asked Vega.

"Canvas shoes with rope soles," said Adam. "She had size seven feet, same as my mother. She borrowed her shoes."

"*Talia* borrowed your mother's shoes?"

"No," said Adam. There was a mild whine of frustration in his voice. It was the most emotion Vega had seen him exhibit. "My mother borrowed Talia's espadrilles. They're still in her closet."

"Why did your mother borrow Talia's shoes?" asked Vega.

"She should have borrowed her Tory Burch ballet flats. They wouldn't have fallen apart."

"Adam!" The voice was sharp and male. Crowley barreled into the room, one hand on his cell phone as he finished a call, the other extended to shake Vega's and Greco's hands. Both men rose to oblige him. Crowley put his phone away and turned to his son.

"Were you annoying these detectives?"

"He was giving us a good education on shoes," said Greco.

"Yes, well, he does that sometimes." Crowley spoke to Adam out of the side of his mouth. "Go find your mother."

Adam slunk out of the room, head down, arms stiffly at his sides. Vega had a sense Crowley often spoke to his son that way.

"Sorry about that," Crowley said to Greco and Vega. "Adam's a good kid. But he can be trying at times. Charlene has the patience of a saint. Talia did, too."

"Our condolences again on your wife's passing," said Vega.

"Thank you." Crowley gestured for Greco and Vega to take a seat on the white linen couch. Crowley took a brown leather wing chair opposite them and perched on the edge, like they were planning some sort of strategy session and he didn't have much time.

"I'm assuming you're here to wrap up the investigation?"

"We just need to go over a few odds and ends." Greco pulled out his phone. "You don't mind if we record this, do you? My memory's not that good anymore and Detective Vega's notes are chicken scratch."

"Whatever will move this along."

Greco hit the record button, and noted the time, date, and parties present. He set it on the coffee table, then flipped back and forth through his notes while Crowley crossed and uncrossed his legs.

"The lights," mumbled Greco.

"The . . . lights?" asked Crowley. "In this room?"

"In your house," said Greco. "They were all off when the first-due responders showed up Thursday night."

"So?"

"So, somebody turned them off. They had to be on when she died, if you get what I'm saying."

"I . . . I don't know," said Crowley. "Maybe Lissette turned them off Friday morning."

Vega and Greco weren't asking the question to gauge Crowley's response as much as his manner. In both their experiences, guilty people talked too much. Greco gave Crowley plenty of time to take the bait. He didn't.

"You left at six on Thursday night, correct?" asked Greco.

"That's right—"

"With an hour's stopover at Mario's in Taylorsville."

Crowley paused. He seemed to sense a trap. "We ate. I can't tell you how long we were there."

"So you ate? And then got right back on the road?"

"I thought we already went through all of this."

"We're just trying to be thorough here," said Greco. "So you went to Mario's, ate, and then drove straight to Albany?"

"To the best of my recollection."

Vega and Greco had worked with enough prosecutors to know that, like cops, they noticed everything and forgot nothing. If Crowley was going to play the amnesia game, it was because he had something to hide. All they had to do now was zero in on the kill.

Greco turned to Vega, like a thought had just occurred to him. "Wasn't there a photograph you wanted to show Mr. Crowley again?"

"You mean that picture of those two little girls?" Vega asked the question breezily, like they'd never discussed it before. He pulled out his phone, scrolled down to the snapshot of Deisy and Nelly, and handed it to Crowley.

"I think I showed you this picture Friday night," said Vega. "But just to be sure—you don't recognize them?"

"They're kids," said Crowley. "I don't pay attention to kids. What's this got to do with Talia?"

Greco ignored Crowley's question and turned to Vega. "You got a more recent shot of one of them, don't you, Vega?"

"Somewhere on my phone." Vega took back the phone and pulled up Deisy's immigration mug shot. He handed it to Crowley.

"How 'bout this picture?"

Crowley's eyes narrowed. His jaw tightened. He thrust the phone back at Vega. "I meet a lot of people," he said. "Maybe I met her somewhere. I don't know."

"The problem is," said Vega, holding Crowley's gaze, "we do."

"We have the video," said Greco. "From her phone—"

"You *what?*"

"The phone," said Vega. "The one she carried in her wallet, along with that snapshot of her and her sister. We have the video from it. Of you and her—"

"Sweet Jesus." Crowley bolted from his chair. "This is ridiculous! I mean . . . how could I know she was an under-age hooker? She looked twenty-one."

Bingo. They had him. Vega's stomach turned to think of it. "Deisy Ramos was a sophomore at Port Carroll High School and a human trafficking victim," said Vega. "She was coerced into prostitution by a sham promise of permanent asylum. Who was your contact?"

"I don't know what you're talking about. She was just a girl." Crowley sank back down on the chair and held his head in his hands. Belatedly, it seemed to occur to him what Vega and Greco were really here about. He lifted his head from his hands.

"You think I killed my wife, don't you?"

"Talia was shopping for a private investigator," said Greco. "Wives don't do that to send valentines."

"She killed herself, plain and simple," Crowley insisted. "I wasn't even there."

"You got somebody else to do it," said Vega. "Who? The pimp who supplied you with Deisy? One of his contacts?"

"This is nonsense!"

"You couldn't stand the idea that she was going to ruin you," said Vega. "So you killed her."

Crowley pushed himself off the chair, fists curled at his sides. There had always been something coiled about the man. An energy that couldn't be ascribed simply to an exacting nature. He kept it hidden at work. Channeled it into his attention to detail and a love of winning cases. But here, inside his former house, the intensity felt less contained and more lethal. He pointed a finger at Vega.

"*You're* the killer, Detective Vega. You shot an unarmed man in cold blood. I should have convened a grand jury when I had the chance. Gotten you kicked off the force doing mall gigs where you belong. Instead, you and the Pillsbury Doughboy here have the temerity to accuse *me?* I'll have both your badges before this is over."

Crowley walked to the door and opened it. "From now on, you will talk to me only through my attorney. Good day, gentlemen."

Chapter 39

"We nailed him with Deisy Ramos," said Greco as he and Vega headed back to the station house. "Got it all on tape."

Vega hunkered down in his seat. "Yeah."

"What are you sore about? Because he called you a killer? We got him admitting to sex with an underage human trafficking victim. His career is toast."

Vega stared out the window as Lake Holly came back into view over the ridge, all church steeples and peaked roofs.

"I don't think he killed Talia."

"What?" Greco turned the wheel of the Taurus so hard he had to overcorrect. "Now I finally agree with you and you're changing course?"

"Not changing course," said Vega. "Somebody killed Talia. I'm just not sure it was Crowley. His body language was entirely different when we talked to him about Deisy than about Talia. He seemed genuinely blindsided. I want a polygraph."

"Which he won't do," said Greco. "He's got nothing to gain and plenty to lose."

A dispatcher's voice came over the radio, requesting Lake Holly send a patrol to Beth Shalom. Vega sat up straighter. He was sure those ICE agents were back.

"Can we swing by the synagogue?"

"Stay out of this," Greco warned him. "Aviles is the subject of a federal warrant, and nothing you say can change that."

At the traffic light, Greco turned right, in the direction of the station house. Away from Beth Shalom.

"What if I told you that Ryan Bale set Adele up last night?" asked Vega. "So that he could remove documents from her car so Aviles couldn't petition ICE for a stay of removal."

"I'd say you had rocks between your ears," said Greco. "I've known Bale ever since he was a rookie. And sure, he can be a little rough around the edges. But he's not corrupt. For what purpose? He doesn't give a crap about some illegal—or your girlfriend."

"Aviles isn't just 'some' illegal," said Vega. "His name was on Elmer Ortega's list. The same list Deisy Ramos was on. What if both made contact—directly or indirectly—with this federal agent who keeps popping up through all these names, promising a reprieve from deportation in exchange for help with some criminal activity?"

"And you think that agent is Bale?" asked Greco. "That makes no sense. Bale is a local cop. You don't think word would get around if he were shaking down immigrants in these parts?"

"I think it would," Vega agreed. "Which is why I think someone else is doing it." Vega told Greco about the retired ICE agent whose name appeared on both Cesar Zuma's and Edgar Aviles's deportation letters. "Neither letter is in their ICE files," said Vega. "And both were signed five months *after* Wilson retired."

"What's Wilson have to say about all this?" asked Greco.

"I don't know," said Vega. "Michelle is trying to track him down. But what if Wilson had a silent partner? That would give the partner a strong incentive to get Aviles out of the country as quickly as possible."

"And you think that silent partner is Bale? Get outta here, Vega. You can't prove any of that."

Vega saw the station house coming into view. That's when it hit him.

"Bale's body cam."

"Huh?"

"Beat patrol officers download the video from their body cameras at the end of each shift, right?"

"That's the policy," said Greco.

"When did Bale's shift end?"

"I think he was working an overtime day shift yesterday," said Greco. "He's on duty for a regular shift this morning. Why?"

"So his video footage from yesterday would be in your system?"

"What's your point?"

"I need you to take a look at the thirty-second pre-feed before Bale turned on his camera when he encountered Adele," said Vega. "This would have been about four p.m. yesterday."

Greco shook his head. "I can't just waltz into the station and yank another officer's body cam footage without some sort of explanation."

"Then I'll give you one," said Vega. "What you make up when you go inside is up to you."

Vega walked Greco through what Adele had told him about Ryan Bale squatting down to check her tires before he turned on his body cam.

"If Bale wanted to set Adele up," Vega explained, "he'd need to know where she was when she broke down so he could offer to change her tire. Which means he'd have to plant a GPS tracking device on her car. That's not something you want to leave on a vehicle as evidence."

"You're paranoid, Vega. You've been sleeping with the enemy for too long."

"If I'm wrong, I'll back off. But what if I'm right?"

Greco cursed as he pulled sharply into the station house lot. He cut the engine, then turned and wagged a finger at Vega.

"You will stay in the car and say nothing to nobody—you hear? Lake Holly's *my* town and Bale's one of *my* people. And I'm very protective of my people."

Greco pushed himself out of the driver's seat, slammed the door, and trudged up the steps and into the building. He looked like a man who'd just been told his wife was cheating on him and didn't want to believe it.

Vega pulled out his phone and dialed Adele. "What's going on?" he asked when she picked up. "Lake Holly just got a request for backup at Beth Shalom. Is ICE there?"

"ICE. Max Zimmerman. Two dozen preschoolers. And two TV stations. Max called them."

Vega didn't care about the TV stations, but he didn't like the idea of children there. He'd forgotten Beth Shalom had a preschool. "Maybe this is the time to cut Aviles loose."

"Edgar offered to go," said Adele. "He doesn't want to put anyone at risk. It's Max who's arguing for him to stay put until I get hold of Michelle."

"*Nena,*" Vega said softly. "She may not call."

"I know that," said Adele. "But I'm afraid to release him. This isn't just about Edgar getting deported anymore. His life is at risk. His *family's* life is at risk. He showed me this cell phone that Lissette had. Dangerous people want this phone, Jimmy."

Vega's heart felt like it had dropped into his shoes. "Whose phone?"

"I don't know," said Adele. "Some teenage girl's selfie is on the screen. I can't find out more without the girl's password."

The phone belonged to Deisy Ramos. Vega was sure of it.

"Don't let that phone out of your sight," said Vega. "Try to stall if you can. I'll get hold of Michelle."

He got her on the first ring.

"ICE is at Beth Shalom," Vega blurted. "Why didn't you text me? Or Adele?"

"Because I'm not the fairy godmother of deportation reprieves," she shot back. "I'm doing the best I can to track down Wilson, but he's on a fishing trip in the Adirondacks. Those are the limits of my expertise."

"You could go to your boss, Bowman."

"And you could let Tyler and Donovan do their jobs," she replied. "If Aviles needs a stay, he can get one when he's in detention—"

"Bullshit, he can! He needs ICE called off now, Michelle. Not in a day. Not in a week. Now!" Vega glanced at the station house door. Greco had yet to emerge. Vega wondered if his pal was right. Perhaps he had lost all objectivity. He ran a hand down his face and tried to get his temper under control.

"Look, Michelle, I'm asking you to trust me on this. Something's going on here. I can't explain it all now. I'm not even sure I've put all the pieces together. But I think it involves the DA and maybe ICE and cops too. We need Aviles. If he gets deported, we'll never unravel this case. Please. I'm begging you. If you have any power to call this off, please ask Bowman for an emergency stay."

There was a pause. Vega wasn't even sure she was on the line anymore.

"I'll see what I can do."

She hung up. Vega lifted his gaze from his phone to see Greco barreling toward him. His whole body had a forward thrust to it like he wanted to punch something.

Vega opened his door. No way was the big man going to drive over to Beth Shalom now. Vega would have to drive himself.

"Get back in the car," Greco ordered. He yanked open the driver's-side door and lumbered into his seat. He started up the engine. "You were right about the body cam."

"Bale's on there? Removing a GPS from Adele's Toyota?"

"Affirmative."

"Shouldn't you be inside, speaking to your chief about this?"

"Not until we contain the problem," said Greco. "The unit Lake Holly dispatched to Beth Shalom was Bobby Fitzgerald and his partner, Ryan Bale."

Chapter 40

Adele hadn't called the television stations. That was Max Zimmerman's doing. He arrived right after the two ICE agents did. By the time he'd gotten out of his car and shuffled up the steps of the synagogue, the first television van with its big call letters on the side and satellite dish on the roof had rumbled into the parking lot.

"What the hell?" Tyler, the black agent frowned at Adele. "You want to make a spectacle of this?"

"I didn't notify anyone," said Adele.

"I did," said Zimmerman from the foot of the stairs. "Why should it matter? If what you are doing is just, then who witnesses it is of no concern."

Zimmerman proceeded to make his way slowly up the stairs. There was a ramp for the disabled on the side, but Adele sensed he wanted the agents—and perhaps the news van—to see him struggle. Tyler and Donovan looked panicked. This was a complication they hadn't anticipated. They plastered themselves against the railing. Adele walked down the stairs and gently coaxed Zimmerman up them and through the doors. Once inside, he leaned in close and grabbed her arm.

"I cannot sit by on this, Adele. As a Holocaust survivor, I cannot. Even if Edgar is willing to give himself up, I can't let him go down this route without a fight."

"I understand," she said. "But please let me handle this. How did you know this was going on, anyway?"

"Eve told me."

"The rabbi's wife?"

"What? You think it was Adam's?"

Adele thanked him and then turned back to the doors where Tyler and Donovan were still waiting for Aviles to step outside. They had their arms folded against their Kevlar vests, but their postures were relaxed. They were in this for the long haul.

Adele stepped out the doors and attempted a smile. She hoped to reason with them. She suspected Agent Tyler, the black agent, was the senior man. He was older, for one thing. Plus, he didn't seem quite as inclined to assert his authority—which made Adele think he had more. When she unfolded a copy of Daniel Wilson's letter to Aviles, she showed it to Tyler.

"I want to share something with you gentlemen," said Adele. "This is a copy of the original letter informing Mr. Aviles of ICE's intent to deport him. It was signed by Daniel Wilson who, as I understand it, retired six months ago."

Tyler scanned the letter. "So?"

"If Daniel Wilson signed that letter, he wasn't authorized to do so, since he was already retired. If he didn't and someone signed it for him, the whole letter is invalid."

"I sent him a letter a week ago," said Tyler. "I can assure you, ma'am. It was very real."

"Yes, but it was based on Agent Wilson's previous, invalid letter," said Adele.

"I don't see what difference it makes if Mickey Mouse signed it," said Tyler. "We have a warrant. Signed by a federal judge—"

"Who believed he was affirming actions taken by a federal employee," said Adele. "Not a civilian."

"Doesn't matter at this point," Donovan said, inserting

himself into the argument. "Our ace beats your joker any day."

Adele raised an eyebrow. "Who exactly is the joker here? Agent Wilson?"

Donovan's face flushed. He was through with wordplay. "Aviles needs to turn himself over now. Or we'll do it for him."

Adele noticed a Lake Holly Police cruiser pulling into the lot. Donovan read the concern on her face. "That's right, Adele," he said, switching to the informal, like she was already a prisoner under his command. "You obstruct us? The Lake Holly Police can arrest you right here and now. For interfering with a federal agent carrying out his duties."

The cruiser pulled up to the curb. Bale and Fitzgerald got out. Adele paled. She couldn't quiet the fear that curdled in her gut at the sight of Ryan Bale.

Donovan leered at Adele. "I hear you got arrested last night so this won't be a new experience. Guess you're one of those gals who's into handcuffs."

Greco flipped on the Taurus's dashboard flashers. It was a ten-minute drive to the synagogue, but they wanted to get there before ICE arrested Aviles. On the way over, Vega told Greco about the phone in Aviles's possession.

"That's what everyone wants," said Vega. "The phone. I'm betting it belonged to Deisy Ramos. And I'm betting there's incriminating video of Crowley on it—and maybe texts and emails with whoever set the deal up."

"You think that was Bale?"

"Maybe," said Vega. "Or maybe someone who can tie Bale into this."

A dispatcher got on the radio and requested a second cruiser at Beth Shalom for "traffic control."

"What the hell?" asked Vega. "What's going on there?"

Greco got on the radio.

"This is car forty-seven. Can I have a status update at Beth Shalom?"

"There's a preschool on the premises," the dispatcher replied. "They are evacuating. There's also heavy media presence."

"Ten-four." Greco disconnected. "Little children, Jews, and an illegal immigrant. Lake Holly's gonna be all over the six o'clock news with this one."

Greco cut a sharp right and dropped his speed near the school. The whole trip felt like they were driving through molasses. Everything seemed denser. The leaves on the trees. The bushes. Even the humid air around them.

"You know," said Greco. "You could have this thing all wrong. Everyone else on Elmer Ortega's list was involved in some way with a crime. What if Aviles is too? What if he was going to turn over the alarm code to the synagogue so Ortega could rob it?"

The idea chilled Vega. Talking to Aviles, he didn't get the sense that the man was anything but hardworking and honest. Then again, every immigrant on that list appeared to have been hardworking and honest before they were thrown into a compromising situation.

"When Michelle and I went through the names," said Vega, "Wilmer Diaz was on the list. Probably because he was in danger of deportation. But it was his wife, Nelda, that this so-called ICE agent actually blackmailed. He used Wilmer to get her to cooperate."

"What's your point?"

"Maybe Aviles was the one in danger of deportation," said Vega. "Maybe Lissette was the one they blackmailed."

"Blackmailed, how?"

"Play this out with me for a minute," said Vega. "I know from my cop friend in Port Carroll that Elmer Ortega may have been working with the Ramirez brothers and their crew out of Port Carroll. Let's say for some reason, the Ramirezes thought the DA was onto their scam.

They know Crowley is into underage hookers. They need something damaging on Crowley to keep him from going after them—"

"I'm with you so far—"

"So they use Daniel Wilson or someone else with a connection inside ICE to find a young, vulnerable asylum seeker and blackmail her into going to Crowley's house to have sex with him and record it."

"Not too hard to imagine—"

"But Lissette walks in on them. Or something else spooks the girl. She leaves so quickly, she forgets her wallet and phone."

"And Talia finds it," said Greco.

"Talia finds it, hides it, and doesn't tell her husband where," said Vega. "But he knows about it because she's threatening to take his behavior public. She caught an STD from him. She got pelvic inflammatory disease from him. Maybe lost her baby because of his actions. She's mad. And she's got the evidence—in the form of a video recording on Deisy's phone."

"Evidence that Ortega and the Ramirez brothers want too," Greco noted. "Assuming they set Deisy up to get it."

"Only now, that phone doesn't just have a recording of Crowley on it," said Vega. "It has contacts that can be traced back to the gang. So Talia has the phone and both the Ramirezes and Crowley are searching for it—for different reasons."

Greco cursed as they slowed behind a UPS truck. They were on a curvy road with a double line and traffic in both directions. They couldn't do anything but wait.

"So we've got Crowley and the Ramirezes searching for the phone," said Greco. "Talia's hidden it. And suddenly Talia's dead, the phone's missing, Lissette's missing, and the phone turns up in an envelope that was, at some point, clearly in Lissette's possession."

Greco turned his face from the wheel and looked at Vega. "You do realize what you're suggesting?"

Vega didn't. Until this moment. His heart felt heavy. "Lissette Aviles killed Talia Crowley."

Greco ticked off the evidence as they began moving again. "She had easy access to the Crowley house. Talia trusted her. And most importantly, she had motive. She knew that phone would buy her uncle's freedom. She believed she was dealing with someone corrupt inside of ICE who could fix his immigration status—and maybe hers as well."

"She was willing to kill another human being for that?"

Greco shrugged. "People kill for a lot less."

By the time they arrived at Beth Shalom, three television vans were parked by the entrance. Hefty men shouldering cameras and reporters with freeze-dried hair stood beside a police cruiser acting as a checkpoint on the driveway. A cop Vega recognized by the name of Ianelli was leaning in car windows and letting some people pass while turning others away.

Greco pulled up and powered down his driver's-side window. "What's the situation?"

"ICE wants to arrest an illegal taking sanctuary inside the temple," said Ianelli. "Bale and Fitzgerald were called down there to assist. But they're in a stalemate, as far as I can tell. The guy's not coming out and nobody wants to break down the doors and go in."

"Where's your partner?" asked Greco.

"Hart's helping Bale and Fitzgerald evacuate the children from the preschool on the premises. We suggested to the rabbi that maybe he should get the kids out. It's chill down there at the moment. But still—we're talking a fugitive arrest. You never know."

Greco jerked a thumb at the row of television vans lined

up alongside the road. "Then what's with all this media coverage? Did the temple call this in? Or did Adele Figueroa?" Greco shot a sideways look of disapproval at Vega.

"I don't know," said Ianelli. "I saw them interviewing an old man earlier, before we suggested that the rabbi move the media off Beth Shalom's grounds. He may have been the one who called. I think he's a Holocaust survivor."

Max Zimmerman. It figured. Vega smiled to himself, thinking about that story Max had told him on their drive home from the synagogue Friday night. Vega supposed Max was trying to get the horse to talk. He had to admire the old man's determination, even if he didn't always agree with his choices.

Ianelli waved them through the checkpoint. Greco slowed as they made their way along the temple's driveway. SUVs and minivans lined the curb. Teachers walked preschoolers to their parents' vehicles. Vega was relieved that at least the kids were being evacuated.

"Look, Vega," said Greco as they drove past the knot of vehicles and into the parking lot. "If you can make this fustercluck with ICE go away, then do it. But I don't want you saying a word to Bale about that body-cam video or Deisy's phone or any of this—you got me? That's a Lake Holly problem and our department will deal with it."

"Gotcha." Vega pulled out his phone. "Let me call Michelle and see if she's made any progress getting Bowman to sign a stay."

The news from Michelle wasn't good.

"Wayne Bowman's in a meeting," she said. "I've tried to reach him but he's not responding."

"Well, make him respond," said Vega. "I'm in the parking lot of Beth Shalom. ICE is here. And we're running out of time. Did you reach Wilson?"

"Still trying," she replied. "But I'll tell you right now, Dan Wilson's not involved in any of this. I pulled up some of his old ICE orders. The signatures don't match. Wilson never signed those letters. Someone else did."

"So then, why can't you vacate Aviles's order of removal?"

"Because a federal judge signed a judicial warrant, Jimmy. I can't go over a judge. Bowman might be able to. But like I said—"

"He's in a meeting."

"Hey, don't get mad at me. This is Adele's fault. She forced Tyler and Donovan to go before a judge. You want to blame someone, blame her." Michelle hung up.

Greco got the gist of the call.

"There's nothing else we can do," he told Vega. "You can't walk through those temple doors. You'd be telling every cop here that you're working for the other side. And besides, it wouldn't help anyway. Aviles is going to come out or not. Nothing you do will change that."

Vega glanced at the front steps where Max Zimmerman was talking to the two ICE agents. The old man looked exhausted. Vega wondered if the kindest thing he could do right now was take him home.

"How about this?" Vega suggested. "You go back to the station house and do what you have to to preserve Bale's body-cam footage from last night and convince Chief B. we need to keep the Crowley case open. I'll convince Max Zimmerman to go home. He can drop me off at the station house on the way. All he's going to do is rile up ICE and that's the last thing we need right now."

Chapter 41

Max Zimmerman was so deep in discussion with the two ICE agents on the steps of the synagogue that he didn't notice Vega maneuvering past the preschoolers toward him.

"Jimmy!" Zimmerman called excitedly. "You're a police officer. Please tell these two officers here that I'm not anti-police. I am only anti-injustice."

Vega felt the two agents' wary gazes. Vega's military-short haircut and the gun on his hip gave him away as a fellow cop. But if he was Zimmerman's friend, he wasn't theirs.

"Who the hell are you?" demanded the white agent, a young man with thin lips and translucent blue eyes.

"Jimmy Vega. I'm a detective with the county police, working on a case in Lake Holly. I was just going to offer to take Mr. Zimmerman home."

"I don't need to go home," Zimmerman insisted. "I need to beg mercy for a man who can't beg it for himself." Zimmerman raised a bony finger. "As a wise man once said, mercy bears richer fruits than strict justice."

"I'm not interested in your Hebe quotes," said the white agent.

"That was Abraham Lincoln."

Embarrassment flashed on the agent's face, then quickly turned to anger. Vega wanted to diffuse the situation. He hooked an arm under Zimmerman's. "Mr. Zimmerman? Please let me take you home."

"I will go—"

"Good—"

"If Adele and Rabbi Goldberg ask me to."

"*Ay, puñeta!*" Vega pulled out his phone and dialed Adele.

The black agent pointed to Vega's phone. "You have the head of La Casa on your speed dial?"

"Detective Vega is dating her," Zimmerman said proudly.

The two agents exchanged a look like they'd tasted something rancid. Vega turned his back and tried to ignore them while he explained to Adele that he was trying to remove Zimmerman for his own good.

"I'll be right out," she promised. She sounded breathy and excited. "Good news—Michelle just faxed over an emergency stay."

"She got through to Wayne Bowman?"

There was a pause. It sounded like Adele was reading the paperwork for the first time. "It's . . . not from Bowman. It's from Michelle." Her voice faltered. "She can do that, right? Issue an emergency stay?"

Vega glanced over his shoulder at the agents. Their jaws were slack, their postures nonchalant but unyielding as they checked their phones. Nothing but a higher judge's order or an emergency stay from their ultimate boss was likely to dissuade them.

"I don't know," Vega replied. "Either way, I think you'd better come out."

"Michelle Lopez is in investigations, not enforcement," The black agent, Tyler, told Adele when she thrust the faxed paperwork into his hands. "She doesn't have the au-

thority to set aside a judge's order. And for that matter"—
Tyler gave Adele a suspicious look—"what's she doing interfering in the first place?"

Vega tried to explain that he and Lopez were working
an investigation together. "Edgar Aviles's testimony may
be crucial to the case."

"So?" asked Tyler. "Let him give it in detention if it's so
crucial."

Back and forth they went. The rabbi came out and
butted in. So did Zimmerman. It took three tries before
Vega finally managed to coax the old man away.

"All right!" said Zimmerman. "I'm going. Please tell
Edgar I tried."

"I will," Adele promised him.

Vega walked Zimmerman through the scattering of
preschoolers still being led to parents' cars. The mass exo-
dus had tapered off to a handful now. Vega saw Fitzgerald
at the curb, directing traffic.

"Is this the last of the kids?" Vega asked the young cop.

"There are still almost a dozen kids and two teachers inside," Fitzgerald replied. "Some parents"—he heaved a
sigh—"they leave an emergency contact number and then
don't pick it up in an emergency."

"Where's your partner?" asked Vega. "Where's Ianelli
and Hart?"

"Hart's at the entrance with Ianelli," said Fitzgerald. "I
think they're being dispatched on another call. I'm not
sure where Ryan is. I think he's getting a head count from
the teachers."

"A head count," Vega repeated. Bale could get a head
count by stopping one of the assistants on the sidewalk
helping children into cars. He didn't need to wander off.
Short of an emergency requiring police response, he had
no business in the synagogue right now. Not with ICE at
the front door.

Something urgent and worrisome percolated through

Vega's veins. Like he'd just discovered that his wallet was missing. He walked Zimmerman over to his car, a gray Cadillac Seville that was buffed to a high gloss.

"Do you think you can drive home without me?" Vega asked.

"You're not coming?"

"I just remembered something I need to do."

Vega opened Zimmerman's car door for him. The old man paused, the door between them. He reached over and gripped Vega's arm. His dark eyes turned glassy.

"I'm alive today because an illiterate pig farmer made a split-second decision to hide me in a hay bale instead of handing me over to the Nazis." Zimmerman's voice, normally so commanding, sounded shaky and hoarse. "What I'm saying is, it's not the big choices that define us. It's the little ones."

"I don't know that I have any choices here," said Vega. "Big or little."

"Ah." Zimmerman wagged a finger at him. "That's where you're wrong, Jimmy. God gave us two arms to lift and one mouth to speak. You think He did all that just so we could cuss out the Yankees' pitching?"

Vega smiled. "I'll try to remember that come playoff season."

Zimmerman got into his Cadillac. Vega watched the old man slowly pull out of the parking lot. Then Vega doubled back to the synagogue. Adele and the rabbi were so deep in conversation with the ICE agents they didn't notice Vega turn off the main sidewalk and onto a path that encircled the building. Beyond a copse of evergreens, Vega saw a fenced playground. It was empty of children. They were all inside.

No sign of Bale.

The back of the complex was much bigger than Vega realized from the front. The lower level bowed out where the preschool was located. An entire wall of glass windows afforded a perfect view inside. Vega could see a young female teacher negotiating a disputed toy between two four-year-olds while another teacher—or perhaps a teaching assistant, she looked barely out of college—poured juice into paper cups.

Vega didn't want to startle them. He walked up to the sliding glass doors and held up his badge. The teacher negotiating the dispute walked over to the door and slid it open. She had dark curly hair that she pulled back into a ponytail and a peasant-style blouse with embroidery and tassels on it. A Hamsa medallion—the hand with the eye in the center—dangled from a gold chain around her neck.

"Sorry to bother you, ma'am," said Vega. "But have you seen any police officers enter the building?"

"I let one in," she replied. "I wasn't sure if I was supposed to. He said he wasn't ICE. He just wanted to get a head count of the children and make sure the building was secure."

Vega tried to hide his concern. He didn't want to alarm the teachers. "Do you know where he went?"

"Upstairs, I think." She flicked her gaze down Vega. Unlike Bale, he wasn't wearing a uniform. "Can't you call him on a radio or something?"

Vega didn't have a radio. And even if he did, it would be on county frequency, not Lake Holly's.

The teacher blocked the door. "How do I know you're not ICE?"

"I'm with the county police—just like it says on my badge."

She didn't move.

"Look, ma'am," said Vega. "Beth Shalom's handyman may be in more danger from the uniformed patrol officer you just let in than from those two jokers on the front steps. I'm not ICE. I'm not here to arrest Aviles. I need you to step aside."

"But the children—"

"The children will be fine," Vega promised. "Just stick to your routines and everything will be over before you know it."

She stepped aside and Vega slipped through the doors. He turned left, away from the classrooms and down a hallway lined with pint-size cubbies. On the tile walls above hung children's finger paintings and the Hebrew letters of the alphabet. Vega wished he knew the layout of the synagogue better. Except for picking up Zimmerman the other night, he hadn't been inside Beth Shalom in years. Even when he was married to Wendy, he seldom set foot in the building.

One hallway seemed to lead to more classrooms and a kitchen. Vega noted a large room beyond. It may have been the room where Joy had her bat mitzvah celebration. Vega couldn't recall. It was all so long ago. It was empty now. Everything down here looked empty.

At the end of the hall was a stairwell. Vega plastered himself against the cool tile of the wall and listened. Bale was on duty. In full uniform. He would have had a radio clipped to his collar. It should have been squawking away with chatter from other cops on duty as well as occasional updates or requests from dispatch.

He heard nothing. Either Bale had muted it or he'd left the building already.

Vega walked up the first half flight of stairs, past a tapestry with Hebrew letters beneath an olive branch. He held his breath and tried to discern each noise around him. The chatter of little children below him and the clap of their teachers' hands. A woman's voice above him. Not Adele's. It sounded like she was talking on a phone. Maybe the rabbi's secretary.

He bounded up the second set of stairs and found himself in a hall paneled in blond wood with a glass case full of decorative menorahs and a bronze plaque attesting to the many families who'd financed the various additions and renovations of Beth Shalom. Somewhere in that long list of names were those of Dr. David and Sarah Kaplan, Vega's former in-laws. Not that they ever really felt like family. More like neighbors who occasionally lent him their barbecue tongs and then moved away to a city he knew he'd never visit.

His whole former marriage sometimes felt like that.

Across from the stairs was a side entrance to the sanctuary. Light angled in broad brushstrokes from the skylights onto the pews. Even empty, the worship hall had a hushed reverence about it. Vega had fallen away from his own Catholic upbringing decades ago. But he still found himself moved by the power and majesty of any space devoted to faith—perhaps because he had so little himself.

And then he heard it. A voice followed by a slight echo. Vega recognized a Spanish accent in the soft consonants and singsong vowels even as he failed to discern the words. It was coming from somewhere inside the sanctuary. Not on the stage or in the pews.

Above. Forty feet above. On the opposite side of the worship hall.

Vega heard another echo as well. This second one looped beneath Aviles's like a dark undertow, fracturing the sound waves like an unexpected sharp or flat. It changed the vibrations in the room. From melodic to discordant. From major to minor. From light to dark.

The second voice belonged to Ryan Bale.

Chapter 42

Vega flattened himself against the door of the sanctuary and lifted his gaze to a spot high on the opposite wall. There on a metal catwalk near the skylights stood Bale and Aviles. Aviles was cornered at the endpoint of the catwalk. His back was to the railing, his hands out in front in a pleading gesture. Bale stood a few feet away, his massive bulk blocking off the exit. Their words to each other were unintelligible at this distance. If not for Aviles's gestures, Vega would have assumed Bale was up there trying to talk down a suicidal immigrant facing deportation.

That's how Bale would play it too. When Adele and Rabbi Goldberg found Aviles's bloody body sprawled out across the pews forty feet below, Bale would tell them how he'd tried in vain to save Aviles. Maybe even throw in some dramatic moment of personal peril. How he'd nearly gone over the rail himself in a desperate attempt to hang on to the man.

Only Vega would know the truth. A truth he couldn't prove. Not with a dead man for a witness.

His first instinct was to shout up to Bale to come down. But why would he? Up there, Bale held all the cards. Vega couldn't hear their conversation. He couldn't read their eyes or facial cues. If Bale really intended to throw Aviles over the railing, there was little Vega could do about it from forty feet below. Bale was two hundred and fifty pounds of solid muscle. Aviles was shorter, flabbier, and easily a hundred pounds lighter. Vega had no radio, no way to summon help. With Aviles dead, the whole situation would amount to one cop's word against another's. And given Vega's rep as a cop who shoots civilians, he had no doubt which officer law enforcement would choose to believe.

His only hope was to find the entrance to the catwalk and get the jump on Bale before he could hurt Aviles. Vega edged his way down the hall outside the sanctuary, landing the rubber soles of his duty boots as quietly as he could on the shiny marble tile floors. His pulse quickened. His thoughts batted about like pinballs inside an arcade machine. Aviles was the link to Lissette. Lissette was the link to Deisy's phone and how it related to Talia's death. All of that in turn was linked back to Bale and the Ramirez brothers. It was a fragile chain of supposition and evidence. One broken loop and it could all fall apart.

Aviles had to survive.

Vega turned the corner and turned again until he was in an empty hallway. He was vaguely aware of voices in the distance. The rabbi's secretary finishing up her phone call. Adele and Rabbi Goldberg arguing with the ICE agents at the front door. The children below, the sound of their happy voices floating through the air like swimmers on a beach.

Vega followed the corridor past the restrooms where he found several unmarked doors. He tugged on each handle. One led to a coat closet. Another, to a storage area full of mops and buckets. A third, to a concrete landing with plumbing and heating ducts overhead and a big gray electrical box on the wall. Vega went to close it when his eye caught the mirror on the opposite wall. His image reflected back at him, wide-eyed and jittery. He saw himself. He saw the door.

He saw the black metal staircase spiraling up behind it.

Vega grabbed the handle and began to climb. Five steps. Then ten. He was right-handed—convenient for holding the banister. Inconvenient for drawing his weapon from his holster as he climbed. Speed and stealth mattered more here, he decided. He kept his Glock 19 holstered and climbed using only the toes of his duty boots to minimize the sound.

Fifteen steps. Then twenty. He was almost two stories into a four-story ascent. Sweat slicked his skin and plastered his polo shirt to his back. The tight turns felt like some kind of funhouse climb. His breathing turned ragged and shallow. Voices faded in and out from above. About five steps from the top of the landing, Vega went into combat pose. He reasoned that Bale wouldn't draw his gun on Aviles. Bale's narrative was better served if his weapon never left his holster.

Which meant Vega would have the advantage.

Vega un-holstered his weapon and planted himself on the four-foot-wide catwalk.

"Freeze!" He yelled. "Hands above your heads where I can see them!"

Aviles held up his hands. Bale turned from Aviles and clamped his hands on each side of the railing.

"Jimmy?" Bale took in the pistol aimed at his head. Not Vega's preferred target but he had no choice. Bale was in uniform and wearing a Kevlar vest. A shot to the torso wouldn't even slow him down.

"What the hell do you think you're doing?" Bale demanded.

"Hands behind your head!" Vega ordered.

"What is this? Have you gone full psycho?"

"I'm not telling you again, Ryan. Do it!"

"He was going to kill me," Aviles choked out. "Throw me over the side. He knows where Lissette is. He *knows.*"

Bale slowly raised his massive arms off the railing and laced them behind his shaved head. "Of course I know," said Bale. "Same as any cop with half a brain. She's been in on the whole charade from the beginning. She killed the DA's wife."

"She wouldn't do such a thing," Aviles protested.

"Where is she?" asked Vega.

"Put the gun down, Jimmy, and I'll tell you." Bale unlaced his hands and started to lower them.

"Keep 'em raised!" yelled Vega. He was feeling disoriented. He thought he'd figured everything out and here was Bale, telling Vega some things he suspected and some things he didn't. "If you know something, Ryan, spit it out."

Bale shook his head. "Not with you pointing a gun at me. Put the gun down—"

"He's lying," shouted Aviles. "He was going to kill me—"

"Aw, for chrissake, Jimmy!" Bale demanded. "Who are you gonna believe? The Frito Bandito here? Or a fellow cop?"

A fellow cop. Always. Even a racist one.

Vega nodded his chin at Aviles. "Let him go. Then we can talk."

"He's an illegal," said Bale. "He's treating a house of worship like a freakin' Holiday Inn. You think I'm gonna let him go? With law enforcement waiting to escort him through checkout? Help me cuff him and turn him over to ICE. Then you and me, we can talk about this."

Vega hesitated.

"Either you're a cop or you're not, Jimmy. So which is it? Which side are you on?"

"Which side are *you* on, Ryan?"

"Huh?"

"The body cam," said Vega. "You turned it on yesterday—right after you removed a tracking device from Adele's car."

A muscle twitched down one side of Bale's thick neck. His tiny raisin eyes registered a moment of surprise. He tossed off a low-rumble laugh.

"Is that what this is about? That GPS?"

"So, you admit removing it," said Vega. "Which means you put it there as well."

"You're barking up the wrong tree, Jimmy. I was doing Adele a favor."

"By arresting her?"

"I've heard rumors that a couple of mechanics in town are stashing drugs in customers' cars and using GPS to recover it. I didn't want to tip off your girlfriend and have her confronting them. Figured I'd trace the GPS myself. Who knows?" Bale shrugged. "It could've proved her innocence."

Vega blinked at Bale. The man was either one of the smoothest liars Vega had ever encountered or he was telling the truth. Which was it?

"Jimmy." Bale took a step forward. "Whatever you think of me, we're brothers in blue. Put the gun away, I'll forget this ever happened, and we can take care of business, all right?"

Bale reached for Vega's gun. Vega stepped back.

"Listen, Ryan." Vega took a deep breath. "I believe you. I do. But we're still gonna have to play this my way until I know for sure. I need you to lie down. Face forward and lace your hands behind your head."

Bale's raisin eyes screwed up until they were pinholes. His voice was steely. "You really have lost your freakin' mind—"

"Do it!" Vega ordered.

Bale hesitated a moment then took a knee and slowly dropped onto his stomach. He placed his palms on the back of his shaved head and pressed his square jaw into the honeycomb grid of the metal. Lying prone like that, in uniform, he took up the entire catwalk. But at least he was less lethal. Vega turned his gaze to Aviles.

"Go downstairs," he ordered Aviles. "Find Rabbi Goldberg or his secretary and tell them to fetch Officer Fitzgerald and bring him in here. Not ICE. Not a squad of police. Just Fitzgerald. Got it?"

"Fitzgerald," Aviles repeated. "Yes. Okay." He stepped in between Bale's arms and legs like a mouse scampering past a sleeping cat. Vega heard his footsteps die away as he descended the stairs.

Vega removed a set of handcuffs clipped to his belt. Bale heard the familiar jingle.

"Jesus H. Christ, Jimmy! You're gonna *cuff* me now? An officer in uniform? The Lake Holly PD's gonna go apeshit on you if you do that. Even Greco won't talk to you ever again. I'm lying down. I'm complying. And besides, how the hell do you think I'm gonna be able to climb down that spiral staircase with my hands cuffed behind my back?"

He had a point.

"All right," said Vega, backing off on the cuffs. He'd settle for disarming Bale instead. He stepped to the right side of Bale and removed the officer's Glock from his holster. Vega tucked it in the back of his waistband.

"You carrying a bug?" asked Vega. A backup gun.

"Negative."

Vega had a hard time believing a bruiser like Bale wouldn't arm himself with a second gun. He felt the man's ankles and patted down the sides of his iron-piling legs.

No gun.

"You see, asshole?" Bale growled.

Vega emptied Bale's pants pockets. It was a reflexive impulse—the sort of thing he did when he was frisking suspects, looking for contraband and ID—totally unnecessary here. Ryan Bale was wearing his ID and he wasn't likely to be carrying drugs.

"C'mon, Jimmy. You don't need to do that." Bale tossed off a nervous laugh. "C'mon, man. You know me."

Vega found a set of keys, some sticks of chewing gum, his wallet, cell phone, and—in another pocket—a badge case. Bale didn't need a badge case when he was in uniform. Unlike detectives, his shield was already clipped to his uniform shirt, along with his picture ID.

"What's this?' Vega felt the badge case.

Bale's voice seemed to pitch an octave higher. He tossed off another nervous laugh. "Cops . . . you know how we like to joke around. Play gags on one another. C'mon, man. Put it back."

Vega suspected Bale kept a fake badge in the case. Probably some sort of sexist or racist tin novelty that he knew might get him into trouble with the brass. Vega wasn't here to make life harder on the guy. He'd open it, glance at it, and put it back if that's all it was.

It wasn't. It was something much, much worse.

Staring back at Vega was a gold badge with an eagle on top and an American flag in the center. A crown of blue enamel sat beneath the eagle's wings. Three gold letters were stenciled across the enamel.

ICE.

Across from the badge was a federal identification card with a headshot photo of Bale and the name *Daniel Wilson, Enforcement Officer.* Vega felt the weight of what he was staring at in his hand.

He was staring at the evidence of a dirty cop.

"Ryan? What the—"

Vega never finished his sentence. In one fluid motion, Bale rolled himself off his stomach, lifted his knees, and shot his feet straight up at Vega, catching him in the gut and lower ribs with the heel of his duty boots. Vega heard a sound like dried twigs snapping in his chest. The badge case dropped from his left hand.

Vega fought to stay on his feet and keep control of his weapon. But already, his body pulsed like one giant bruise. Nausea rose at the back of his throat. Each breath felt like shards of glass were piercing his lungs. The pain was blinding, slowing his reflexes. When Bale charged at him,

Vega knew he had, at best, one shot, given that Bale's torso was protected in Kevlar. He wrapped both hands around the grip but couldn't get off a clean shot before Bale's fist connected to the left side of Vega's face.

Fireworks exploded in front of his eyes. Big sparking lights with halos around them and strobe flashes that danced like lightning across his field of vision. Vega saw the big man in double—unsure which image was real and which was imagined. And then he felt it. A torque to his right wrist that forced the Glock from his hand. It skittered across the honeycomb grating and dropped to the floor of the sanctuary four stories below.

Blood ran down Vega's face and stained the collar of his shirt. His left eye began swelling shut. His head pounded like someone was playing a conga rhythm between his ears.

Bale yanked his weapon from the back of Vega's waistband and returned it to his own holster.

"You're not even worth the price of a bullet." He spat out a thick wad of saliva at Vega's feet for emphasis.

Vega braced his arms against the railing and tried to steady his vision. "You can't kill me," he choked out, wiping the blood from his face with the back of his hand. "Aviles will tell—"

"Tell what? He's gone, amigo. *Deportado*. You think he cares what happens to you? You're a burned-out head case who came up here to cut a deal for you and your heroin-dealing girlfriend. And believe me, after you're gone, that's exactly where they'll find the rest of that missing stash—inside your truck. Or your house."

Bale clamped a hand on Vega's shoulder and spun him to face the railing. Bale was counting on their mismatched sizes to make the job easy. But Vega had been a street fighter in his youth. He'd beaten boys who were bigger and heavier because he knew all the soft spots on the human body where size and strength offered no advantage. The eyes. The ears. The gonads. Fingers. Nails. And the best, most vulnerable spot of all. A spot that required only the bony joint of an elbow.

Vega waited until Bale hunched slightly at Vega's back, positioning himself for leverage. Then Vega raised his elbow level with his shoulder and delivered a hard up-and-back jab to the soft tissue at Bale's throat. He felt the satisfying give to Bale's flesh, like a fist in pizza dough.

Bale stepped back, wrapping both his hands around his throat, a stunned look in his beady eyes. Vega used the precious seconds to advance on Bale and grab his gun again from his holster.

A burst of voices echoed from below. High-pitched chatter. Children. Walking up the stairs from the preschool. Filing into the sanctuary for some morning ritual Vega could only guess at. *Just stick to your routines.* Is that what he'd told the teachers? And now those routines were throwing these children straight into the line of fire.

"Police!" Vega shouted. "Get out. Call nine-one-one!"

He knew how this would look to the teachers below. He knew that when they looked up, they'd see a bloody, dark-skinned man in street clothes holding a gun on a white uniformed cop. Vega had to hope they'd take into account the badge he'd shown them earlier. Whatever. So long as they all left.

Except they didn't. A couple of the children scattered in the commotion, hiding under the pews and by the bimah.

"Get them out of here!" Vega shouted again.

He turned his attention from Bale for only a second, but it was enough. Bale charged at Vega, flipping him up and over the railing.

His vision spun. He saw the world in slow motion. The great blue sky through the windows. The cool blond oak of the pews forty feet below. A little girl with dark brown pigtails in a yellow dress hiding beside the bimah. There were probably screams from the teachers and children below, but Vega couldn't hear them. His primitive reflexes took over, relinquishing everything not needed to fight the force of gravity.

Bale's gun went first, dropping from Vega's hand to the sanctuary floor below. He locked his arms around the railing and tried to swing a boot to catch the edge of the catwalk. His shoulders and biceps burned with the effort. It felt like someone had poured lighter fluid on his tendons and set them ablaze. His fingers turned numb until he could no longer feel them—only the sweat that greased his palms. He couldn't see—blinded by the swelling in his left eye and the blood dripping into his right.

Bale sliced his index finger down the front of his uniform shirt. The Velcro seams ripped apart, revealing Bale's Kevlar vest beneath. He leaned over the railing and grabbed Vega by his armpits, relieving the strain on his body. Vega's muscles quivered at the sweet reprieve.

Bale's eyes were flat and lifeless. All the tough-guy bravado seemed to drain from them. What was left behind didn't even look human. Vega felt like he was staring at a mannequin.

"You got a choice here," Bale hissed softly into his ear. "Let go and no one else dies."

Bale's gaze floated over Vega's shoulder. In the direction of the bimah. Vega couldn't turn to see what Bale was looking at. But he could guess. The girl in the yellow dress. Maybe others as well.

"I got a backup gun in my vest," said Bale. "So, what's it gonna be? 'Cause I won't just take the girl when I check out. I'll take as many as I can with her. Either you die. Or they all do."

Chapter 43

Edgar Aviles appeared at the front doors of Beth Shalom, breathless and sweaty.

"Rabbi." He banged on the double-paned glass until Rabbi Goldberg noticed. Only two sheets of glazing and five feet of concrete stoop stood between Aviles and the two ICE agents waiting to arrest him.

"Edgar?" The rabbi's voice cracked as he said his name. "I don't think you should be out here—"

"You need to get Officer Fitzpatrick. Quickly, Rabbi. Please."

"Officer Fitz . . . ?" Rabbi Goldberg turned to Adele.

"Do you mean Officer Fitzgerald?" Adele asked Aviles.

"Fitzgerald, yes," said Aviles. "Detective Vega asked me to bring him inside."

Adele scanned the parking lot and driveway for Bale's partner. She didn't see him. She didn't want a cop inside that synagogue. She didn't even want Vega inside. What was he doing there anyway?

"Where's Fitzgerald?" Adele asked the two ICE agents.

Tyler and Donovan shrugged. "Probably hunting around for his partner," Tyler answered.

"Please, señora," Aviles begged. "Please. It's very important. If you can't find Fitzgerald, then another police officer."

"*We're* law enforcement," said Donovan. He smiled at Aviles like he was on the menu.

Adele raised her hands. "Hold it. Hold it one moment." She turned to Aviles and spoke in Spanish. "What's going on?"

"The bald cop—he tried to kill me," said Aviles.

"Bale?"

"I think so. Yes," said Aviles. "He tried to throw me over the railing above the sanctuary. Detective Vega rescued me. He told me to get Fitzpat . . . Fitzgerald."

Adele pulled out her cell phone and hit Vega's number. She didn't want to risk Aviles's freedom for a situation that he already had under control.

One ring. Two. Three. Vega's voice mail came on the line. Adele's heart began a slow creep into her throat. She turned to the two agents. Tyler was older than Donovan. Calmer. She trusted his judgment more, even if he did work for ICE.

"Can you get the Lake Holly Police on your radio and ask them to come over here?"

"Will do," said Tyler, pulling out his radio. "Though if it's a real emergency, we're cops and we're already on the scene."

Adele turned back to Aviles and spoke again in Spanish. "Where is Detective Vega?"

"I left him on the catwalk in the sanctuary," said Aviles. "I left both of them there."

A tumble of little bodies began pouring down the red-carpeted stairs, moving quickly to the front doors. Adele noticed the two teachers and the rabbi's secretary walking behind, hurrying some children while they carried others in their arms. All of them had panicked looks across their faces.

"What's going on?" the rabbi asked them.

"A police officer and some other man are fighting on the catwalk in the sanctuary," said one of the young women. "They're trying to push each other over the railing."

Adele's lungs constricted. She felt like she was breathing through a cocktail straw. She wanted to push past everyone and run inside to help Vega, but she didn't have a clue what to do.

"Fitzgerald's at the top of the driveway," said Tyler, returning his radio to his belt. "He's heading down, but it's going to take a few minutes. Same with a unit response. We're here. Let us help."

Aviles turned to Adele and Rabbi Goldberg. "Please. Let them enter. I understand they will arrest me. But the detective needs our help."

Rabbi Goldberg took off his glasses and wiped his tired eyes. Nobody had taught him how to handle something like this in seminary school.

"Agent Tyler," said the rabbi. "You can come in. Agent Donovan? Please stay here and keep the local police informed when they arrived."

Tyler followed Adele, Rabbi Goldberg, and Aviles into the synagogue and up the short flight of stairs to the sanctuary. Right away, they heard it—hard breathing and voices coming from inside. The rabbi rushed forward. Tyler put a hand on his shoulder.

"Easy," cautioned the agent. "We don't know what we're walking into. You and Ms. Figueroa stay here. Outta trouble." Tyler turned to Aviles. "Where's the entrance to the catwalk?"

"This way," said Aviles. He led the agent down a hall. The rabbi waited until Aviles and the agent had turned their backs to peek inside the sanctuary. His face paled beneath his dark beard. His glasses dipped along the bridge of his nose.

"*Got in himmel,*" he whispered.

Adele came up beside him. There, forty feet above the pews, was Vega, hanging on to the outer edge of the catwalk railing, trying to swing his foot up and gain a purchase. His face was bloody and swollen. His arms quivered from the strain of holding himself up. Bale watched him casually from the walkway.

Time stopped. The earth felt like it was spinning on the head of a pin. She couldn't think. She couldn't breathe. Vega had probably only a minute or two more before his arms gave out. No one could survive a four-story drop onto hard wooden benches and marble floors.

She pushed past Rabbi Goldberg and ran across the sanctuary floor, cursing herself for all the minutes she unknowingly wasted outside.

"Dear God, help him!" she shouted up at Bale. "He's going to fall!"

"Get out of here, Adele!" Vega huffed. "Get out!"

Bale leaned over the railing a few feet away from Vega. His uniform shirt was open and untucked. His face was slack. He didn't seem to be able to register the human suffering right next to him.

"Here's your chance, Jimmy," said Bale, loud enough for Adele to hear. "You want to walk out of this? The kids left. But you've got another victim to take their places."

"Get out!" Vega screamed again at Adele.

Bale pulled a gun from beneath his vest. "Maybe you should die together."

Adele registered the gun a second before Bale pointed it at her. She dove beneath a pew and waited for the firecracker explosion. On the catwalk, she heard shouting. She lifted her head to see Aviles and Tyler rushing the landing. Two shots echoed through the interior. Aviles staggered, then hunched his shoulders and threw himself full force at Bale.

The big man's legs flipped out from under him, sending him halfway over the railing. He might have stood a chance but for his high center of gravity. His mass was all on top. The muscular biceps and torso. The Kevlar vest. There was only one direction he could go in—straight down, headfirst, onto the pews.

He landed like a bag of cement. A thud that seemed to suck all the noise out of the room. Adele flinched at the impact, four rows away. But her eyes were on the railing, watching as Tyler and Aviles grabbed Vega beneath his shoulders and pulled him onto the catwalk.

Rabbi Goldberg touched Adele on the shoulder. She hadn't even realized the rabbi was behind her. She had no idea when he first entered the room. Her heart and mind had been on Vega.

The rabbi rolled up his sleeves. "Go see the detective. Make sure everyone is okay. I'll stay down here. If there's a chance I can save this man, I will."

"You know CPR?" Adele asked him.

"I left medical school for seminary," said Rabbi Goldberg. "After I lost my first patient." He looked up to the lamp on the stage, shimmering in front of the cupboard of religious scrolls. "Now, I let Him do all the decision making." The rabbi gestured to the catwalk. "Go check on the detective."

Adele found the spiral stairs to the catwalk. She expected to see Tyler and Aviles leaning over Vega, trying to get some feeling back into his arms. But it was Aviles who was on the ground. Vega had shrugged off his bloody polo shirt and V-neck T-shirt. Tyler was pressing both to a spot just below Aviles's shoulder.

"He took one of the bullets," said Tyler. "I'm not sure he realized it until the adrenaline began wearing off." Tyler looked down at Aviles. His face was pale and sweaty.

"I'll get the rabbi up here," said Adele. "He has medical training."

"Yeah. Do that." Tyler leaned over Aviles. His voice was tender when he spoke. "An ambulance is coming, man. My partner just radioed me. You're gonna be okay. More than okay. My partner just got word. Our boss signed the emergency stay."

Chapter 44

Lights. Sirens. EMTs negotiating the spiral stairs. Vega's head throbbed. His arms ached. He registered the man and woman with stethoscopes around their necks carrying Edgar Aviles down in an improvised stretcher, an oxygen mask on his face.

Bale, they took out in a body bag.

"Deisy's phone," Vega managed to choke out to Adele before the EMTs loaded him into an ambulance. "Make sure the police get that phone."

"I know where it is," said Adele. "Rabbi Goldberg will turn it over."

Vega lost track of Aviles after they got to Lake Holly Hospital. The handyman was whisked into surgery. Vega was led into a curtained triage cubicle with nothing more high-tech than a blood pressure cuff and a jar of tongue depressors. He already knew they'd X-ray his skull and torso and then bandage him up and send him home. There was nothing modern medicine could do for cracked ribs, strained tendons, and a probable concussion but time and rest.

Adele sat in the cubicle with him, holding his hand, the depth of concern in her eyes a pretty clear indication of how bad Vega looked. He had an ice pack over the swollen left side of his face. His hair was flaked with dried blood. He'd given up both his polo shirt and his undershirt to help stanch Aviles's blood. He was now wearing a lost-and-found number the nurses had dug up—a black T-shirt with a Metallica logo on top and four skeletons on a battle-field. All he needed was the ink sleeves and ponytail to go with it.

"Go home, *nena,*" Vega told her. "They've still got to X-ray me. And then I have to go back to the station and give a statement."

"*Today?* You're hurt."

"We've got to move fast on this," said Vega. "Bale's dead. His coconspirators are gonna know it soon if they don't already. If we don't piece this thing together quickly, we may be chasing it all over Central America."

"I can't believe Ryan Bale made all those poor immigrants think he was an ICE agent," said Adele.

"I know." Vega fell back against the cool sheets of the gurney. His head throbbed. But even in his pain and confusion, he realized that parts of Bale's story didn't add up. It was easy enough for Bale to make up a fake badge and ID. Easy enough to buy a jacket that read: *ICE.* But how did a local cop get his hands on real information about people in ICE's files? Someone inside of ICE had to have fed him the cases. Someone not on their radar.

"I guess Bale was the one who planted that heroin in my car," said Adele.

"Looks like it," Vega grunted. Though the whole fiasco left him with more questions than answers. How did Bale know Adele's car would be in her driveway Saturday night while they were out at that gig? How did he get ahold of those bundles of heroin? According to Lieutenant Giordano, Lake Holly wasn't one of the agencies involved in that sting.

Adele got a text on her phone. "It's Maria," she said. "Edgar's wife." She looked tense as she opened it. Her shoulders seemed to relax as she scrolled through the words. "Edgar's out of surgery. The bullet missed his vital organs. He should pull through okay."

"I'm glad," said Vega. "I owe him. I'd be happy to write a letter on his behalf."

"I'm sure he would appreciate that." A shadow crossed Adele's face. "I guess Bale didn't tell you anything about Lissette?"

Vega shrugged. They were sitting inside a flimsy hospital cubicle with ears all around. He didn't want to leak information in an ongoing investigation. Still, Bale's allegation that Lissette killed Talia Crowley bothered him. Not because it was ludicrous.

Because it wasn't.

On the surface, Bale and the Ramirez brothers would have had no vested interest in killing Talia Crowley. They were all about blackmailing immigrants into helping them rob high-end houses and businesses. That likely changed when Elmer Ortega's prints showed up after the jewelry store heist in Lake Holly. Ortega could have dropped a dime on all of them. It made sense the Ramirezes would kill him. But that upped the ante. Bale needed assurance the district attorney would never go after them. What better way than blackmail? A phone video of an underage human trafficking victim having sex with the DA would keep Crowley in their pocket forever. Except Deisy left her phone and wallet behind, Talia found it, and the only one who could get it back was Lissette.

There was just one person in her way: Talia Crowley.

"I hope Lissette's alive," said Adele.

"Me, too," said Vega. But maybe not for the same reasons.

When the attendant came to wheel Vega in for X-rays, he insisted Adele go home and take care of Sophia. She was gone by the time he came out. He was wheeled into an actual room with four walls and a door. Greco was inside, taking up the only visitor's chair and tapping messages, one finger at a time, into his phone.

"Jeez, you look like crap."

"I got an excuse," Vega shot back. "What's yours?"

Greco closed the door and dragged his chair closer to Vega's gurney. The screech of chair legs across the linoleum felt like an ice pick in Vega's brain.

"Got you an actual recovery room instead of that shower stall they had you in," said Greco. "So—you dying? Or are you gonna talk to me about this fustercluck you've handed my department."

"*I've* handed?" Vega sat up. Lights spurted across his field of vision like shooting stars. His head throbbed. "One of your finest did this to me."

Greco placed a meaty paw on Vega's shoulder and gave it a squeeze—his best attempt at bedside manner. "I should've realized when I saw that body-cam footage that Bale needed to be taken out of action right then and there."

"Forget it," said Vega. "How could you know it was this bad? This has taken everybody by surprise."

"And now it's going up the food chain," said Greco. "FBI's been notified. U.S. Attorney's Office is involved."

"Our involvement has been terminated?"

"Not terminated," said Greco. "Demoted. We've gone from chefs to busboys. They still need our legwork to figure out which end is up. Feebies can't tie their shoes without ten pages of instructions." Greco walked Vega through what he and Sanchez had done so far, from bagging Deisy Ramos's phone at the synagogue to writing up search warrant requests on the phone's contents, Bale's house, cars, and electronic equipment.

"We've got BOLOs out on the Ramirez brothers," said Greco. "We've alerted the airports and agents at the Mexican border in case they decide to flee to El Salvador.

Michelle's over at ICE, trying to figure out how Bale got his inside information."

"How about Crowley?" asked Vega. "The feds are gonna question him, right?"

Greco pointed to a video monitor mounted high up on the wall. "I have no idea if those things are wired for sound. And I'd rather not have our mugs accusing the DA of anything on the six o'clock news."

"He admitted to being with that girl, Grec."

"That girl is dead," said Greco. "And we weren't investigating the girl. We were investigating Talia Crowley's death. Which in no way involves the DA."

"How can you be so sure?"

"Because he passed his polygraph—"

"*What?* When did this happen?"

"This afternoon. While you were doing your high-wire act with Bale." Greco leaned in closer. Vega could smell the garlic on his breath from lunch. "It's legit. I got the state police to administer it. We kept the questions to Lissette's disappearance and Talia's death. He's clean on both. He didn't kill his wife. He doesn't know where his housekeeper is."

"Well, *somebody* killed his wife," said Vega. "What about that light switch at the top of the basement stairs?"

"By the time the neighbor called nine-one-one, the whole electrical panel was flooded," said Greco. "The house *would have been* dark."

"But that basement light switch was in the off position—"

"Which could have happened accidentally when the firefighters lugged their gear down the stairs," Greco pointed out. "Look, Vega, we've got feds crawling up our asses at the moment. We've got a corrupt dead cop, a major scam we haven't even properly unraveled, and a shot-up synagogue. I'm not turning the feebies loose on our DA over a friggin' light switch."

"What about the fact that he was whoring around and Talia wanted to expose him?"

"You think he's the first politician to engage in those sorts of extracurricular indiscretions?"

"Those *indiscretions*"—Vega gritted his teeth—"involve a sixteen-year-old human trafficking victim who was murdered yesterday. And I'm betting that phone of hers links Crowley to the scam—"

"If the feds want to pursue him, I'm all for it," said Greco. "But I'm not gonna wave a stick at a pit bull and neither should you. You fight that fight and lose, you'll never work in this county again."

Greco rustled around in his pocket and pulled out a half-eaten Hershey bar. He handed it to Vega.

"What's this?" asked Vega.

"A get-well present."

"Where's the other half?"

Greco shrugged. "I got hungry waiting for you to come out of X-ray."

Chapter 45

Greco took Vega's recorded statement while Vega gobbled the rest of the melted Hershey bar and waited for the stack of insurance forms, prescriptions, HIPAA privacy statements, and doctors' follow-up instructions he had to sign and review before he could be discharged. The stack was as thick as a robbery case file.

Greco offered Vega a ride back to the station house to fetch his truck but, aside from the candy, Vega hadn't eaten all day. He needed some real food in his stomach first. Something filling and soothing. The hospital cafeteria's cuisine would go down just fine.

"I can walk back afterward," Vega told Greco. "It's only a couple of blocks."

"Walk, nothing," said Greco. "Just call the station house when you're ready. One of the patrols will drive you over."

"Okay. Thanks."

Vega had forgotten how bright the hospital cafeteria's fluorescent lights were. They made his headache worse. So did the lingering smell of tomato soup. But at least it was quiet at four in the afternoon. The lunch crowd was over and the dinner crowd hadn't started.

Vega chose something basic for his battered stomach: overcooked chicken and a plate of soggy white rice. The blandness of the food comforted him and their coffee wasn't half bad.

He was struggling with his plastic knife, tearing at the limp chicken, when a figure walked toward him. He didn't take her in until she stood across the table, resting her fingers on the plastic chair.

"Detective Vega? What happened to your face?"

Vega lifted his gaze slowly so as not to assault his eyes with the lights. He took in the pale blue scrubs first. Then the tea she was cradling in her brown hands and finally, the black kinky hair pulled back tightly in a ponytail, revealing those articulated shoulders and oversized earlobes.

"Ms. Osorio—"

"Cecilia." She put her tea on the table. "You're sort of a family acquaintance at this point, I suppose." Her hawkish eyes took in Vega's swollen and bruised face. "Did you get into a car accident?"

"Line of duty." He wasn't about to delve into the details.

She frowned at his T-shirt. He forgot he had the name of a heavy-metal band plastered across his chest. "Undercover?"

"No, unfortunately. The guy who hit me knew he was hitting a cop."

"I hope he got worse."

Vega stared at his plate. She seemed to guess that she'd entered a conversation there was no graceful exit for. She pulled out the chair. "May I sit down?"

"Uh, sure."

"You've been on my mind ever since the weekend. I was thinking about calling you."

Vega couldn't hide his surprise. "About the case?"

"Nooo." She pulled off the plastic lid on her tea and

took a sip. "About that . . . other matter." She swept a gaze over her shoulder to make sure they were alone. Satisfied, she pulled her chair closer.

"After we talked the other night, I went through a box of my dad's old things. I don't know what I expected to find or why I was even looking. When he died, all his possessions fit into a couple of shoeboxes."

Her voice caught on the words. Vega put his plastic fork and knife down and pushed his tray aside. He could see it was taking all of Cecilia's composure to speak. She lifted her gaze from her tea.

"I wish I could tell you I found something about your childhood that could help you, Detective—"

"Jimmy."

"Jimmy," she repeated. "But what I found said more about my dad than about you. Still, it was something I wanted to share with you."

Cecilia took a deep breath. "As I think I mentioned, my father never spoke much about his childhood. But I knew he was angry about his mom just abandoning him like that. All his drug and alcohol problems seemed to be about quelling that anger."

She dunked her tea bag, then wrapped the string nervously around one finger. "When he died two years ago, I was just so heartbroken that we'd only begun reconciling, that I stuffed all of his possessions into those boxes and stuck them at the back of my closet. I couldn't bear to look at them."

Vega understood. His own mother had died a couple of years ago—murdered in a brutal attack. He still had a hard time looking at old picture albums and items he'd boxed up from her apartment.

"Anyway," said Cecilia. "When I went through the box after speaking to you, I found a letter my father's mother had written to him. The envelope was postmarked about a year before she died. I thought they had no contact."

"What did the letter say?" asked Vega.

"She asked his forgiveness." Cecilia pushed her tea to one side and settled her dark eyes on Vega's. "She told him she was a teenager when social services took him away. She was abused by her boyfriend and messed up on drugs. She told him in the letter that she was dying and begged his forgiveness."

"Do you know if he forgave her?"

"I don't think he ever did," said Cecilia. "But the date on the envelope corresponds with the month he first reached out to me—to ask *my* forgiveness—for not being in my life more as a kid."

"And you gave it to him," said Vega.

"And I gave it to him."

She laced her fingers together and tried to compose her words. "Jimmy, I don't know why you ended up in foster care. I don't know what happened to you there. But I know one thing from looking at my grandmother's letter and thinking about the last couple of years of my father's life. Time is short. We never know how much we have. If you spend it looking for ways to hate and blame people in your past, it will drag you down and poison you. Your mother and grandmother must have been good people. They got you back. They raised you up well. And, until now, you never had to face that dark time."

"But that's just it," said Vega. "I have these half memories. Things, like being locked in a closet—"

"By your mother?"

"No," said Vega. "I went down to child services in the Bronx and found out that the people who fostered me were taken off the approved list of foster homes two years after I was there. I think they did that stuff to me."

"And if you find them—then what?" asked Cecilia. "They're old. They might be dead."

"I guess," Vega admitted. "I found out one thing from looking at the records at least. I didn't get taken away because my mother hit me. It was likely a baseball injury. Somebody anonymously called it into child services by mistake."

Cecilia regarded Vega for a long moment. "I'm an ER nurse," she said. "You're a cop. How many *baseball* injuries have you ever mistaken for abuse?"

"What are you saying?" asked Vega. "That it wasn't a sports injury? That my mother did that?"

Cecilia raised an eyebrow. She didn't believe him. Vega felt angry. He didn't need to defend his family to this stranger.

"My mother was a nurse," said Vega. "Not an RN, maybe. But an LPN. She didn't drink or do drugs. She worked every day of her life. She didn't even bring men into the house until I was long out of it. Never once do I remember her or my grandmother hitting me across the face like that. Never!"

"Okay, Jimmy. I believe you," said Cecilia. "Then your mother had an enemy."

"Huh?"

"Nobody makes an anonymous phone call to child services for a baseball injury. Unless they were looking to hurt your mom by hurting you."

Vega blinked at her. Luisa Rosario-Vega was a gentle, soft-spoken woman. Private and unassuming. Who would hate her so much they would try to take her only child away?

Someone who blamed her for poisoning their cat.

Someone whose kid sister had been seduced by Luisa's husband and spirited away.

Gloria Rodriguez.

Cecilia must have seen the fury creep across Vega's face. She reached out a hand.

"Jimmy, please. Listen to me. The past is the past. You've got to let it go. If you don't, it will burn a hole right through you. That's what happened to my dad. It ruined his life. Don't go down the same path."

"I don't know if that's in my power."

Chapter 46

Vega knew he should walk to the station house, get in his truck, and drive straight home. He was officially on medical leave. His chest stung with each intake of breath. His head throbbed. The swelling on the left side of his face made it difficult to drive. Yet he burned with a deeper hurt and pain that no amount of painkillers or rest could help him with.

He walked the few blocks to the Lake Holly police station and got in his truck. Then he pulled out his cell phone and dialed Michelle. The child in him wanted to confront her with everything he suspected about her aunt. The adult in him knew better. ICE was scrambling to find their mole. That was her focus right now and it should be his. It served no purpose to derail it with personal crap that was thirty-five years in the past.

Her voice was breathy and concerned when she picked up.

"Jimmy! Oh my God, I heard. Are you okay, *mano*? We're going crazy here, ever since the news broke about Ryan Bale."

"I just got discharged from the hospital." Vega tried to keep his voice cool and professional. This wasn't the place to rehash ancient wounds. "Thank you for intervening on Edgar Aviles's behalf. He saved my life."

"I understand he's now fighting for his," said Michelle.

"Adele got word that he'll pull through," said Vega. "So, what's the update on your end? Have you got any leads on who your mole might be? Because Bale definitely had one."

Michelle hesitated a moment. Vega realized she was probably speaking from her not-so-private cubicle. "Can I call you right back?"

"Okay."

Vega checked his phone messages while he waited. There was an email he'd missed earlier, from Greco, reminding the investigators that Talia Crowley's funeral was tomorrow. Vega knew that after the blows he took today, no one would expect him to go. But he would. He had to. He felt a great sadness that he'd let Talia down by not figuring out what had happened to her. And now, with the FBI involved, he might never get close enough to the investigation again to find out. She deserved better than that.

Michelle called him back a few minutes later.

"I'm in my car in the garage below," she said. "It's the only place I can find privacy."

"Have you got a suspect?" asked Vega.

"Well, it's not Dan Wilson," said Michelle. "That much, we're sure of. He's been in the Adirondacks the whole time. Whoever set this up just used his name."

"Tyler and Donovan?"

"They're straight shooters," Michelle insisted. "Same with Eddie Hidalgo in our office. Chuck Cassidy's always griping about something. He has some gambling problems. My field director's focusing on him."

"What about Wayne Bowman himself?" asked Vega.

"He certainly has the access as field director," said Michelle. "But he's like Wilson. He's got a religious zeal about this work that he wouldn't compromise. Even Cassidy feels wrong for it. He's too lazy and sloppy to pull it off."

"Can you match agents' work schedules to what we

know about the timeline? That might eliminate people who were on-duty."

"I'd love to," said Michelle. "But Karen's the only one who has access to all that and she left early. Doctor's appointment."

"You mean the candy dish lady?"

"Yep. Without her, we're lost when it comes to the vagaries of our computer system."

Vega felt a buzzing in his head that couldn't be ascribed to the concussion. "Does the candy dish lady have access to individual petitioners' files?"

"Karen has access to everything."

Silence. The realization seemed to hit them both at the same moment. "You don't think . . . ?" Michelle's voice seemed to rise in pitch. "I mean, how would Karen Hurst even know a bruiser like Bale? She's just this sweet old lady who bakes us cupcakes."

"Hold on a minute," said Vega. "I'm going to put you on speaker and switch screens."

Vega trolled his phone's icons until he came to Facebook. Karen Hurst struck him as the Facebook type—the sort who posts pictures of pets and babies. Several Karen Hursts popped up when he entered the name. He eliminated some through age and geography until he came to a profile picture of a heavyset, silver-haired woman who lived up near Vega in a town called Markham. Under the tab *Works At,* it read, *administrative assistant, ICE.* Vega hit the *Friends* tab and typed in *Ryan Bale* in the search bar.

Up came a close-up of a barbell with Bale's name beside the photo.

"Karen Hurst is Facebook friends with Ryan Bale," said Vega. "And I think I know why."

Vega went back to Hurst's Facebook page and typed in just *Bale* this time. Up came a whole bunch of Bales, one of them an older-looking woman named *Ellen Hurst Bale*. Vega clicked on the page. And there it was. A photo from Easter. Ellen Bale surrounded by her three grown children.

One of them was Ryan Bale.

"Karen Hurst is Ryan's aunt," said Vega. "It's her. The candy dish lady. She's the mole."

Chapter 47

Vega's head was hurting. Michelle and ICE didn't need him to track down their own employee. They'd find her easily enough. Coming out of her doctor's appointment. Stocking up on candy at a drugstore near her home in Markham. Defrosting a steak for dinner. A woman like that had a predictable schedule—even if the person behind the schedule hadn't been quite as predictable.

Vega drove home and hit the shower as soon as he got in the door. He changed into jeans and a T-shirt from a 5K race he ran last fall. It beat wearing Metallica across his chest. Then he fed Diablo and checked in with Adele. He must have popped his first pain pill right before that because he couldn't even recall what he and Adele had talked about. All he knew when the phone awoke him at nine p.m. was that he hadn't left the couch for at least two hours.

He fumbled between the lumpy cushions for the phone, nearly stepping on Diablo, who was napping beneath his feet. He studied the name on the receiver. He'd been expecting Michelle with word on Karen Hurst's arrest. But it was Solero instead, calling to check up on him.

"I heard what happened, man. Are you okay?"

"I got busted up a bit," said Vega. "But the fingers still

work so you don't need to go looking for another guitarist just yet," he joked.

"Ryan Bale . . ." Solero let out a long whistle. "Who'd have thought?"

Vega let the words hang on the line. He suspected his friend was looking for gossip. Cops were notorious busybodies. Vega couldn't be sure what was public and what wasn't yet—even for fellow police officers—so he said nothing.

"Listen," said Solero. "I just finished up a personal training session with Chuck McCormick."

Just hearing McCormick's name put Vega in a better mood. Solero's client was the guy who recorded the band's eight songs in his home recording studio.

"Did he finish the mix?"

"I'm sitting in his driveway about three miles from your house, holding it in my hand," said Solero. "You want me to swing by and you can give a listen?"

"Aw jeez, that's tempting," said Vega. "But my ribs are killing me and my head's not much better."

"Then this will take your mind off the pain, my man. What do you say? I drive home and it's gonna be days before I can shoot a copy to you."

"Okay," said Vega. "You're on."

Vega hung up from Solero and pushed himself off the couch. The pills had muffled the throb in his head and chest, but they hadn't killed it. He shot a glance at his weight bench and weights in the corner and realized it would be a while before he lifted anything heavier than a pencil.

He walked into the kitchen and got himself a glass of water and dog treat for Diablo. If a dog could look worried, Diablo did. He cocked his head at Vega, a questioning look in his eyes.

"I'm okay, pal." Vega gave Diablo a scratch between the ears. "Just a little banged up, is all."

Vega's phone rang again. He saw Michelle's name on the screen and picked up.

"Did you collar her?"

There was pause. Vega heard voices in the background. A high-pitched *beep-beep* of a truck backing up. Maybe ICE was still on stakeout.

"Jimmy . . . she's dead. She shot herself in the head."

Vega's legs seemed to give out beneath him. He pulled out one of his dining table chairs and sank into it. His reflection stared back at him from the sliding glass doors of the deck. His face looked like a Halloween mask. No wonder Diablo seemed worried.

"Everybody involved in this scam is dead or bailing," said Vega.

"I know," said Michelle. "The FBI thinks the Ramirez brothers may have already boarded a charter to Mexico. It could be months before we get anywhere with Interpol."

"Are you sure the shot was self-inflicted?"

"I'm not sure of anything," said Michelle. "The FBI won't let ICE anywhere near the scene. They think we're all suspect. I had to drive up in my own car. I'm mostly relying on the sheriff's deputies to feed me information. Their lieutenant tells me they found no sign of a break-in. Karen had gunpowder residue on her right hand and one clean shot to the right temple."

"What kind of gun did she own?" asked Vega. "A pistol? A revolver?"

"She didn't," said Michelle. "The gun she shot herself with is a Smith & Wesson semiautomatic that was reported stolen in Wickford a month ago."

"The cops find anything else out of place?" asked Vega. "Maybe a neighbor saw some handyman walking around?"

"They found a key in the bushes," said Michelle. "Right by the rear door to the garage."

"Her house key?"

"They said it was unusual. I haven't seen it yet."

"When you do, can you text me a photo?"

"I'll see if I can sweet-talk one of the deputies."

Vega heard an intake of breath on the line. "So listen," Michelle continued. "I've got a twenty-pound bag of Purina Dog Chow sitting in the trunk of my car and no dog owner to give it to. I'm heading right past Sullivan Falls on my way home. Want me to drop it off?"

Vega hesitated. "I'm busy tonight."

"Adele?"

"My drummer. He's stopping by to play a mixtape for me."

"It will only take five minutes."

"I can't, Michelle."

She seemed to register the drop in temperature between them.

"Hey, not for nothing," she said. "I tried my best to help Aviles today. I put my job on the line to write that order when I couldn't get ahold of my boss."

"I know that," said Vega.

"So why the cold shoulder? You've been a different person ever since you got out of the hospital today. Is it on account of the concussion?"

"No."

"Then what?"

Vega fumbled for words to describe the hurt and anger he'd been feeling ever since his conversation with Cecilia Osorio this afternoon. Nothing—not the pounding in his head or the pain in his chest—could come close to the ache he felt in his heart. But when he opened his mouth, only one word came out.

"Gloria."

"What are you talking about?"

"You aunt," said Vega. "She was the one who called the cops on my mom and got me sent into foster care."

"You're crazy," said Michelle. "Why would she do that? Because of my mom and our dad's affair? That happened four years before you got sent away."

"Yeah," said Vega. "Four years of bad blood. And then Gloria's cat scratches me in the eye and soon after, someone poisons her cat. She always blamed my mother. Maybe calling social services was her way of getting even."

"I don't believe it," said Michelle. "My mother would have told me—"

"You think your mother's going to admit what happened? That's why they don't want to talk about that picture of me. It's not just that I got sent away. It's why. They know, Michelle. Your mother. Our father. They *know.*"

Silence. Vega heard her breathing hard on the line. He needed air himself. He slid open the door and stepped onto the back deck. The moon's glow cut a shimmering path across the lake. A mist wafted through the trees, glazing them with dew. Vega shivered as it settled on his skin. He could feel Michelle's hurt across the phone line. For him. For her. For the messed-up choices of their families that had brought them to this juncture.

"I don't know what to say," she whispered finally. "If Gloria did that, she did a terrible thing. An unforgivable thing. If my mother and our father knew—they should have said."

"I'm guessing they didn't know then," said Vega. "They probably found out later."

"I'm so sorry."

"Yeah," he grunted. "Me too." Vega felt a peppery feeling in his nose and eyes. He wiped at them, hoping he wouldn't start the bleeding again. He took a deep breath. "Text me if you find out anything more about the shooting."

"I will," she said softly. There was a newfound distance in her voice. Vega felt like he was standing at an airport gate, watching Michelle board a one-way flight to a place he would never visit. A place she would never leave.

"Get some sleep, *mano*."

She didn't say "good-bye." They'd both been through enough good-byes to recognize one without the word.

Chapter 48

Vega stood by the deck railing for a long while after that, until the hair on his arms turned wet with mist and the cold seeped down into his marrow and made him shiver. All his life, he'd coped—for better or worse—as the only child of a single mother. He'd drifted between cultures and communities, adapting, yet never belonging. He'd been happy enough—or so he'd thought. But then Michelle walked back into his life. She filled a hole he didn't know he had. A hunger for family, for a shared sense of history. He grieved a door closing that he'd never noticed until she opened it.

He was glad when his drummer showed up to pull him out of his melancholy mood. Solero was dressed in sneakers, black sweatpants, and a dark hoodie—not surprising, since he'd just come from a training session with one of his private clients. His bristle-short black hair glistened on its shafts. There was a charged look to his eyes. Diablo, normally such an effusive greeter, hung back. Solero hadn't been up at Vega's cabin since he got the dog. When his friend bent over to pet Diablo, the dog barked and circled Vega's legs.

"Whoa." Solero backed up. "He looks like he'd take a chunk out of me."

"He's normally very friendly," said Vega. "Too friendly. But I don't know his puppy history. Maybe you remind him of someone. I can let him out."

Vega opened the sliding glass door and nudged Diablo onto the deck.

"He won't get lost?"

"Never. He knows where his meal ticket is." Vega walked into the kitchen area and opened the refrigerator. "You want a beer?"

"Sure." Vega tossed him one, then walked back to the couch empty-handed.

"You're not drinking?"

"These pain pills I'm on really knock me out," said Vega. "I'd better not."

Solero studied Vega's face. "Bale did all that?"

"The metal catwalk did some of it," said Vega. "But yeah, he helped it along." Vega patted his sore ribs. They were wrapped in an ACE bandage, which helped. But only time would heal them. "When I start to feel bad about him going over the rail and dying like that, I remember that it could have been me."

"Amen to that." Solero popped the tab on his can and took a long pull before setting it down on the table in front of Vega's lumpy corduroy couch. Vega sat down next to Solero and opened his laptop.

"Thanks for coming over and bringing the tracks, Richie. That's the best medicine in the world."

"Always is." Solero pulled a flash drive from inside a pocket of his sweatpants and cradled it in his large square hands. Vega took it and inserted it in his drive.

"I thought you said McCormick couldn't mix the tracks for another couple of weeks."

"I guess he had some spare time," said Solero. "It's only a rough mix. It still needs polishing."

Vega plugged the flash drive into his laptop and opened

the audio files. He expected to see eight finished song tracks with all the raw vocal and instrument recordings mixed into a single track. Instead he saw dozens of tracks for each song.

"This isn't the mix," said Vega, gesturing to the screen. "These are the original tracks we laid down over a month ago."

"Aw man, I don't believe it!" said Solero. "Chuck must have downloaded the wrong files. Jeez, Jimmy. I'm so sorry."

"That's all right." Vega tried to hide his disappointment. He was tired and hurting. He probably would have begged off seeing Solero this evening if not for the thrill of hearing the mix.

"I wanted to go over a few things on the original tracks anyway."

Vega nodded. Solero was nursing a beer. He couldn't very well throw his friend and fellow band member out. "Sure."

Solero pulled up Vega's vocals on the third song, an up-tempo, salsa-inspired piece with both English and Spanish lyrics that Vega wrote with Danny Molina. Adele said it was her favorite of all the songs Vega had written. It was called "Hot Blood, Cold Heart."

They'd just started listening when a text dinged on Vega's cell phone. He checked the screen. It was from Michelle. It had been sent about ten minutes earlier. Out here in the woods, his messages sometimes got delayed, especially if they contained attachments.

"Something important?" asked Solero. "About the case?"

"Don't know." Vega typed in his password and pulled up the text. It contained two photos of the silver, T-shaped key the cops found in Karen Hurst's bushes by her garage. One photo was an establishing shot and the other was a closeup.

What do you think this is a key to? Michelle had typed beneath the two photos.

Vega didn't have to guess. He knew. As would any musician.

Especially a drummer.

Solero eyed the photos over Vega's shoulder. Then he did something that catapulted every synapse in Vega's body into overdrive.

He patted his pants pockets.

Vega pushed himself off the couch. His stomach lurched. His palms turned sweaty.

"Listen, Jimmy." Solero tossed off a small girlish laugh. "I know what you're thinking. But you've got it all wrong. I had nothing to do with what happened to Karen."

Vega blinked at Solero. Nobody outside the investigation knew that Karen Hurst was connected to the case. Or that she'd died. Vega felt the enormity of what his friend had just confessed to—and the danger he was in, alone in the woods with a killer. His gun was in his lockbox upstairs. His dog was outside. He couldn't outrun or outfight a hulk like Solero, especially in his present condition with a swollen left eye and broken ribs.

Solero lunged at Vega, spun him around, and locked a massive arm around Vega's neck. The phone clattered to the floor.

"You could've listened to a few music tracks and let me leave," hissed Solero. "That's all I needed you for. To establish an alibi. But it's too late for that now."

"You were the other ICE agent," Vega sputtered. He saw everything clearly for the first time. Solero was the one who met with Lissette. The one who stole the heroin that Bale planted in Adele's car. "You gonna shoot me in the head with a stolen gun like Karen?" Vega choked out. "That only works once."

"Don't need to."

Solero threw Vega facedown onto the rug in front of the fireplace. Then he fished out a set of cuffs from the back pocket of his sweatpants and cuffed Vega's arms behind his back. Outside, Diablo barked and pawed at the sliding glass door. Solero ignored him as he scanned the tops of Vega's amps. His eyes brightened when he saw what he was looking for.

Duct tape.

"A musician's best friend," said Solero. He yanked Vega up by his shoulders, then dragged him over to the shelf with the duct tape. Vega saw what was coming. Solero was going to tape his legs together. He kicked wildly, with an animal fierceness he didn't think he could conjure up after Bale this morning. His left ankle connected cleanly with Solero's. The big man almost went down. But not before he'd managed to grab the tape and wind it around Vega's jeans at the ankles.

"What are you going to do?" asked Vega. "Throw me in the lake? You'll never make it that far."

Solero's eyes settled on something else in the corner. Not Vega's guitars or his amps. His weight bench.

"You're going to have a little weight-lifting accident, Jimmy. You tried to bench-press too much weight and dropped it on your throat. Crushed your trachea. You should always have a spotter."

Solero slammed Vega down on the weight bench, faceup, and sat on him. Vega arched his back, desperate to throw Solero off but the man was too big and Vega, too hurt and spent. His ribs felt as fragile as toothpicks. Every twist was like a knife to his chest.

Outside, Diablo's barking grew more furious. His body thudded against the sliding glass door.

"Shut up!" Solero snarled at the dog as he wrapped the duct tape around Vega's body. Sweat poured down the big man's face and dripped on Vega's T-shirt.

"Richie, think what you're doing," Vega pleaded. "We're friends. Fellow musicians. I can help you. There's still a way out of this."

Solero didn't answer.

A foot above Vega's head, the shiny chrome barbell sat suspended like a giant guillotine. Vega gulped for air. He imagined the moment of impact, the barbell crushing his larynx, the shattered bits of cartilage blocking the thin passageway from his lungs to his brain. He imagined the panic as he struggled for air through a blocked windpipe. It was a hell of a way to die.

Solero eyed the gray metal discs attached to each side of the barbell.

"A hundred and sixty? That's all you press?" He sneered. "Well, tonight, Jimmy, you're gonna press a whole lot more."

He reached down and slipped an additional fifty pounds on each side. Two hundred and sixty pounds of weight—all of it ready to drop on Vega's throat.

The glass door slid open.

"Freeze!" a female voice shouted. Diablo's bark followed close behind. Vega could barely lift his head, but he recognized the familiar Bronx vowels, so like his own.

Solero straightened and grabbed the barbell. All he had to do was clear the holders. Gravity would do the rest.

One second. Two.

Diablo sprang forward, sinking his teeth into Solero's shin.

"Get him off me! Get him off!" Solero squealed, dropping the barbell back in its holders and searching for anything to protect himself from the dog.

"Step away from the bench," Michelle commanded Solero. "On the floor. Hands behind your head. Jimmy!" she shouted. "Call off your dog."

Vega let out a loud whistle and Diablo bounded over to the weight bench, leaning over Vega to lick his face.

Michelle fished two sets of zip ties from her duty belt and cuffed Solero's ankles and wrists. Then she patted him down.

"I don't have my gun on me," Solero insisted. "I didn't plan on hurting Jimmy. He forced my hand."

"Right," Michelle grunted. "Tell it to your attorney." She looked over at Vega. "He's clean." She found a set of handcuff keys in Solero's pocket to unlock Vega's wrists. Then he directed her to a drawer for scissors to cut him out of the duct tape. Michelle dialed 911 while Vega finished freeing himself. Diablo paced in front of Solero, growling.

"It's okay, boy," said Vega, balling up the duct tape and tossing it on the floor. He gave the dog a knuckle rub between his upturned ears.

"He's a smart dog," said Michelle while they waited for deputies from the sheriff's department to arrive. "He deserves better than that dried chow I have in the back of my car."

"He gets a steak dinner after this," said Vega. He held Michelle's gaze. "You too. How did you know?"

"I showed the picture of the key to a deputy whose brother's a drummer. I didn't even know drums had tuning keys. But as soon as he said that, I got a bad feeling."

"You saved my life," said Vega.

"Yeah, well—repayment for helping me get rid of Corn Dog all those years ago. So now we're even." Michelle looked around the big room with its fieldstone fireplace and beamed ceiling. "Nice place. You got a bathroom? All this excitement went straight to my kidneys."

Vega directed her upstairs. Then he walked over to Solero and sat on the rug in front of him, staring at his former friend and fellow musician. His voice was soft, almost pleading, when he spoke.

"All I want to know is why, Richie." Vega wiggled his fingers in front of Solero's face. "We were supposed to be five fingers on a hand. Inseparable. Isn't that what Danny always said? A family. You could have told us if you needed money."

They all had money problems of one sort or another. Alimony. Child support. Home repairs. College expenses. A cop's salary was steady, but nobody got rich off it. A lot of guys worked second jobs. Their wives worked full-time. They made it work. And Solero could have too.

Then again, maybe it was more than just money, thought Vega. Solero spent his work life around gangs and gang members. Maybe being around all that power and illicit excitement got to him. Made him lose his way little by little until he couldn't find the path at all.

"Nobody was supposed to get hurt," said Solero. "Then that piece of crap, Cheetos, threatened to open his fat yap to the DA after the jewelry store heist and the Ramirezes whacked him. Everything went south after that."

Vega wasn't interested in his pity party. "Where's Lissette?" he demanded.

"I don't have her."

"You know where she is," said Vega. "You convinced her you were an ICE agent. Made her believe her uncle was about to get deported. All she had to do to save him was find the phone Deisy Ramos left in Crowley's house and turn it over."

"But she didn't," said Solero. "She got spooked and ran when the kid showed up. We didn't even know where the phone was until her uncle turned it on and we tracked it to the temple."

"So where is she?"

Solero's lips curled. "Get the U.S. Attorney's Office to give me immunity and I'll tell you."

"Not gonna happen, Richie. So do this poor girl and her family a favor and tell me what you know." Vega leaned in close. "It's Crowley, right? He had Lissette killed after she killed Talia. Or maybe he had them both killed. To protect his reputation. He's the only one with motive."

Solero tossed off a laugh. "You believe that, you haven't been paying attention."

Chapter 49

Talia Crowley's funeral was held at the Lake Holly Congregational Church, a nineteenth-century fieldstone church surrounded by ancient oaks and rhododendron bushes just beginning to bloom. The reverend was bald and sweaty and earnest—though it was clear he didn't know Talia.

Vega wondered how much Glen had either. He got up to speak and delivered a believable performance as the loyal, grieving husband. But he left out any mention of his dead bride's passion for cow trinkets. Or her talent as a watercolor artist. Or her deep desire to have children. That was left to her sister, Lori, the one person who really grieved her loss.

It would be days, maybe weeks, before news of the district attorney's encounters with Deisy Ramos and other human trafficking victims—in the county and in places like Taylorsville—broke and forced him from office. It would be months before all the different police agencies got a grip on the magnitude of the scam and the dozens of immigrants who'd been blackmailed—many of whom were too fearful to come forward and admit their involvement.

A search warrant of Ryan Bale's and Karen Hurst's homes and electronic devices turned up names, but the paper trail was long and tedious. Solero was in jail and wasn't talking. The Ramirez brothers had been detained by the Mexican police. But Vega knew from past experience that international extraditions could be slow.

"Lucky us," Greco griped. "We get to try those two dirtbags, send them to prison, and—because they were born here—we can't even deport them when it's over."

Vega shook his head at the irony. Men like Aviles got deported. Men like the Ramirezes got to stay. Though at least Aviles had a chance at the moment. The feds needed his testimony. They would expedite a visa for crime victims that would allow him to live and work in the U.S. legally again. Vega had no doubt that when Aviles recovered from his injuries, he'd go back to work at Beth Shalom where he'd be welcomed by Rabbi Goldberg and the congregation, with Max Zimmerman front and center.

Vega smiled at the memory of Max telling him the story of the talking horse. Faith and hope. They turned out to be more important than Vega had realized. He needed a little of both himself at the moment.

People began filing out of the church and lining up to offer sympathies to Lori Danvers and Glen Crowley on the steps. Vega saw Maria Aviles and her three children in the receiving line. Vega pulled out his phone and texted Detective Omar Sanchez, who'd been sitting near them with his wife.

Did you confirm the connection with Maria? Vega texted.

Yes, Sanchez texted back. **This morning. Search warrants are in place.**

Vega pocketed his phone and turned to Adele seated next to him in the pew. She was fanning herself with the program. The church wasn't air-conditioned. Everyone was overdressed. Vega shrugged out of his dark blue suit jacket.

"I've got some police business to take care of." He kissed her on the cheek. "I'll catch you later, I promise."

"Everything okay?"

"No. But I think it will be."

Vega ducked the long receiving line and headed out the arch of front doors. He found Charlene Crowley and her son, Adam, on the lawn outside, beneath the shade of a tall oak tree, accepting stiff hugs and air kisses from somber, sweaty men and women. Vega knew Charlene would be at the funeral. Not just because she was bringing Adam.

Because it would be bad manners to do otherwise.

She'd done herself up for it too. A stylish black blazer dress with double-breasted buttons, black kid gloves, and a small beret with a veil on top. Her silver-blond hair was cinched back in a bun. Her makeup was camera-ready. Adam stood beside her, sweating through a white shirt and black suit. His curly hair glistened along his scalp. His eyes were focused on people's feet.

Vega planted his lace-up black oxfords in front of the young man. "Well?" said Vega. "Do they meet your approval?"

Adam didn't smile. He didn't remark on Vega's bruised and swollen face. He just stared at Vega's feet. "Nine-and-a-half, medium," he said. "No tactical boots today."

Charlene took in Vega's battered face and brought a gloved hand to her chest. "*Detective?* Oh, my Lord—what happened?"

"Line of duty injury, ma'am," said Vega. "But I'm all right. It's healing."

"Well, thank goodness. And thank you for coming. I'm sure it means the world to Glen."

"I only wish we could have given him closure. Given Talia closure."

"But you have, Detective. She's at peace now."

"I wish that were true, ma'am," said Vega. "But the detective in charge—Detective Greco—he thinks she was murdered."

"You mean that lovely man who adored my sweet potato pie?"

"That's him."

"I don't understand," said Charlene. "I thought the police ruled it a suicide?"

"They were going to," said Vega. "But Detective Greco's being"—Vega kicked at an imaginary stone at his feet—"such a hard-ass, excuse my French. He says if we can't find the utility knife that Talia used to cut the washing machine hose, we have to open up the whole investigation all over again and start from the beginning."

"That's absurd."

"Tell me about it," said Vega. "I told him that knife's probably still down there somewhere, tucked in the debris."

"And what did he say?"

"Told me to find it. Or he's opening the case again."

"That's a lot of work for y'all." Charlene fanned herself with the program. Vega noticed her makeup was beginning to streak with the heat.

"A lot of work for the feds and the state police," Vega corrected. "I think Greco's bringing them into it this time. Listen," he said, leaning in close. "Don't trouble Mr. Crowley about this right now. He's got enough on his mind. I'm sure the knife will turn up."

"I'm sure." She smiled. Vega noticed it falter on one side.

It took just forty-five minutes for Charlene Crowley, still wearing her black kid gloves, to punch in the electronic passcode to her ex-husband's house, walk down the basement stairs, and place the utility knife she'd used Friday night inside a soggy rolled-up throw rug by the washing machine. She gave a small gasp of surprise when Vega emerged from an alcove behind the basement stairs, but she quickly recovered.

"How did you know?" she asked, more curiosity than venom in her voice. "One itty-bitty knife couldn't mean all that much." Her Southern twang had intensified, the only hint that she might be nervous.

"The light switch," said Vega. "You turned it off before you left Friday night. Talia wouldn't have hung herself in the dark."

She folded her arms across her chest and thought about that for a moment. "Really, Detective." She batted her eyes at him. "You can't possibly believe an old gal like myself is strong enough to hang another full-grown woman from a pipe."

"You didn't need to be strong," said Vega. "Just smart." He pointed to the rack of weights in the corner. "Pulleys—ma'am. You tied weights to the other side of the rope and lifted her by dropping them. Only you put one of the weights back hastily. It was turned on its side. That's what gave me the idea."

"Oh, honestly." She pulled off her gloves, one finger at a time. "Why would I do something like that?"

"You tell me," said Vega. "You had wealth. Prestige. Social standing. Even after Glen left you for his pregnant mistress—"

"Do you know how hard that was to deal with? To hold my head high after what he did with that little tramp?"

"Then why protect your ex-husband?" asked Vega. "Why not let him get what's coming to him?"

"Because his disgrace would be mine," said Charlene. "I'm still the former wife of a prominent man. The mother of his children. If people knew . . ." Her voice caught. "All the years I put up with his abuse. His sex romps with under-age girls . . . *I* would be ruined. Our family's reputation. I'd dealt with all of it for thirty years, Detective Vega. I was not going to be undone by some truck driver's daughter who wanted revenge."

"How did you get her to take the Valium?" asked Vega.

"Did you come over with a bottle of wine on some pretext? Maybe to ask her advice about Adam? That's what I'm guessing. Then you slipped the pills into her glass when she wasn't looking. She'd have no reason to fear you. Your charm. Your grace. No reason to believe you'd drug her into unconsciousness, then drag her down the stairs and hang her when she was too weak to fight back."

Vega gestured to the utility knife barely sticking out of the rolled-up throw rug. "You watch too much *CSI*, Mrs. Crowley. You assumed the flood would wash away all the evidence. It never does. Not everything that counts can be counted."

"Spare me your tired clichés, Detective. Who's going to believe you? Detective Greco? All he cares about is my sweet potato pie."

Vega walked over to what looked like a smoke detector. "You hear that, Grec? Guess that means no more pie for you." Then he turned back to Charlene. "He's upstairs, by the way. If you haven't guessed already, this is all on video."

"A video that proves nothing. You have no evidence. I'm just humoring you, Detective."

"On the contrary," said Vega. "We have two detectives at your house right now with a search warrant for a size-seven, water-damaged canvas pair of—what do you call them?" Vega feigned forgetfulness. "Oh yes—espadrilles. Talia's espadrilles, to be exact. The ones you borrowed Thursday night when you realized that by cutting the washing machine hose, your own wet shoes would give you away."

Charlene's face slackened. She seemed to age before Vega's eyes. "Adam," she whispered.

"He's quite the expert when it comes to noticing shoes."

She folded and unfolded the black leather gloves in her hand. "I suppose this is the point where I ask for an attorney."

"We can do it that way," said Vega. "Which means I'll have to cuff you and frisk you right here. Or maybe on the lawn—in front of all the neighbors."

"You have an alternative?"

"Yes, ma'am" said Vega. "Accompany us down to the station and swear out a full confession. You'll leave here with no cuffs and we'll just be a taxi service. In return, you tell us what happened to Lissette."

"Talia's housekeeper?"

"She wasn't just Talia's housekeeper, Mrs. Crowley," said Vega. "She was your employee. You paid her, too. We confirmed it this morning with your former housekeeper, Maria. Her aunt."

"I was only trying to help the family after Maria got sick," said Charlene.

"That's what Maria believed too. But that's not the real reason and you know it," said Vega. "You paid Lissette to spy on Talia. To figure out if she was trying to have another baby after she miscarried. That was your main purpose. You wanted to know if she was going to get pregnant again. But Lissette told you other stuff as well. How Glen had sex with young girls at the house. How Talia was planning to leave him and go public with the scandal. Even the alarm passcode came from Lissette."

"I have no idea what you're talking about. I want an attorney."

"That's your constitutional right. Absolutely, ma'am." Vega looked up at the video camera. "Hey, Grec? You still have that *Eyewitness News* reporter's cell phone? She covers Lake Holly. Maybe she can get some footage of the arrest—"

"Okay. Okay, already. I'll do it your way." Charlene sighed heavily. "But I did not hurt Lissette. She's perfectly safe."

"Then where is she?"

"She's my guest."

"Your . . . *guest?*"

Charlene smiled, but there was something vacant and hollow in the gaze. She reminded Vega of a porcelain doll. Perfect hair and skin and nothing behind the eyes.

"I always take care of my guests."

Chapter 50

It was Adam who led Vega and Michelle to the bolted root cellar door in the basement of Charlene's farmhouse estate. Lissette was there, down a short ladder, in a below-ground room with a cement floor, a wall of empty wooden shelves, and a bare incandescent bulb overhead. She was shoeless and naked with only a blanket around her. Her long black hair was greasy and tangled. A thick yoga mat doubled as a bed in one corner. A bucket stood in for a latrine in the other. A wooden door was wedged between two empty storage shelves to form a table of sorts. A tray of canned beans and the remnants of a blueberry muffin sat congealed on the plate with plastic utensils beside it. Yellow and purple wildflowers hung limply from an old yogurt container on top of the board, as if, in some chilling way, Charlene really did think of Lissette as her "guest."

Lissette wept and made the sign of the cross as Vega and Michelle helped her up the stepladder. Michelle climbed back down and fetched another blanket to put around the young woman until they could find her some clothes. Lissette shook violently. Vega could feel her body quaking right through the blanket. He shrugged off his suit jacket and wrapped it around her shoulders. The room was cool but not cold. This was fear talking. Fear of being locked in a windowless space with no escape.

Vega knew that fear in his marrow.

He peeked down into the room. Just seeing it made him feel faint and dizzy. His tongue swelled. His stomach churned. His whole body broke out in a sweat. He closed his eyes and saw that closet again, the one he conjured in his dreams where the floor was littered with damp, mildewed towels and the big green fingerprint-smeared door wouldn't open. Only now, he could locate those dark images and give them a name.

It happened when you got sent away. Through no fault of yours. Through no fault of your mother's.

"Jimmy?" Michelle emerged from the root cellar with a second blanket for Lissette. "Are you okay?"

Vega took a deep breath. His chest hurt—but only from his broken ribs. For the first time, the ache went no deeper. His fears had a context. He could never say for sure all that had happened to him in those eight weeks his mother lost custody of him. He wasn't sure he wanted to know. But he knew the most important part: His mother and grandmother loved him. They fought hard to get him back—and even harder to help him heal. And he had.

Michelle wrapped the second blanket over Vega's jacket, which was big enough to cover Lissette to the midpoint of her thighs. Already, Vega heard the EMTs above them, scrambling through the kitchen. Vega met the frightened woman's eyes and spoke softly in Spanish.

"Your family will be waiting for you at the hospital," he assured her. "I know you're scared. It's going to take time to heal. But you're safe now, I promise. You're going to be okay." He looked across at Michelle. "*Nita,*" he said softly, hoping his endearment would convey what his words could not. "It's going to be okay."

* * *

Charlene Beech Crowley was charged with the murder of Talia Crowley and the kidnapping of Lissette Aviles. Somehow, she managed to convince a judge to allow her to post bail instead of waiting out the months in the county jail. Even so, Vega wasn't quite sure the former Junior League president really processed what was happening. She greeted the detectives warmly when they showed up to interview her and sent them handwritten thank-you notes afterward.

"*Another thank-you note?*" asked Vega, waving Charlene's latest flowery missive at Greco. "For helping to put her away?"

"She doesn't believe she's going to be convicted," Greco pointed out. "Remember, she's spent her life rearranging the facts to suit her private narrative."

"Well, this time, we're writing the script."

"For one Crowley, at least," Greco muttered.

Glen was another matter. He'd stepped down as district attorney, citing concern for his "family's welfare," and his desire to not "taint the judicial process." Privately, he'd managed to cut a deal to help the U.S. Attorney's Office in their case against Solero and the Ramirez brothers in return for immunity from any charges.

"Mark my words," said Greco. "Come the fall, Crowley will be a talking head on some cable news show. Who knows? He might even get his own show."

"I hope he gets electrocuted by his microphone." Crowley's ease at evading prosecution enraged Vega. He could still see Deisy Ramos's baby face on that Bronx pavement the day he and Michelle tried to save her life. Deisy mattered—even if powerful men like Glen Crowley and the U.S. Attorney's Office were willing to sweep her under the rug. Vega attended her funeral. He kept tabs on her mother through Danny Molina, who'd managed to raise funds for a college volleyball scholarship at the high school in her honor.

Vega took comfort in the fact that Lissette had survived and was doing well. The feds had granted her the same visa they'd given Edgar. With it, she'd become "legal" for the first time. She found work as a teacher's aide in a nursery school. Teaching was her real love. Adele said that working with children had begun to heal her in a way nothing else could.

Vega was glad someone was healing. He sure wasn't. His concussion gradually faded and his ribs stopped being painful to the touch. But his heart was another matter.

Richie.

Solero hunkered down in prison, refusing all visits from his fellow band members. Especially Vega. For weeks, Vega couldn't even pick up his guitars without feeling an acid burn in the pit of his stomach. Armado cancelled all their upcoming gigs. Their audio tracks sat dormant in Chuck McCormick's home studio. Vega wondered if he could ever go back to playing again.

When he was seven, music had saved him. But he wasn't seven anymore.

Then he thought about Cecilia Osorio's words, about how the past could burn a hole right through you if you let it. He was determined not to. Four weeks after Solero's arrest, Vega picked up his guitar and played again. First hesitantly. Then every day. He called up Danny and Brandon and Chris, the other members of Armado. They admitted that they, too, had stopped playing. They missed the band. It would take time, but they agreed that they would regroup and come back. The music was eternal. It was bigger than any of them.

It would outlive them all.

With Vega on medical leave and his band on hiatus, he had a lot of time to spend with Adele.

"Too much time," Adele quipped one day as she packed for Sophia's weekend camping trip with the Girl Scouts. Adele had been roped into chaperoning. Vega had spent the last few days checking and rechecking their supply list. He'd even color-coordinated their bungee cords.

"Jimmy," Adele said, gently nudging him from yet another examination of the batteries in their flashlights. "Do something fun this weekend while we're away."

"Like what?"

"Have lunch with Joy."

"She's going to the beach with friends this weekend."

"Then grab a beer with Danny. Catch a movie with Chris or Brandon. Or . . ." She held his gaze. "Call Michelle. Invite her and her boys up to the lake. You know they'd love it. And so would Diablo."

"The case is over—"

"It's not about the case," said Adele. "Call her. It will be good for both of you."

Michelle jumped at the offer, as Adele said she would. The problem was her car. It had a busted alternator. She offered to take a train, but Vega decided to pick her and the boys up instead. She suggested he meet them outside her mother's place in the Rosedale Projects.

"It's easier to park there," she explained. "You can pull up to the curb by the basketball courts. Text me when you're close and we'll be waiting."

It was a warm June Saturday and the basketball courts were hopping, the balls bouncing across the asphalt to the blare of rap and reggaeton from stereo speakers.

Michelle was there, standing beside a suitcase that looked like she'd packed for a three-month trip. She was wearing jean shorts and a halter that made her brown skin glow. The boys, Alex and Artie Jr., were both wearing track shorts that hung below their knees and basketball sneakers that encased their ankles. Their eyes were hesitant beneath the brims of their baseball caps. Vega's heart dipped. He was technically their uncle. He was also a stranger.

He hoped after this weekend, he'd become a friend.

Vega nosed his pickup to the curb and stuffed Michelle's suitcase in a space behind the rear seats.

"What the hell have you got in here?" he asked. "A dead body?"

"I wanted to come prepared," she said. "You know. Mosquito repellent. Tick repellent. Sunscreen. Iodine wash—"

"We're not going to Alaska."

"*Mano,* compared to here, it might as well be."

The boys got into the backseat. Michelle cupped a hand over her brow and gazed at the benches by the basketball courts. She lifted an arm and waved. Vega followed her gaze to an older, rounded woman with a soft, expectant look on her face. Michelle's mother, Carmen Rodriguez. Vega couldn't recall the last time he'd seen her.

Carmen set her eyes on Vega and slowly raised her arm to wave at him. He felt a swirl of emotions. Anger at what she'd likely covered up all these years. Confusion at what had set it all in motion. But something else too. Forgiveness. Not just for her but for himself. He'd made some terrible mistakes in his own life. Some, he could walk back. Some, he couldn't. Cecilia Osorio was right. The time had come to accept and move on.

Slowly, he raised an arm and returned her wave. It wasn't much. But it was a start.

Acknowledgments

Writing fiction about current events is a roller-coaster experience. All too often, I begin a book with a premise that feels implausible only to discover that by the time the book is published, the circumstances have become all too real. Whether the story has been about the vulnerability of women and children in immigrant families, the tribulations of young people with DACA, or the way politics can tear apart a community, I have often felt more like a journalist chronicling events than a fiction writer inventing them.

Voice with No Echo is no exception. What started as fiction—a story about a custodian in Max Zimmerman's synagogue who gets caught up in a deportation—turned into reality a few months into the writing. That's when an undocumented immigrant who had worked for two decades as a custodian at a local synagogue was arrested and deported. The man, who had no criminal record, arrived in Mexico without money, his cell phone, or ID. The officer who escorted him over the border predicted he would be kidnapped within a week. In a country he hadn't set foot in since he was eighteen.

The synagogue members scrambled, much as they do in the novel. They hired lawyers. They raised money to take care of the man's wife and American-born children. They wrote dozens of letters to officials. There were rallies. Articles in the local paper. Months went by with no news. I finished my book. It had a happy ending. The man's fate is far less certain. He did get back to the United States, but it took ten months and a change in a federal court ruling to make it happen. His long-term prospects for asylum remain unknown.

Unlike fiction, nothing is for certain.

Stories like these—of people caught up in events beyond their control—are what drive my fiction. Thank you, readers, for your support. And many thanks, too, to the individuals who continue to provide me with guidance and encouragement throughout the series. Special thanks, as always, to Gene West, for his insights into law enforcement and his pitch-perfect sense of story. Thanks, also, to Janis Pomerantz, who reviewed the synagogue portions of my story for wording and accuracy, and to my agent, Stephany Evans and Ayesha Pande Literary, who are always there to lend an ear, even as I had to put the book on hold for a personal emergency.

Thanks to my editor, Michaela Hamilton, marketing director Vida Engstrand, and Kensington CEO Steven Zacharius for championing what some might call a controversial series. I don't know many publishing houses that would take such a risk—and be so supportive throughout.

And most of all, my thanks to my family: my husband, Tom; son, Kevin; daughter, Erica; and stepfather, Bill. I couldn't do this without you.